Truth in the Word

Truth Book Two

F. D. Adkins

Truth in the Word
Print Edition
Copyright © 2022 F.D. Adkins

CKN Christian Publishing
An Imprint of Wolfpack Publishing
5130 S. Fort Apache Rd. 215-380
Las Vegas, NV 89148

cknchristianpublishing.com

Paperback ISBN 978-1-63977-120-2
eBook ISBN 978-1-63977-913-0
LCCN 2022944872

To my Heavenly Father,
who stands with me on the mountaintops
and carries me through the valleys.
Thank you for allowing me to write and making this book a reality.

To Steve,
my husband, best friend, the love of my life.
Your love and support never cease to amaze me.
Thank you for your understanding and encouragement in all my
hours of writing.
And thank you for pushing me to believe in myself and lifting me
when I didn't.

To Landon and Layna,
the greatest children a mother could ever hope for.
Thank you for being as excited about my books as I have.
Never forget…
"… The Lord thy God is with thee whithersoever thou goest." Joshua
1:9 KJV

Truth in the Word

Chapter One

Fear hides in the dark crevices of my mind, and when night falls, that fear attacks and squeezes like a boa constrictor tightening around my body.

Where am I? How did I get here? The heat is sweltering, but chills shoot down the center of my back, stinging like needles piercing my skin. An eerie sensation in the pit of my stomach tells me I am not alone. Balling my hands into fists, I dig for the courage to take a step. I hold my breath, trying not to make a sound, and ease my right leg forward. As I shift my weight, I exhale with a sigh of relief when the board does not creak beneath my bare foot. My eyes burn from straining in the darkness, and I squeeze them closed for a minute. A bloodcurdling scream shakes the floor and vibrates through my body. My eyes spring open. A tiny, horizontal stream of light appears a few yards in front of me. *A door… the scream came from in there. Someone needs help.* A bead of perspiration drips from the end of my nose, and my stomach leaps into my chest when it hits the top of my foot. Shaking off my fear, I swallow hard and inch forward. *Only a few more steps to go.* I force my legs to move until I am in front of the door. With a trembling hand, I reach out, moving my arm from side to side, feeling for the knob. Before my fingers make contact, an ear-splitting shriek wails from the other side, rattling the door and sending my heart flying from my chest.

MY EYES POP OPEN. My body jumps, and I spring straight up. *Who is screaming?* Streams of sweat trickle down my forehead. Something gasps for air right next to me, and I stiffen my muscles at the sound. *Who's there?* My hand rests against wet fabric.

"Spencer, Spencer, calm down. Ellie, you scared Spencer." Steve's voice pulls me from my confusion.

"S-s-sorry. I had that nightmare again." My voice quavers as I try to get the words out. "She was still screaming. I almost touched the doorknob this time."

Steve's hand caresses the back of my head. "Ellie, your hair is soaking wet. I think you should talk to someone about these horrible dreams. You cannot go on like this."

Spencer leans against me. Whimpers escape his mouth in rhythm with his shaking body. "Spencer, it's okay." I wrap my arm around him. "Steve, don't you think it's about time Spencer sleeps in his own room? I mean, we have been married almost four months, and we have a monkey sleeping between us."

"Ellie, you know he can't sleep in his room alone. He has PTSD. What if he wakes up having one of his episodes?"

"I know. It's just that I would sleep better if I could snuggle up next to you." I take a deep breath and exhale. "I'm sorry. That sounded really selfish."

"Ellie, I have been thinking. PTSD can pop up any time after a traumatic experience. Maybe these nightmares are… well, maybe you should talk to Spencer's doctor."

"I am not going to see Spencer's doctor. Besides, it's not PTSD. This nightmare is not related to anything we went through." My eyes start to water.

Skepticism rings in Steve's voice. "Okay, but it's the same dream every night?"

"Yes, except each night, I get a little closer to that door. I told you tonight I almost touched the doorknob."

"What doorknob, Ellie? Do you know where this door is?"

"No, it is so dark. I can't even see what the door looks like. I just know it's a door because of the glow of light through the crack beneath it." I lie back on my pillow. "I wish you could understand how real it is... how real this girl's screams are... screams of pain. I feel like it means something."

"Maybe hypnosis would help you figure out where you are in the dream. You know, put you in touch with your subconscious."

He did not just say that. I reach over and click on the lamp so I can see Steve's face, because I am sure he must be kidding. "I hope you are not serious. I can't believe you would even mention the word hypnosis."

"I'm sorry, Ellie." His voice lowers with a sound of defeat. "I want to help you, and I don't know how."

"What would really help is if you would wrap your arm around me until I fall back asleep." I turn off the lamp and wipe the tears from my cheeks. *Lord, please comfort me and help me to rest.*

Steve doesn't say anything, but the blankets pull and the mattress bounces as he switches spots with Spencer. The commotion stops, and his arm drapes across me. His touch pushes the thoughts of the screams, the door and the nightmare away.

Thank you, Lord. Thank you. My brain gives in to the exhaustion.

Chapter Two

A squirt of soap falls into my hand from the automatic dispenser, and I rub my wet hands together. The soap lathers as I rub, and I count to seven over and over, seven times. I know it is the same as counting to forty-nine, but when I am nervous, I have to do things in increments of seven. I rinse my hands and hold them under the heated hand dryer.

Time to make breakfast, I tell myself trying to focus. I open the refrigerator and grab the carton of eggs, taking note that I better add a trip to the grocery store on my list of things to do today. Closing the door, I turn and start to take a step when a flash goes off in my head. I fall back and lean against the refrigerator. For a second, I am blinded by bright light, and a bitter taste fills my mouth. When my vision clears, the room spins around me. I lay the eggs on the counter and grip the edge as I ease toward the round oak dining table in the corner of the kitchen. My mom gave us the table when Steve and I were married. She said she needed a bigger table for family gatherings, one that had more than four chairs now that Steve and Spencer were part of the family. I lower myself into one of the mission-style chairs and click on the small television on the wall, hoping to distract myself until the nausea passes. I swallow to push the rising acid back down and then close my eyes.

"Breaking news. A mass shooting has taken the lives of five people at a grocery store in Chicago this morning and hospitalized seven others." I lift my eyelids and stare at the television in disbelief. "According to one of the shoppers in the store, the man became disgruntled when another customer cut the line and got in front of him. The witness said the man left his cart and walked out of the store. When he returned, he had a small semi-automatic handgun and started firing the weapon." *Unbelievable.* Pushing myself to my feet, I click the television off and get back to breakfast.

As I cross the kitchen, making my way back to the eggs, my phone vibrates. I slip it from the pocket of my pajama pants. *Seven o'clock on the dot.* Mom started sending me these texts several years ago when my sister suddenly disappeared. Even though Eileen is back home safe and the whole nightmare is over, my mom still sends a text precisely at seven o'clock, noon, three o'clock in the afternoon, and nine o'clock at night before bed to make sure I am okay. And, after all these years, it is always the same text. *I am pretty sure she copies and pastes.* My finger swipes the screen to unlock it, and I click on the text.

Please text back that you are okay and always know Mom loves you.

I tap out my reply.

Better than okay. I will always know. Love u 2.

As I slide the phone back into my pocket, I cannot help but crack a grin and shake my head as I admire Steve's latest contraption on the countertop. *And to think, my mom still uses a frying pan?* I pop the eggs in the "Eggscrambler" machine, turn the dial to extra fluffy, and push the scramble button. Looking through the little window, I watch the eggs crack and the shells get swept away by the wide metal fork. A quick stream of milk whisks into the eggs, and then the burner glows red as the eggs rock back and forth, tossing and folding them as they cook. The timer sounds, and I split the eggs between two plates.

My eyes are so heavy from lack of sleep. "Thank goodness this is my day off." I mumble to myself. Dragging my feet, I trudge over to the breakfast table and set the plates down on the placemats in front of two of the chairs. *Hmmm. Steve is still not downstairs yet.* I shrug. *I did kind of wake everybody up last night. Then, Steve got stuck sleeping in the middle between me and Spencer.* I can't help but giggle at the image in my mind. As I turn around, I swipe the brown twigs of hair away from my eyes and head back to the sink. I wet my hands and get another drip of soap. *One, two, three, four, five, six, seven… one, two, three, four, five, six, seven… one, two…*

I finish my ritual of counting, dry my hands, and turn my eyes back to the soap dispenser. Steve's voice grabs my attention just as I am about to start the ritual all over again.

"Why isn't Herb making breakfast?"

"His battery was dead this morning," I turn and glance at Steve, "and trust me, I was extremely disappointed when the coffee was not ready."

"I don't understand." Frustration echoes in Steve's voice as he swipes his fingers through his short, dark-brown hair. "Why would his battery be dead? He is programmed to connect to his charging station at exactly eleven o'clock at night, and disconnect at six o'clock in the morning."

I laugh at his distress. "You can relax. It had nothing to do with his programming. Herb was connected to his charging station. The problem was that somehow the charging station had come unplugged."

"Well, we need more eggs. Mom is coming for breakfast. I told Herb, but I forgot to tell you."

"No worries. She can have mine. My stomach is still quivering from that nightmare." I grab my thirty-two-ounce coffee mug from the cupboard. "I just want coffee right now. I will make a piece of toast later, after I go for a run."

Steve eases closer and engulfs me in his arms. "You need more than toast." He kisses the top of my head. As he steps back, he takes the coffee cup from my hand. "Go sit down. I will get our coffee."

I nod as I stare back into his deep brown eyes that always seem to make the rest of the world disappear. *He is too good to me.* I plod over and sit down in the wooden dining chair. Propping my elbows on the table, I rub my temples in an attempt to massage the tension from my head.

"Ellie," Steve sets the coffee cups on the table, "are you okay?"

The doorbell chimes just as he finishes his question, but he stands there staring at me, waiting for me to answer.

I smile and squeeze his hand. "I'm fine. Thanks for pouring the coffee." Pushing off of the table, I rise to my feet. "I'll let your mom in." The doorbell chimes again, so I pick up the pace through the living room and open the front door. Steve's mom is dressed to the hilt, as usual, in a cashmere sweater and designer boots with spiked heels. She is wearing bright red lip gloss, and her shoulder-length brown hair is curled under with every hair in place. "Good morning, Cynthia," I say, hugging her as she passes through the door.

"Good morning, dear. You look lovely as usual." She kisses my cheek.

As she steps away and heads toward the kitchen, I glance down at the plaid pajama pants that I am wearing. *I wonder if she is talking about my pajamas or the dark circles under my eyes.*

"And this house is always spotless. How do you work and keep it so clean?" she remarks over her shoulder.

I follow her into the kitchen and notice that Spencer has made his way down for breakfast. He is sitting in one of the chairs at the breakfast table with an orange and a banana lying on the table in front of him.

"Hey, Mom." Steve hugs her with one arm and sits her coffee

on the table by a plate of eggs. "I can't wait to hear this big news of yours."

"I can't wait to tell you. You are going to be so excited." A big grin covers Cynthia's face, and she claps her hands together. "Oh, look at Spencer." She pats his back. "Good morning, Spencer."

Spencer smiles at her and makes a squeaky monkey noise.

"Where's Herb?" Cynthia looks back and forth around the kitchen and then sits down in the chair next to Spencer.

"His battery was dead." Steve plops down next to his mom.

I follow suit and take the remaining chair between Steve and Spencer.

"That's too bad." She starts to laugh. "You know, I just love the drive out here from Arlington. Fairfax County is absolutely beautiful. And when I pull up the driveway through the trees to the front of your house, with the old clapboard siding and the mountains in the distance, I feel as if I am about to visit the Waltons." Resting her elbow on the table, Cynthia props her chin on her fist as her eyes scan the kitchen countertop lined with Steve's inventions. "Then, I walk through the front door and find the Jetsons instead. It is like I pass through a time portal that shoots me one hundred and thirty years into the future."

Steve shakes his head at her perception and laughs. I think he knows her description is right on the mark.

"I am aware that the outside is a bit dated, but this house... well, you wouldn't understand," he looks at Cynthia as he speaks, "but it sort of has a special character about it... I guess you could say a sentimental value that no one else could appreciate."

Spencer makes a grunting noise and reaches out his hands, grabbing my hand in his right and Cynthia's hand in his left.

"This little guy is something else." Cynthia remarks as she and I hold hands with Steve. "That monkey doesn't touch his food until you hold hands and say the blessing. I mean, I know he probably doesn't understand what you're doing any more than

I do, but he knows the routine and leaves his food alone until you pray."

"Spencer is one of a kind. That's for sure." Steve gazes at his mother. "And I pray every day that you will understand." He lowers his head and closes his eyes. "Lord, we thank you for this beautiful day and your many blessings. We praise you that your mercies are new every morning. Thank you for bringing us through the storms that have raged against us. Thank you for this food and for giving us this day to share this meal. Guide each of us today so that we will bring glory to you. In Jesus' name. Amen."

As soon as "Amen" leaves Steve's lips, Spencer drops our hands and begins tearing the peel from the banana.

Cynthia stretches her neck a little and peers over at the spot in front of me. "You're not eating, Ellie?"

"I will in a while." I take a sip of my coffee. "I just need coffee first."

"I noticed that you seem tired…" Cynthia scoops up a bite of eggs on her fork. "Of course, you always look stunning, but you are usually in your running clothes this time of the morning. Are you feeling okay?"

"I had a nightmare. After I finally drifted back off, I overslept." *Why did I say that? Now she is going to ask.* Thinking fast, I make a quick change of subject before I have to explain my nightmare. "So, did I hear Steve say that you have some big news?"

"Yes." Cynthia lays her fork down, and with both hands balled into fists, she starts bouncing up and down in her seat with excitement. "Are you ready for this? I am going to run for president."

"President of what?' Steve gives her a quizzical look.

Cynthia sighs, and her eyes widen as she speaks. "The United States of America."

A forced smile appears on Steve's face, and I can tell he doesn't know how to react. Then, it hits me. I realize that I am sitting here with my mouth hanging open. *Say something.*

"Ummm. Congratulations, Cynthia. Have you been thinking about this for a long time, or is this a spur-of-the-moment decision?"

Cynthia clasps her hands together and props her elbows on the table. "It was always my dream to become president, and actually, it was in my future plans to run. That is, until that evil husband of mine, Dennis Denali, did away with me and ran for office himself. How could I have been married to such a devious man?"

"Mom, I am so proud of you… the way you have picked up the pieces and now… president… wow." Steve puts his hand on her shoulder. "Ordinarily, I know you would win by a landslide, but with the last name 'Denali', do you think you have a chance? Don't get me wrong. I don't mean to be negative. It's just, I have a hard time finding work because of who my birth father is. People can be mean. I don't want to see you suffer any more than you already have."

"Steve, that is sweet of you, but I am a grown woman. I can handle it. Besides, it is all in how we present ourselves. And we are victims. I have to make the public see that I was a devoted wife and mother, and my evil husband faked a car accident and had me frozen as an experiment. On top of that, he erased the memories of my poor, innocent children."

Steve cocks his head sideways. "And you think that will be enough to win the presidency?"

"Of course not. The issues are what will win the election. People want change. For goodness' sake, the last president they elected tried to kill them all. Since then, Americans have been stuck with Craig Kutchins, who I honestly believe is scared to death. Every time the media asks him a question, he answers with a question." Cynthia lets out a half-giggle. "Dennis must have chosen him to run as his vice president because he thought Craig would stay out of the way." She gives her head a quick shake. "Anyway, enough about Dennis and his puppets. I have a lot to get done before I make an announcement. I want to time it out just right… you know, not too early but not too late either. And I don't have much time to prepare. The election is in 2052, and we are already at the end of June 2050. The other candidates were probably getting financial backing while I was still frozen in that test tube." Cynthia takes a deep breath appearing to try to calm herself. "My advisor suggested announcing my campaign around the first of May next year. That gives us barely over a year and a half before the election on November 3, 2052.

"So, do you… like already have a party backing you?" I am so tired that I know my words come out all wrong.

"I am running as an independent." She straightens her posture. "Political parties are going to be one of the issues that I address in my candidacy. In his farewell address, George Washington warned Americans about having political parties. And he was right. Our country is divided between the two parties, and the ravine between them is getting deeper and wider. This country doesn't cast votes based on the issues. Their vote is strictly based on if they are Democrat or Republican." Cynthia glances at her phone. "Oh, I have to run. I have a meeting with my publicist." She pushes her chair back and stands up. "We'll talk more later. I am going to need you two to help in the campaign."

Steve and I scoot our chairs away from the table.

"No need to get up." Cynthia leans over and gives Steve a quick hug. Then she gives me a quick pat on the back as she walks past my chair. "Finish your breakfast. I can show myself out. As she leaves the kitchen, she yells back over her shoulder, "Bye, Spencer."

The front door opens and then closes with a thud. Steve and I look at each other.

"So, what do you think of that?" I try to keep a neutral tone since I am not sure how he feels.

"Well, it's not that I don't want to support her. After all, she is my mother… even though I can only remember…" he drops his head, "…in my mind, I have only known her for about four months. You know, I thought eventually I would start to get my memory back." Steve touches his fingertips to the sides of his head. "Anyway, to answer your question, I don't want to be in the spotlight. After escaping the facility and the world finding out that my fath..." he stops and mutters under his breath, "it's so hard to refer to him as my father." He continues, "After the world found out that President Denali was planning to wipe out the population, I think we have had enough publicity to last a lifetime."

I reach over and lay my hand on his. "I know. I was thinking the same thing."

Steve squeezes his eyes closed and exhales.

"Hey, because she is your mother, doesn't mean that you have to be involved in this." I pick up his hand with both of mine and hold it. "Cut yourself some slack. You have been through a lot. Give yourself a little time to absorb everything."

"I know you're right." He opens his eyes but stares straight ahead. "But I keep reminding myself that she has been through a lot too. Taking into consideration all that I have lost, she has lost even more of her life than me. That man that was supposed to be her husband. My father faked her death in a car accident and then let his cryonics team use her as their first human subject."

I shake my head. "No. You aren't looking at the big picture. You still lost more of your life than her."

He raises his eyebrows and looks at me with a confused expression.

I continue before he has a chance to question me. "I understand you are thinking that she was frozen all those years before you were even taken to the president's training facility, but your mother never had her memory erased. You, on the other hand, lost every memory of your entire life."

"I didn't think about it that way. President Denali didn't freeze her because she didn't forget about God. She was just his test dummy to see if he could cryogenically preserve people." Steve taps his fingers on the table. "And now that we know my mother had intentions of running for president back then, it is pretty obvious that he needed to get her out of his way."

"Good morning, everyone." Herb comes rushing past the kitchen table. He still has his black toupee and wears the same red bow tie that he sported in the medical wing of the facility, but instead of a lab coat, a white button-up oxford covers his metallic mid-section. The red centers in his dark brown eyes glow as his robot head does a one-eighty twisting backward. "Oh my," he says in a deep voice with a proper accent. "I see you have already attended to breakfast. My apologies. For some reason, it appears that I have overslept." Herb collects the dirty dishes from the table and takes off toward the sink.

After the investigation was complete, Steve asked if he could keep Herb, and since he could prove Herb was his prototype, no one put up an argument.

I push back from the table. "I am going to do my Bible study and then go for a run. I need the stress release. My schedule is all out of whack from oversleeping, and my OCD is kicking in."

"Okay." Steve's face takes on a strained expression. "I wish you would run on the treadmill though. No one else is around out here, but I still worry about you running with those earbuds in. We live in a crazy world." He tilts his head to the side and winks at me. "At least let me know when you leave so I can time how long you are gone."

"I'll be fine. You know I love the fresh air when I run." I kiss him on the cheek. "But I'll tell you when I leave." I start out of the kitchen, but a thought hits me. "Oh, yeah." I spin around on my heels. "Don't forget about dinner tonight with Alice and Gerald. We are supposed to meet them at Gerald's restaurant at seven o'clock."

"Glad you said something. I had forgotten." Steve stands and pushes his chair under. "Do you think we will be home by nine? A new episode of *Dateline* comes on tonight."

"I doubt it." I raise one eyebrow. "I know you love that show, but how can it even compare to the drama we went through. The President of the United States had a demented plan to destroy the world and repopulate it with his personal army of followers that had no knowledge of God. He put us, along with a whole lot of other young people, in this so-called training facility located in an old military complex hidden inside of a mountain, where he hypnotized us and shocked our brains to erase our memory. And then he froze the people that did not forget God in tubes using cryogenics. We took off on a wild goose chase trying to find his plane before it dropped the poison that would destroy humanity, and along the way, you found out that the President was your father." I shake my head. "Sorry, but no television show will find a true crime story that can come close to that."

"I know. But I still like it." He picks up Spencer. "Come on, Spencer. We have work to do." He follows me from the kitchen and heads toward his office.

I walk out onto the little glass sunporch on the back of the house and pick up my red-letter King James Bible with my name, "Ellie Hatcher" embossed in gold in the lower corner. My mom gave it to me when I was ten years old. I rub my hand across the grain of the black leather cover. *I will never forget how much I missed having this in President Denali's training facility. I will never again take for granted the freedom to be able to hold this book in my hands and read the Word of God.*

I plop down on the round braided rug in the middle of the floor, crisscross my legs, and get taken aback when I open the front cover and my eyes fall on my mom's handwriting just inside:

'Thy Word is a lamp unto my feet, and a light unto my path.' My dearest Ellie, read the words of this book and record them in your heart. Remember, even in the darkness, you are never alone. 'For the Lord thy God is with thee whithersoever thou goest.' God is always with you, and His Word will light your way.

When I was a little girl, I had a horrible phobia of the dark. I giggle to myself as the image of my bedroom fills my mind. The room was lit up like a runway because I had a nightlight plugged

in almost every wall outlet. Even with all the nightlights, sometimes I would still go wake my mom up in the middle of the
night. She would sit on my bed and read the Bible to me until I
would fall back asleep.

Shaking myself back to the present, I lift the ribbon book-
mark to turn to the book of Ephesians, where I left off yesterday,
but my finger misses the gap made by the ribbon, and instead,
my Bible flips open to chapter fourteen in the book of John. I
glance down at the page filled with red letters and start to read as
I relish in the knowledge that these are the words spoken by
Jesus.

> *"And I will pray the Father, and he shall give you*
> *another Comforter, that he may abide with you*
> *forever;*
> *Even the Spirit of truth; whom the world cannot*
> *receive, because it seeth him not, neither*
> *knoweth him: but ye know him; for he dwelleth*
> *with you, and shall be in you.*
> *I will not leave you comfortless: I will come to you."*

A smile spreads across my face as I absorb the words. *His
Holy Spirit lives in me.* I look on down the page.

> *"But the Comforter which is the Holy Ghost, whom*
> *the Father will send in my name, he shall teach*
> *you all things, and bring all things to your*
> *remembrance, whatsoever I have said unto you.*
> *Peace I leave with you, my peace I give unto you:*
> *not as the world giveth, I give unto you. Let not*
> *your heart be troubled, neither let it be afraid."*

I close my Bible and shift up on my knees. With my hands
pressed together, I thank God for His blessings and for sending
His Holy Spirit to live inside of me. I ask for His forgiveness. I
ask for His protection around my friends and family. I pray for

Cynthia, that she would have a personal experience with Jesus. And I ask Him to carry my burdens and lift my fears. I raise my hands above my head and open my fingers in a physical act to remind myself that He cannot carry these burdens unless I let go and give them to Him. Then, I thank Him again for always being with me.

Feeling so much lighter, I jump to my feet and dash to the bedroom. In a flash, I slide on my running shorts and t-shirt and grab my earbuds from the dresser. I stride through the house to the closet by the front door to get my sneakers. *Oh yeah.* I turn around and head into the den that Steve uses for his inventions. "Hey." I call out as I round the corner, then come to an abrupt stop. Steve is lying back, fully reclined in a black leather chair that is positioned in the middle of the room, facing a giant screen hanging on the wall. The image on the display moves along a dirt path winding through trees with mountains in the background. The screen reminds me of the one at the facility in front of the large treadmill belt on the floor that made it appear like I was running outside on these different trails.

Suction cups attached to wires that lead from a small metal box on a table beside the chair are stuck on Steve's forehead, chest, arms, and legs, and he has headphones covering his ears. I walk into his field of vision since he can't hear me and give a slight wave. I guess I startled him because he jerks all over. Either that or the contraption hooked to him gave him an electrical shock.

He pulls the headphones from his ear. "You scared me. I didn't hear you come in."

With wide eyes, I look back and forth between him and the screen. "What are you doing?"

"Oh. I am doing my workout. It's cardio day."

Crinkling my forehead in confusion, I cannot help but state the obvious. "Ummm. But you aren't moving. You are sitting in a recliner."

"Yeah. I hate it too. I can't stand to sit still." He pushes the footrest down with his legs. "But I think maybe this is my best gadget yet because so many people say they don't have time to workout. Well, with this baby, I can run ten miles and catch up on my sleep at the same time. You want to try?"

"That's okay. I don't want to interrupt." I walk over, square up the table with the metal box to align with the tiles on the floor, and then kiss the top of Steve's head. "I am leaving for my run. I love you." I walk toward the door. "Be careful with that thing." I yell back over my shoulder. As I exit the room, I mutter under my breath, "Anything that has wires with suction cups and attaches to your body frightens me."

I pull my running shoes from the closet, slip them on in front of the door, and take off.

Chapter Three

I powerwalk up the gravel driveway back toward the house. I usually run two miles, but for some reason, I keep losing my balance. I am not dizzy. I just keep having episodes where I space out and see white spots. I grab my side. *Great. Now my stomach is cramping.* I almost double over, but then, as quick as it came, the pain goes away. As I run up the porch steps, I feel fine and wish I had run the second mile.

"Back already?" Steve says as I walk through the front door.

"Yeah. I only m-m-made it..." white spots fill my vision again, and the room seems to fade, "... a m-m-mile." My knees give out beneath me, and the lights go out.

~

"Ellie! Ellie! Wake up, Ellie!"

Someone is calling my name.

"Ellie, can you hear me? Please, wake up."

I open my eyes and look straight into another set of eyes staring down at me... deep brown eyes. *Déjà vu.* My heart almost leaps from my chest, and I gasp.

"It's okay, sweetheart. An ambulance is on the way."

My surroundings come into focus, and I push myself up with my hands to a sitting position. *That was so weird... just like the first time I met him.* I know my eyes must be as big as dinner plates.

"Ellie, lie down. You shouldn't be trying to sit up." Steve eases his arm around me. "What is it? You look like you have seen a ghost."

"I-it w-was weird. Wh-wh-when I woke up, you were looking down at me... like when I woke up after Herb and Shelly put the chip in my head." I smile at how bizarre it sounds, and then I let out a little giggle. "Just now, before I got my bearings together, for a second, I thought I was back in that horrible place."

Steve glances down at the white lab coat he is wearing and bites his lips together. For some reason, he likes to wear it when he works on his robotic inventions. "I guess if you are disoriented, the scenario would sort of appear similar."

The doorbell buzzes. "Paramedics!" a voice yells through the door.

"I am not riding in an ambulance. Look, I am fine." I make a move to stand up.

"Ellie, lie back down." Steve glares at me as he opens the door. "You just fainted."

"I am fine." I argue.

Two paramedics lumber through the door carrying duffle bags with equipment.

"Ellie, please just let them check your vitals. If everything seems fine, I will drive you to the hospital. But you are going."

Sighing, I drop my shoulders in defeat. "Fine." I agree as one of the EMTs checks my pulse.

~

LYING on the bed in the emergency room after being poked and prodded for several hours, I stare at the ceiling. Steve sits in a chair in the corner of the little room.

"I don't think I can lay here another minute." I complain.

"Well, we are not leaving until the doctor tells us what is going on with you." Steve taps on his phone. "Oh, man. What is wrong with this world?"

"What?" I peer over at him.

"Twelve people were killed this morning in a road rage accident in Florida. The article says that a driver got angry when a car pulled out in front of him. The driver chased the car down and side-swiped it, pushing it into oncoming traffic. It hit another car head-on, and five cars behind that one piled up like dominoes."

I open my mouth to comment, but before I get a word out, an older man with salt and pepper hair steps through the curtain.

"Mrs. Denali, I am Dr. Ericson." The doctor makes eye contact with me and then sits down on a little stool that has wheels. "How are you feeling?" he asks as he rolls on the stool over to the side of the bed.

I sit up, tucking the blanket beneath my legs. "I am feeling much better, thank you."

"Well, I understand that you fainted this morning, and before that, you had a few episodes where you experienced some light-headedness and blurred vision." Dr. Ericson moves his finger across the tablet screen. "Anything else?"

"It's not exactly blurred vision." I try to explain. "It's more like… bright spots. I see bright white spots, and the last time it happened, my stomach started to cramp." I twist my mouth to the side as I think of what to say. Since I want to get out of here, I don't want to open a bigger can of worms. "Dr. Ericson, I don't think it's anything to worry about. I haven't been sleeping all that well. I have had a few bad dreams that woke me up in the middle of the night. My body is probably reacting to lack of sleep."

"Well, that could be a contributing factor." He glares at his tablet through a pair of tiny, square, wire-rimmed glasses. "However, I have been reviewing your lab results, and I believe your fainting spell is a result of low blood sugar. Mrs. Denali, what have you had to eat in the last twenty-four hours?"

I think for a minute. "A tuna sandwich."

"A tuna sandwich?" he repeats after me. "When did you have the tuna sandwich?"

"I had it for lunch yesterday." I take a deep breath as I realize that it sounds like I am starving myself. "Those nightmares have had me a little nervous, and I haven't felt like eating."

"I see." He lowers the tablet and holds it on his lap. "Mrs. Denali, I am going to be honest. Your bloodwork is impeccable. I haven't seen cholesterol numbers like this in a long time. However, your urine specimen contained ketones. That means your body is burning fat because you are not getting enough food to supply glucose for energy. Your fainting spell was most likely the result of low blood sugar."

"So…" I clear my throat, "all I need to do is eat better."

"Yes." Dr. Ericson smiles. "That's all. I am guessing from your perfect cholesterol and the fact that you were running this morning before you fainted that you exercise regularly. With your active lifestyle, you should be eating every few hours because your body probably burns calories quickly." He stands up. "You are free to go home as soon as the nurse comes in with your paperwork. But you mentioned trouble sleeping because of some nightmares. Do you need something to help you rest at night?"

"No. That's not necessary. I don't like to take medication unless it is absolutely necessary."

"Very well. I can't argue with that. I do recommend that you take a few days off from work and let your body rest and recuperate." He lifts the tablet and starts swiping his finger across the display. "What do you do, Mrs. Denali?"

"I am a field agent for the FBI." I answer, already knowing that missing work is not an option since I have only been on the job for a few months. I finished getting my degree in criminal justice through an online program, and because of my involvement in bringing down President Denali and stopping the plane before the poison was dropped, the FBI waived the two years experience requirement. In addition, as part of the government's appreciation of my service in protecting our citizens, they also waived the twenty weeks of training at Quantico as long as I could pass the exams. They said I had already spent enough time away from my family, and I shouldn't have to lose anymore. Luckily, most of the courses I completed with my degree covered the textbook information, and since I work out daily, the fitness test was not a problem. I did have to complete an extensive weapons and fight training course though, but that was during the day at a facility in Washington.

"Then, I definitely suggest that you take a couple of days. It was nice to meet you, Mrs. Denali." He turns toward Steve. "Mr. Denali, take your wife to get something to eat. I bet she will feel much better."

"That will be our first stop." Steve shakes the doctor's hand. "Thank you, Doctor."

I GAZE at the house as we creep up the narrow drive, and my mind drifts back to the first time I saw it. I remembered thinking that it should have been torn down years earlier, but then Steve, Alice, Eileen, Spencer, and I went inside. I close my eyes and picture that living room. I still get tears in my eyes when I think about that dusty, tattered Bible lying in the middle of that coffee table. I had longed for my Bible in that facility, but we weren't allowed to have one there. When I saw that Bible, I hugged it to my chest. I knew God had put it there.

Steve must have known God had led us to that house too, because when we got back from our honeymoon, he told me he had a big surprise for me. I couldn't believe he had bought the house and completely renovated it. He said we had to complete the package. We had already found the owner of the Volkswagen Bug that seemed to magically appear in a garage just when we needed it, and luckily, the owner sold it to us along with the old Kubota tractor that Steve and Spencer fell in love with. After a little elbow grease and TLC, we had the car looking new again. The tractor is still a work in progress. Anyway, Steve thought it was only fitting that we save that house too.

Steve grabs the pizza from the backseat as I step out of the car.

"If we eat all that, we aren't going to be hungry for tonight." I say as Steve pulls out the box with the extra-large supreme inside.

"You need to eat, and it is only three o'clock. We don't even meet Alice and Gerald until seven o'clock, and you know we will talk for at least an hour before we eat."

I nod because I know he is right.

"I hope Spencer is okay. We have been gone a while." I remark as we walk up the steps into the house.

"I was thinking the same thing. I hope he hasn't had any episodes with his PTSD."

"Nothing that pizza won't cure, I'm sure." As we pass through the living room, my eyes start to water when they fix on that Bible in the middle of that old coffee table. I had to leave it just as it was when we found it.

"You really must let someone know when you plan to be gone this long." Herb's proper accent reflects an angry edge as he stands in the doorway of the kitchen holding Spencer, who appears to be trembling. "I have not been able to do anything but console this monkey."

"Sorry." Steve puts the pizza down and takes Spencer from Herb. "I'll take care of him. Could you please get us some plates and bottles of water?"

"Of course." Herb's tone calms. "Is everything okay?"

"Ellie fainted and had to see the doctor, but she will be fine. She just needs to eat." Steve explains.

"All because I overslept and didn't get an appropriate breakfast prepared." Herb mumbles as he moves to the cabinet for the plates.

Steve hands Spencer to me. "Here, Ellie. Let him know you are okay. He is scared."

I sit down in one of the dining chairs with Spencer and rock him back and forth while Steve puts the pizza on the plates. I notice he cuts a third off of one of the slices for Spencer. I guess pizza is not all that healthy for monkeys. *Not that healthy for humans either*, I think to myself as I look at the puddles of grease standing in the middle of the pie.

"Okay, let's eat." Steve says as he sits down.

I lift Spencer over into his chair and he starts clapping his hands when he sees his plate. *Wow. The healing power of pizza.* "What's this?" As I lean back in my seat, I catch sight of a folded white piece of paper on the floor.

"I don't know." Steve shrugs. "What does it say?"

I unfold the paper, but before I can look at it, Spencer has his hands out, bouncing up and down in his seat.

"I guess we better say blessing first." Steve grabs my hand as Spencer snatches hold of both our hands. "Dear Lord, thank you for taking care of Ellie and letting her feel better. Thank you for this food. Please, Lord, help her to be able to eat and let her rest well tonight. We praise you for your blessings. In Jesus' name. Amen."

Spencer sticks the slice of pizza in his mouth, and Steve rolls his eyes.

"Anyway," Steve turns his attention back to the paper, "you were looking at the paper."

"Yeah. It's a letter or something." I squint my eyes to see the small print and read out loud.

"My dearest ice princess,

I am counting the minutes until I see you again. For so many years, I looked upon your beauty, frozen in time. I think of the endless nights that I would sneak into that lab and slip into a trance as I gazed into your eyes that sparkled like snowflakes

through the frost. I wanted to help you, but I didn't know how.
Please forgive me for not knowing how. For some reason, I have
been given another chance, and I promise to never fail you again.
Together, we will make this plan work. Now, there is no one to
stand in the way. I can't wait until tomorrow. I will be waiting in
the usual spot.

    All my love,
    Mitchell"

"Who's Mitchell?" Steve crinkles his forehead and takes a
bite of pizza.

I lay the paper on the table. "I have no idea. That's all it
says." My stomach knots up at the thought of taking a bite, and
acid rises in my throat. "It must have fallen out of your mom's
purse this morning."

"Whoever he is, he was obviously at that facility." Steve
stares at the wall as he chews his food. He seems to drift a
million miles away in thought.

I pick up the slice of pizza. *Ellie, you heard the doctor. You
have to eat,* I remind myself. I lay the pizza back on my plate and
tear a bitesize piece of the crust off the edge. Swallowing hard, I
lift it to my mouth and pause as I touch it to my lips. *Mind over
matter, Ellie.* Nibble by nibble, I get down the little piece in my
hand. My stomach settles down, so I tear off another bite of the
crust and pop it in my mouth.

After a minute, he looks over at me. "I don't like it, Ellie.
What plan? What is she up to?"

"Maybe it's just this whole running for president thing."

Steve stands up, pulls his phone from his pocket, and sits
back down. Biting his bottom lip, he taps his finger on the
screen and puts the phone to his ear. "Hey, sis. I am so glad you
answered. Do you remember anybody named Mitchell that was
at the facility?"

As I listen to Steve's conversation, I blot the top of the cheese
with my napkin to absorb the grease and try a taste of the cheesy
part. *Alice is right. This is like Manna From Heaven.* I start

scarfing down the rest of my pizza when my eyes catch sight of the vein pulsing in Steve's forehead, and his eyes look like they are about to pop out of his head. *I am guessing she knows who Mitchell is.*

"I'm sure it's nothing. I will explain later. Thanks, Teresa." He peers over at me with his mouth open. "Dr. Mitchell Blakely. That is the only Mitchell she knows of."

A bite of pizza almost gets stuck in my throat, and I feel all the blood drain from my face. "Unless he holds his age well, isn't he a bit young for your mother?"

"There is definitely a significant gap in their ages," Steve's jaw clenches, "but I am more concerned about what this plan is of theirs." He pushes back from the table. "Do you mind if I go work on the tractor for a bit? I need to process all this drama surrounding my mother, and tinkering with that tractor clears my mind."

"Sure, go ahead. It's only a thirty-minute drive to the restaurant, so we have a while. I think I might have another piece of pizza and call Eileen." My phone rings as I put another slice of pizza on my plate. I reach for my pocket but realize I gave it to Steve at the hospital.

"Oh, I put it in your purse." he says as he bends to pick my handbag up off the floor and passes it to me.

I pull the phone out and note all the texts from my mother. *Oh no.* Quickly, I swipe the screen and put the phone to my ear. "I am so sorry, Mom. My phone was in my purse, and I just realized how late it is."

"But you are okay?" her voice trembles through the line.

"Yes, Mom. Why wouldn't I be?"

"Oh, Ellie." Mom is in such a panic that she almost shouts through the phone. "Have you not been watching the news?"

"I saw about two minutes this morning, but no, not really." I reply as Steve stands in the doorway, casting me a worried look.

"How can you work for the FBI and not know what's going on?"

"Mom, it's my day off, and I have been busy. What on earth has got you so upset?" I ask her.

"Well, you know how we were talking the other day about all the shootings and violence that has been on the news. A few hours ago, someone strapped on a bunch of explosives and walked into the police station in one of those new suburbs outside of Washington. Blew the whole place up. According to the news, they don't even know how many people have died." Her tone weakens. "Ellie, I was so scared that you got called into work on that case. I don't like this job of yours. Too many bad things are happening."

"Mom, bad things have always happened." I click on the television to the national news station. My heart starts to race when I take in the scene behind the reporter.

"No, ma'am. Not like this." Her words blend into the background as I watch the body bags being carried from the smoking, fragmented structure. I hear Steve gasp behind me.

"Just be careful, Ellie."

"What?" I snap back from the news report and absorb Mom's words. "Oh. I will. Stop worrying."

"Not possible. I am your mother. Text me tonight. I love you."

"Love you, too, Mom." I lower the phone, and Steve's hand rubs my shoulder.

"I take it Jillian is worked up with worry about her daughter's new job." he whispers in my ear.

"That and the number of mass killings that have occurred in such a short time." I give my head a slight shake in disbelief. "I know mass shootings have been on the rise… but yesterday, there was that shooting at a mall in Texas. This morning I saw that there was a shooting at a grocery store in Chicago that killed five people. Then you read about that road rage incident that killed twelve people. Now, this. Why would someone strap enough explosives to themselves to blow up a building?"

My phone vibrates in my hand. I let out a long sigh when I see the screen. "I have to go to work."

"What? No." Steve says almost in a whiny voice. "But you aren't on call, and we have dinner plans."

"I know. But I am a new agent, and apparently, with the extenuating circumstances, a lot of agents have been sent to assist in the investigation." I smile. "Don't worry. The text says they need extra help in the office." I stand on my tiptoes and kiss his cheek. "I'm sure Alice will understand, and we can postpone until tomorrow night. After all, it's Gerald's restaurant. He is pretty much always there."

"Okay," he utters in defeat. "Just please be careful."

"I promise. I'll call Alice while I change into my work clothes."

I walk into the bedroom with the phone to my ear. Alice answers on the second ring. "Ellie, I was about to call you."

"Hey, Alice. Not you too. My mom already called in a panic about that police station, but I only have to go help out in the office. They have the experienced agents on the scene."

"No, it's not that. Well, I mean, I worry about you and your job, but I also know God's got you." She rattles her words off like she is in a race against the clock. "Ellie, did you hear about that road rage accident earlier today in Florida?"

"Yeah. Steve saw an article on his phone and said something about it."

"The media just released the name of the driver a few minutes ago." A sniffle filters through the phone. "Ellie, the driver's name was Linda Bateman. When they flashed the photograph on the screen, I thought I was going to be sick. Ellie, it was Darla. I guess Linda Bateman was her real name. But we knew her as Darla. She hit that car and forced it onto the wrong side of the road."

My legs give in and I collapse to my knees beside the bed. "Steve read the article like the driver was a man... I guess the media just assumed. I-I c-can't believe Darla killed all those people."

"Ellie," Alice gulps, "Darla was killed too." Her voice cracks.

"I know she killed all those people, but she was still my friend. We all shared the same room in that place."

I drop my head and stare at the floor. The room starts to swirl around.

"Ellie... are you still there, Ellie?"

"Uh-huh." is all I force from my mouth as tears flood my face.

Alice clears her throat. "I know you have to go to work. But keep your guard up. I need you." Another sniffle sifts across the line. "I guess we have to cancel our dinner."

"Can we do it tomorrow night, instead?"

"Absolutely. I will tell Gerald to make something extra special. See you guys tomorrow."

I toss my phone on the bed, wipe the tears from my eyes, and push myself to my feet. *Just put one foot in front of the other,* I tell myself. I scoot my feet along under the weight of my exhausted body toward the closet to get dressed. *I can do all things through Christ which strengtheneth me.*

Chapter Four

Steve and I push through the carousel-style revolving doors into Gerald's restaurant. Actually, Steve pushes the door with one hand and helps me keep up with the other. I didn't get home from work until two o'clock in the morning. Agents, including Kate, who has befriended and mentored me since I started, were on the scene of the explosion most of the night investigating. Nineteen people had been killed. Twelve were police officers, six were people who were in the station for questioning and various other reasons, and, of course, there was the man that had walked in with the explosives strapped to his body. My assignment was in the office, doing background checks on the alleged perpetrator and the victims. I was so disturbed by the search results that I tossed and turned until four. When I finally did fall asleep, I had that horrible nightmare again and woke up screaming. Steve held me until I went back to sleep, and then he got up early and had pancakes waiting on me when I came into the kitchen this morning. Apparently, Herb's charging station had come unplugged again.

When we step out of the revolving door, Alice strides across the dining room toward us, waving her arms. Her blonde hair lays about six inches past her shoulders now, but her petite frame makes it appear longer. As soon as she is within reach, she engulfs both of us in a hug at the same time. I couldn't have made it inside that facility without Alice. I know God put her there with me. He gave me a Christian friend, a sister in Christ, to help me through it. And, of course, Gerald was there too, on the same team as Alice and me. He feels like the brother I never had.

"I know it was only last week that we had dinner at your place, but I have missed you guys. Come on. Gerald set us up a special table in the back." She puts her hand on my shoulder as we walk. "Oh, and I hope you don't mind. I talked to Eileen this morning. She and Teresa are going to have dinner with us too."

The thought of all of us together calms the butterflies in my stomach, and my lips curve up. "Mind? Of course, I don't mind. All of us together… this is perfect." *And it will give me an opportunity to talk to them about my discovery.*

Steve grabs my hand and gives it a squeeze. I can tell by the look in his eyes he is thinking the same thing. It's so weird how he reads my mind.

Alice leads us down a tiny corridor and through a door into this small room with a formal table set for six positioned in the center. The lights are dimmed, and two candles are lit in the middle of the table.

Gerald rushes through the door and pulls me into a hug. Then he steps over and shakes Steve's hand. "Did you guys drive the little 'bug'? I love that car."

Steve shakes his head. "No. We brought the Hydromax since it is a half-hour drive to get here. It's too hard to find gas, and if you do, the price is through the roof."

Gerald's face starts to develop a pink tint. Politics gets him worked up. "It's just not right. I know they've banned the production of gas-powered vehicles and want them off the road altogether, but most people can't afford to go out and buy a new car. The government acts as if they care by telling people that they understand the financial burden of buying a new car and assure the public that they won't ban gas-powered cars from the highway produced before 2049, then they raise gas prices sky-high and add all kinds of taxes to businesses that sell it. One way or another, they find a way to control us. That's what it's all about… controlling us."

"Well," Steve remarks, "it seems to me their ploy is backfiring, just like when they tried to switch to electric cars. Parking lots couldn't harbor enough public charging stations. People who commuted long distances struggled, especially if they forgot to charge. You can fill a gas tank in a couple of minutes, but it could take eight hours to charge an empty battery." Steve shakes his head. "Now hydro fuel is cheap and easy to fill up, but the cost of the cars is pretty steep. And since they raised gas prices, companies are shutting down because employees can't afford gas to get to work."

"These government officials never learn." Gerald rants.

Teresa and Eileen step into the room and Gerald turns to give them each a hug.

"Alice made me put together a special menu for tonight." Gerald says as he pulls out the chairs for us to sit. He grabs a pitcher of water and puts it on the table as he sits.

"Ooooh. I can't wait." Teresa rubs her stomach. "I have been studying all day and I am starving."

"So, did you decide what you are going to school for, Teresa?" Gerald asks across the table. "Alice told me you got your GED and started some college courses."

Teresa glances at Eileen and gives a half-smile. "I struggled for a bit, trying to figure out something that I would want to do every day for the rest of my life. But Eileen gave me some great advice. I have decided to be a clinical psychologist."

"Wow." Gerald nods. "You care so much about other people. That is the perfect career for you. Eileen did give you great advice."

"Oh, I didn't tell her to be a psychologist." Eileen chimes in. "I struggled enough choosing my own major. I wouldn't dare choose for someone else."

We all look confused.

"What was the great advice then?" I prod.

Teresa straightens her posture. "Eileen told me to think about all that we had been through and how I could use it for good. She said that is how she decided she was going to get a degree in molecular biology and do medical research."

"I was frozen for two years and brought back." Eileen tilts her head. "Denali used all his scientific research for evil, but imagine the good that could be accomplished. It is hard to fathom that a person can be frozen for years, and their memories wiped clean, but we still don't have a cure for cancer."

"Mr. Jameson," a petite waitress, wearing a white button-up oxford and a black apron, calls out from the doorway.

Gerald looks in her direction.

"Sorry to interrupt, but," she pulls at her ponytail as she speaks, "there is a slight complication in the kitchen."

The muscles in Gerald's face visibly tighten. "What kind of complication?"

The waitress takes a step into the room. "Colby miscalculated the cooking time for the main course."

Gerald's face turns red, and his nostrils appear to slightly flare. "I'm sorry. It seems I better check on dinner." He springs up from his chair and strides from the room.

I swallow hard. *He looks angry.* My heart starts pumping faster. *Stop. Don't overreact. He is only going to check on the kitchen.* I slide my chair back. "Excuse me for a moment," I say politely. "I need to go to the ladies' room."

Steve must know where I am going because he casts me a worried look.

"I'll be right back." I look him in the eye as I speak, and he gives a quick nod.

I pad with soft steps down the tiny corridor toward the restrooms. As I pass the kitchen, I look through the rectangular glass window in the middle of the door. Gerald is talking to a young man in chef's attire. *Gerald doesn't seem to be upset.* I trudge on toward the restroom, trying not to make my spying obvious.

Just as I put my hand out to push on the restroom door, it swings open with a jerk, and my heart leaps from my chest.

"Oh, dear. I am so sorry." A lady with graying hair and a soft smile apologizes. "I didn't mean to startle you."

"No worries," I reply with a giggle. "It wasn't your fault. I am just a little on edge." I pass through the door as the kind lady holds it open. With my hand still on my chest from the startle, I walk to the sink and stare in the mirror for a minute. *I wish I hadn't looked in the mirror. I'm a mess.* I run my fingers through my hair, but there is nothing I can do for my pale skin and puffy eyes. "I need sleep." I mutter under my breath. I pull off a paper towel and use it to open the bathroom door.

When I pass back by the kitchen door, I notice Gerald is laughing. He has one hand on the young man's shoulder, and he is gesturing with the other like he is telling a story. I exhale with a sigh of relief. *I can't believe I was worried. I know Gerald better than that.* Shaking my head in frustration with myself, I plod back to our table in the back room.

Steve jumps up to help me with my chair, and at the same time, gives me a quizzical look. I crack a little smile, and he nods in understanding. A moment later, Gerald comes back pushing a cart with six plates heaped with pasta and shrimp tossed in some sort of white sauce and melted cheese.

"Everything okay?" Alice lifts her eyes toward Gerald.

Gerald laughs, "Yes. My new chef baked the lasagna a little... well, a lot too long." Gerald places a plate in front of each of us as he talks. "I was a tiny bit upset until I saw the poor kid's face. He looked scared to death, and it reminded me of my first cooking job. I was so nervous. I got preoccupied with dressing the plates and trying to make the food look like the fancy restaurants did on television that I forgot about the oil I was heating. The fire department came, and the whole place had to be evacuated because of the smoke." Gerald put two baskets of bread in the middle of the table between the candles. "I told him the story, which made him laugh, and he seems to be more relaxed now."

"Gerald, you are something else. Too bad all employers aren't like you." I say with pride in my voice.

I silently thank God for the people gathered at this table. We are a Christian family that is always supporting and encouraging each other in our faith.

We join hands for the blessing, I have a thing about germs and touching people's hands. I get nauseous, and sometimes I even have an anxiety attack. But it's weird. With this group, it is the complete opposite. When we hold hands to pray, I feel comfort, and this calm settles over me.

"GERALD, you outdid yourself. That pasta was delicious." I am so full that I have to lean back in my chair.

"Oh, Ellie," Gerald shakes his head. "You always say that."

"No, really." I lay my napkin on the table. "I would lick the plate clean, but that would probably be inappropriate."

At that, everyone doubles over in laughter.

"Okay, Ellie." Alice raises one eyebrow and stares me down. "I have been waiting all evening for you to spill about what is bothering you."

"It's noth…"

Alice narrows her eyes into slits.

"Yeah, okay." I cover my face with my hands and take a deep breath. "I just don't want to be a downer when we are having such a great time."

"Talk to us, Ellie. What's going on?" Alice reaches across the table and gently pulls my hands from my face.

I turn back and look at the door. "Can anyone hear us in here?"

"No, but just in case..." Gerald strides over and closes the glass-paned door. He pats my shoulder as he rounds the table to sit back down.

"Yesterday, I got called into work because so many agents were helping out at the scene of the explosion. Normally, mass shootings and things of this magnitude fall to local and state authorities, and the FBI works behind the scenes when needed with background searches and things like that. But in this case, a whole police department was wiped out, so most of the agents in our office were out there, hands-on in the investigation." I swipe a twig of hair from my face. "Anyway, when I arrived at the office, I was instructed to research and find out as much information about the suspect as possible and see if he had any links to anyone in the department." I am talking so fast I have to stop and take a deep breath.

"They said on the news today that one of the officers in that department had pulled the guy over and had given him a speeding ticket earlier yesterday morning." Teresa comments in a questioning tone.

"Yes. That's right." I confirm. "One of the agents on the scene discovered the video on the officer's squad car camera." Sharp pains pulse through my head, and I push my fingers against my temples. "As I was doing his background check, I discovered that this guy was reported missing about four years ago. Then a year and a half ago, he was found. He was rescued from President Denali's complex at Raven Rock." I pause, but only silence fills the room, so I continue. "When I saw that, I immediately thought of Alice telling me about Darla, so I started doing more research. In the shooting incident at the grocery store, the perpetrator was in President Denali's training facility. The mall shooting... same. I started to panic. So, I looked up the bus hostage thing in Georgia last week and the massacre in that fast food restaurant in Arkansas... both perpetrators were recruits in President Denali's army. I could keep going, but you all get the idea."

"So," Eileen grabs the edge of the table as she speaks in a flat tone, "you are saying that the people who were in President Denali's training complex are snapping and committing mass murder."

"I don't know what is happening. And I really didn't want to upset you guys with it, but my gut tells me that it is not a coincidence that all these people were in that facility."

As if all of our minds are linked together, we turn and gaze at Teresa.

Teresa casts her eyes at each of us. "Why are all of you looking at me? I haven't done anything."

"We know you haven't done anything." Steve stands up and walks around to the other side of the table, where she is sitting next to Gerald. He squats beside her chair and puts his hand on her shoulder. "Teresa, you knew everything about that man's plan. He had essentially put you in charge of the recruits and the facility. Do you know of anything he could have had done to us in there that would cause this?"

Teresa drops her head. "I-I don't know what it could be." She closes her eyes.

"Even though you have told us the story before, maybe if you start from the beginning, you will remember something else." Steve takes his sister's hand. "You are the only source of information that we have."

Squeezing her eyes tighter, Teresa swallows hard and starts to talk. "Now that I have my real birth certificate, I figure I must have been about eighteen or nineteen. And that adds up with Mr. Hatcher's timeline of when President Denali acquired access to Cheyenne Mountain Complex. Honestly, everything at the beginning is like trying to see through a thick fog. But I do remember getting that so-called electrotherapy for a while. And President Denali would call me into his office there at the facility quite often and talk to me. Please remember, I had no recollection he was my father." She takes a shallow breath. "He introduced himself to me as the President of the United States, Dennis Denali. In the beginning, he would commend me on how well I was doing at the facility and would make small remarks about my outstanding credentials and accomplishments in the medical field. Before long, he had me believing I had my Ph.D." A tear trickles down Teresa's face.

Steve reaches up and wipes it away with his finger.

"Don't forget," Teresa opens her eyes and glances at us, "I had lost all knowledge of God. At this point, it was as if I had never heard of God." She closes her eyes again. "He would make comments about how corrupt the world had become and that it was because of all these so-called saints or followers of Jesus. I would go to these hypnosis sessions with Dr. Eckert, and I think I was literally being brainwashed because it wasn't long before I developed a hatred for Christians. I had no idea who God was or what Christians believed, but I hated them. Little by little, in these private meetings, President Denali would say things about getting rid of the entire population, except for his chosen few, and starting over. Pretty soon, he had me right on board with him wanting to destroy people that I didn't even know, and bit by bit, he made me feel like I was making a contribution to creating a better world. He started to reveal how the recruits coming in for training would be part of his personal army, and once society was destroyed, his chosen recruits would repopulate the earth. He told me how he was erasing their memories and giving them all new names. That's when he made me the head of the facility in the position right under him. He said he could not be at the facility and take care of his duties as president at the same time and that, with my work ethic and my credentials as a doctor, I was the perfect person to help him out and oversee the training of his army."

"Okay," Alice leans in closer as she has to look around Gerald to see Teresa, "what about the tracking chips, the cryonics, the reprimanding… anything there that could have done something to people?"

"Well, the tracking chips only let us know the exact location of the trainees and allowed us to overhear their conversations. I can't say that something else wasn't added with the chip, but I was never aware of it. As far as the cryonics, all I knew was that

President Denali had a research team, and they were freezing those that kept any knowledge of God after the electrotherapy should have cleaned out their memory. So, only Denali's team of scientists would know that, but I don't see how that could have anything to do with this because Darla was never frozen."

"That's true." Alice nods in agreement. "Is there anything else you can think of? What about the reprimanding?"

Teresa rubs her forehead with her fingertips, "I don't know. That reprimanding was supposed to be a punishment for trainees who broke the rules. I think Dr. Eckert might have headed that up, but I am not even sure of that. I wasn't dragged into it until it didn't work like it should on everyone. I was told the trainee would have a sort of nightmare that would leave them humiliated and let them know their real status in the world. I never experienced it, but I heard it was like monsters clawing and chanting cruel insults."

"Oh… let me tell you, it was a lot worse than that," Gerald rants. "It was like demons swiping these long dagger-like nails at you and whispering all your shortcomings and every mistake you have ever made. Words cannot capture the horror of it. I woke up wanting to die."

"But not everyone had that. Some were coming out more hopeful than they went in… like Alice and Ellie." Teresa looks back and forth between us. "That's when President Denali got livid and started jumping down my throat, but I had no idea why the punishment wasn't working on some people."

Gerald's face goes blank, and I notice he seems to be lost in thought. Then, he pops straight up from his chair like a spring and strides out of the room.

"Wonder where he's going?" Alice mutters in a low voice.

A minute later, Gerald steps back into the room, and his eyes lock on Alice. He eases over next to her and lifts her hand with his. "Alice, I love you." He smiles. "Do you remember the day in level one when we sat in that dining room talking about the new names they had given us? I was complaining about being Bob, and you were fussing because you didn't think you looked like a

Delores. They hadn't given us last names, so we decided to make up our own. You named yourself Ducati after the motorcycle. I didn't know your real name then, but I knew you were someone special. And now, I could never imagine my life without you. I have been trying to plan the perfect moment to do this, but… in case I snap and start killing people, I need to make sure you know how I feel about you." Gerald drops to one knee and pulls a ring from his pocket. "Alice Jacobs, I am in love with you, and I grow more in love with you every day. Will you marry me?"

"Gerald," Alice looks down at him with tears in her eyes, "you are not going to snap and start killing people." She smiles. "And I could never imagine my life without you either. Now, make it official and put that ring on my finger so I can start planning our wedding."

Chapter Five

"Wow. What a night." Steve mumbles with his mouth wide open in a yawn.

I put my purse on the chair as I step into the living room. "You can say that again. I definitely didn't expect the night to end like that."

"That's odd." Steve pauses and tilts his head like he is trying to hear something.

"What?" I silently mouth.

"Spencer usually meets us at the door."

I follow Steve into the kitchen. Herb must have finished his chores because he has shifted into low power mode and stands frozen in the middle of the kitchen. As soon as Steve walks in front of him, Herb's eyes light up.

"I thought you were keeping an eye on Spencer. Where is he?" Steve questions Herb in a quavering voice.

"Oh, dear. I must have fallen asleep." Herb twists his head back and forth. "But no worries. He's fine. He was playing that little handheld game just a few minutes ago."

"Spencer?" Steve calls out as he takes off through the house toward his office.

I turn down the hall in the other direction toward the bedroom, but Spencer does not appear to be in the Master or the spare bedroom. Steve and I get back to the kitchen door at almost the same time. Worry shows in the frown lines etched into his face.

"Spencer?" he calls out again.

As we round the doorway into the kitchen, Herb is pacing round and round in a small circle. If a robot could have a panic attack, I am sure this is what it would look like.

"Herb," Steve scolds, "stop pacing and help us find Spencer. Where was he when you saw him last?"

"He was sitting right there in the chair at the table, bouncing up and down with that game in his hands, making his little monkey noises." Herb rolls over and looks under the table. "He couldn't have just disappeared."

My heart flutters as I walk over to check the back door. I twist the knob and let out a sigh of relief. "The back door is locked, so he couldn't have gone outside." As I turn around, I notice a light glowing under the utility room door.

Herb must notice too, because he races at top speed and flings the door open. "Oh, thank goodness." He puts his metal hand on his chest.

I look in through the opening in the door. Spencer is curled up asleep on the floor beside Herb's charging station, still clutching the game in his little hands. The plug to Herb's charging station is lying on the floor, and the charger to Spencer's game is plugged into the wall.

Steve eases up behind me and peers over my shoulder. "Hmmm. Well, I guess now we know how Herb's charging station keeps getting unplugged."

With the frown lines gone from his face, Steve tiptoes over and lifts Spencer from the floor. "Come on, little guy," Steve whispers, "let's go to bed."

I follow him into the bedroom and watch him tuck the little monkey into bed. As he turns toward the bathroom, I notice he pauses next to his nightstand and runs his fingertips across the edge of the notebook lying beneath his Bible. He twists his head in my direction. "Never forget... be not afraid... For the Lord thy God is with thee whithersoever thou goest."

Chapter Six

The heat is smothering. I fight the urge to gasp for air as I listen for what might be lurking in the dark. Her scream stabs through my ears and pierces my heart. Sharp pains shoot through my chest. *I have to help her.* I ease toward the door on my tiptoes. My heart rate goes up with every step.

Don't be afraid. I am right here with you.

The words flash in my mind, and I turn my head from side to side. *Who said that?* I freeze to listen. *Nothing.* I swallow hard. *I must be hearing things,* I think as I push myself to take another step toward the horizontal crack of light. With my arms in front of me, I gently pat the air searching for the door. "BUZZ… BUZZ… BUZZ."

~

"BUZZ… BUZZ… BUZZ…" I leap from the bed landing on the floor with a thud.

"What was that?" Steve sputters. "Ellie, where are you? Shut your alarm clock off."

Alarm clock. It's just my alarm clock. I push up on my elbows and knees. Then, I reach up with one hand and run my fingers across the top of the clock until I feel the snooze button. The horrible blaring noise stops, and a whiny squeaking sound fills the room.

"Where is he now?" Steve grumbles as he clicks on the lamp. "Spencer, get down from there."

I lift my head as Steve is pulling Spencer's hands from one of the blades on the ceiling fan. Pushing up on the side of the bed, I stand and slide the alarm button to off.

"Are you going for your run?" Steve lays Spencer back on the bed.

"No." I shuffle toward the bathroom. "I'll have to run when I get home. I have to be at work by seven."

~

TWENTY MINUTES LATER, I come out of the bathroom in khakis and a black knit top. I need coffee, but I can't go out of the room without making the bed. Moving from one side to the other, I smooth the sheets and blankets and position the throw pillows in the center of the bed.

I rush down the hall to the sunporch and open my Bible. I pick up where I had left off in Ephesians and read about the armor of God in chapter six. Then, I get on my knees to give thanks and ask God to guide me through the day. When I am finished, I sit on the floor in silence for a minute and let myself feel God's presence. With my mind renewed and refreshed, I rise to my feet and speed to the kitchen.

"There you are." Steve stands up from the table and kisses my cheek. "Herb made eggs, but I thought you might want a bagel with peanut butter too."

I sit down and take a sip of coffee. "Thank you. Actually, I think I just want the bagel. Eggs seem a little heavy right now."

He clutches my hand. We bow our heads and give thanks together.

"I am guessing you had the dream again." he says as he lifts a bite of eggs to his mouth.

"Yes, but this time I thought I heard a voice."

The doorbell rings, interrupting my explanation.

Steve raises his eyebrows. "Who could that be this early in the morning?" Steve glances at the clock. "It's only six-fifteen."

I push back from the table. "I don't know. Would your mom stop by this early?"

"Surely not without calling." Steve follows right on my heels.

I don't know if he is curious or doesn't want me to go to the door alone, but I am not opening the door without checking the camera. I push the button on the monitor mounted on the wall on the right side of the door, and the image of a middle-aged man standing on the porch fills the screen. He has dark hair, neatly combed to one side, and is wearing black pants and a light blue button-up shirt with a bulletproof vest. Behind him are two men dressed in black. They have on black caps, black pants, and black t-shirts with black bulletproof vests covering them.

Steve taps the intercom button. "Can I help you?"

The man in front twists his head from side to side like he is trying to figure out where the speaker is. "Yes. My name is Allen Morgan, and I am with the Department of Homeland Security. Do you have an identification pad?"

"Push the button below the doorknob." Steve instructs.

We watch on the screen as the man presses the button. The cover to the identification pad slides up, and the man places his thumb on it."

The man's identification information pops up on the screen.

Allen Morgan
Special Agent
United States Department of Homeland Security
Office of Intelligence and Analysis

"I need to speak with Steve Denali and Ellie Hatcher Denali."

Steve rolls his eyes toward me. "May I ask why you need to speak with them?"

"An executive order has been issued by President Kutchins." The man pulls an envelope from his pocket and holds it up. "It is imperative that I speak with them right away."

"An executive order? I haven't heard anything about President Kutchins issuing an executive order." Steve remarks as he grabs my hand and gives it a squeeze.

The man purses his lips like he is losing patience. "In the interest of public safety, and to avoid mass panic, this order is being kept confidential under the president's right of executive privilege. You have my identity verified on your screen with confirmation that I am a federal officer. I am going to need you to open the door now."

"I am aware of your credentials. However, I have seen nothing that requires me to open the door. I am assuming that the document in that envelope permits you to be on my porch barking out demands." Steve asserts in a strong, controlled tone, even though I can feel his hand trembling. "If you would, please slide the envelope through the mail slot so I can review the document and consider your request."

The man's face flushes. "Sir," he dictates in a harsh voice, "I am going to slide this envelope through the slot because I do not want this to be difficult, but take note that this is not a request."

The envelope flies through the slot, and my heart pounds as I watch it drop to the floor. I lean down and pick it up with my thumb and index finger holding it like I am expecting it to explode. Steve takes it from my fingers, tears through the flap, and slides the paper out. My phone starts ringing in my purse on the chair, but I ignore it and move around beside him so I can see as he unfolds the letter.

Office of the President of the United States of America
Executive Order: Immediate Action Required

Issued June 29, 2050

IN REGARD TO PUBLIC SAFETY AND NATIONAL
SECURITY

*By the power vested in me as President of the United States of
America, I hereby issue the following order in consideration of the
recent surge in malicious activity across the country:*

1. *Pursuant to the National Security Act of 2042, all
   parties that were held in any capacity and for any
   length of time at President Dennis Denali's Soldiers
   Against Crime Training Facility, located in the
   Cheyenne Mountain Complex, must return to the
   facility for testing to determine the cause of the
   outbreak.*
2. *All parties must remain at the facility until deemed safe
   to re-enter society. Approval for re-entry will be on an
   individual basis and decided by the scientific medical
   staff approved by the president.*
3. *The Department of Homeland Security has complete
   authority in the apprehension of all parties that were
   subject to the above-said facility and has permission to
   use whatever force necessary to accomplish the mission.*

This order shall take effect immediately.
Craig T. Kutchins
President of the United States of America

Fear roars inside of me, forcing acid into my throat, and I
swallow hard to push it back down. Steve must notice my knees
buckle because he drops the letter on the floor and grabs me
around my waist before I fall.

"Ellie, it will be okay." he whispers in my ear. "Whatever
happens, never forget. The Lord thy God is with thee whithersoever thou goest."

"Open up, Mr. Denali." Something hits the door with a heavy thud.

Chills tingle down my spine. I bite my lower lip and focus on the verse my husband quoted.

A squeal pierces my ear from behind. I know it's Spencer before I turn, but I still can't help but look to see if he is okay. Herb stands in the doorway with Spencer draped around his robot neck. Steve waves his hand, motioning for Herb to get back in the kitchen.

I turn back and cast my eyes on the screen just as Agent Morgan plants his foot in the center of the door with another heavy thud. The door rattles but doesn't give. I stand frozen. My instincts tell me to run, but I can't get my muscles to move. *What's the use? Running won't do any good.*

Steve sidesteps in front of me, putting his body in front of mine. My mind whirls at top speed, searching in desperation for a way out of this. I can't go back to that place. Somewhere in the background, my phone rings again. With Steve shielding me, I can't see the men on the screen, but something spurs Steve into motion. He spins around and pushes me with urgency away from the front door. We are halfway across the living room when the floorboards vibrate beneath my feet, followed by a thunderous deafening boom that motivates my legs to move faster. An object whizzes through the air like a bullet and smashes into the wall above the opening to the kitchen. Steve keeps pushing me forward, and in the same second that we are about to pass through the doorway into the kitchen, the knob to the front door falls on the floor in front of me.

My heart drops to my feet at the sound of the front door bursting open. Rushing footsteps pound the floor behind us. As we move through to the kitchen, my eyes are fixed on the back door, but I catch sight of Herb in my peripheral vision. He is hovering in the corner, holding Spencer like a mother protecting her baby. He has one hand supporting Spencer's body and the other hand covering his little monkey head.

I extend my hand to open the back door, but one of the men

in black grabs Steve behind me. I try to hold on to him, but the man jerks Steve away from me and slams his body to the floor.

"Stop!" I scream, reaching for Steve. "Please don't hurt him." *Lord, please don't let them hurt him.*

Wailing like a car alarm, Spencer's high-pitched shrieks tear through the room and slice through my eardrums. Agent Morgan stands to the side and watches as the other man in black grabs my arms and twists them behind me. He thrusts me down like a ragdoll, and the side of my face bounces off the ceramic tile. Pain radiates from my jawbone and runs across the top of my head. I try to get my elbows under my body to push myself up, but the man's knee plants hard in the center of my back, forcing me back down. My stomach contracts, and I gag as the breath is knocked from my lungs. When I finally suck in a breath, I stop resisting and lie motionless on the cold tile. As a tear drips from my eyes, I recite Hebrews 13:6 in my mind. *The Lord is my helper, and I will not fear what man shall do unto me.*

Amid the chaos, the rhythmic clap of running feet grows louder, and someone bursts into the kitchen. "Get your hands off of her." a woman's loud voice agonizes. "Leave her alone."

Mom.

"Please, Ma'am, you need to get out of the way." Agent Morgan speaks in a calm, pleading tone. "Sir, I need you to take this lady and go outside."

Mom grunts like she is straining against something. "No, Tom. I am not going anywhere. These monsters barged into our house and took Eileen. I will not let them take Ellie."

Dad is here too.

The sound of her voice moves closer to me. "You listen to me. My daughter and her husband have done nothing wrong. You have no right to do this. For goodness' sake, my daughter is a field agent with the FBI."

"Ma'am, I am aware of your daughter's affiliation with the FBI. However, the president has issued an executive order, and your daughter's name is on the list." He takes a step toward my mother. "I need you to let go of the officer, or I will have to charge you with obstruction of justice." I look up from the corner of my eye and watch the man in the blue shirt pull my mother away from the man holding me down."

"Please. You are supposed to be protecting innocent people like them. They are victims." Her words muffle through heavy sobs. "Think about it. Everyone would be dead right now if it weren't for those two. You would be dead."

"I don't know what you are talking about, ma'am, but you have to leave." Agent Morgan motions her away.

"Yes, you do. Those two were part of the team that stopped President Denali from dropping that poison, and now you are treating them like murderers."

Agent Morgan is silent for a minute and then responds in a low, flat tone. "It doesn't matter what I know. I have orders to follow."

"The male subject is sedated." The words must come from the other man in black behind me. "I'll take care of the monkey."

"You will do no such thing!" Mom shouts. "That monkey stays with me!"

"I don't think so." The man in black steps into my line of sight and moves toward Spencer. "This is a wild animal that needs to be contained."

"He is not a wild animal... H-h-he is... a service monkey."

"A service monkey?" Agent Morgan's voice rises in question.

"Yes. My husband is speech impaired." Mom coughs. "He needs that monkey to help him communicate."

With my insides trembling, I roll my eyes as far as I can to follow the man in black. I can't handle the thought of what will happen to Spencer if they take him. Pursing my lips together, I fight the urge to scream as the man in black reaches out to grab Spencer out of Herb's arms. But before the man's fingers even get close, Herb holds Spencer under one arm and rotates his mechanical torso backward, shifting Spencer away from the man. Then Herb whips his other arm around, keeping it straight out, and cuts through the air like a helicopter blade. Herb's metal appendage makes direct contact with the man's upper body slapping him right across the front of his bulletproof vest. The impact slings the man crashing back into the wall.

The man's face turns red, and he bares his teeth as his hand pulls his gun from his holster.

"No! Hold your fire!" Agent Morgan yells as he steps toward the man, and then he calmly orders, "Let it go. We have what we came for." He looks at Mom. "Take the monkey and leave."

Mom stands still and peers down at me with rivers running down her face.

"M-m-mom," I sputter with my face pressed against the floor. "Pl-please take Spencer. Take him and you and dad… g-go home." The man pressing me to the floor leans over and jabs something sharp into my neck. "P-p-please." The room blurs and white noise echoes in my head. I try to fight it, but the light slowly fades to black.

Chapter Seven

The door... I must be right in front of it. Another scream pierces my eardrum. *Hold on. I'm coming.* I try to reach for the knob, but I can't. My arm is stuck... *why can't I lift my arm?* Panic rises in my chest. I can't breathe. *"I am here. I will never leave you, nor forsake you."* A faint voice speaks in my ear, or maybe it's a voice in my head. I don't know, but I suddenly gasp for a breath. A rush of air floods into my nose, and my lungs fill. I wriggle and pull with all my might trying to free my arm. All of a sudden, the ground shakes beneath me, jolting my entire body.

∼

A BUMP JARS my back and neck, and my heels bounce against something hard. A twig of hair falls against my face. I attempt to swipe it away, but my arm won't move. *Where am I?* My eyelids flutter as I try to orient myself and bring my surroundings into focus. The hum of an engine and the slight vibration beneath my body alerts me that I am moving.

Lying flat on my back, I rub my fingers against smooth

fabric that seems to stretch under me. My arms and legs are held by some kind of straps, and I think my head is in some type of vise. In an instant, the details of the morning flood through my mind. Agent Morgan, the letter, the two men in black, my face on the cold tile floor, Mom... *oh no... poor Mom.* An ache presses in the center of my chest. When I finally win the battle against the light and get my eyes to adjust, I find myself looking up at a low-budget robot standing beside me. It's nothing like Herb. With only one eye, this thing looks like a cyclops made from a tin can. Its arms resemble vacuum hoses, and if it were not for the high-tech fingers attached to metal balls on the ends of the arms, this robot could easily pass for a middle school science project. Each finger is a different tool ranging from different sizes of screwdrivers to pliers to drill bits. My primary concern is the scalpel that is in the index finger location on the robot's right hand. At the sight of the sharp instrument, my stomach churns as a million thoughts swirl around in my mind.

"What have you done to me?" I cry out as I squirm, trying to get my head free. "Let me up from here."

The robot lets out a series of beeps, and then a cold metal tip presses against my temple. The face of the man in black that tried to take Spencer appears right over me.

"Stop! If you even think of becoming violent, I will pull this trigger." He moves his face a little closer to mine. "Do you understand?"

"Ellie." I can't see him, but Steve calls out from somewhere on my right. "We're okay. Please be quiet and don't fight them."

I swallow as tears pool in my eyes. "Okay, but where are we?"

Another man's voice, that I assume must be the other man in black, answers. "We're almost to the train that will transport you to the facility in Colorado for your testing."

I decide not to say anything else. Since I am strapped down, I guess Steve is right. Causing a stir is not going to going to help matters. Instead, I close my eyes and pray.

THE MOVING vehicle comes to an abrupt stop making my heart skip a beat. A few seconds later, a door screeches open, and Agent Morgan's voice fills the space. "Why are they still strapped on the tables? Cy should have been done with them over an hour ago."

"Sorry, Boss." The man with the gun points at me. "The lady here was getting violent. I thought it best if they were kept restrained."

I roll my eyes.

"Surely both of you could have contained them. You have weapons, and they don't." Agent Morgan says in a condescending tone. "Now, unstrap them so we can get them in line for the train."

The man reaches for the contraption on my head. I am already twisting my neck when the bracket pops loose. I need to see Steve. As I look over, the other man releases Steve's head, and he turns toward me. My eyes meet his and he forces a smile. I know he is trying to comfort me, but the worry is written in the lines on his face. As soon as my arms and legs are free, I push myself up and do a quick scan of my surroundings. We appear to be in some sort of medical vehicle or utility van. A small aisle separates the two narrow gurneys that Steve and I had been strapped to. The man grips my arm as I stand. The other guy doesn't seem to be using as much force with Steve. He stands back and lets Steve get to his feet.

The man jerks me by my arm toward the door where Agent Morgan is waiting. I have to know if that robot put another tracking chip in me, so I lift my other arm to feel the back of my head. I barely get my hand up when the man sidesteps behind me and twists both arms behind my back.

Agent Morgan narrows his eyes and lifts his open hand toward me as he looks up at the man standing behind me. "Let go of her arms so she can step down." The man drops my arms, and Agent Morgan takes hold of my wrist and steadies me as I get out of the vehicle. "I'll take her from here." he says in a firm tone with his stare still fixed on the man. "Stay here and get the van cleaned up."

The other man steps down after Steve and then eases up beside him.

Agent Morgan casts a glance back and forth between me and Steve. "Come on. We need to get you two to the train." He points in the direction of a huge dome building that shimmers with mirrored windows.

Agent Morgan walks beside me, and Steve and the other man move along behind us.

I notice Agent Morgan seems to have softened a bit, and I can't help but wonder if my mother's words hit a nerve. As we cross the parking lot toward the building, I decide to test the water and speak. "Agent Morgan," I cough and clear my throat. "Why are we taking a train? I don't remember having to take a train before." *Of course, I was unconscious before,* I think after the words had already left my mouth.

"I'm still learning about how this whole mess worked," he answers in a quiet voice, "but the way I understand it, only a few people at a time were sent for President Denali's training. Because of the urgency of this situation, all the subjects that were ever in that facility are being sent back there at once. It's way too many people to transport any other way."

Steve tilts his head. "The government has kept almost everything hush-hush. We know from the journals we found that President Denali probably had around fifteen thousand people in his so-called personal army, and a little more than a hundred of the people that had been frozen could not be revived. Most of those were the ones that had the cryonics procedure done early on. If I am allowed to ask, how many people are we talking about?"

Agent Morgan shrugs. "I don't see what it hurts for you to know. You are going to be there with them all anyway. I was told that there were about thirty-seven thousand people that needed to be tested."

"Thirty-seven thousand?" I question under my breath.

"I couldn't believe President Denali had recruited, or deceived, I guess is a better word, that many people, so I did a little research." Agent Morgan speaks in a barely audible voice. "You are right about the fifteen thousand in his army, but on top of that, he had around twenty-two thousand cryogenically frozen."

Steve sucks in a deep breath. "Ellie and I saw a room full of tubes, but I never imagined twenty-two thousand people. How could that many fit in there?"

"The report said he was using the upper levels in most of the buildings in the complex to store them, but he had also built underground rooms in some old railroad tunnels that run through the other side of the mountain." Agent Morgan lightly touches my back as we step up onto the sidewalk.

We walk in silence the rest of the way to the door. A black sign with silver letters attracts my attention. *FORTE RAIL of Arlington.* I get that sinking feeling in my chest. I read an article not long ago about this new train system. It was designed to compete with air travel. I think the article said it travels at an average speed of three hundred and fifty miles per hour.

Agent Morgan reaches for the handle but stops and puts his hand back down. He turns his body where he is facing both Steve and me. "Look, I know you have been through a lot, and this whole thing has not been a bed of roses so far. But considering what you two have already done for this country... the world for that matter, I am sure once they run the tests and see that you are not dangerous, you will be able to go back to your normal life and forget this nightmare ever happened." He shifts toward the door but stops again, slumping his shoulders. "Try to look at it from the government's perspective. Innocent people are being killed. They have to figure out what is going on before more people die."

Agent Morgan pulls the door open, and I guess I am standing too close because he backs into me, and I almost topple over. Steve grabs my waist to stop my fall at the same time that

Agent Morgan catches me by my wrist. I feel his thumb slide beneath my shirt sleeve and press something to the inside of my forearm. My mouth opens to speak, but something about his expression keeps me silent.

We go through the door into the dome building, and with one look, nausea twists in my stomach. A line of people runs around the perimeter, and uniformed officers, wearing helmets and carrying automatic rifles, march back and forth beside the line.

Agent Morgan guides us to the back of the line. "Face forward and wait quietly in the line. Don't make any sudden movements, and you'll be fine. Once you get to the front, they will check your identity and load you on the train." He pivots on his heels and exits the building with the other man behind him.

Steve puts his hand on the small of my back, and my stomach relaxes. *At least I am not here alone. Steve and I are together, and I am thankful for that.*

We inch along in silence. The only sound that can be heard is the clacking of the officers' boots against the large square tiles as they stomp back and forth, making sure their presence is known. When we finally get to the front of the line, a short, stocky woman with a blonde pixie cut stands behind a podium. A laptop sits on top of the podium and a thumbprint pad is affixed to the front. And to the right of the podium is a glass door. The windows are tinted, but I can still make out the outline of a train car on the other side. An officer comes through the door and escorts the person that was in front of me to the train.

The woman motions me forward, and as I step toward the podium, I notice she is also wearing a blue uniform with a United States Department of Homeland Security badge like the other officers pacing around with guns.

"Name?" she huffs without taking her eyes off the laptop screen.

I open my mouth but freeze up.

"Name?" she yells out in a voice like a drill sergeant.

"Oh, uh," I hesitate, "Ellie Denali."

The woman's eyes bulge out, and she rotates her gaze toward me. "Think you're funny, don't you? State your real name, please."

"Ellie Hatcher Denali."

The lady stiffens her posture and gives me a frustrated look. "Just put your thumb on the screen."

The woman's jawline hardens. "Your last name is Denali?"

"Yes, ma'am. I..."

Before I can explain, the woman turns to the officer coming through the door. "Place her under high-risk." she instructs him in a flat tone. Then she glares at me with narrow eyes as he pulls me through the door.

As we edge down the walk beside the train, I try to keep my strides short and move in slow motion. I don't want to go without Steve, but the officer is pushing me so hard that I can barely keep my feet underneath my body.

The train has a mirrored appearance with a shiny silver exterior and a long protruding pointed nose, similar to a jet. Starting at the nose of the locomotive, the top of the train has a slight curve that peaks at the fourth passenger car and then descends with a gentle slant to the end of the sixth passenger car. The lower body of the train wraps around the track, and the train can't be taller than ten feet at its highest point. The officer guides me all the way to the first car behind the locomotive.

As we reach the door, a deep male voice calls out, "Wait up. I have another one for high-risk." Another officer leads Steve up and hands him off to the officer escorting me.

The muscles in my chest relax a smidgen. *Thank you, Lord, for keeping Steve with me.*

The officer pushes both of us through the door to the train. A large, uniformed man gripping a nine-millimeter handgun stands in the aisle at the front of the car. The car is full, except for two seats in the back row on the right.

"Take a seat there." The officer behind us points. "And place your arms on the armrests."

I move in first and sit in the seat by the window, and then Steve slides in next to me. We place our arms on the rests just as we are told. As soon as our arms touch down, clamps spring out and clasp tight around our wrists, restraining our arms. The officer leans over and pulls at the clamps making sure they are secure. Without another word, he turns and goes back through the door.

I watch the man in the police uniform at the front of the car. His knuckles are white, and the skin on his hands is stretched so tight from his death grip on the gun that it looks like his flesh will split open any minute. He rotates his eyes from side to side, and with his feet planted shoulder-width apart and his knees slightly bent, he appears to be in attack position. I decide it's best not to make eye contact, so I look away. I don't need any more stress. The butterflies in my stomach are wreaking such havoc that it feels like they are having seizures. I bend my wrist and twist my hand until I can at least grab Steve's fingers. I know he is sitting next to me, but I need to touch him. With his fingers intertwined with mine, I close my eyes and thank God again that I have Steve here with me. As I pray, the train lurches forward. Steve squeezes my fingers. *God is in control.* I know He will use this situation for good, but sometimes, I have to remind myself.

Fighting the urge to talk to Steve because I fear that is sure to get us into trouble, I keep my eyes closed and, for the moment, try to pretend that none of this is happening. It doesn't work. My mind keeps drifting between Eileen, Alice, Teresa, and Gerald, wondering where they are.

A deep, roaring voice echoes from the loudspeaker and jerks me from my troubled thoughts. "At this time, please direct your attention to the display at the front of your car."

When I open my eyes, President Kutchins is on a flat screen that is suspended from the ceiling right behind the armed officer. The president is sitting at his desk between two American flags, and the image of the charred remains of the explosion at the police station fills in the background.

President Kutchins stares straight ahead. Beneath a toupee full of curly black hair, his face lacks any expression at all. However, with the unnatural absence of wrinkles on his skin and the amount of make-up caked on his face, I am not sure he is capable of forming any facial expressions. He proceeds to tug at something in his ear and then starts to speak. "Hello… huh." He tugs at his ear again and nods. "As I am sure you know, I am the President of the United States, Craig T. Kutchins. I understand that you have all had an eventful day, but I am here to…" he pauses and pats the side of his head with his palm like he has water in his ear, "to calm your fears. We are all aware of the recent violence that has ended in mass mortality and the significant increase in these incidents over the past few months. The majority of these occurrences have one factor in common. The perpetrator was one of President Denali's victims. Yes, you heard correctly. I said, victims. I understand that each of you has been victimized by a man that was capable of evil beyond anything imaginable. That being said, I need each of you to understand that I cannot allow these violent acts claiming innocent lives to escalate. So, please be patient and cooperate with the medical and scientific staff at the facility until they can determine and correct the cause of the problem. Remember, finding the problem and developing an antidote will benefit you as well. Excuse the metaphor, but I am sure you want to know if you are a ticking time bomb waiting to be set off. I hope you see the importance and the imperativeness of your cooperation, and that you will proceed through this process as gentle sheep. Let me remind you that this is a matter of national security. Anyone who does not cooperate will be dealt with harshly. Thank you for your attention. Good day."

The screen blinks and goes black.

"Liar. He's a liar!" a man shouts from somewhere in the middle.

The armed officer pounces forward and aims his gun. "Silence!"

I lean my head toward Steve so I can look between the rows

of people. A man about six rows up is bouncing up and down in his seat.

He stops yelling, and his body stops moving. His monotone voice reflects his broken state. "I've done nothing wrong. They call this the land of the free. Where's the freedom that all those soldiers died for so long ago? If they saw this, would they still give their life for this country?" The back of his head tilts like he must be looking up at the soldier. "Do what you have to do, but I'm not going back to that place." At that, the man starts grunting and thrashing his body from side to side. The people beside, in front of, and behind him lean away as best they can with their arms restrained.

The officer's face goes pale. His forehead crinkles, and water trickles down his face. As I stare at him, wondering if the moisture on his cheeks is sweat or tears, his face contorts into a grimace, and the gun fires. A deafening blast rips through the train car and reverberates off of the metal wall, leaving behind a high-pitched ringing in my ears. The man slumps over, revealing a huge, gaping hole between his shoulder blades, and then a shriek of pain in a shrill female voice echoes from somewhere in the distance. My eyes fix on the bullet hole through the back of the man's seat. The cries of pain are coming from the woman seated behind him. Her voice only sounds farther away because of the ringing in my ears.

And it's not only the woman's voice. Everything sounds muffled and barely audible, as if I am outside the train watching and hearing the chaos break out through the window. People are screaming. Five more officers pound their feet through the door from the adjoining car. I turn my head and bury my face in Steve's shoulder. Another shot, and the woman's shrieking stops. A few more shots and a thick silence fills the car. I can't lift my head. I don't want to see. I don't want to know.

The tip of a weapon nudges my arm. "Sit up and face forward!" a gruff voice barks at me.

I raise my head in slow motion, and a set of cold eyes stare down at me. I shift my face away from him and look straight ahead, but in my peripheral vision, I catch sight of two limp bodies being dragged down the aisle toward the door at the back. The train is still moving, so I wonder where they are taking them.

The officer who fired the gun is gone, and another armed officer stands in his place at the front of the train. All the other officers must have exited when the bodies of the man and woman were removed. I gaze up at the empty seat where that poor man was killed. *Killed for what?* I ask myself. *What danger did he pose with his arms tied down? All he did was state the truth.* As I look at that empty seat with my mind drifting in thought, I notice the man in the next seat over from the vacant spot. His head is drooping forward like he has fallen asleep. Rolling my eyes without moving my head, I scan the rows toward the front where the man and woman had been sitting. All the people in that area appear to be sleeping. I can only see the backs of their heads, but some are drooped forward, some lolled to the side, and one lady's head is folded backward with the tip of her nose sticking straight up in the air.

I purse my lips together and close my eyes. *What did they do to those people?* My mind goes berserk as questions bounce off of each other inside my brain. *Are they dead? If it was as simple as knocking them out, why didn't the officer render the man unconscious? Why did he have to shoot him? Did he kill him to make a point?* My hands go from trembling to jerking, and Steve squeezes my fingers tighter. *Calm down, Ellie. Seven deep breaths. In... Out... In... Out... In... Out... In... Out... In... Out... In... Out... In... Out... Never forget. The Lord thy God is with thee whithersoever thou goest.* I say the words over to myself.

We ride in silence with only the sound of the train moving on the tracks and an occasional whimper from a sob that cannot be contained, but I have no tears because I have decided that this has to be another one of my nightmares.

Chapter Eight

After five hours of riding with our arms strapped down, the train comes to a stop, and the side door to the outside opens. Another officer stands by the door as the officer that was at the front of the car releases the clamps from our wrists one at a time and directs us to exit the train. Steve is in the seat next to the aisle, so he has to exit first.

As soon as my wrists are free, I take giant strides, hoping that I don't lose sight of Steve. When I step off the train and pass the guard by the door, I notice that Steve has already disappeared. Instead, I find myself looking up at a towering lady dressed in black pants and a black fitted shirt. Her blonde hair lays in a long braid across one of the straps of her shoulder holster that is holding a semiautomatic handgun by her rib cage on each side. By the looks of her muscular build and her massive size, I can't imagine she has much of a need for the guns. I guess that is why they are snapped snugly in their holsters.

"Mrs. Ellie Denali, I am agent Miranda Benton. First, let me apologize for the mix-up. You should never have been placed in the high-risk car. Agent Gomez apparently didn't get past your name on the identification screen. Otherwise, she would have seen your status as an agent with the Federal Bureau of Investigation and the great service you have performed for our country. If you come with me, I will get you where you need to go." We move side by side down the walkway between the train and a dome building identical to the one we left from. Her legs are so long that I almost have to jog to keep up.

As we walk past, I notice the other cars are still full and don't seem to be unloading yet. Casting my eyes up toward the woman, I ask, "Agent Benton, could you tell me where they took my husband? He got off the train right in front of me."

"No worries. He should be inside the train station by the time you get there. We are just going to stop by the restroom up ahead and let you get changed into your uniform. With so many people coming into the facility for testing, the staff has asked that everyone be dressed and ready to begin upon arrival." She reaches up and twirls her braid. "I can imagine that you will be glad to see a restroom anyway since the passengers in car one aren't allowed any breaks. That is an extremely long trip without a visit to the restroom."

I let out an exasperated sigh. "Not being able to use the restroom is the least of a person's worries in that car."

She stops in front of the ladies' room and pulls open the door. I place one foot inside, and my airway constricts. The grout between the floor tiles is stained and grungy, and the walls and the doors to the four separate bathroom stalls are covered in graffiti and other questionable substances. I pull my arms tight to my body and stand in the center of the room to ensure that I do not touch anything.

A utility shelving unit has been set up along one wall with stacks of boxes labeled with a name on each one. Agent Benton lifts the one with *Ellie Hatcher Denali* printed on the front and hands it to me. "Your uniform and shoes are in this box. You are going to feel like it is too small, but it is meant to be tight-fitting. Excess clothing will make the testing more difficult. The suit also has snaps and patches already in place for the placement of the wires and electrodes, so please do not tamper with those.

You can change in the first restroom stall." She points to the normal-sized stall closest to the sinks. "Place the clothes you are wearing now back in the box, and I will take it from you when you come out."

I glare at the bathroom stall, and my heart beats so fast that I feel dizzy. *Don't panic,* I tell myself. *Seven deep breaths.* I close my eyes and breath in seven times, exhaling slowly each time. Then I repeat in my mind, *I can do all things through Christ which strengtheneth me. I can do all things through Christ which strengtheneth me. I can do all things through Christ which strengtheneth me. I can do all things through Christ which strengtheneth me. I can do all things through Christ which strengtheneth me. I can do all things through Christ which strengtheneth me. I can do all things through Christ which strengtheneth me.*

"Mrs. Denali, are you okay?" Agent Benton's voice rises with worry.

"Sorry…" I choke on my words. "P-Paper t-towels. I n-need paper towels."

She looks around. "There is a hand dryer. You won't need towels."

I drop my head. "You don't understand. I don't like public restrooms. I need paper towels so I don't have to touch anything."

As the words leave my mouth, I want to kick myself. *The one person who has shown any understanding in this place is now going to think I am crazy.*

Her gaze falls on something smeared on the door to the first stall. "Yeah. I see your point. This place is pretty crusty." She walks over and opens a cabinet in the corner filled with cleaning supplies. "Here we go." She pulls out a roll of thick blue shop towels.

I grab the towels with my trembling fingers and turn in the direction of the stall. "Ummm, Agent Benton, would it be okay if I used the large one in the corner?"

"Yeah, sure." Her tone is relaxed and carefree. "Others will be coming in, so don't be alarmed. I am required to stand right outside the stall door."

I nod. Fighting against my OCD, I have to force every step as I trudge to the back, into the large, handicapped stall. Using a paper towel to touch the handle, I slide the latch closed on the door, then I lay the towel on the floor over to the side and place the box on it. As I lean down, the sound of someone talking and the clack of footsteps entering the bathroom catch my attention. A woman with a harsh, grating voice instructs someone to change in stall one. I glance under the partition door and notice Agent Benton's boots on the other side.

After I put the box down, I tear off a few more towels and spread them out in the center of the floor, trying to cover enough space to stand on when I remove my shoes.

Now. I raise back up and droop my shoulders, mentally exhausted from my preparations. Agent Benton is so tall that the top of her head is visible over the stall partition. She appears to have her back to the door, but she could easily look over if she wanted.

More voices echo through the room, and someone goes into the stall next to me. *Don't think about it. Just hurry and get out of here.*

I move as fast as I can to use the restroom and change. I fold my clothes as I take them off and then switch them out with the ones in the box. *No way. Please tell me this is not the uniform.* Agent Benton wasn't exaggerating when she said the uniform might seem small. I hold out the long sleeve spandex unitard that appears to be in a toddler size and try to stretch it with my hands. Snaps and Velcro patches alternate in spots across the chest, on the inside of the arms, and on the inside of the legs.

"Mrs. Denali, are you almost finished?" Agent Benton calls from outside the stall door.

I let out a silent sigh. "Yes. Sorry. I am just trying to stretch this uniform a bit so I can get it on." I crinkle it up in my hands like pantyhose and slip in one leg at a time, and then wiggle it up over my waist, trying not to rip the fabric as I pull. As I slip in my left arm, a little disc on the inside of my forearm flickers under the lights. It resembles a coin battery but is only a quarter-inch in diameter. *Agent Morgan.* The scene unfolds in my head as I recall him walking us into the train station. *I almost fell, and he stuck something into my sleeve.* Knowing it will show through the spandex, I peel it from my arm. *What is it?* I flip it over with my fingers. *His expression. Agent Morgan looked me straight in the eye and pulled his eyebrows together like he was telling me something. Maybe this is supposed to help me, but how?*

"Mrs. Denali, we need to get moving." Agent Benton calls through the door. The person in the stall next to me is already exiting.

"Okay." I press the adhesive side of the disc up near my armpit, where it can't be seen. "Sorry, I am almost done." I squeeze my arms into the suit and shimmy it the rest of the way on, and then I reach down and grab up the shoes from beneath my clothes in the box. *Soft, padded slippers?* I turn them over. *They don't even have rubber soles. What... were they afraid we would go berserk and start hitting each other with our shoes?* Shaking my head in disbelief, I shove them on my feet, pick up the box, and dart out of the stall.

"I need to wash my hands." I give the box to Agent Benton and dash to the sink. I flip on the water, pump a few squirts of soap, and do my counting ritual in my mind as I rub.

Agent Benton is already holding the door open when I finish, so I fight the urge to get more soap and wash again. The hand dryer is by the door, but I shake my hands dry instead as I walk outside. "This way." She points to the train station entrance. "We are going in there to get you some food before you leave."

A large metal box resembling a vending machine stands right inside the door. A thumbprint pad is in the center of the front, and a wide chute curves down out of the side like a playground slide. When I walk in front of the machine, the thumbprint pad glows, and an electronic voice shouts, "Please identify yourself."

I place my thumb on the screen.

"Ellie Hatcher Denali," the machine enunciates. A box slides down the chute. "Your meal is served." With wide eyes, I cast a quick glance up at Agent Benton, who is waiting next to me with her arms folded over her chest. I bend down and grab the small cardboard box. *Did I really expect a hot meal?* I ask myself as I recall my face against the tile floor in the kitchen.

"You'll be waiting in here for a bit, so take your time and eat your food." Agent Benton says as she leads me from the entryway into the main room of the station.

I swallow hard. *Please, Lord, let me find Steve.* My eyes frantically scan the room. Guards are stationed about every twenty feet around the perimeter of the wall, but only a few passengers dot the wall along the back. "Thank you, Lord." I blurt out loud with a sigh of relief.

"Excuse me?" Agent Benton peers at me with a quizzical look.

"My husband. He is right there, leaning against the wall." Tears of happiness stream down my face. However, under different circumstances, I might burst out laughing because he is wearing a unitard too.

"Oh." She steps in the direction where he is sitting as she pulls out her phone and taps the screen. "Mr. Steve Denali."

He shifts on one knee to stand. "No need to get up. As I told your wife, neither of you were supposed to be in the high-risk section. The officer at check-in made a slight judgment error." Agent Benton swipes the screen. "It looks like you were both assigned to car two, and for clerical reasons, it is important that we keep you with the group you were assigned to. So, as soon as they unload, you will be transported with that group to the facility." She turns on her heels and strides to the exit.

I collapse to the floor beside Steve and he grabs me in a hug as I wrap my arms around his neck. "I was so scared that I had lost you." My body shakes, and I bury my face in his shoulder, trying not to sob.

"It's okay. We are together, and that lady said we are in the same group." Steve pulls his arms back when a guard starts walking toward us. "Ellie, if they do separate us, don't panic. I promise I will find you. It's all going to be alright." He smiles at me and lifts my chin with his finger. "It can't be any worse than what we have already been through."

"I know," I say as I lean back, tapping my head against the wall. "But I would still prefer not to go through it at all. And my mind keeps going in circles between Eileen, Alice, Teresa, and Gerald, wondering where they are and if they are okay."

"Yeah, me too. I keep thinking they should have been on this train with us since we would all be traveling from the same area. I even tried to peer through the windows of the other cars when I got off the train, but I didn't see any of them." Steve sidles up a little closer to me and takes my hand. "I still think they have to be here. We'll find them." His face turns toward mine. His eyebrows are almost pinched together. "Do you think Spencer is alright?"

"Are you kidding? He is with my mother, and she treats him like a grandchild. He will be so spoiled when we get back, we won't be able to do a thing with him." The corner of my mouth turns up as the question pops into my head, and I have to ask. "Steve, I am a bit curious. You programmed Herb to protect Spencer. Why didn't you program him to protect us? Did you see him slam that guy against the wall?"

"I know. I have been asking myself the same question. At the time, I was thinking that Herb takes care of Spencer when we aren't home, and I guess I thought, or at least hoped, that we would never have to worry about being in danger again. So much for wishful thinking." Steve laughs as he lets go of my hand and picks up his boxed meal. "We better eat dinner."

"A hot meal would be nice, but since I didn't even get breakfast, it is better than nothing." I flip the box over. "What is it anyway?"

"It's an MRE." He rips open the box. "Oh, it has the heater bag in it. Open yours up, and I will show you how to do it."

I pop open the end and slide out the contents: a vacuum-sealed bag that reads *Pepperoni Pizza,* a plastic bag with some sort of pad inside, a pouch with *Heating Agent* written on it, a cardboard sleeve, and a sixteen-ounce bottle of water.

Steve holds up the bag with the pad inside. "Take the heater bag and tear off the top." He rips a small section from the top. "And slide the pizza inside."

I drop the vacuum-sealed pizza into the bag.

"Now, open the heating agent and pour it in." He holds up the bag and demonstrates.

I follow his instructions and fold over the top of the bag just like he does. Then I slide the bag into the cardboard sleeve.

"Prop it up." Steve leans the cardboard sleeve against the baseboard on the wall. "Now, by the time we say the blessing, it will be hot."

"That fast?" I lift one brow in question.

"The old ones took longer... about fifteen minutes. They used salt water to activate the heating process, but this new chemical agent works almost instantly." He takes my hand, and we bow our heads. "Dear Lord, thank you for keeping us safe and for keeping us together. Thank you for this food, and this time to share this meal with my wife. Lord, I pray for the families affected by what happened on that train. Please don't let anyone else be hurt, and please guide us through this and return us home safe. And please be with our friends. We pray these things if it be your will. In Jesus' name. Amen." He rubs his hands together as he lifts his head. "Let's eat."

"Wow. This thing is steaming." I remark as I peel open the package.

"But my God shall supply all your need according to his riches in glory by Christ Jesus." Steve turns up one corner of his mouth. "That verse is in my notebook."

A rush of warmth flows through my body. *It's going to be okay.* My muscles relax, and my heart slows.

"What's wrong?" Steve looks at me with wide eyes. "Why do you have this blank stare?"

"Nothing's wrong. It is what is right." I turn my head and gaze at him. "God is in control. You lost every memory of your entire life, but yet, you were able to remember enough scripture to fill a notebook." I straighten my posture and nod. "We have Jesus in our heart, so no matter what happens, the story has a happy ending."

Steve winks at me. "I already have a lot to be thankful for." He motions in a circle with his hand. "I am on a date with my wife in the middle of a train station in Colorado." He points to the window. "We have a hot meal and a beautiful mountain view."

I can't help but giggle out loud. I take a bite of pizza as I look at his big brown eyes and think to myself, *I have to be the luckiest woman in the world.*

~

AFTER WE FINISH OUR PIZZA, we sit with our backs to the wall and our legs stretched out in front of us. More and more people line up against the wall as the guards unload the passengers and bring them in one by one.

I stare at the brown fuzzy slippers on our feet and smile. "I forgot to compliment you on your unitard."

"I hope you like it," Steve remarks with a sarcastic chuckle, "because I don't think it is coming off unless I have it surgically removed."

A shadow moves in my peripheral vision as someone shuffles into the spot next to me. "I can't find him," the voice behind me murmurs, followed by the sound of fabric catching as it slides down the textured wall. "Please, help me find him."

My eyes widen. "Alice." I fling my head around as her body slumps to the floor. "Oh. Alice. I am so glad to see you. I have been worried sick." I bounce to my knees and grab her in a quick hug. I let go before one of the guards can get bent out of shape.

With her knees still drawn to her chest and her arms stiff, she sits in a rigid form staring straight ahead as her palms push against the floor on each side of her. Her face is streaked where tears have washed away her makeup.

"Alice," I speak softly as I tuck a piece of her hair that is hung on her helix piercing behind her ear, "talk to me."

She turns her watery eyes toward me. "Gerald, I can't find him." She sniffles.

Steve scoots over and puts his hand on her shoulder.

"We were talking on the phone when someone burst into his office at the restaurant. I heard Gerald yell something. Then, he screamed like he was in pain, and the phone went dead." Alice wipes her eye with the knuckle of her index finger. "I was going to check on him. I picked up my phone and was dialing 911. When I ran out the door, an agent was standing outside and grabbed me." She puts her face in her hands, and her shoulders heave as she sobs. "The way he screamed… and I haven't seen him here. Something horrible has happened to him."

"Listen to me. I am sure he is fine." I lean closer to her and lower my voice. "A lot of people were on that train. It may take a little bit of time with all this security, but we will find him."

Steve nudges her. "After all, we just now found you."

Alice gives a half-hearted nod. "What about Eileen and Teresa?" she asks, still swiping at her tears.

"We haven't found them either, but if the three of us are here, they must be too." I say with a confident tone.

"May I have your attention, please." A woman's voice that resembles Agent Benton's blares over the intercom.

I turn around and notice that she is standing by the glass entry doors, talking into her phone. It must be connected to the loudspeaker.

"All passengers from car two have been unloaded and are now ready to depart." The sound reverberates in the glass dome. "Please stay in line with your hands to yourself and remain silent as you move toward the door."

We stand and form a straight line. I am inbetween Alice and Steve. The guards inch in closer to us, brandishing their rifles. The line moves at a snail's pace, and we are closer to the back than the front. It appears that an officer is checking everyone's identity again. This time it is a male officer. The longer I wait in line, the more I think about Gerald, and my anxiety starts to build again. I didn't want to upset Alice any more than she already was, so I tried to be positive. But her recount of the story unnerved me. On top of my nerves, I am sweating profusely under this unitard. I am afraid to look, but I am pretty sure that I have large wet circles on my back and under my arms.

Out of the corner of my eye, I notice a guard staring at me, and I can't help but make eye contact. He narrows his gaze and stretches his fingers tighter around the gun, but I don't look away. Something about his eyes bothers me. As I stare back at him, I realize he has the same look in his eyes as the officer that fired his gun in car one. *Fear or anger. I can't tell which it is.* His hands start to get fidgety with the gun, so I decide it is time to look away.

We finally make it to the exit. While Alice places her thumb on the pad, I peer out the window and take in the aerodynamic design of the enormous bus sitting outside. The top of the bus slopes downward from the back to the top of the windshield. Then the windshield slants to a point at the bottom, making the front of the bus look like a wedge. Large glass panels cover the sides down to a shiny black band that extends to only a few inches from the ground and wraps around the entire bus, concealing the wheels. Alice moves to the door and Agent Benton escorts her toward the bus. The officer with the pad motions me up, and I place my thumb on the pad. This time the officer doesn't have a conniption over my name, and I am allowed to move on to the exit where Agent Benton is already back and waiting to escort me.

"When you get on the bus, a guard will point you to a seat." She walks beside me and waits for me to step up into the bus.

The fuzzy slippers are not the best for climbing the rough stairs. Without a sole, the padding wads up, and I almost trip. My brain seems to automatically be programmed not to touch doorknobs, handrails, or anything that other people have touched, so without even thinking about it, I lean my shoulder into the rail and get my balance.

The bus is almost full since we were near the end of the line. I notice there is no driver's seat or steering wheel, so the bus must operate completely on autopilot. An aisle runs down the center of rows with two seats on each side, and a guard is stationed in the aisle between every three rows. These guards are gripping nine-millimeter pistols in their right hands and small devices that look like phones in their left. Alice is seated only a few rows back on the left side, and a man is in the window seat next to her. The guard points me to the row on the other side of the aisle from Alice. I step over to the seat by the window, and as soon as I sit, Steve steps on. The guard nods for him to go next to me.

A few more people load, and then the bifold doors close. We sit in silence for a minute, with only the faint hum of the motor, and then a computerized female voice echoes over the intercom, "Enable security mode in three, two, one…"

At the word 'one', the guards in the aisle lift the tiny phone-like devices and tap the screens. Steve's head falls over on my shoulder. I twist my head to find out what is wrong with him when I realize everyone around me seems to be sleeping. Everyone has their eyes closed but me, and the guard in the aisle of our section is staring a hole straight through me. My heart pounds in my ears. *What do I do?* From the corner of my eye, I glimpse the guard tap the screen again with a little more force, *like it will make a difference*. I don't know what stimulates me to do it, but as soon as the guard's finger pokes the device, I hold my breath, close my eyes, and drop my head over on top of Steve's.

Is he still staring at me? I think to myself as the bus starts to move. I want to look, but I know I can't. *Lord, I don't know what is going on. Please let Steve, Alice, and everyone on this bus be okay. And please help me to be still and keep my eyes closed.*

"What happened?" someone murmurs in the aisle.

It has to be one of the guards talking. I strain to hear.

"It's okay now. She's out. Must have been some kind of interference or a malfunction or something." another voice answers.

"Are you sure we shouldn't call the doc? Let him know there might be a problem."

"No. It was probably something I did. She conked right out the second time."

"Alright. But keep your eyes locked on her and your weapon ready."

Out? What does he mean by 'out'? My heart hammers in my chest. *Relax. I can't let him see me shaking. I have to relax.* I force myself to take slow, shallow breaths. *Oh. Out. Everyone is knocked out. So, why didn't it work on me?* My thoughts race. *Maybe it is my anxiety. Dr. Eckert's hypnosis wouldn't work on me because I couldn't relax. And I am definitely not relaxed. But this isn't a result of hypnosis. The guards did something through those devices. What have they done to us?*

Chapter Nine

Two sets of hands lift me from the gurney and drop me onto a metal table. It takes all the strength I can muster not to groan when the back of my head smacks against the hard surface.

"Careful." a familiar-sounding robotic voice orders.

"Chill out, tin can." A man on my right-side grumbles as he straps my wrist to the table. "She can't feel anything anyway."

"Well, maybe you should consider using your brain instead of your muscles." the robot ridicules. "Just because she can't feel anything doesn't mean you can't hurt her."

"Ha-ha. Words of wisdom coming from a hunk of metal with spiked hair and an earring."

Waves. I knew that voice sounded familiar.

"Just get on out of here. I will take care of strapping her head," Waves puffs, then mumbles, "you all never do it right anyway."

Footsteps pad across a hard floor, followed by the creak and the thud of a closing door. A cold rubber band tightens around my forehead.

"Okey-dokey, Mrs. Ellie Denali, I know you can't hear me,

but my name is Waves. I need to get some pretty pictures of your brain, so your head is going in this little tunnel for just a minute." He seems to freeze for a second because the room is filled with complete silence. Then he comments, "Mrs. Ellie Denali, you look exactly like someone I used to know. I remember her because, well, because there was just something special about her. Miss Sarah was like the sun in the middle of a storm. Oh, well, here we go."

I want to open my eyes and talk to him, but I know I can't. Someone could be watching. A low humming sound grows louder and then begins to echo around my head. A bright light penetrates through my eyelids and I fight the urge to flinch. After a few seconds, the light withdraws along with the humming echo.

The door creaks again and heels click across the floor, mixed with the pitter-pat of normal shoes.

"Are you finished yet, Waves?"

Dr. Blakely.

"Almost, sir. The scan is complete, I need to upload the images."

"Very well. We'll wait." Dr. Blakely insists.

My nose itches. *Fight it. Don't move.*

"Row, row, row your boat gently down the stream. Merrily, merrily, merrily..."

"Waves, must you sing?" Dr. Blakely barks out.

"Yes, it is part of my programming. Singing makes people happy and puts everyone at ease." Waves replies in a singsong rhythm. "Maybe you should try it."

Great. Now I am about to laugh. I hold my breath and try not to picture Dr. Blakely's face at that comment.

Dr. Blakely lets out a loud sigh. "The images, Waves. Just get the images."

"Okey-dokey. Row, row, row your boat gently down the stream. Merrily, merrily, merrily, merrily, life is but a dream." Waves continues singing and then deepens his voice, making his words sound like the ding-dong of a doorbell. "ALL-done."

"Thank you, Waves." Dr. Blakely says in a flat tone. "Why don't you move on to the next room while I examine the pictures?"

"Yes, sir. Duty calls. Row, row, row your..." The door creaks again and finishes with a thud.

"So... Mitchell, are you going to tell me what is going on?"

No. It can't be. The blood drains from my face, and before I can catch myself, my mouth falls open. I jerk it closed in hopes that they aren't looking.

"Cynthia, I told you that we can't talk here. I have gotten you released. You have clearance to leave, so you need to get out of here before someone starts questioning your test results." Dr. Blakely utters in desperation. "I will contact you later and explain everything."

"No one is in here, Mitchell. Can you please tell me if we can use any of this to help us?"

With a groan of defeat, he says barely above a whisper, "All of the perpetrators that were involved in the recent string of violent acts and had ties to this facility went through testing, except for the man responsible for the police station bombing, of course. There was nothing left to test in that case. As of right now, the only thing we know is that all of the perpetrators had damage to the lateral septum of the brain. Without getting technical, the lateral septum is sort of a connector in the brain. It receives messages from the hippocampus, which is the part responsible for memory. This was the area that President Denali was targeting. However, the lateral septum is also linked to the hypothalamus, which plays a role in emotional balance. For years, the lateral septum has been a key element in many theoretical studies on rage, for the purpose of controlling outbursts that accompany certain psychological disorders." He pauses. "Hence, why Dr. Eckert and I have been brought back in. We have to determine which of these people have brain damage, what could have caused it, and why are we just now seeing the effects after this length of time. So, in order to answer your latter question, the answers to all of these other questions have to be determined first."

"Isn't it a little odd that you and Dr. Eckert were asked to be involved in this testing process? It surprises me that they would put that much trust in you since you worked for Dennis when you were here before."

Dr. Blakely groans. "First of all, you know we were both exonerated, and it was concluded that we believed everything we did here at the facility was to train recruits for Soldiers Against Crime. Your loving husband had us convinced that our jobs were doing a great service for our country. Second, the government wanted Dr. Eckert and me to take part in this testing because we know better than anyone what these people were exposed to here."

"Understood. That makes sense." Cynthia agrees, and then in a humble tone, she asks, "What exactly did my lateral... whatever look like?"

"I told you that your tests were fine."

"No, you told me to leave before someone started questioning my results." Her voice gets hoarse. "Is there something wrong with me, Mitchell? Please tell me the truth."

"I didn't look."

"You didn't look?" Cynthia's pitch rises in question.

"No. There was no need to. Obviously, this is related to something Denali did to erase these people's memory. He did not attempt to erase your memory. He only used you for a lab rat in his cryonics experiment."

"Oh, I guess you're right." she mumbles and then lets out a loud sigh. "How long is this whole thing going to take... you know, to get all this testing done and figure out the cause?"

"Honestly, I have no idea. It is apparent that this executive order was expedited without any forethought by our genius president." Dr. Blakely criticizes. "Even though it will take a little while for Homeland Security to round up everyone, they already had more trains headed here than we could handle. Thorough testing takes time. There is no way we could assess the subjects that fast or even accommodate that many people here. So, some of the trains have been diverted to prisons with enough open space and staff to house and monitor those people until we can get to them."

"Are you saying that these people could be imprisoned for a long time?"

"That is a good possibility." he answers.

"Have you tested my son or daughter yet? You know their memory was affected. I need to know now that they are okay." Her voice cracks on the last words.

As her voice cracks, my heart rips in half. *Please, no. Why is it just now hitting me that something could be wrong?* I feel tears puddling behind my eyelids. *Steve has to be okay.* My hands start to tremble, and I press my palms on the table to steady them. *What if he's not? We just got married. We are supposed to have children and grow old together.* The seconds waiting for Dr. Blakely to answer seem like hours. *What time I am afraid, I will trust in thee. Psalm 56:3.*

"No. If she is in here, he is probably next." he answers matter of factly.

"Look, Mitchell. I don't care how you do it, but Steve and Teresa's tests will be normal. I could care less about Ellie, but I want my children released." Cynthia demands. "Do you understand?"

"Of course." he answers in a quavering voice.

A bit of pressure releases from my chest. *Her comment about me doesn't matter. I am just so relieved that Steve will get out of here. But what if something is really wrong? Dear Heavenly Father, I am scared. I am scared for my husband, my sister, my friends, and myself. Please don't let anything be wrong with our brains. Please let these tests show that we are all okay."*

"I am curious though." Her tone returns to normal. "What does Ellie's test show? Do you see any damage in her images?"

I hold my breath.

"Alright, alright, be patient. I need to get all the images on the screen." he mutters, followed by the clicking sound of a computer mouse. "Okay, right here in the center. Do you see that darker area?"

"Yes, but I don't know what it means." Cynthia replies.

"To answer your question, the perpetrators all have light lines right through here in this area." He coughs and makes a gurgling sound like he is clearing his throat. "As you can see, Ellie does not."

"So, she is fine." Cynthia says in a neutral tone. "Does this mean she will be released?"

"It's not quite that simple." Dr. Blakely answers.

My brain is normal. He said so. What does he mean it is not that simple?

"Something is happening to the brain, causing these lesions to develop. We have not figured out the cause, and we don't know how long it could take for the damage to occur. Therefore, because the CT scan doesn't show damage now, that doesn't mean lesions still won't develop. The president will not allow anyone to be released until we have some definitive answers. As I explained earlier, you are the one exception because your memory was never affected."

"Okay, I understand that reasoning, but," Cynthia probes, "if that is truly the case, Ellie's memory was never erased either."

"Hmm. That's interesting."

"What's interesting, Mitchell?" she grumbles.

"Just a minute ago, you said that you could care less about Ellie." Dr. Blakely says bluntly.

She did. I heard her. But weird. Dr. Blakely's attitude seems a bit different than in that letter I found in the kitchen. Maybe the magic is dying now that she isn't frozen anymore.

"I don't care. I am just trying to figure out if you are keeping something from me." Cynthia snaps back.

Dr. Blakely's voice softens. "Cynthia, I would not keep anything from you. Surely, I have proven myself. And you are right. Ellie's memory was not erased, but it was targeted. She escaped before her memory was harmed, but she was still exposed to elements that were supposed to erase her memory."

"Oh. So, you have to make sure that she wasn't exposed long enough to be at risk for those lesions." Her words rise like she has had an epiphany. "Well, that's fine. Follow Kutchin's procedure. He can't be the brains behind this hoopla anyway. But I want Steve and Teresa out. I don't care that their memory was affected. I need them out and all clear... I mean, we need them out and all clear."

"Yes, my ice princess. I will take care of it. I promise."

I guess the magic is back.

"Thank you, and I'm sorry for being so short with you." Cynthia lets out an audible sigh. "I am a bit stressed. This would be the perfect setup if Dennis hadn't dragged my children and me into this place too."

"No worries, my love. I am the one that should be sorry. I guess I am on edge as well." He pours on a thick layer of honeyed words. "Look, I'll have one of the guards take you to the airport. I already have a plane waiting to take you back to Arlington. I am going to be covered up the rest of the evening and night with all these people to test, but I will call you with an update in the morning."

"Do you promise?"

"I promise, my dear. Now come on. I will walk you out." Footsteps clank across the floor, and his voice grows fainter. "I need to have Waves wake Ellie up anyway. I still have to complete her psychiatric evaluation."

The door squeaks and then closes with a clatter.

I start to open my eyes but then remind myself that cameras are probably everywhere. My worries ricochet off of each other in my head. I don't know whether damage to our brains or Cynthia's plan should be my biggest concern. I try to convince myself that I am probably blowing both situations way out of proportion and wasting precious brain cells in the process, but my OCD won't let go. The worries are already in orbit. *Stop it, Ellie.* I command myself. *Give it to God. Casting all your care upon Him, for He careth for you.* As I quote the scripture, a new set of thoughts starts bouncing around in my head. Steve is going to be released, and my brain is fine. *I have a lot to be thankful for. Dear Lord, thank you. Thank you for letting Cynthia push to get Steve released. Thank you for not letting my brain have those lesions. Thank you for giving me peace and reminding me that You are bigger than any of my worries.*

The doorknob rattles, followed by a click. "Merrily, merrily, merrily, merrily." His singing and the whir of his robotic movements get closer. "Such a catchy tune." he says right over me. "Alright, Mrs. Ellie, it is time to wake you up. Here we go… in three…"

How do I do this? How do I make this look real?

"Two…"

Should I squirm or just pop my eyes open? Relax, it's just Waves.

"One."

I blink my eyes a few times, which is not an act. The light is bright, and I can't get my eyelids to open all the way.

"Mrs. Ellie, can you hear me?"

The spots from the bright light fade. My vision clears, and I start to laugh. Waves is leaned over me, blinking and bobbing his head from side to side.

"Yay!" he shouts. "I made you smile."

"Yes, Waves, you did. Thank you. I needed to smile." I move to sit up but realize that I am still strapped to the table.

"Well, then, you are very welcome." He stares at me in silence for a minute. "I am not supposed to unstrap you, but your test was fine, and you don't look dangerous." He tilts his head. "And it will really annoy Dr. Blakely." He chuckles. "Let's do it." His metal hand reaches down next to my ear, and the rubber band loosens from my forehead.

I twist my head from side to side, stretching my neck while he releases the straps holding my wrists and ankles. Once he has me free, I sit up and rub the back of my head as I swing my legs over the side of the gray metal table. "Looks like they could at least put some padding on that thing. My head is sore."

"I will put that in the suggestion box." Waves comments.

I lift one eyebrow. "There is a suggestion box?"

"Not yet. I will have to make one." He glances at the computer stand next to the metal table and then scans the room. "Aha." he says, wheeling himself between a sofa and a chair to a small desk in the corner. He lifts a gray box of tissues and jerks the contents out in a wad with his long, pointy index finger. Leaving the wad of tissues on the desk, he strolls back across the room, opens the drawer in the computer stand, and pulls out a black marker.

I watch in disbelief as he prints in all capital letters, *SUGGESTION BOX.* Then he takes a slip of paper out of the drawer, writes *PROVIDE PILLOWS DURING TESTING FOR HEAD SUPPORT*, and drops it in the tissue box.

"Tada. All finished." He holds up his suggestion box.

I grin and shake my head. "Waves, you are something else. Do they not watch you on camera or monitor you in here?"

"Oh yes. This room feeds into Dr. Blakely's office, but I think after the first day, I got on his nerves so bad that he turned down the volume and stopped paying attention."

I can't help but stare at his mohawk. The red spikes quiver as he talks. "Hey, Waves, can I see that marker and a slip of paper?"

"Sure thing." He pulls a pad of paper from the drawer and hands it to me with the marker.

On the top sheet, I draw a tic tac toe board. Then, on the second sheet, I write, *I know Steve will be released, but I need to know if his test is really okay.*

He looks over the top of my hand as I write. When I lift my eyes, he nods.

"You got it," Waves shouts. "I love tic tac toe." He snatches the second sheet that I wrote on and sticks it between his teeth. The paper grinds into tiny bits, and he swallows.

I wonder where it goes.

He grabs another marker and winks. "I'll be X's, and you be O's." He stretches his hand and makes an X in the top corner.

I put an O in the middle just as Dr. Blakely flings the door open.

"Waves, what do you think you are doing?" Dr. Blakely rants.

"I am playing tic tac toe." Waves answers cheerfully.

"It is bad enough that you have broken the rules and unstrapped her." Dr. Blakely purses his lips for a second and rubs his right hand across the top of his head. He still wears his shoulder-length black hair slicked back into a ponytail. After a long sigh, he continues, "But why would you give her a writing utensil? A writing utensil is a sharp object that could be used as a weapon."

"Well, if she doesn't have a marker, how is she supposed to draw the O's?" Waves puffs. "Really, Dr. Blakely, I am not sure how you graduated from medical school."

"Waves, please leave so I can do my evaluation."

"Very well, sir. I am needed down the hall anyway." Waves extends his hand. "Let me get the marker from Mrs. Ellie before I go. I wouldn't want you to get hacked up by a soft-tipped marker or anything."

"Waves." Dr. Blakely's face turns blood red. "I am losing my patience."

"Oh. That is too bad. If you lose all your patients, that means you will be out of a job." Waves puts his metal hand on the side of his torso and lets out a bellowing guffaw as he rolls toward the door.

I have to put both of my hands over my mouth to keep from laughing out loud.

Dr. Blakely pinches the bridge of his nose. "The proper procedure is to keep the subject restrained until I have completed the evaluation. However, considering that you are no longer contained and your brain scan was normal, how about we do your evaluation over in the sitting area?" He extends his hand toward the sofa and chair.

I hop down from the table. "I suppose I get the sofa?"

"Of course. Feel free to lie back and get comfortable." He sits down in the chair and crosses his legs as he leans back. "The goal of this session is to evaluate how you have been doing since you left the facility."

"Well, this should be an easy evaluation then." I flip around and recline on the sofa, resting my head on the arm. I would prefer to sit up since I have been strapped to that table for so long, but I don't want to look at Dr. Blakely. Unfortunately, this sofa is not as comfortable as the one that was in Dr. Blakely's office before.

"Oh. And why is that?" he prods.

"Because my life couldn't be better." I watch a spider crawl across the ceiling as I talk. "Well, except for being forced to come back here. But before this little bump in the road, I have married the man of my dreams, my family is all back together, and I have a great career."

"I see." He lifts his chin and straightens his back. "So, I believe the last time we spoke, you were all filled with this peace that passes understanding. How's that holding up?"

"Wow, you have a good memory." I comment. "Dr. Blakely, I accepted Jesus as my Savior and asked Him to come into my heart a long time ago. That peace that I get from my relationship with Jesus is permanent, and I am filled with peace because He is always with me. I take it from the way you asked the question that you haven't found the peace that comes from a relationship with God?"

Dr. Blakely twists and uncrosses his legs. "Mrs. Denali, we are here to do your evaluation, not mine."

"I'm sorry. I didn't mean to sound like I was evaluating you. It's just..."

"Just what, Mrs. Denali?" he questions in a patronizing tone.

"It's just that," I swallow hard, trying to choose my words carefully, "I could not imagine facing one day in this world without God to walk with me, carry me, lift me, listen to me," I smile, "give me that peace in the darkest of valleys, reminding me that He is in control and that He will never leave me."

"I seem to be facing each day just fine, so let's get back to your evaluation." He picks up a tablet from the side table next to his chair and uses his index finger to type something. "I understand that this sudden trip back to the facility has been a major interruption in your life, but I need you to be completely honest with me in answering my questions so that we can help you if there is a problem." He drags his thumb across the screen. "Has anything about your physical or mental health changed, or have you noticed anything different?"

"No. Nothing abnormal."

He taps on the tablet. "I know you were involved in stopping President Denali, so I guess it could be said that you dealt with a bit more turmoil than the other trainees. Is there a specific moment that stands out to you as being the worst?"

"Oh. There were several moments." I say, keeping my tone relaxed even though the memories of those moments make me boil inside.

"And those would be?"

"Well, let's see." I put my finger to my chin to display my sarcasm. "I suppose discovering my younger sister frozen in a tube ranks close to the top. That and finding my best friend unconscious in one of these labs, not knowing if she was dead or alive. But, if I had to choose one as the worst, I would have to say it was seeing my father get shot and thinking he was dead."

"That's a pretty dramatic list of worst moments. I suppose you must harbor a lot of anger and resentment inside." Dr. Blakely prods.

"Of course, it makes me feel angry if I put all my focus on those bad things. I am human. But, when I think of the big picture, I can find many things to be grateful for. I met my husband, my family has gotten closer, my sister has discovered what she wants to do with her life, I made a new best friend, and Gerald and Teresa accepted Jesus as their Savior." I sit up on the sofa and turn to face Dr. Blakely. "The Bible says, 'And we know that all things work together for good to them that love God, to them who are the called according to his purpose. Romans 8:28.' What President Denali intended for evil, God used for good."

"Good... huh?" He narrows his eyes at me. "What about the people in those tubes that died?"

"It is sickening. What Denali did was a horrific act of evil. But..." I breathe out, "we can be at peace knowing that those people are with Jesus in Heaven now."

With a smirk on his face, Dr. Blakely glares at me. "And how exactly do you know that?"

"Because that was the whole reason President Denali froze them. He couldn't erase God from their lives."

He bites his lips together and peers at me with a blank face. "Moving on." He glances down at the screen. "Do you ever lose your temper or feel like you have a hard time controlling your anger?"

"No."

"That's it." He adds a hint of skepticism. "You never lose your temper?"

"Umm. No. I am more of a 'let it build up and have a good cry' kind of person."

He types on the screen. "In these episodes where you explode into tears, do you ever have thoughts of harming yourself or someone else?"

"First of all, take note that I never said anything about episodes where I burst into tears. I simply meant that I cry instead of having a temper tantrum. As for the question, no, I never have thoughts of harming anyone, including myself."

"Very good." He taps the display on the tablet one time. "And how do you sleep? Would you say that you get eight solid hours of sleep per night?"

I feel my heart pump faster at the mention of the word 'sleep'. Scratching my head, I answer in a matter-of-fact tone. "I would guess more like seven hours."

"And that is continuous sleep. You don't have nightmares or wake up intermittently?"

When Cynthia came for breakfast, I mentioned my nightmare. I wonder if she told him. I have to be honest, but how do I keep from raising a red flag? Thinking fast, I reply, "Everyone has nightmares occasionally. I suppose something would be wrong if I didn't."

He nods. "I see in my notes that you are a field agent for the FBI. So, I can understand how your job might affect your sleep sometimes. I would assume that you deal with a lot of unpleasant situations." He lays the tablet on his lap. "I know you had some hypnosis sessions with Dr. Eckert, and then you were given the electrotherapy that delivered electric shocks to the hippocampus of your brain. As we have learned, President Denali was utilizing these techniques to erase the long-term memory of the trainees here at the facility. Is it true that you suffered no memory loss whatsoever?"

"That is correct." I relax a bit.

"Okay. One more thing, and we will be finished." Dr. Blakely shifts in his chair. "At one point, you were sent for reprimanding. I understand that this was some sort of fright-ening virtual-like simulation intended for punishment. However, a glitch or malfunction was changing the simulation for some of the trainees, and instead of a punishment, they seemed to have a rewarding experience. Records indicate that several updates were made on this system, but even in the last groups of trainees, which included you, some trainees continued to leave reprimanding with a smile on their faces while others were leaving in terror. One young man even committed suicide after. What do you remember about your experience?"

I press my palms together and touch the tips of my fingers under my chin. Pulling in a deep breath, I squeeze my eyes closed and try my best to explain. "I remember it was dark, really dark... and hot. These long fingers were grabbing and clawing at me. I could hear these faint voices pointing out my shortcomings... all my faults one after another." The corners of my lips curve up as I remember what happened next. "And then there was a light and a cool breeze. A loud voice said, 'You are mine, and I hold you in my hands.' The hands and the whispers faded at the sound of the voice. And I was filled with joy... this indescribable happiness." I open my eyes, and Dr. Blakely is staring at me with his mouth agape.

"Well, I guess that... umm... that's all I have." He lifts the tablet and begins tapping the screen again. "Let me make a few notations." A minute passes as he focuses on the device in his hands. "Okay. I appreciate your patience. With so many to test, it is helpful to get my notes entered as I go."

"Yes. I can imagine the task of testing this many people at once must be overwhelming." *He has no idea I heard his conversation with Cynthia.* I babble on to see how he will respond. "I mean according to that Executive Order," as I say the words, the image of the white paper pops into my mind, "you know, the paper they showed us right before they tore our door down and tossed us on the floor like criminals." I take a shallow breath. "Anyway, it appears that everyone is ordered back here effective immediately."

"Unfortunately, that is not a realistic scenario. As much as we would like to take care of this overnight, it is not possible to test everyone at one time. You just got lucky. Your train was selected to test upon entry. Except for our offices, almost every room in this building has been set up for testing, but even with the robotics and technology, getting through the people on that train tonight is pushing our limits." Dr. Blakely slides forward in his chair.

"So, what about all the other people coming in?"

"Some will have to arrive later, as we have space, but we will be housing as many as we can in the various buildings. Group by group, day by day, we will make sure everyone is in a safe mental condition to re-enter society.

"I suppose that is all that can be expected of you." I force my mouth into a fake smile. "What now? Since you said my brain scan was normal, I assume I am free to leave?" I ask, widening my eyes and lifting my brows.

"No, it's not quite that simple. You will have to stay until we determine the cause of the problem in those affected. Because you are fine now doesn't mean a problem cannot still develop.

However, with your clear scan and your stable evaluation, you will have a little more freedom in the facility than those whose tests show otherwise or those that have not been tested." He stands to his feet, and I follow his lead and push myself up from the sofa.

I know that I should probably keep my mouth closed at this point, but... "in other words, we are being held prisoner here indefinitely."

"Mrs. Denali, I am sure if I were in your shoes," he shifts his eyes downward toward my feet, "or slippers, I would feel the same way. But we have to consider all the innocent lives that are at risk. At least, I assume that is the president's motive here." He reaches for the doorknob but pauses before he turns it. "Now, I have to get to the next room, so I can examine your husband's scan. A guard is waiting outside the door to escort you to building two. You will stay in a shared room, much like the one you had before."

As Dr. Blakely turns the knob, Waves is on the other side, pushing the door open.

Waves thrusts his hand over his heart. "Oh. You startled me. I thought you would be finished by now." He rolls past us over to the computer stand. "You really need to speed it up, Dr. Blakely. We have a lot of people to test."

"I am headed over to Steve Denali now. Do you have his images entered?" Dr. Blakely looks back over his shoulder with his hand holding the door.

"Oh. Dr. Eckert has already read the images. He is doing his evaluation now." Waves answers.

"What?" Heat rises in his face. "I thought I told you that I would be taking care of Mr. Denali's evaluation."

Every muscle in my body stiffens, and I stand frozen beside Dr. Blakely in shock at his outburst. I roll my eyes back and forth, hoping Waves will spill the results of Steve's brain scan.

"Yes, but then, Dr. Eckert was free and said he would do it." Waves explains as he reboots the computer.

"Again, I specifically said that I would take care of it." He speaks slowly and enunciates each word.

"Well," Waves retorts, "if someone hadn't spent so much time gawking at ice lady earlier, maybe someone would have made it to the other room before Dr. Eckert."

"Waves, why did you not tell Dr. Eckert…"

"Tell me what?"

My head jerks toward the sound of the voice.

"Oh. Dr. Eckert. I didn't hear you walk up." Dr. Blakely's voice cracks.

"I didn't mean to startle you." Dr. Eckert steps into the room. I notice his gray hair seems to have thinned a bit on top in the last year and a half, and his mustache is gone, but he still has the ancient navy-blue bowtie and that weird eerie glint in his eyes. "What was Waves supposed to tell me?"

Waves spins around to face Dr. Eckert. "He is mad because he wanted to do Mr. Denali's evaluation, and you beat him to it."

"I didn't see any special notes on the computer. Was there some specific concern that I should have been aware of?" Dr. Eckert crosses his arms. "His scan and evaluation were normal. The guard has already escorted him to his room."

"No. No reason for concern." Dr. Blakely gives Waves a stern look and then shifts his eyes to connect with Dr. Eckert. "I had looked over Mr. Denali's records when he was brought up for his scan, and I realized that he was considered an employee of the facility. Based on that knowledge, I was planning to have him released if his testing was normal."

"I am afraid you don't have the authority to do that." Dr. Eckert drops his arms to his side and glares over the top of his rectangular framed glasses. "His test results are normal so far, but his memory was erased, which places him in a group that requires further testing."

No. My knees feel like they are going to collapse. *They have to let him go.*

"Dr. Eckert, I have to disagree." he states in a professional tone. "I really do not see the need to detain him. I mean, for Pete's sake, he was responsible for the robots that inserted the tracking chips."

As I listen, my anxiety sends my heart into overdrive. I roll my eyes back and forth between Dr. Eckert and Dr. Blakely, wondering who is going to win the argument. Dr. Eckert opens his mouth to respond, but before he gets any sound out, a distant wail echoes down the hall. He seems to tense up at the woman's faint cry of pain, and Dr. Blakely appears to raise his eyebrows at Dr. Eckert.

"Dr. Blakely, you are free to have your opinion, but my word is final. Mr. Denali will remain here for further testing." He turns toward the door. "Now, if you will excuse me, it appears that I have a situation to attend to." He starts down the hallway, grumbling in a loud voice, almost as if he wants us to hear, "I really wish the guards could avoid violence. The subjects do us no good if they are dead."

As soon as Dr. Eckert is out of sight, a guard steps into the doorway. "Mrs. Ellie Denali, follow me, and I will escort you to your quarters."

I pause for a moment to see if Waves or Dr. Blakely say anything else, but Waves is getting his computer ready for the next test. Dr. Blakely's face is blood red, and he looks like he is gritting his teeth. I glance back at the guard, whose eyes are fixed on me so hard that they are like lasers burning holes right through me. Since he has a loaded gun in his hand and his finger seems to be twitching, I figure it's best if I follow him.

Chapter Ten

The guard walks behind me on my left side, using the tip of his gun to point the way. Now that I know we are inside a mountain, I don't question why we don't go outside to pass from building one to building two. After we enter the second building, the guard guides me down a hallway dotted with metal doors on both sides.

When he stops in front of one of the metal doors, my airway constricts, and I am sure that I am going to choke. It's the door to the same room I shared with the other girls in level two of training. It's the door to the same room where I lost a friend. I remember standing in this hallway sobbing as Telisia's lifeless body was wheeled out. I hadn't known her long, but our circumstances had made us family. She was like a sister.

The guard places his thumb on the pad and motions for me to go in. With a trembling hand, I crack the door open, grimacing, I try to bury the painful memories deep inside. The nudge of the gun against my rib cage prompts me to push on into the room.

The quarters look pretty much the same, with lockers along one wall. Rows of cots still cover the concrete floor, except before, there were two rows of five cots with plenty of space surrounding each bed. Now, four rows of ten cots are squished into the room with barely enough space to edge sideways between them.

The door clanks shut behind me. The room is dim, and I notice only half of the lights are on. One girl is curled up in the fetal position on a cot only a few feet from the door. Her eyes are open, but she doesn't move or acknowledge that I am even here. My eyes follow the sound of muffled sobs to one of the cots in the back of the room. *Alice.*

I breathe a sigh of relief when I see her, but at the same time, needles poke into my chest at the sight of her tears. Alice is always so strong and in control. She is always the one lifting everyone else. It is so out of character for her to look so broken. I hurry toward her, twisting, turning, and shuffling between the cots.

"Hi." a soft voice startles me.

I shift my head, searching for the source. A tiny young woman with long, curly red hair stands outside the doorway to the bathroom.

"Oh, hi." I reply and give a little wave as she walks toward me.

"I'm Bailey."

"Nice to meet you, Bailey. My name is Ellie."

"Do you know her?" Bailey nods her head toward Alice. "I tried to talk to her, but she wouldn't stop crying."

"Yeah. That's Alice. I'll talk to her."

"Okay." She tries to curve her mouth into a friendly smile, but her lips quiver like she might burst into tears too. "I'll go see if I can get Cindy to move." She turns in the direction of the motionless girl on the cot in the front.

"Alice," I whisper, touching my hand to her shoulder. "Did they hurt you?"

"On the train, I heard gunshots. I didn't know what it was. But when I got here, that girl up there lying on the cot told me that she overheard the guards talking about someone being shot because he was resisting." Her body jerks as her words come out between her wails. "I am afraid it was Gerald." She rolls her eyes up at me. "You know that sounds like something he would do. That is if he even made it here after what I heard in his office."

"Alice, it wasn't Gerald that was shot." I sit on the side of the cot and wrap my arms around her.

"How can you be sure?" She sobs into my shoulder.

"Because Steve and I were in that car. I didn't see the man's face, but I heard his voice and saw the back of his head." I pause when her sobs quieten. She lifts her head and gazes at me through her tears. "Alice, it wasn't him." I reassure her.

Alice sniffles. "You're positive?"

"One hundred percent."

Alice's posture stiffens, and her jaw line hardens. In an instant metamorphosis, the broken Alice transforms into the strong and determined Alice that I am accustomed to. "Ellie, are you okay? Do you know if your scan was normal? Something feels..." She stops herself and purses her lips together. Her eyes move around the ceiling and then back to me. "Ellie, God's got this. We may have to take a few leaps of faith." The corner of her mouth curves into a half-smile.

I smile back even though I am a little worried. Alice's one-sided smile usually foreshadows us doing something risky. Add in the phrase, 'leaps of faith,' and I am certain she is devising a plan that involves breaking the rules. Sometimes I wonder how our personalities connect so well. Alice exhibits a no-fear attitude, and I am obsessive-compulsive, which means I avoid risks. But God brought us together. He sent Alice, a sister in Christ, to be with me the first time we were here. Now, here we are again, and it's no coincidence. I know God has put us here together for a reason.

Alice waves her hand to Bailey, motioning her over, and then says to me in an undertone, "I want to introduce myself and tell her I'm sorry for not being all that friendly earlier." Bailey walks up. "Hi," Alice says looking up at her. "It's Bailey, right?"

"Yes. That's me." Bailey responds. "Glad to see you are feeling better."

"Thank you. I owe you an apology. I was letting worry get the best of me, and I don't normally do that. Anyway, my name is Alice. Could I have a do-over?"

Bailey puts her hand on Alice's shoulder. "You can have as many as you want, but you don't need one. And you don't need to apologize either. I understand. Worry gets the best of us all from time to time. I think worry is one of the devil's best tactics... that and fear." She laughs. "At least he gets me with both of those anyway."

"Me, too." I add.

Alice taps her chin. "Have either of you checked out those lockers?"

"I did." Bailey shifts her eyes toward the wall. "It's more baby clothes, extra slippers, and some towels."

"Great. I didn't think I would get into this onesie the first time. Now, I have to peel this one off and put on another one." I slide off of the cot and kneel on the floor. "Here, Bailey, have a seat." I say as the large bolts holding the legs of the cot to the floor catch my attention.

Bailey lowers herself to the edge of the thin mattress.

"They didn't even give us soaps and shampoos this time?" Alice asks. "What are we supposed to shower with?"

"I wondered that too, so I checked the bathroom." Bailey says, then explains. "Well, not that I like examining bathrooms... but... I needed to keep my mind busy... for obvious reasons."

Alice and I nod.

"They have bolted dispensers to the shower walls with soap and shampoo. I guess they didn't feel conditioner was essential or shaving either, for that matter." Her hands fidget, and she swipes her hands across the legs of her pants. "Umm, were you girls human ice sculptures too, or were you part of the army?"

"Neither." Alice replies.

Bailey's face contorts with a confused expression.

"We were in the last group," I chime in. "We were the escapees."

Bailey's mouth falls open, and her hand flies up to cover it. "You two were in the group that stopped the plane and got President Denali caught. Oh, my goodness. You two saved my life."

"Oh, no. We didn't. That whole thing was God's show. We were just a bunch of misfits with a monkey." Alice clarifies.

"Well, God paved the way, but you chose to follow His lead and carry out His plan." Bailey grins. "Thank you for following His lead."

"Bailey," I hesitate, "the way you asked the question a while ago, I am guessing you were one of the cryonics victims?"

"Yes. He took a few years of my life." She drops her head. "I didn't understand why it happened to me. I was engaged. The man I was going to marry moved on with his life while I was being held prisoner as a popsicle. I was angry for a while, but then I looked at the pieces of the puzzle." Bailey lifts her gaze. "You guys came along and saved me along with the rest of the world. The man of my dreams turned out not to be the man of my dreams. He had done some not-so-nice things to the woman he ended up marrying. And I met someone that I believe might be the person God has for me." She tilts her head and twists her mouth to the side. "I don't know though. Now I am back here, so maybe he's not. Maybe God is keeping me from another mistake." She laughs. "Time will tell, right?"

"In God's time, not ours." Alice remarks.

As Alice speaks, my attention is pulled to the girl still curled up on the cot. "Did you say her name was Cindy?" I ask, feeling a pang of guilt that we are sitting here having a conversation and that poor girl is up there alone.

"Yeah." Bailey casts a quick glance toward her. "When I came into the room, I tried to talk to her, but the only thing I got out of her was her name."

"Alice, you talked to her, didn't you?" I ask.

"She was the only one here when I came in, and she almost gave me a heart attack. She was laying on her side on the floor with her eyes closed, so I fell to the floor beside her, started checking her pulse, kept asking her if she was okay…" Alice's distress echoes in her tone as she rattles off the details. "She wouldn't respond, so I rolled her over onto her back. I think she finally spoke up because she thought I was about to do CPR." Alice puts her hand to her chest. "Then she just kept repeating that she was scared. Scared he wouldn't know. After a few minutes of struggling through the conversation, I put together what she was trying to tell me. Apparently, her husband wasn't home when the agents came for her. She said she was afraid that he wouldn't know what happened to her. At that point, she began to wail that we were all going to die, and she didn't get to tell him she loved him one last time. I questioned her about the 'we were all going to die' comment." Her voice drops until it's barely audible. "That's when she told me about the man being shot on the train, and I went to pieces."

"Maybe we should all go try to talk to her." I push off the side of the cot and rise to my feet.

The door bursts open, and our heads turn in unison. Two women are shoved into the room, and a guard yanks the door closed behind them.

"That door only opens from the outside." I say my thought aloud without realizing it.

"Yep." Bailey sighs in disgust. "I already tried to open it."

The two women stand motionless in front of the door and appear to be surveying the room. The taller of the two has long black hair pulled back in a ponytail and bangs cut in a straight line covering her forehead. She locks her eyes on us and starts in our direction. The other woman, with a blonde bob-cut streaked with blue highlights, drops to her knees with a thump. The taller, dark-haired woman stops in her tracks and looks back as the woman on the floor buries her face in her hands. She turns on her heels, squats by the woman on the floor, and pulls her into her arms.

"For where two or three are gathered together in my name, there am I in the midst of them." I mumble to myself.

"You're right." Alice leaps from the cot.

I turn my head toward her, not even realizing that she heard me. "What?"

"You're right. We need to pray together. Come on." She takes off sashaying between the cots toward the girls at the front.

Bailey and I follow suit, making our way between the cots behind her.

Alice kneels beside the two women on the floor. "Hey," she whispers, "my name is Alice, and this is Bailey and Ellie." She gestures toward each of us.

Bailey smiles. "Hello."

"Hi." I add.

"We are going pray together. Why don't you guys join us?" Alice looks around and then motions with her hand. "Let's go over by Cindy."

The two women nod and get to their feet. The taller woman with dark hair speaks first. "It's nice to meet all of you. My name is Liz, and this is Mable."

"Hi." Mable chokes out.

We all move with Alice and kneel at the foot of Cindy's cot.

Bailey leans over Cindy and whispers to her. I guess she must be inviting her to pray with us, but Cindy doesn't respond.

"Why don't we hold hands?" Alice suggests.

I swallow, fighting my OCD, and grab Bailey's hand in my right and Liz's hand in my left.

"Dear Heavenly Father," Alice begins, "we thank you that you have kept us safe in all of this and that you have put us here with each other so that we are not alone. Lord, we cry out to you. We need help. Lord, if it be your will, please provide healing to those that might have negative effects from being here before. And Lord, if it be your will, please help us to get out of here safely. Guide us, Lord, and show us what it is that you would have us do here. Show us our purpose in this to glorify you." Alice pauses, and her voice cracks as she continues, "Please, Lord, I am scared for Gerald. Please let him be alright and help me find him."

A few seconds of silence pass, and I add my cry to God. "Lord, thank you for surrounding me with other Christians to share this time of prayer with. Please be with Steve, Teresa, Eileen, and Gerald. Please keep a shield of protection around them. Please comfort my parents and help them not to worry." Tears puddle in my eyes and trickle down my cheeks. "And Lord, please help me to obey your command and to be strong."

Bailey speaks up. "Father, thank you for Alice, Ellie, Cindy, Liz, and Mable. Please help us to get out of here." Her sobs echo through the room. "Lord, I am so scared. Please, I can't go through this again."

"Lord, I praise you for these sisters in Christ." Liz lets go of my hand and lifts her arm above her head. "Help us to get home to our families. And Lord, my dad needs someone to take care of him until I get back. Please take care of my dad's needs." Liz takes my hand again.

A hoarse, trembling voice utters from somewhere right outside the circle. "Lord, help him to know I'm okay. Please let him know I love him. Please let him wait for me."

Cindy. Oh, thank you, Lord, for giving Cindy the strength to join us.

The door creaks, and someone kneels behind me. Bailey and I separate hands and let the new girl in the circle. As we pray, more and more come in, and we continue to take turns praying. Soon, we have too many for one circle, so instead of a circle, we sort of huddle. The hands of people behind me touch my back. As I listen to each person pray, I am in awe of what is happening in this room.

Fingertips graze my back, and her tone echoes relief. "Father, thank you. Thank you so much for letting me find my sister."

Eileen. I let go of the hands beside me and fling my arms around my little sister. I don't know if I should have during our prayer, but I am so relieved that my emotions take over. Despite my outburst of joy, she continues to pray with her arms around me.

Another hand falls on my shoulder, and a new voice calls out to God. "Lord, thank you for letting me be in here with my new sisters."

Teresa. I reach up over my shoulder and place my hand on top of hers.

Her words quaver between sobs. "This place... it reminds me of the person I used to be before I knew You. I know you have forgiven me, Lord. Please silence the past that haunts me. Help me remember that I am Your child now. If there are any ill intentions intended, please protect us."

The door flings open and bangs against the concrete wall. My heart leaps, skipping at least three beats. One of the girls screams as she lies on the floor and covers her head.

"What is going on in here, and where is Ellie Denali?" Dr. Eckert's voice booms.

I raise my arm in slow motion and wave to Dr. Eckert. "I-I-I'm r-r-right h-here." I stutter. The hair on my arms tingle as I take in Dr. Eckert standing beside Dr. Blakely and two guards gripping their guns.

Dr. Eckert hardens his expression more, which I did not think possible. He turns to face Dr. Blakely. "I thought you said she wasn't in this room."

"I-I... her location wasn't on the screen." Dr. Blakely scratches his head.

"Well now, you must have overlooked it. Maybe you should double-check yourself before you waste my time." Dr. Eckert turns back to us. "As for whatever is going on in this little huddle, you all need to separate. This type of activity is prohibited. I will cover this in my announcement in a bit, but if you would like to remain unrestrained, then you must not huddle up in large groups." He turns to go out the door. "Let's get back to work, Dr. Blakely."

"You know," Dr. Blakely mutters to Dr. Eckert, "maybe that huddle they were in was blocking her signal. She was kind of in the middle."

They go out the door. The two guards glare at us with

clenched jaws and taunt us with their guns before they turn and follow. The door slams with a loud clatter.

In an instant, I leap to my feet and dash across the room. *No cameras are in the bathroom.* Cold sweat beads on my forehead. *That was before. What about now? I'll just have to risk it.* With the focus of my panic elsewhere, I don't even give a thought to my normal phobia of going into the shared bathroom.

As soon as I am through the bathroom door, I reach up with both hands and run my fingertips all over my head. Alice, Eileen, and Teresa are right on my heels. I back away, holding up my hand, reminding them that we can't be too close. *Not until I figure out the problem.*

"Ellie," Alice peers at me with unblinking eyes, "are you okay?"

I put my finger to my lips, signaling her to be quiet, and then I point to the back of my head. When we were here in training, tracking chips were inserted in the back of our heads. That is how they tracked our location and listened to our conversations.

Alice nods and purses her lips together.

I don't know sign language, so I do my best to talk to Alice through hand motions. I point at my head and then at her head. I start sliding my finger over my head and neck again, hoping that she figures out what I am doing. Alice starts rubbing her hands across her head too.

A tear drips from the corner of my eye. I know I don't have much time before Dr. Blakely checks his screen. *Think, Ellie, think.* I tell myself. *Why didn't I go to sleep like everyone else, and why can't Dr. Blakely see my location?*

Alice walks around behind me and lifts my hair. Little by little, she shifts sections of my hair and touches my scalp.

My heart pounds in my ears. *He is probably back to building one by now.* I try to slow my breathing. *Wait. What if I don't have a chip? Maybe that's the problem. Maybe that tin can robot forgot to put it in.* I flip around and motion to Alice to let me check her. I rub and press my fingers all over the skin beneath her hair. I don't know what they have done this time, but I can't find any kind of cut where they could have inserted it. Swallowing hard, I drop my shoulders. *Lord, what am I going to do?* I suck in a deep breath through my mouth. *'Above all, taking the shield of faith, wherewith ye shall be able to quench all the fiery darts of the wicked.'* I absorb the words from Ephesians 6:16 as they roll through my mind. *Faith. God has always taken care of me. Have faith. That's what I am going to do.* I let the verse play over again inside my head.

Shield. My head jerks up. *Agent Morgan.* With wide eyes, I dash into the back dressing room and fling the curtain closed. Alice's footsteps pad across the hard tile floor, and I can hear her breathing on the other side of the curtain. Curling my fingers around the fabric, I tug at the neck of my unitard, trying to stretch it far enough that I can stick my hand inside. Pulling it as far as it will go off my shoulder. I manage to get my index finger under my arm and peel the small disc from my skin. Holding it gently between two fingers, I lay it on the seat. My heart rate slows as I peer down at the little silver disc. *It must be some kind of device that blocks out the chip's signal.* I tap my chin as I think. *Now what? I may need it, but I can't have it on me all the time.* Alice will know.

I slide back the curtain, and Alice's face is almost nose to nose with mine.

"What's wrong?" she mouths without making a sound.

How can I explain it and get her to help me without talking? I smile, remembering that Alice is an expert at puzzles. *She will figure it out.* I wave her inside, and as I peep out into the bathroom, I notice that Eileen and Teresa are gone. They must have gone back out to avoid drawing attention to us.

When Alice is inside the dressing room, I pull the curtain closed and point to the disc on the seat. Then I act out putting on my armor. I wrap the belt around and pretend to buckle it. I rub my hand over my chest for the breastplate, and then I extend my hands down, swiping them across my feet like I am putting on shoes. *This is fun, like playing charades.* I pull the helmet down over my head. Reaching out, I grab my imaginary sword and place it where the sheath would hang at my side.

Alice has her focus locked on my every movement. As she studies my motions, she bites her bottom lip and rubs her hands together. Squinting her eyes at me and holding up the palm of her hand, gesturing her uncertain guess, she forms the word 'soldier' with her lips. Or, at least, I am hoping that is what she said.

I nod, affirming her guess. *Now for the important part. Please let her get this.* Pointing the index fingers of both hands, I draw a shield in the air in front of me and then make eye contact with Alice.

She gives me a puzzled look, so I draw it again.

"Shield." she says silently.

I nod, and then holding up one finger, I point to the disc on the seat, draw the shield in the air, and tap the back of my head where the chip was inserted during training. I look at Alice and repeat the motion.

She stands frozen for a moment gazing at the little disc. With narrowed eyes, she extends her hand and lifts the device with her fingertips. Holding it in front of her face, she twists it back and forth, studying both sides of the disc. All of a sudden, her face lights up, and the corners of her mouth curve into a sly smile. In a swift motion, she takes the disc in her right hand, clutches my wrist, and presses the disc to my wrist firmly with the heel of her palm.

"Where on earth did you get this?" she asks aloud.

"Shhh." I put my finger to my mouth.

"It's okay. They can't hear us… unless they have the bathroom tapped… but I doubt it. If they were going to listen to us that way, they would have done it before."

"What is that thing?" Still nervous, I can't help but whisper.

"It's a signal-blocking device." Alice explains. "The tracking chips are inserted inside the body, presumably in our head. When this little disc touches our skin, it sends pulses or vibrations through our body that interferes with the waves emitted by the tracking chip."

"So, any ideas where we can hide this thing? I mean, we definitely need it, but…"

Alice finishes for me. "Dr. Blakely is going to notice if you are not accounted for on his screen."

"Exactly."

"I'll be right back." Alice takes her hand away and sets the disc back on the seat. She slips out of the dressing room and returns in a few seconds with a paper towel. With her jaw set and an intense look of concentration on her face, she lowers herself onto the floor and pulls at my slipper.

Confused, I lift my foot and let her slip it off. *I know I hid a piece of paper in my shoe before, but how is this going to work? The disc will still touch my foot inside the slipper.* I watch as she rips a hole in the top of the slipper from the inside. With the extreme care and precision of a surgeon, she uses her fingernail like a knife and hollows out a tiny area in the foam padding.

She tears off a little corner from the paper towel, rolls the disc up inside it, and stuffs it into the padding of the slipper.

Alice is a genius.

~

WHEN ALICE and I come out of the bathroom, the room is so quiet I can hear my own heart beating. Everyone has chosen a cot and is either lying or sitting on it. I guess the guards and Dr. Eckert have made everyone afraid to get near each other. Thankfully, Eileen and Teresa have been able to secure four cots beside each other.

I sit on the edge of my cot, counting the hours on my fingers, trying to guestimate the time. I don't suppose it matters. But since I have nothing else to do, I go over the day in my head. *Agent Morgan and his goons burst into our house around six-fifteen. How long could we have been in that van? I don't think they would have traveled far; else it would not serve the purpose to switch us to a train. Maybe an hour? That would make it… seven-fifteen. I'll say seven-thirty. Then, maybe another hour by the time we got on the train… eight-thirty. Probably five hours on that train… nine-thirty, ten-thirty, eleven-thirty, twelve-thirty, one-thirty. By the time we changed, ate, and loaded the bus… two thirty, three thirty. Half-hour bus ride, an hour of testing… I would have gotten to this room at five o'clock. We've had to have been in this room two or three hours, so that would make it…"*

"Building two… may I have your attention please for a few announcements and instructions."

Cots squeak all over the room as the girls sit up to listen.

"First, I realize that it is almost eight-thirty. I apologize that dinner has not been provided yet, but it will be at your door by the time I finish this message."

Eight-thirty… I was close.

"Building two has finished the first phase of testing and will continue onto the second round. You have been separated into living quarters based on your test results. The second round of tests will resume tomorrow. No congregating is allowed. If you are in a situation where you have been given the liberty to move about freely in your quarters, adequate personal space must be maintained at all times. Violation of this rule will result in consequences. We must be cautious and eliminate any risk of gang activity. Bedtime is ten o'clock. However, dim lighting will remain on for monitoring purposes. That is all I have for now. Enjoy your dinner."

The door swings open, and two guards step inside. Shelly strolls through the door and between them, pushing a cart filled with small cardboard boxes. Her appearance hasn't been altered since I was here before, except for the white ruffled apron covering her bronze metal torso instead of scrubs. Her brown curly ponytail swings from side to side as she moves. She stops the cart in front of the wall of lockers. The red dots in the center of her glistening deep blue eyes glow as she turns her head right to left.

"Hello there, Ladies." Her loud mechanical voice still mimics a southern accent. "I come in peace. But," she thrusts a stiffened hand up in the air and slings it down in a chopping motion, "I must warn you, I do know karate." She blinks her eyes a few times. "Now, I know it's a bit late for greasy foods, but I've got fried chicken and tater wedges." Her arm extends, and she points to the back. "Let's start with the back row and come up one at a time." Shelly keeps talking as Bailey walks up to get her box and water bottle. "And I do apologize. All I have is water. I tried to tell the bosses that lemonade goes with fried chicken, but they thought water was best."

One by one, we take the boxes of chicken and go back to our cots. After we all have our food, Shelly pushes the cart out, and the guards step backward from the room. The door clanks shut behind them.

A moment passes as everyone stares at the white boxes, and then Teresa's voice breaks the silence. "If it's okay with everyone, I will say the blessing." she utters barely above a whisper.

In an instant, her words bring the room to life as 'yes', 'please', and 'thank you' echo across the room in response to her offer.

Chapter Eleven

Silent tears flood down my face. I miss my husband, but more than that, I need to know that he is okay. I keep telling myself not to worry. He said he would find me if we got separated. But I can't help it. After all, when we got married, we became one. He is part of me, and I am part of him.

I wish I could go to sleep. *Escape the stress and worry for a few minutes.* But even if I could relax long enough to fall asleep, the muffled sobs filtering from various locations around the room aren't exactly melodic lullabies. And I don't recall these cots being this… *I don't really know the word for it…* but it takes me back to when I was ten years old, and we took a family camping trip. My dad was not the outdoorsy type, and I am pretty sure he had never been camping before. However, he was determined to take his family on this trip because he thought it would be a great bonding experience. He went out and bought a tent large enough for the four of us. We hiked down a trail with our camping gear to this huge lake where Dad spent hours setting up the tent on rocky terrain. It was painful. No matter which way I shifted, a sharp rock would stab into me. Anyway, that tent was more comfortable than this cot.

I am so tired. *Maybe if I close my eyes... imagine I am some-where else. Lord, please take these worries and help me sleep.* I pretend I am lying on the beach. The dim lights are the sun's rays penetrating through my eyelids, and the muffled sobs are a mix of crashing waves and seagulls laughing as they steal food from unattended blankets. Fragments of seashells poke my back through my beach towel, but my body soon adjusts to the discomfort. The waves and the seagulls fade into the distance, and then I am in the midst of nothing.

～

THUMP. *Thump. Thump. Thump.* With every loud beat, a strange ache radiates from my chest into my shoulder and down my arm. Even though my eyes can't penetrate through the thick shroud of black that surrounds me, the feeling that someone is watching me makes the hair on my arms stand at attention.

A horrid shriek causes my beating heart to trip over itself. I spin in a circle, searching for the source of the suffering cry. *There.* A sliver of light dances in the distance. Someone needs help. Someone is in pain. I try to move, but my knees are locked.

"Ellie, be strong."

I jerk my head back and forth. *Who said that?*

I force myself to move toward the glow. As I shuffle closer, the sound of someone weeping grows louder. A few more steps and the illuminated strip is in front of my feet. I reach out with my hand feeling for a way in. A piercing scream rattles the door. Just as my fingers graze the knob, I squeal in pain and jerk back, grabbing my blistering fingers in my other hand. The burning won't stop. I fall to the ground thrusting my fingers into my mouth to soothe the sting.

～

My ELBOW COMES DOWN on something hard, sending a wave of tingling shocks down my forearm. My back scrapes against metal, and a loud grunt is forced from my mouth as my side collides with the concrete floor.

"Ellie... are you okay?" Alice's voice pulls me back into the room.

I open my eyes, and Alice's face is hanging over the edge of her cot.

Eileen scrambles over her pillow and leaps to the floor at my head. "Are you hurt? What happened?" Her lips tremble with panic.

"I'm fine." I reassure her. "It was just a bad d-d-dr..." My tongue protrudes out of my mouth. I gag as if fingers are being stuck down my throat. Heat rushes through my body, and my stomach convulses in pain. My arms and legs vibrate out of control, striking against the floor. The room fades. I strain to focus on Alice and Eileen, but their faces keep multiplying until they are only diminishing spots.

"Ellie... don't leave me, Ellie..."

My eyelids fall, my body relaxes, and sleep takes over.

~

"ELLIE, keep your fingers crossed. It's going to be okay."

Alice.

A discord of whimpers and wails filters around me.

Heavy footsteps pound nearby. "Ma'am, step away from her now."

"No," she cries. "What have you done to her?"

A husky voice growls, "She is only sleeping. If you don't step away, I will shoot."

"Please, leave her alone." another voice wails.

"Eileen, Alice," Teresa's tone pleads. "Please, you have to get back. They are going to hurt you if you don't move away from her."

What's happening? I crack one eye with a flutter making it look like an involuntary tremor. A hand grabs Alice by the arm, and I squeeze my eyes closed. *Please, Alice... Eileen, stay back. Don't fight them.*

"Just keep your fingers crossed, Ellie. It'll be okay." Her desperate words echo in my ears as she is pulled away.

My fingers are crossed. I feel it. I press tighter, keeping my index and middle finger wrapped around each other.

"Keep your gun on her." a man orders as one set of hands grabs me under my arms, and another grabs my ankles. My body is lifted from between the cots and tossed onto a hard surface. One strap stretches around my arms and abdomen, and one strap crosses my knees, holding my legs down. Then, with the rhythmic squeak of turning wheels, I am pushed from the room. The door slams.

Once they are out of the room, the men don't speak. The only sounds are the pounding of boots down the hall and the faint creak of the wheels. Then, the gurney stops, followed by the swoosh of an elevator door. My heart rises and falls as the elevator ascends and comes to a halt. *I wonder if that was one story or two.* The gurney goes into motion again.

"Bring her on in."

That sounds like Dr. Eckert.

The straps loosen, and the rough hands shove my body over onto another cold table. More straps tighten around me. Suction cups press to my forehead and behind my ears.

"Is she almost hooked up, Claude?"

"Almost, doc, just a couple more wires."

A chill runs down my spine as a long skinny finger reaches under my head and presses a patch on the nape of my neck.

"Her little episode is almost too good to be true. Now, I don't have to wait to see if my latest updates have eliminated the glitch." Dr. Eckert's voice moves closer. "And since she is one of the ones that was affected by the glitch before, how fortunate I am to have this one as my test subject." he mimics a villainous laugh.

"But, doc," Claude interjects, "I thought you tested the new program earlier today."

"Oh, I did, and the results were astounding." Excitement rings in his tone. "But," he sighs, "it means nothing if it doesn't work on her."

What is he talking about? My heart catches in my throat. *I have to know.* I take a shallow breath. *Lord, I am so scared. Please, help me to be strong.* Using my thumb, I wiggle the disc from between my fingers with slow and gentle movements until I get it pressed between my hand and the table. *Okay, here it goes. Three, two, one.* I cup my hand so that the disc is covered, but my skin isn't touching it. The sounds around me grow distant, and all awareness disappears.

~

"How COULD he allow this to happen to you?"

"How could he let you go through this again?"

The murmurs echo in my ears.

"Married and a new career… you just got to the mountain-top, and now the faithful servant is in the dark valley."

"Yes, look at you now."

What? What are they talking about? Why can't I breathe?

The shroud of darkness pushes in, suffocating me. I suck in, but the hot air burns my lungs. Hot, rancid breath hits my face with every crushing word.

"That new husband doesn't love you anyway."

"He hasn't rescued you yet, has he?"

"You heard her. You heard what she said."

"His mother will get him out, and he will leave you to suffer."

Glowing hands with fingers of fire reach up from some-where below, clawing and slashing at me. The sound of flesh ripping and tearing floats up from beneath the hands, and bloodcurdling screams of pain plead and wail for help. A haunting stench rises in the smoke and creeps up my nostrils, torturing me with a horrific scent, a smell that could only signify death.

Tears flood down my face as the whispers surround me, shooting darts at my heart from every angle.

"Your faith has been a waste. Your God has abandoned you, and your husband doesn't love you."

"You are alone."

"Alo-o-o-ne."

No. My God will never leave me nor forsake me.

"Ha-ha. Then why are you here… again?"

"You have been forsaken."

No. I have not been forsaken. My Savior says, "In the world, ye shall have tribulation: but be of good cheer; I have overcome the world."

"Overcome the world… where is your mountaintop? Where is your mansion? Huh?"

"Face it, he does not care."

"No one cares."

My Father cares. My Father loves me. He loves me so much that He gave His only Son to die for me. My mountaintop… my mansion is in Heaven. My Father loves me so much that He wants me to live in Heaven with Him for eternity.

A loud crack of thunder booms sending tremors like an earthquake. The darkness above me splits open in the shape of a jagged lightning bolt. Bright radiating light pours down on my face, and a breath fills my lungs with cool, fresh air.

A penetrating but unexplainably comforting voice resonates out of the light, "My seal is upon her. She belongs to me. She is my child. Flee from her."

The darkness, the whispers, the hands, the screams, the sounds of torture, it all fades away, and there is only light. Cool air swirls around my body, and I am floating in the breeze.

The penetrating voice softens. "My child, I will never leave you nor forsake you. My spirit dwells in you." A gentle touch of a finger swipes under my eyes, clearing away my tears. "Well done, my good and faithful servant."

Joy consumes me, and I laugh. I laugh, not because anything is funny, but because I have so much joy inside that it is bubbling out of me.

❧

"Wake her up! I want to know why she is laughing."

Is that Dr. Eckert? He sounds mad.

"I'm trying, doc. It takes a second for the body to catch up to the brain."

I blink a few times and push my eyes open. That robot with red curly hair and hand-drawn freckles is standing at my head, peering down at me.

"Oh, I remember her." Claude twists his head away from me to face Dr. Eckert. "She laughed at me before, but she's really nice."

"Aaaah. Nice. Isn't that sweet?" Dr. Eckert mocks through gritted teeth.

"No, I mean it." Claude turns his head back and fixes his gaze on me, that is if a robot can gaze at someone. "I don't remember anyone else ever asking my name but her. And it wasn't fake or as if she was being polite when she asked. It was more like... she really cared to know."

"Oh, for Pete's sake!" Dr. Eckert growls and then appears at my side.

"Who's Pete?" Claude asks.

"No one. It's only an expression. Focus, Claude, please." The vein in Dr. Eckert's neck pulses as he glares down at me. "Mrs. Denali, since you are so caring, would you care to share why you are laughing?"

"Well," I search for the words, "it's kind of hard to explain.

"Give. It. A. Whirl." Dr. Eckert enunciates each word with force.

"Joy. I am overflowing with joy."

"Let me get this straight." He bites his lip and takes a shallow breath. "You were forced from your home and escorted back to this facility at gunpoint, where you were locked in a room with thirty-nine other women. While detained in your shared quarters, you had some sort of fit in your sleep, which ended with you having to come here for punishment. And now, you have woken up from your reprimanding that should have been a horrible experience, hence why it is referred to as a punishment, but you say you are overflowing with joy. Is that correct?" he challenges and then stares at me with his mouth twisted to the side.

"Yes." I nod as best as I can, considering I am strapped to a table.

"Interesting. Would you care to elaborate on your surplus of happiness, Mrs. Denali?"

"Okay." I swallow hard. "You are right about all the events leading up to this moment, except for how your reprimanding ended. And, let me just point out that I find it a bit peculiar that one would be punished for having a nightmare. It seems the nightmare would be punishment enough. But, anyway, your reprimanding thing started bad, but my Father showed up, the sun came out, and the darkness was no more." I grunt to clear my throat. "Dr. Eckert, I am aware that you are far more educated than I will ever be, so I hope you do not take this the wrong way. But you have a little misunderstanding of joy and happiness. You see, happiness depends on the circumstances. Joy comes from God, so because I have a personal relationship with Him, I have joy despite my circumstance."

Dr. Eckert's face reddens. "Mrs. Denali, I will make a note about your delusional state in your file. As for now, Claude will alert the guards to come and escort you back to your room." He turns and walks through the door, slamming it behind him.

Claude moves over to the little desk and taps on the keyboard.

Unaware of how much time I have, I flatten my hand out on top of the disc and try to line it up in the crack between my index and middle finger. Luckily, my hands are sweaty, so it sticks to my skin long enough for me to get my thumb underneath and push it up between my fingers. Breathing a sigh of relief that I didn't drop it, I cross my middle finger over my index finger to tighten my grip on it, and at the same time, keep it hidden.

Just as I get the disc hidden, Claude is towering over me. "Mrs. Denali," his body lowers so he is closer to my face, "I liked that story about your Father. You must have a really great dad."

I can't help but smile at him. "Yes, yes, I do."

The door bursts open, and two guards push a gurney into the room.

"Oh, you won't need that. She's awake now." Claude loosens my straps. "She can walk."

Both guards stiffen and grip their guns.

"Don't get your feathers in a bunch." he winks at them. "Two tough guys like you don't need a gun for little Ellie here. She is the nicest person I have ever met."

"Thanks, Claude." I grab his metal hand as he pulls me up from the table. "Hey, who knows? Maybe you will still get to take me to the moon one day."

"I'm afraid the moon is setting my hopes too high. Maybe a rocket booster would be a more reasonable dream. I would still be part of the shuttle."

I shake my head. "You are too much, Claude, too much."

Chapter Twelve

The guards shove me into the room. It must be morning because everyone is awake. Eileen, Alice, and Teresa are kneeling in the back of the room, holding hands in prayer. When the door clanks shut, their heads all turn at the same time. Eileen is on her feet first and leaps across three cots running toward me. She flings her arms around my neck, and her tears wet my cheek as she embraces me. Alice and Teresa are right behind her, pulling us all into a group hug. With our arms locked around each other, Alice utters a prayer of thanks under her breath.

"We better separate." I whisper a warning.

"You're right." Alice lets go and wipes her fingertips under her eyes.

"This is ridiculous." Eileen grumbles, backing away. "I can't even hug my sister without getting in trouble."

Teresa doesn't speak. She wraps her arms around herself and stares into space like she is deep in thought.

Alice rests her hand on my shoulder. "Ellie. Are you okay?"

"Yeah, but I need to go to the bathroom." I roll my eyes, signaling her to follow. "I have been tied up for a while and haven't had a chance to go." Getting tired of crossing my fingers, I quicken my pace across the room.

Without stopping, I grab a paper towel from the holder as I pass by and then dart into the back dressing room. I don't look back, but I know Alice is behind me. As I pull the curtain closed, Alice slides through.

I sit on the bench, and Alice drops beside me. With the disc in my palm, I press my hand on top of hers.

"What happened?" she spouts as soon as the disc touches her skin. Worry wrinkles crease her forehead.

"Reprimanding." I answer, meeting her gaze.

"Like before?"

"Sort of." I lean my head back against the wall. "That robot, Claude, was in there the same as before. He hooked up all the wires, but Dr. Eckert was in the room too. I still had the disc between my fingers when I first got in there, so I could hear him talking. It seems he has tried to modify the program to correct the glitch."

"Glitch?" Alice raises one brow.

"Glitch, meaning it did not work on everyone the way he planned."

"Like with Ash, you, and myself." Alice confirms.

"Exactly." My hand starts to sweat, so I push harder on her hand to make sure I have good contact. "Anyway, I had to know what he had done, so I laid the disc on the table under my hand. His new version begins much worse, and I can't imagine how horrific the experience would be for the people not affected by the glitch."

Alice curves up one side of her mouth. "Are you saying...?"

"Yep." I nod. "It still did not work on me." I touch my other hand to my chest. "You should have heard Dr. Eckert when I woke up laughing. Then, when I opened my eyes, his face was as red as blood."

"You woke up laughing? Oh, I wish I could have seen that."

"Alice," I say, taking on a serious tone, "you know the voice at the end… when we felt the cool breeze, and we were overcome with this unexplainable peace?"

"Yes." she answers, taking on the same serious tone.

"It's God."

"I thought so before." Her gaze drops to the floor. "But then I was confused because this was something they were doing to us… something they were forcing us to experience."

"I am aware of that. I keep going over and over the fact that this is some kind of program created by Dr. Eckert, but those hands before with the glowing fingers and the heat… it all seemed demonic." My voice starts to crack. "Alice, this time… the screaming and the sounds of torture at the beginning… it certainly resembled how I would picture hell. And those whispers, I think they were demons or the devil himself. Dr. Eckert couldn't know those things. A computer couldn't attack me with words from a conversation that no one but me knows I overheard."

"Okay." Alice utters as if she is still trying to process what I am saying.

"Then," I continue, "when the voice, the voice I know was God, spoke, he said, 'My seal is upon her. She is mine.'"

Alice's eyes widen into huge circles, and her shoulders lift. "That's why it doesn't work on us."

I look at her in confusion.

"The seal. We are sealed with the Holy Spirit." Her mouth spreads in a smile from ear to ear. "We are the property of God."

I stare at Alice for a minute as I toss her words around in my mind. *Ephesians 1:13. When I accepted Jesus as my Savior, I was marked with His seal. The seal of the Holy Spirit.* My lips curve up, matching Alice's smile. "You're right. That's it." The wheels in my head start turning again. "But, Alice, I am still puzzled about something. If this is supposed to be some kind of computer program that creates a sort of virtual experience, what's going on? You are a computer expert. How is this possible?"

Alice puts her other hand on top of mine and squeezes, and her words come out barely audible. "I'm not sure, Ellie. I am trying to wrap my brain around it, but it seems that we are dealing with a much deeper and darker battle than we thought." She swallows hard, and I can tell she is blinking back tears.

"Alice, we have to stay strong. I promise we are going to find Gerald and Steve, but first, we have to find a way out of this room."

"I've been thinking about that." Alice sniffles. "Do you think they would have changed the location of the cameras?"

"I don't know." Narrowing my eyes, I stare at her in wonder. "Are you telling me that you still remember where the cameras are?"

Her eyes gaze back at me, and the puffy bags beneath them illustrate the pain she holds inside. "I will never forget where those cameras are... or were. I will never forget anything about this place. The problem is that they might have changed or added some." She lifts her free hand and glides her fingers around on her scalp. "That, and we still haven't figured out where they put the chips. I have almost rubbed blisters on my head trying to find it."

The bathroom door creaks.

"Ellie?" Eileen's voice echoes through the bathroom.

I lift my palm off of Alice's hand and lay the chip on the bench next to me. "Yes."

"I was getting worried about you. Shelly is here with muffins."

"Oh, good. I am hungry." I answer. "I'll be right there."

"Hey, Ellie," she calls out in a strangled tone and then chokes out, "we need to pray. Two guards just took Teresa for more testing."

As soon as the door clicks shut, Alice is already tearing off a piece of the paper towel. I jerk off my slipper while she rolls the disc up inside of it. She hands me the wrapped-up disc and then hurries out so we both don't leave the bathroom at the same time. I tuck it in the padding of my slipper and take a moment to pray.

When I walk out, two guards are standing at the front of the room behind Shelly. Everyone else is sitting on their cot except for Alice, who is walking away from the cart with a muffin and a water in her hands.

Shelly motions to me. "Only two muffins left. One must be yours."

I walk up to the cart. "Thank you." I say as she reaches me the muffin.

"Oh, dear. I must have miscounted. I still have a muffin left, and everyone seems to have one." Shelly turns her head in slow motion from side to side.

"Oh, Teresa has already been taken to testing. It must be hers."

"What?" Shelly growls. "Why would they do that? That is not the schedule. Breakfast is at seven o'clock. Testing does not begin until seven-thirty. By not keeping to the schedule, poor Teresa has missed the most important meal of the day."

The door flings open and two more guards walk in. "Bailey Montgomery, proceed slowly to the door with your arms at your side." one of the guards order in a harsh tone.

"NO! NO! NO!" Shelly's head does a one-eighty, and her ponytail swings from side to side as she rants at the guards. "Testing does not begin until seven-thirty. It is only seven twenty-eight. We have schedules for a reason."

Bailey stands frozen beside her cot, holding one foot forward.

"Very well." the guard spouts back through gritted teeth. "Bailey Montgomery, you have two minutes to finish breakfast, then proceed to the door slowly with your arms at your side."

"That's more like it." Shelly spins her head back around. She reaches under the cart, pulls out a couple of napkins, and uses them to wrap up the extra muffin. The red dots in her eyes light up as she scans the room and fixes in the direction of Teresa's cot, the only vacant bed in the room. With the muffin and a water, she crosses the room and lays them in the middle of the empty bed. Moving back to the cart, she grabs the handles and pushes it out the door. "Gentlemen, it is now seven-thirty." she states as she exits the door with her two escorting guards.

Bailey tiptoes to the front with her thin legs visibly trembling beneath her. One of the guards holds out a thumbprint pad, Bailey lifts her right hand and presses her thumb to the screen. The guard with the pad nods to the other guard, and they nudge her to move through the door.

A soft sob next to me pulls my head sideways. Eileen has her hands over her face, but the tears are streaming between her fingers. I shudder as I realize how frightened she must be. My little sister has already lost over two years of her life in this place, cryogenically frozen in a tube. And even worse, all of the memories of her childhood are gone. *She must be terrified.*

I go over and sit on the edge of her mattress. With my hand on her shoulder, I pray, *Father, thank you for bringing my little sister back to me. I know she is scared. Please calm her fear and let her feel your hands carrying her over these raging waters.*

When I open my eyes, Alice is sitting on the other side of her. I open Eileen's water bottle and help her take a drink. I know she is an adult, but I want her to know I'm still her big sister, and while I can't make this mess go away, I am here with her. Alice gets up and moves back to her cot, so I follow her lead. I keep forgetting about this whole no huddling rule.

A few minutes pass, and I still have the muffin that I am picking at. It is so quiet that I can hear myself chew. The door creaks and a harsh mixture of gasps and squeals fill the air as Teresa's staggering body is pushed into the room. My eyes burn at the sight. Her nose is gushing blood, and the side of her face is bruised and swollen.

Alice, Eileen, and I race across the room, but before any of us get to her, Teresa falls against the wall.

"Teresa!" I cry out.

Alice grabs her under one arm, and I get under her other arm. Together we carry her to her cot.

Eileen runs toward the bathroom. "I'll get some wet paper towels."

Alice and I lower Teresa onto the mattress.

"Teresa." I get on my knees beside her and pull her hair from her face. "Can you talk? Tell us what happened?"

"P-p-punch." she grunts.

Alice gets on the floor on the other side of the bed. "Who punched you?"

"D-d-d-on."

Eileen sprints back and hands me some of the towels. My breath catches in my throat. *I don't have gloves.* I get angry with myself for my thought. *Now is not the time to let my OCD take control. She is family, and she needs me.* I hold the towel by the edges and dab it around her nose to absorb some of the blood. I don't want to wipe too hard until I can see how badly she is hurt. Eileen hands me more towels as the ones that I am using become soiled.

"It would be nice if we had some ice, but thankfully, your nose doesn't appear to be broken." I lift myself a little higher on my knees and survey Teresa's eyes. "Your pupils aren't dilated, but by the looks of this swelling, you took a hard hit. Teresa, do you think you can sit up on the side of the bed?"

"Uh-huh." Her reply comes out sounding more like a groan.

I rise to my feet and pull Teresa to a sitting position while Alice helps to sturdy her from behind. Once she appears to have her balance, I lower myself back to the floor, and Alice and Eileen sit on each side of Teresa.

Alice takes Teresa's hand. "Now talk to us. Who is Don?"

"He w-was o-one of the f-first trainees." she stutters and slurs her words.

"I don't understand." Eileen scrunches up her face. "I thought you went for testing."

"M-me t-too." Teresa wipes the drool from her swollen mouth. "Th-they… the g-guards took me into this room, and a man was already there sitting at a table. I j-just thought we were both there for testing." She wipes her mouth again and takes a strained breath. "A few minutes passed while we sat waiting. I knew his face looked familiar, but I couldn't remember his name. But since I was the infamous Dr. Fleming when I was here before, he remembered me as being in charge of the nightmare that ruined his life. I tried to explain that I had lost my memory like everyone else and that I was no longer the person he remembered. I told him how Jesus had forgiven me and made me new." Tears trickle from the corners of her eyes. "He said that he used to believe that but not anymore." She hesitates for a second and then goes on to explain. "Even though it seems like the conversation should have been tense, he did not use an angry tone. His voice actually sounded sympathetic toward me. Then, something happened to him. It was as if some kind of switch flipped. With no warning, blood rushed to his cheeks, and his eyes got big, really big. His face contorted into a grimace. He stood to his feet with a giant shove, flipping the table over. Before I had a chance to react, he grabbed me around the throat and lifted me from my chair. The second that he let go of me, I turned to run for the door, but he clutched onto my arm. Something hit my face, which I assume was his fist, and everything went black. When I came to, I was lying on the floor in that same room, Don was gone, and a guard was standing over me. As soon as the guard saw that I was waking up, he jerked me to my feet. Another guard that I didn't even know was there gripped my other arm, and they practically dragged me back here."

I lean over and rest my head in my hands. "It doesn't make sense." I rub my temples hoping it will stimulate my brain.

"I'm not making it up." Teresa's voice cracks.

I lift my head and touch her knee. "Oh, Teresa, I didn't mean it that way. I meant that it doesn't make sense why they would let that happen to you and then bring you back here with no medical attention at all. You could have a concussion."

Teresa's leg quivers beneath my hand. "I know. I keep trying to come up with a reasonable explanation." Then she cracks a small grin, at least as much as she can with a swollen lip. "But God provided. I am in here with you guys. You have some medical training from when you were going to school for nursing, and you and Eileen have watched your mother as a nurse your entire lives. You knew what to look for, and you guys fixed me up."

As Teresa finishes her sentence, the guards escort Bailey back into the room. She does not appear to have any injuries. In fact, she seems a little peppier than when she left.

The guards are still standing at the front of the room with the door ajar. "Alice Jacobs, proceed slowly to the door and keep your arms at your sides."

I push down on Alice's knees, holding her down as I stand up. In the process, I signal to her with my eyes. Clearing my throat, I speak up as I turn toward the back of the room. "She is in the restroom. I will tell her." Without looking back, I hurry into the bathroom, hoping they won't shoot me. *Alice, please don't move until I get back.*

I drop to the floor right inside the door, pull my slipper off, and take out the disc. My heart flip-flops in my chest with every thumping beat, and I don't even get my slipper all the way on before I rush out with the disc tucked between my fingers. The guard with the thumbprint pad stares at me like he has some kind of x-ray vision and can see my thoughts. I walk between the cots where Alice, Teresa, and Eileen are still sitting on the edge of the bed. Stopping a bit past Alice with my body blocking her from the guards' view, I tuck my hand behind my back and wave my crossed fingers to Alice.

One guard raises his eyebrows.

Alice's hand touches mine as she stands, and the disc slips from my fingers into hers. She steps around me and walks slowly to the front with her hands at her sides.

The other guard narrows his eyes into tiny slits and glares at me. It is obvious that Alice did not come out of the bathroom. I shrug my shoulders at him and plop down on my cot.

With skepticism written all over his face, he holds out the pad. When Alice puts her thumb on the pad, he seems satisfied and doesn't cause any trouble. The two guards turn and walk out of the room with Alice between them. As soon as the door clanks shut, Eileen's head pivots toward me. "Ellie, what was that all about?"

"Nothing." I mumble, hoping she won't press the subject. Dropping to my knees, I clasp my hands together and rest my head on my fingertips. *Lord, thank you for letting that work out just now. Please take care of Alice. Please keep a wall of protection around her.* Someone clasps their hands on the outside of mine. I look up, and Teresa is kneeling on the floor on the opposite side of my cot, holding my hands as she whispers a prayer under her breath.

After she says "Amen", Teresa's eyes meet mine, and her mouth freezes part way open like she wants to tell me something, but she can't speak out loud. With a pained expression, she says, "Let's go check on Bailey."

I know it's a cover, so she doesn't have to open up, but we do need to find out what happened with Bailey. And until we find the chip in our head, there is no way to talk in private until Alice gets back with the disc.

Bailey is a few cots down from us. She is lying on her back, and I am curious why she is staring straight up at the ceiling with a huge smile on her face.

"Bailey?" I say as I walk up.

"Oh, hey, girls." Bailey sits up and crisscrosses her legs. "Have a seat." She pats the mattress with her hand.

"I'll keep my distance and squeeze down here on the floor." I say as I lower myself to my knees in the narrow space between the cots. "I wouldn't want us to get in trouble for gang activity." I chuckle.

Teresa plops down on the foot of the bed. "It looks like your testing went better than mine." Teresa tries to joke with Bailey.

Bailey gasps. "My goodness, Teresa. What happened?"

Teresa giggles. "You're smiling. I would rather hear a happy story... so you share first."

"Oh, you are not going to believe it, but I am pretty sure that I heard the voice of God." Bailey lifts her brows as she speaks.

I squint my eyes in a look of confusion. *Reprimanding. But she wasn't being punished. She was supposed to be in testing.*

"What do you mean?" Teresa probes.

"Okay. So, the guards took me into a room with this weird robot that had freckles and red hair, almost the same shade as mine." Bailey talks fast with excitement in her tone. "I laid down on this table, and then I must have been knocked out because next thing I know, I am consumed in a pit of darkness. People are screaming in pain, hands are clawing at me, and these voices… well, let's just say they reminded me of some pretty bad stuff I did when I was younger. And then, I was suffocating, actually suffocating. I couldn't see anything, but it was like a hand was cupped over my mouth and nose. Some kind of invisible force was pulling me down as if I had weights attached to my body." Bailey's smile gets bigger. "That's when it happened. The voice. A crack of light appeared over me, and this loud, commanding, wonderful voice said, 'She has my seal. She is my child. Leave her now.'" Bailey looks back and forth from me to Teresa. "The darkness turned to bright light, and all that bad stuff went away. Then the voice told me that I had nothing to fear because he would never leave me. See, girls, it had to be God."

"Bailey, I know you said you were cryogenically frozen, but did you go through reprimanding when you were here in training before?" As I speak, she stares at me with a blank face.

"Reprimanding? I don't think so. What is reprimanding?"

"Well, if you broke one of the so-called rules, you were sent to reprimanding. My experience was similar to what you described, but for a lot of people, the dark and gory stuff at the beginning didn't go away. It intensified, which is what is supposed to happen. One person was so traumatized that he ended up taking his own life." I watch as Bailey's mouth falls open. "I went through it when I was here before and then again last night. It seems that it is supposed to be worse now, but it is still not having the agonizing effect they want on everybody." I tap my fingers on my chin. "It doesn't make sense."

"What?" Teresa whispers.

"Reprimanding is a punishment. For instance, I caused a disturbance with my nightmare last night, so they took me to be punished."

"But Bailey didn't do anything. They called her out of the room for testing." Teresa finishes my statement and then seems to get lost in thought. Her face grows pale, and she pushes to her feet. "If you guys will excuse me, I-I n-n-need to lie down."

"Are you okay?" Bailey reaches up and pats Teresa's arm.

"I-I'm fine." Teresa utters with an expression that shouts she is not fine. "Just a little tired." she claims.

Teresa walks away, and I pull myself up. Pins and needs prickle my legs from my position too long on the floor. I stand for a minute to let the blood get flowing again.

Bailey looks up at me. "She doesn't seem okay."

"Maybe some rest will do her some good. This place has left scars on us all, and on top of that, she has a black eye and a busted nose."

Bailey drops her head. "Yeah, I feel bad for acting so happy when she is obviously hurting."

"Hey. You had an experience with God. How could you possibly contain your joy?" I pat her back and drag my tingling legs back to my cot.

As I sit, I notice Teresa curled up with her knees to her chest. Her back is trembling. She has her face buried in her pillow, but her whimpers still escape. I want to go to her, but then I think we all need some space sometimes. And there isn't much of that in here.

Chapter Thirteen

I cannot do this. After only a few minutes of sitting on my cot, the walls start to close in, so to speak. Panic starts to bubble as my obsessive thoughts barge in. *What if Steve isn't alright? What if Gerald is hurt... or worse? What if Alice gets caught with the disc? What if... what if...? Put on your armor, Ellie.* I close my eyes and take a deep breath... *seven times... say it seven times. Cast thy burden upon the Lord, and He shall sustain thee. Cast thy burden upon the Lord, and He shall sustain thee. Cast thy burden upon the Lord, and He shall sustain thee. Cast thy burden upon the Lord, and He shall sustain thee. Cast thy burden upon the Lord, and He shall sustain thee. Cast thy burden upon the Lord, and He shall sustain thee. Cast thy burden upon the Lord, and He shall sustain thee.*

I open my eyes and scan the room. *They say that we are here to make sure we are mentally stable, yet they lock us in a room with nothing to do but go stir crazy.* "Hmmm. Well, it's not happening." I mutter to myself. I leap off my cot. The largest open space is at the front of the room, but I don't want to disturb everyone. I move to the floor space at the foot of my cot, which isn't much, but it's larger than the space beside it. I start loosening up by making circles with my arms. Then, I bend over, keeping my legs straight, and put my hands on the floor to stretch my hamstrings.

"Ellie," Bailey yells from across the room, "what are you doing?"

To be so small, her voice really carries. I wonder if she sings. I smile and turn my head in her direction. "Trying to stay healthy." I shout back as I start to jog in place.

"That's a great idea. We need to keep up our strength."

I glance back over, and Bailey is pulling her ankle up behind her, stretching her quads.

After Bailey's announcement, a few other girls are off their cots, stretching their muscles. Eileen comes out of the bathroom and joins the activity in front of her cot next to me.

"Oh, this is fun." Bailey's voice vibrates as her feet pound the concrete floor. "We need music though. It's hard to run without music."

The rhythm of jogging feet echoes off the walls.

"I know. Let's sing. Everybody knows *Amazing Grace,* right?" Bailey asks with enthusiasm.

"Yes," Eileen chimes in, "but isn't that a bit slow for running?"

Bailey laughs. "Not the way we are going to sing it. We are going to shake up the tempo. Follow my lead."

As soon as we start singing, even Teresa gets up and joins in.

A few minutes pass, and Alice appears through the door. The guard behind her grips his weapon, but after a quick glance around, he backs out and closes the door. I figure he could see we were spaced apart… or maybe he went for backup.

At the sight of Alice, we stop singing and running, and I dash toward her.

"Apparently, I missed something." Alice says, slowly rotating her head.

"Nothing big. We are just refusing to go stir crazy." I wrap her in a hug. "Are you okay?"

"I am better than okay," Alice giggles. "I have His seal."

As I step back, I touch my chest in relief. "Come on in the bathroom. I finally found the toothpaste dispenser."

"Oh, good. Now, if we can find toothbrushes, we will be set." Alice remarks.

"Don't hold your breath." I joke as we walk toward the bathroom. "Toothbrushes could be a dangerous weapon."

"True, so true." Alice agrees in a sarcastic tone.

I have to keep up the game, so I lead Alice over to the sink. I point to a plastic box on the wall. "You already know that one is a soap dispenser, but here on the other side," I point to a smaller plastic box, "this one is toothpaste."

"Oops." Alice puts her hand to her mouth.

"What?"

"I have been washing my hands in toothpaste." She holds her hands up. "Smell, they are minty fresh."

Shaking my head, I take off for the back dressing room. We both slip inside, and I slide the curtain closed behind us. When I turn around, Alice is already sitting on the bench, and she is unwrapping a wadded tissue. I sit down beside her as she takes the disc out of the tissue. She reaches over and caps the disc down on the back of my hand with her fingers pressed together.

"Where did you get the tissue, and how did you get the disc in it?" I blurt out.

"I was laughing so hard when I woke up, tears were streaming down my face. When Dr. Eckert left, I asked Claude for a tissue. Then as I got off the table, I picked the disc up in the tissue and wadded it in my hand."

"Dr. Eckert was in there?" Her tissue tactic was so smart, but I want to know about Dr. Eckert.

"Yes, and I heard some interesting comments come out of his mouth before I let go of the disc." Alice's expression becomes hardened.

The serious look on Alice's face causes my stomach to knot. "Tell me."

"As soon as I went into the room, Claude told me to lie on the table. Then he announced that it was time for me to go to sleep, so I faked it until I could see what was going to happen. While Claude was strapping me down and putting the wires on my head, the door opened, and I heard Claude greet Dr. Eckert and ask if he was sitting in for the test again. Dr. Eckert replied that he needed to know if his last adjustment corrected the problem."

"So, he is still trying to make it work on us. But why?"

"I don't know, but it is all very suspicious." Alice grips the edge of the bench with her other hand and stares at the floor. "There was a tapping noise, like he was typing on a keyboard, and he was mumbling to himself."

"Could you make out what he was saying?"

"Oh yeah. I heard him." Alice swallows. "He was talking about the chip. He said that the wire attached to the chip was working. However, he would need to shock the area with the lesions a little harder. I was hoping he would elaborate, but his focus went back on me. He asked Claude if I was hooked up and ready. Claude confirmed, and as I was letting go of the disc between my fingers, I caught one last comment from Dr. Eckert before it went dark." Alice lifts her head back toward me and presses harder against my hand with the disc. "His exact words were, 'This is my last try. If it still doesn't work, I'll just use them as bait.'"

"Bait?" I raise my voice but catch myself and lower it. "What did he mean by bait? You didn't hear him say anything else?"

"Not before I went into complete darkness. But when I woke up happy and laughing, he slammed his fist down on the table and told Claude they were finished testing the program. He was moving to plan B. He stomped toward the door chattering that he had worked too hard for this little setback to mess things up. He still had enough to do the job, and as soon as his monsters were unleashed, he would finally have the life he had always dreamed of."

Bait. Monsters. Unleashed. I sit there staring at Alice with my mouth agape. I can't think of anything to say. All these puzzle pieces fly and swirl and crash into each other inside my brain, and none of them seem to fit together. *What does it all mean?*

"Ellie?" Alice wipes a tear from my face that I didn't even know was there.

"Sorry. I didn't mean to space out. I-uh-"

"You are trying to figure out what on earth Eckert was talking about." Alice finishes. "Let me know if you figure it out because I am stumped."

"We may be in big trouble then." I whisper.

"What do you mean?" Alice narrows her eyes.

"You are the puzzle guru. If you can't figure out what's going on, nobody can." I try to speak in a lighthearted tone, but inside, I am trembling because I know I am telling the truth.

"No. No negative thinking. You are a newlywed with a brand-new career, and I have a wedding to plan. God brought us through the storm before. And it was in that storm that we met Steve and Gerald. So, let's trust Him to lead us out of this one."

A sense of calm washes over me and my fear is replaced with determination. "You're right. We have to trust the One that already knows what is happening. After all, He has given us this disc. I mean, what are the chances that an agent for the Department of Homeland Security would have stuck a disc to my arm that cancels out the chip?"

"Now, that can only be the work of God." Alice grins and starts mapping out a plan aloud. "Okay, we have to find Steve and Gerald. We can't do that with the chips signaling our every move, and it is going to be hard to sneak out of here with both of us touching this disc all the time."

"The locked door might complicate things too." I add. "I am not being negative… only stating the facts."

Alice smiles and rolls her eyes. "Okay, so…"

"So, what's the plan?" I inquire, a little frightened at what her answer might be.

"First," she touches my shoulder with her free hand, "we ask God for help." She drops her head with her hand still on my shoulder. "Heavenly Father, thank you for being with us. Thank you for sealing us with the Holy Spirit that has protected us in this place. Father, thank you for giving us this disc so we can talk to each other. And thank you for putting Ellie and me here together. Please continue to be with us, Lord. Show us what to do. Guide us, Lord, please guide us on the path that you have placed us here to take. Please help us to accomplish what you have planned for us. We praise you, and we love you, Lord. In Jesus' name, we pray. Amen."

Thank you, Lord, for Alice. "Amen."

The bathroom door creaks open. "Ellie?"

Eileen. I glance at Alice, and she removes her hand with the disc. Slipping from behind the curtain, I answer, "Hey, sis. What's wrong?"

She shakes her head, "For an obsessive-compulsive with a phobia of public restrooms, you sure are spending a lot of time in here."

"Oh, I came in to show Alice the toothpaste dispenser... anyway, that doesn't matter. What's happening?" I ask, walking over to the sink to wash my hands. "Umm, forget washing your hands. Dr. Blakely is out here looking for you and Alice."

My heart drops to my feet, and I freeze with my hand in mid-air, reaching for the faucet. "Why is he looking for us?"

"He's out there grumbling that you guys are missing. So, hurry up and come on. I told him you were in the bathroom, but he doesn't believe me."

Alice pads up behind me. "There's no need to space out our exit. Let's get this over with."

Eileen holds the door for Alice and me, and then she follows us out. Dr. Blakely is standing at the front of the room by the door. He has his arms folded across his chest, and he is rocking back and forth on his heels.

Weird. I wonder why there are no guards with him. He is not even armed.

Alice and I roll our eyes toward each other at the same time. I know she is thinking the same thing. We snake our way between the cots to the front.

"Well, well, well." The vein in his forehead dances as he glowers at us. He drops his arms to his side and stops rocking. "You ladies mind explaining why neither of your locations is showing up on my screen?"

I lift my shoulders. "I'm sorry, Dr. Blakely, but how are we supposed to know? It sounds like a technical issue."

Dr. Blakely shifts his weight from one foot to the other, side to side like he can't be still, and he fidgets with his hands wiping them repeatedly on his slacks. "Never mind." He lowers his voice. "We will discuss it in my office." Taking a step around Alice and me, he calls out, "Eileen. Teresa. I will need to speak with you as well."

Eileen, who is pacing along the back wall, strides to the front. Teresa, on the other hand, rises from her cot and moves like an injured snail across the room. *But who could blame her after what she has been through?*

As Teresa nears the front, Dr. Blakely stares at her face with a puzzled expression. "Teresa, what..." he stops himself and gives his head a quick jerk. "Come on. Let's just get going. You four, follow me and if you think you are being quiet, be quieter."

He eases the door open and then lets us pass through before he softly closes it. Alice nudges my elbow. I roll my eyes up to meet hers, and she raises one eyebrow. I give my shoulders a quick shrug to answer her unspoken question.

Eileen and Teresa walk side by side in front of Alice and me. Dr. Blakely moves with stealth, almost tiptoeing down the hall. And with his blood-drained complexion and scanning eyes, he appears to be acting more like the prey than the predator. The interesting thing is that his scanning eyes never seem to land on any of us four. I find that odd, considering we are supposed to be the danger to society. He places his thumb on the pad at the exit door from building two, sticks his head out, and looks both ways.

We proceed to the entrance of building one, which is not far. Again, Dr. Blakely uses his thumbprint to unlock the door and peeks in before he opens it all the way. He leads us a few steps down the hall to the second door. It is solid steel with no window and no doorknob. To the side of the door, he places his thumb on the pad, and then he looks at the screen on the wall above it. A red laser light streams from the screen into Dr. Blakely's right eye for about three seconds. The light turns off, and the door clicks slightly ajar.

Dr. Blakely places his hand flat on the door. He peers over at us, and under his breath, he utters, "not a word." He pushes the door open wide enough for us to slip through sideways one at a time. The room is dark, but as soon as the door is closed, the light slowly illuminates the space. Before my eyes adjust or I even get a glimpse of the office, I am engulfed in a set of arms. I don't know what is happening, but for the moment, everything is perfect. *Thank you, Father.*

To my right, a soft sob penetrates my ears, mixed with a whisper of praise.

"Waves, what are you doing in here, and how did you get in?" Dr. Blakely exclaims.

"To answer your first question, Dr. Eckert is irritated that you have not completed the evaluations in rooms one and two. I came to find you. And to answer your second question, Dr. Eckert gave me security clearance to all of the offices but his." Waves wheels to the door. "I won't say anything about this little party, but you best get those evaluations done."

The door closes behind Waves, and Dr. Blakely sighs. "I hate to break up this little reunion, but we have to get going. We are running out of time." Dr. Blakely's voice trembles and he keeps rubbing his hand across his slicked-back hair as he speaks. He turns to the laptop on the desk and taps the keyboard. In almost a whimper, he talks to himself as he types. "I should have had him out of here an hour ago. Why couldn't he just go? Why does he have to be the big hero?" The corners of his eyes glisten with moisture. "I'm not going without them." He mimics in a singsong voice.

He wouldn't leave without all of us. I touch my fingertips to my chest and gaze up at Steve. He smiles, and a tear drips from the corner of my eye. I glance over at Alice. Gerald has his arm wrapped around her, and she is still whispering prayers of thanks with her head pressed against his chest.

Dr. Blakely pushes away from the computer. "Alright, it's showtime. Steve, please find your mother first thing when you get out of here. I'm scared. She still won't answer my calls. I had a private flight waiting for her at the airport to take her back to Virginia. But, for her protection, I made sure there was no record of the flight, so now I cannot get anyone to confirm the flight's departure from Colorado Springs or its arrival in Arlington. You have the number to my burner phone." His voice fades in and out. "Please call the second you find her."

Steve nods. "Don't worry. I'll find her."

Dr. Blakely darts his eyes to each of us. "This is a big risk, but Steve wouldn't go unless I got all of you out. We have to move quickly and quietly. Most important is that you all act like you are doing nothing wrong. Hopefully, since I will be walking with you, the guards won't give us a second thought." He puts his hands on the sides of his face and squeezes his eyes closed. He lets out a long breath through his mouth, opens his eyes, and steps toward the door. His heels dig in before he takes a second step, and his body jerks as he comes to an abrupt stop. "The chips." he mumbles and then turns to face us. "I almost forgot. We have to get the chips out of you, so you can't be tracked." His chin drops to his chest, and he sighs. "This is going to take too long."

"No, it won't." Alice assures Dr. Blakely. "Show us where they are located. Ellie and I can help get them out."

Dr. Blakely lifts his head. One side of his mouth has a slight curve. "Okay." He opens the drawer below his computer and pulls out a blue case from which he removes a bottle of alcohol, sterile pads, and a canister. "Alice, sit here on this stool and lean your head over." he says, keeping his voice low as he takes something out of the canister and rips away the plastic wrap. It is some type of tool with a needle on one end and a needle with a tiny, almost microscopic, hook on the other.

Alice lowers herself on the stool, pushes her head down as far as she can, and pulls all of her hair forward. Dr. Blakely presses the tip of his fingernail into the back of Alice's scalp in the center, about an inch above the hairline on her neck. He drags his fingernail down across her skin to the edge of her hairline. Over and over, he repeats the clawing motion until his nail snags. Keeping his finger in place, he picks up one of the sterile pads, holds it to the top of the alcohol while flipping it upside down to moisten it, and wipes Alice's head. Then, as he pushes down with his nail, he takes the needle end of the tool and moves it toward the nape of her neck.

It is all I can do not to grab his hand. He is trembling so badly that he is struggling to get the tip of the needle to the edge of his nail. Eileen must be freaking out too, because her fingers jab into the center of my back, and being her sister, I know that means 'do something.'

Dr. Blakely finally gets the needle pressed to the tip of his fingernail, and his hand seems to calm. I watch as he inserts the point of the needle into her skin and wiggles it in a circular motion. Blood bubbles around the needle.

I pick up another sterile pad, and when he pulls the needle back, I dab the blood away.

Dr. Blakely flips the tool around to the end with the hook, inserts it into the same spot using the same technique as hooking yarn with a crocheting needle, and pulls. A small, almost invisible, hair-like wire resembling a fiber optic thread slides out with the hook. Once the wire is protruding about a half-inch from her head, Dr. Blakely puts down the tool and uses his thumb and middle finger to pull it the rest of the way out.

My throat burns, and a bitter taste fills my mouth. I know the sight of this shouldn't bother me. After all, my mother is a nurse and I was in nursing school before I changed to criminal justice, but the thought of that wire sticking into our brains makes me ill.

Dr. Blakely reaches in the canister and hands me another tool wrapped in plastic. "Do you think you can do this?"

Pursing my lips together, I swallow the rising acid and nod without speaking.

"Good. You take care of Eileen, and I will get Steve."

Alice watches me as I take the chip from Eileen. Actually, I guess it is more of a chip embedded into some sort of wire, but hers is not hard to find at all, and I have it out in no more than a minute. When I glance over, Dr. Blakely is still working on Steve, so I go ahead and take care of Teresa while Alice decides to try getting Gerald's removed. I worry a little when Alice and I are both done with Teresa and Gerald, and Dr. Blakely is yet to be finished with Steve.

Alice pats my shoulder. "I am sure it's fine. Here, let me get yours."

I sit and try to sweep my knotted hair out of the way. I didn't realize it was so tangled. Of course, we aren't allowed a comb or brush. *That could be too dangerous.* I don't even get finished counting to seven, seven times before Alice is holding the wire between her fingers.

"Oh, good. You're all done." Dr. Blakely clears his throat. "Sorry that it took me so long. Steve's was buried pretty deep." He turns for the door. "We have to hurry. Remember the rules. I will get you to the end of the tunnel. From there, the parking lot is at the end of the path, and a white four-door sedan with a pizza delivery sign on the side will be waiting to take you to the airport." He glances back at us one more time and then reaches for the door.

"Wait," I blurt out. "What about those twenty-ton doors? Don't you need to open them before we leave?"

"People are continuously being escorted in for testing, so the doors aren't sealed yet. There is just a beaucoup of guards." Dr. Blakely wipes the sweat from his forehead and cracks the door open.

Chapter Fourteen

D r. Blakely steps into the hallway twisting his head in jerky movements. He was so worried about us acting normal, yet he is the one that looks like an escaped convict on the run. Sweat is gushing off of his face, and the way his eyes are darting around, it is obvious he is up to something.

I should have asked him about the cameras, I think to myself a little too late. *Since Waves said the camera in his room fed into Dr. Blakely's office, and it was Dr. Blakely that knew when my chip wasn't showing up, maybe Dr. Blakely monitors all of the security.*

The door barely closes behind us when a guard comes through the building one entrance. The man's eyes flare with panic. He jumps into attack position whipping his gun up and aiming it at us with his finger on the trigger. "It's okay, Dr. Blakely. I've got you covered."

"No, no, it's fine." Dr. Blakely holds up his trembling hand, motioning for the guard to lower his gun. "Um... they are being released. That's... that's why I'm not armed. They pose no danger."

The guard lowers his weapon. "Very well, sir. Sorry for my interruption."

"No worries. But since you are here," Dr. Blakely asserts, "would you care to escort us to the end of the tunnel... in case we do encounter someone dangerous?'

"I'd be glad to, sir." The guard grips his gun in his right hand and opens the door with his left. Sticking his head through, he peers both ways. "All clear. Follow me."

Dr. Blakely points for us to go behind the guard. Steve goes out first, and I follow him. Once we are all through the door, we walk two by two, with Steve and me in front of the others. Dr. Blakely plods out to the side. I glance in his direction. His face is ashen, and by the way that he is opening and closing his hands, he appears to be on the verge of some sort of breakdown.

The path angles at a curve and is surprisingly vacant until we get near the first blast door, where five guards are standing evenly spaced in the opening. The guard leading us takes a sudden giant step to the side. A thunderous boom echoes off the rock walls, and Dr. Blakely lands with a thud next to my feet. Blood covers what is left of his head.

My chin drops. I can't breathe. Steve tugs on my arm, pulling me behind him. Gasps and screams erupt from the others, but I can't even get a sound to escape.

The guards rush forward from the open door, but the guard leading us steps back in front of us, raising his hand. He mumbles something about us not being harmed. "Boss's orders." he says in a calm, almost mechanical voice. The other guards lower their guns, and our guard turns to face us with his gun pointed. "Turn and walk slowly." he dictates, maintaining his monotone voice.

"Wh-why d-did you shoot him?" Alice wails through tears.

"I said to turn and walk slowly." He pokes her in the chest with the tip of his nine-millimeter.

We follow the guard's orders. Steve keeps me in front of him, shielding me completely from the guards behind us. My legs tremble and tingle as we falter back up the path. I blink, trying to clear my vision, but all I see is a frozen mental picture of Dr.

Blakely lying lifeless on the ground, his face disfigured and covered in red.

Even though I haven't been with the FBI that long, I have seen some gruesome scenes, but this is not the same. I knew this man. Not well, I admit, but all the same, I knew him. And now this bloody image is etched in my mind, and even worse is the recollection of our conversation during testing. He never came right out and said that he didn't know Jesus, but when I shared that I couldn't imagine going through one day in this world without God, he commented that he was getting through each day just fine. *Oh, Dr. Blakely, I hope you found Jesus.* Tears pour from my eyes.

As we approach the entrance to building one, Dr. Eckert steps through the door. "Well, well, if it isn't my famous escapees. Thought you would give it another try, huh?"

"We weren't trying to escape. We were told we were being released!" Teresa barks in a tone that I haven't heard from her since she was Dr. Fleming. "Your guards killed Dr. Blakely." She steps around Steve and me to the front and stares straight into Dr. Eckert's eyes. "Why? I thought we were here to be tested because we don't want innocent people to be killed. Your guards just murdered a man in cold blood." Her posture stiffens, and through a clenched jaw and gritted teeth, she shouts the question again, "Why?"

"He broke the rules. He blatantly disregarded a direct order from me and the president of the United States!" Dr. Eckert barks back at her.

Teresa holds her stance. "And that warranted murdering him?"

"He was expendable." Dr. Eckert's nostrils flare and his tone is full of arrogance. "On the other hand, Joanne, test results from the six of you could be vital to our research."

"My name is Teresa."

"Oh. I forgot." he mocks. "You are a new creation or something. What do you call it... born again?" He looks past Teresa and smiles at me. "Mrs. Denali, you will come with me for testing?" He pulls a semi-automatic handgun from his belt. "And I would not advise trying anything brave." He shifts his focus to the guard. "Put the rest of them in the holding room in building two. Stay positioned outside the door, and do not leave your post for any reason. I will send for them one at a time."

"No. Dr. Eckert," Steve pulls me backward, "let me go for testing first."

"I'm sorry. I give the orders around here, not you, Mr. Denali. But don't fret," Dr. Eckert smirks, "you will get your turn." Pointing the gun at my chest, he grabs my arm and jerks me from Steve's grasp. "Come along now, Mrs. Denali." he says in a honeyed voice. "Let's get you to the testing room. After all, you are all about saving the world, right?" He rotates toward the building one entrance pushing me in front of him. Reaching around me, he puts his thumb on the pad and opens the door.

I walk into the building and trudge in slow motion down the hall. Dr. Eckert instructs me to take a right at the end of the corridor and then points me into the stairwell. My throat starts to close. *Why is he taking me upstairs?* I swallow hard and suck in a shallow breath. *This can't be good.* Balling my hands into fists, I try to control the trembling. *Please, Lord, help me be strong.*

We stop on the second floor in front of a solid steel door. Dr. Eckert uses the pad to open it and holds it open for me to go in.

"Have a seat at the table." He motions with the gun toward a wooden table with folding metal chairs around it. "Your testing will begin in a few minutes." He closes the door, leaving me alone.

I sit in one of the chairs, scanning the room in the process. *Folding metal chairs. I guess safety is not an issue in here.* The room is only about fifteen feet by fifteen feet with plain white walls. Besides the table and two chairs, it is empty. I can't help but think this resembles the scenario that Teresa described, except no one else is here. *I wonder if Dr. Eckert knows we don't have those wires in our heads anymore?*

A couple of minutes pass as my mind replays the horrors of the last hour. The door flies open, startling me, and I jump, causing the metal chair to clank against the concrete floor. A man is pushed into the room and the door crashes shut behind him. The man is about six feet tall with red hair and a muscular build. He stands in front of the door biting his lips together with his arms crossed over his chest and his hands tucked under his armpits.

"Hello. I'm Ellie."

"T-Tolliver. My name is Tolliver." He looks around the room. "Do you know what we are doing in here?"

"Nice to meet you, Tolliver, and no, I'm not sure. Dr. Eckert told me to wait here and that my testing would begin in a few minutes."

"Oh. Okay." Tolliver takes a few steps to the empty chair and sits. "The guard told me I was going for testing. What kind of testing do you think it is?"

"In this place, who knows? We just have to..." I stop midsentence as my eyes lock on Tolliver's wrists. "What made those marks?" I point at the red indentions that look like bracelets.

"That's from the restraints." he says, peering down at my wrists. "Yours must not have been on as tight."

His brain must have the lesions. I don't want to upset him, so I decide not to say anything about not being restrained. "I'm so sorry. They shouldn't have those things on you so snug. Hopefully, this will all be over soon, and we can go home. We just have to be strong and hold on to God."

"You go ahead. I've tried that, and it didn't work out."

"What do you mean?" I ask in a soft voice.

Tolliver stares at me and doesn't answer. His eyes widen into big circles. A vein in his forehead pops out, and his cheeks turn to a glowing shade of red.

"I'm sorry. I didn't mean to offend you. I..."

Tolliver shoots up from his chair. The muscles in his arms are contracted, and his hands are shaking like someone having a seizure. He bites down on his lip until blood starts to drip down his chin.

Pushing my chair away from the table, I rise to my feet and step slowly backward in the direction of the door. He storms toward me, swinging his fist toward the side of my head. Thrusting my left arm up, I block his arm long enough to strike him in the throat. He takes one staggering step back and coughs. *I should have struck him harder. But I know this isn't his fault.*

He recovers in a few seconds and lunges at me. His right-hand grips my throat, and he shoves me against the wall. He starts to squeeze, but I manage to get hold of his thumb with both hands, and using all of my strength, I twist it backward. He yelps in pain, releasing his grip, and I thrust my foot as hard as I can into his knee.

Tolliver drops to the floor on his side with both hands clutching his knee. The rage is still in his eyes, and baring his teeth, he musters up a deep, throaty growl. I watch with my guard up, hoping that I don't have to go any further. He moves to roll up to his feet. *You have no choice, Ellie. He is going to kill you.* Swinging my stiffened leg around in a swift motion, I plant my foot in the side of his head, knocking him back to the floor, unconscious.

Even though I know my technique was right on the spot, panic consumes me. I drop next to him and press my fingers to his neck. *Thank you, Lord.* I let out a long deep breath at the ticking pulse against my finger.

The door flings open. "Congratulations, Mrs. Denali. I guess your self-defense training with the FBI has paid off." Dr. Eckert takes a step into the room with a guard as his shadow. "I especially liked that last knockout maneuver. Few can perfectly execute a kick to the temple. Of course, without it, you would no longer be with us. I suppose when one is faced with imminent death, one can become rather resourceful."

"He needs medical attention, Dr. Eckert. Please check him." My heart hammers in my chest.

"Oh, don't worry." Dr. Eckert motions in two men wearing medical scrubs carrying a stretcher. "I will make sure he is fine. He is one of my strongest, so I can't let anything happen to him now, can I?" He lets out a single chuckle. "The guard will take you to the holding room." As he pivots on his heels toward the door, he mutters, "What a waste. I could certainly use fighting skills like that." He stops with a jerk. "One more try... I have to give it one more try." Dr. Eckert pounds out of the room.

I turn my gaze and watch the two men examining Tolliver. It appears they are following proper medical protocols before they move him to the stretcher. *I wonder why Teresa didn't get any medical treatment.*

The guard grips my arm and pulls me to the door. For some reason, he doesn't aim his gun at me, which is surprising considering I rendered a man unconscious only a moment ago. Instead, he grips the gun by the barrel in his left hand and carries it at his side. As we enter the stairwell going down, someone screams. I mean, I think it was someone screaming. The shriek was distant and muffled, but I am pretty sure it was a person. I come to an abrupt halt only three steps down and look up toward the stairs leading to the third floor.

"Keep moving." the guard orders as he tugs my arm.

"Did you hear that?" I ask, still peering up in the direction of the call as he drags me down a few more steps.

"Hear what?"

"Someone screaming." I cast my eyes to the guard. "It sounds just like the scream I heard when I left the first evaluation room with Waves."

"You must be hallucinating, but don't worry. I've been told hallucinations are common in the test subjects." He leads me around the corner at the bottom of the steps into the corridor.

Since the guard doesn't have his weapon trained on me, and he hasn't been overly harsh, I decide to try to get some dialogue going.

"So, how long have you been a guard?" I ask without turning my head to look at him.

"I don't understand your question." he replies in a dead voice.

"Well, what did you do before you came here?"

"Before here? I've always been here." His response is matter of factly.

"Oh." I try to play along. "Where is your family? Since you are here around the clock, I bet you miss them."

"My brothers are all here."

"Who are your brothers? Are they guards too?" I pry.

"We are all brothers."

Maybe his memory has been erased. But why? Confusion fills my mind. "That's a lot of brothers. Where were you born?"

He puts his thumb on the pad and holds the door open to exit building one. "I was created here, of course... to be a soldier for the United States government."

Chills run down my spine, and my legs almost collapse beneath me. I swallow hard and try to keep the conversation going without letting my voice quaver. "I was born in Fairfax, Virginia, and I only have one sister. But," I twist my head and let my eyes meet his, "I do work for the United States government."

The guard stops in front of the building two entrance and peers at me with a hardened expression. "You do? But I thought you were a test subject."

"A test subject?" My pitch rises in question.

"Yes. You are here to determine compatibility with Dr. Eckert's project."

"Oh. Which project are you referring to?" I pry, trying not to sound uninformed.

"His 'Save America' project. I am sure you are familiar with that." He places his thumb on the pad.

"Oh. I'm sure his project is going to be a great success." I almost choke on the words. Coughing to clear my throat, I keep going. "Have you heard any updates on the progress?"

"I think he may have hit a few snags. I overheard him say that some of the subjects weren't responding to the therapy, but he is determined to end the corruption."

As we walk into building two, I wonder why I haven't asked him already. "I apologize. I forgot to ask. What is your name?"

"Chey Four-Fifteen."

I can't help but widen my eyes at that. "Does it have some sort of meaning?"

"Yes. My first name, Chey, means I am part of the Cheyenne Mountain Division, and my last name, Four-Fifteen, gives my precise identity here in this division."

"What other divisions are there?"

"I know Raven Rock is one division because that is where the compatible subjects are being transported. At least, that is what I understood when I escorted some of the subjects to the train the other day. Raven Two-Twelve told me they were being housed there." He points me around the corner and up another flight of stairs. "You didn't give me your identity?"

"How rude of me? I forgot that I didn't introduce myself. My name is Ellie."

As we reach the second floor, Chey Four-Fifteen taps his thumb and opens the door. We go through the glass vestibule into the large lab where Cynthia, Spencer, and a mix of various animals had once stood frozen in tubes. Now, the room is empty, except for computer screens lining the back wall. To the left, a guard is standing in front of a steel door with no window. His gun is in a holster on his side, but his hand is resting on the grip. *That must be the holding room.*

"Ten-Nineteen." Chey Four-Fifteen addresses the guard in front of the door, "Eckert said I should relieve you of your post so you can nourish. On your way, you are to escort Gerald Jameson to lab two for testing. Claude is ready for him now."

Gerald will panic if he thinks he is going through reprimanding again.

Ten-Nineteen takes his hand off of his gun. "Very well." He swivels around and presses his thumb to the screen. "Gerald Jameson?" he calls out when he opens the door.

Gerald appears in the opening. "Where am I going?"

"Testing." Ten-Nineteen holds up his weapon. "Keep your hands at your sides at all times."

Gerald glances at me.

"Don't panic, Gerald." I take the risk and speak up as he

passes me. "I promise it won't be like last time. Trust me. Just close your eyes."

"Control your subject, Four-Fifteen." Ten-Nineteen lifts his gun.

"Ellie, harness your tongue."

I nod. "Sorry, only trying to prevent unnecessary distress."

Ten-Nineteen's boots clack in a rhythm as he leads Gerald down the steps, and Chey Four-Fifteen motions me into the holding room. My foot barely makes contact with the floor inside the room before Steve's arms sweep me off the ground. "You're okay. Thank you, God, for letting her be okay." his voice cracks. "I was so scared."

The door clanks with a thud behind me.

Chapter Fifteen

S teve steps back from our embrace but keeps a tight hold on my hand. I rotate my head to check out the holding room, but there is not much to note. It is only a ten-foot by ten-foot space, and I am wondering by its small size if it didn't use to be a supply closet. The room is completely empty without even so much as a chair.

Eileen and Teresa each hug me, but Alice is sitting on the floor, leaning against the back wall. Tears are streaming down her cheeks. I don't have to ask. I know she is worried about Gerald.

"So, what happened?" Steve asks in a quavering voice. His Adam's apple bobbles as he swallows.

I squeeze my eyes closed for a second. Pinching the bridge of my nose, I let out a long sigh. "Look, I don't know if they can hear us or not, but we have to get out of here and quick." I glance back at Alice. "Gerald is going to be fine. He is with Claude. But we can't let them take anyone else where they took me."

Alice's eyes fix on me. "What do you mean?" she calls out from her position on the floor.

Motioning for the others to follow, I walk over and squat next to Alice. "I was taken to what I assume was the same room that Teresa was taken to. The scenario was pretty much the same, except I was the first one in the room. After a bit, a man named Tolliver was brought in. He seemed kind of scared. We talked for a few minutes, and I asked about the red indentions around his wrists. He said they were from the restraints."

Steve wraps his arm around my shoulder as I talk.

"So, I assumed that meant his test showed lesions on his brain. I continued talking to him and said something about it being over soon and us holding onto God to get through it. He informed me that he had tried that before, and it didn't work out. That's when something happened to him. He became a totally different person. He tried to hit me and choke me. I used my self-defense training and eventually had to kick him in the temple to knock him out." I cast my focus on Teresa. "The thing is… he got immediate medical attention."

Alice shifts up on her knees. "Do you really think he would have killed you?"

I nod. "Dr. Eckert came in. He complimented my fighting skills and made a comment that I would no longer be here if I hadn't used them."

"If you can fight like that," Teresa tilts her head to the side, "why haven't you fought back before?"

"Everyone has guns. I can't fight guns."

"Oh… true…" Teresa gives a slight shake of her head. "Sorry, I wasn't thinking."

Eileen's bottom lip starts to quiver. "They are going to kill us." she whimpers in a low voice.

"Let me tell you about the guard that walked me back here. His name is Chey Four-Fifteen."

Alice raises one eyebrow. "What kind of name is Chey Four-Fifteen?"

"He told me that he was created here to be a soldier for the United States government. The only family he refers to is the other guards that he says are his brothers. I asked him about his name. Chey stands for his district, Cheyenne Mountain, and the number is his identity here. He explained that there were other districts, but he only knows of Raven Rock because that is where the compatible subjects are being housed. It seems that we are test subjects. According to Four-Fifteen, Dr. Eckert is working on his 'Save America' project to end corruption, and not all the test subjects are responding to the therapy."

"So," Alice massages the sides of her head, "if we mix your information with what I overheard about us being used as bait, I am thinking that the reprimanding virtual demonic thing must be the therapy Chey was talking about, and we are the ones that it is not working on. Do you remember that I told you he was talking about unleashing monsters?" Alice taps her chin. "I believe he is using us as the bait in that room to test his monsters."

"I get that I missed Alice's story before, but I am lost." Steve moves his eyes back and forth between Alice and me. "Why is he unleashing monsters?"

Alice twists her mouth to the side. "I don't know. But we better figure out how to get past Chey Four… whatever his number is and his brothers."

Teresa buries her face in her hands.

"Teresa," I reach over and brush her hair behind her ear, "are you okay?"

She shakes her head but doesn't uncover her face.

"What is it?" I ask not sure if I should pry with us all in a group.

"I should have told you before." she mutters through her hands.

"Told us what?" Steve speaks in a reassuring tone and puts his hand on his sister's shoulder.

Teresa takes down her hands and looks at each of us. "When I was here as Dr. Fleming, I was sort of dating Earl… Dr. Eckert. Please don't judge me. Remember, I was led to believe that I was much older than I actually was." She squeezes her eyes tight like she doesn't want to see us as she talks. "Anyway, Dr.

Eckert was close with President Denali. I often heard them on the phone jabbering about high-tech scientific research that was over my head."

"First," Alice leans toward Teresa and touches her hand, "Teresa, we have no reason to judge you. You were a victim in all of this, and worse than that, your own father is the one who made you a victim. We are your family. Don't ever worry about us judging you." Alice raises her gaze to the rest of us. "Second, if he knew about Denali's plan, why wasn't he charged?" Alice inquires.

"I don't know. I told the authorities everything when they interrogated me." Teresa wipes her face. "I guess they didn't have any evidence."

"He may not have known what President Denali was really doing." Eileen adds. "Because they seemed close and talked about scientific research doesn't mean that he was in on the plan. We know President Denali was an expert at deception. Even if he knew about the plan, maybe he was given immunity like Teresa was given because he had erased his memory and brainwashed him too."

Steve runs his hands through his hair and blows a deep breath out of his mouth. "But isn't President Kutchins the one giving all the orders? After all, his executive order is the reason we are back in this place."

"Right now, it doesn't matter. We'll figure it out once we are out of here. I'm surprised a guard hasn't already come for one of you guys. Any ideas?" I can't help but look at Alice. She has a way of figuring things out.

"Ellie, how do you feel about doing one of your little kung fu maneuvers to knock out Chey Four… the guard?" Alice asks.

"Well, he was nice to me, and I don't want to hurt him." *Lord, what do I do?* "But we could die if I don't."

Alice starts rattling off in a hushed tone. We all lean in close to hear her. "If I remember right, that reprimanding room with Claude is here in building two. Since we are on the second floor, it must be on the third floor."

"I am sure I took an elevator." I confirm.

"Me too." Alice continues. "I know where the cameras used to be. We will have to hope they haven't changed. The guard must have connected with you, Ellie, if he spilled all that information."

I notice Steve stiffen and cross his arms. *She had to use the word connected.*

Alice must catch my expression. "Well, I don't mean he connected with you. But he sensed something that made him trust you. I will lie on the floor and pretend that I am struggling to breathe. Ellie, you yell in a panic that we need help. Hopefully, when he hears your voice, he will open the door. As soon as he opens the door, get him before he can point the gun. Once you knock him out, we will take his gun, go to the third floor to get Gerald, and then... I don't know."

"Okay." I whisper.

Alice and I wait for Eileen, Teresa, and Steve to respond.

Steve kisses the top of my head. "Honey, are you sure you want to do this?"

I nod. "We have no choice."

"I don't like this." Eileen rocks back and forth. "I know we have to, but I don't like it."

"Let's do it." Teresa's tone perks up. "When he comes in, I will keep the door from closing."

"We don't have much time, but we need to pray first." Alice lowers her head and holds out her hands.

Bowing our heads, we clutch on to each other and connect our hearts.

"Father, we thank you for being here with us... for sealing us with your Spirit... for giving us each other. Lord, we need you. We know something isn't right about all of this. So, if something bad is happening, please help us figure it out. If it be your will, Lord, help us to get out of here and stop it before it's too late. Please keep us safe and show us the way. Father, we can't do this, but You can. Lead us, Father. In Jesus' Name. Amen."

We all get to our feet except for Alice, who crawls to the

center of the floor and lies down on her back. I don't think any of us know what to do, so we stand in a circle around her staring in silence, waiting for her signal of distress.

Even though we are looking right at her; Alice catches us by surprise. Her hand slaps hard against the floor, flinging my heart right out of my body and onto the ceiling. She grabs her throat and makes straining noises as she sucks in air, pretending to gasp for a breath.

I run to the door. "Help. Four-Fifteen, we need help in here." When he doesn't respond, I use my fists to beat and add more desperation to my tone. "Please, Four-Fifteen, Alice can't breathe."

Alice is getting louder. She is trembling and gasping and flailing and flopping around all over the floor.

Either he doesn't hear me, or he is choosing not to hear me. *Maybe he isn't out there anymore.* I almost let my guard down when the door cracks open. The tip of his gun comes through first. *Great.*

"Four-Fifteen, please, help. Something is happening to Alice. She can't breathe." I rattle off fast in a panicked voice.

He looks at me with what I perceive as a touch of sympathy in his eyes, and with a sigh, he lowers the gun gripping it only with his left hand. Guilt stabs through my chest.

Ignore it, Ellie. They are going to die. This is your only chance to save them, I keep reminding myself.

He pushes the door wide enough to slip through.

I wait for him to step completely through to give Teresa space to catch the door. "Please help her, Four-Fifteen." I point. "She is suffocating."

With his eyes fixed on Alice, he doesn't even flinch when my foot flies up. And it's not because he doesn't see my foot coming. We didn't put enough thought into our plan to account for his level of fight training. His right-hand catches hold of my ankle, and he shoves me backward. But just as he pushes me, Steve grasps the gun and kicks Four-Fifteen's legs out from under him. Four-fifteen lets go of my ankle and uses his hand to break his fall. Unfortunately, he hangs on tight to the gun. Steve twists as he pushes down, trying to keep the gun pointed at the floor, but at the same time, rip it from the guard's grip. The guard, still sitting on the floor from his fall, thrusts his right hand around toward the trigger as he tries to raise the barrel with his left. But, before his right-hand makes contact with his weapon, I raise my right knee and straighten my leg as I rotate my body. The top of my foot nails him directly in the side of the head. He releases his grasp on the gun, barely enough for Steve to yank it down and away. Before Four-Fifteen gets his wits back, I scissor my legs and plant my left heel square on his right temple. His face takes on a blank stare for a couple of seconds, and then he falls onto his side.

Alice leaps to her feet. "Let's go."

"Wait. Eileen, hold the door for a second." Teresa keeps her foot in the door until Eileen grabs it. With an intense look on her face, Teresa drops beside Four-Fifteen and pats her hands over the pockets of his uniform. She slides her hand into his right front pants pocket and pulls out some sort of handheld device resembling a phone, but it has a screen on both sides.

"What's that?" Eileen peers over Teresa's shoulder.

"I'm not sure," Teresa flips it over in her hands. "Let's take it for now. Maybe we will figure it out."

"It looks like one of those devices that the guards were holding on the bus when everyone went to sleep." I say as Teresa walks toward the door with it.

"Come on." Alice urges, motioning hard with her hand. "We don't know how long we have before he wakes up or someone shows up." She sticks her head through the door and then takes off across the large room and through the glass vestibule.

We follow her lead, trying to run and tiptoe at the same time. Teresa and Eileen are right behind Alice, then I go, and Steve tags along in the back, brandishing the guard's gun.

Alice pauses and presses her ear to the door leading out to the stairs. She stops before her hand touches the door. Her shoulders slump and her head drops.

Steve peeps around me, narrowing his eyes.

Deflated, I turn to him and hold up my thumb. Out of the five of us, not one remembered the thumbpads that have been added to all the doors.

"I could shoot it open?" Steve contemplates out loud.

Uncertain of how to proceed, we stand like statues in front of the door. My heart pounds in my ears, shaking my thoughts. It seems like minutes pass, but in reality, I think it is only about thirty seconds when Teresa steps around Alice. All of our eyes follow her movement. She lifts the device she took from the guard.

I hadn't noticed before, but it has a little metal tip extending from the top. The metal extension looks like the end of a USB cord, only wider. Teresa lowers her head and studies the base of the thumbpad on the wall. Then she lifts the little device and inserts the metal tip into a port in the bottom of the pad.

Yes. My posture straightens.

The screen on the little device lights up with the words 'Enter Override Code,' eight blanks, and a number pad.

I hunch over, deflated again.

Teresa lifts her hand toward the screen with a trembling finger and taps zero, one, zero, nine, two, zero, four, seven on the number pad.

My eyes almost pop out of my head. The small screen turns green, and the door clicks, popping slightly ajar. *How did she know the code?*

With her hands shaking worse than before, she pulls the device from the thumbprint pad and takes a step back for Alice to lead.

Alice stands frozen with her mouth hanging open as if she is hypnotized by the cracked door. In a zombie-like movement, Alice extends her leg and takes a slow step forward. Grabbing the edge of the cracked door, she places her ear up to the door again and pulls it open. With a quick move of stealth, Alice snaps out of her stupor and takes off up the steps to the third floor.

This is the first time that I have been thankful for these fluffy slippers. If we had on regular shoes, even tiptoeing would probably sound like a herd of buffalo with five people treading up two steps at a time in an enclosed stairwell.

At the door, Alice listens, and with no hesitation this time, Teresa moves fast with the little device. Her code works again. I am dying to ask her how she knows the code, but making any sound is not an option right now. My nosiness will have to wait. We step into the room that is only dimly lit with what is probably some sort of emergency lighting. In an instant, I am taken back, and the image of all those stacked boxes fills my mind. This is where we found President Denali's journals. This is where we discovered the evil that we were up against. This is where we learned of President Denali's horrible plan to create a world without God.

All those boxes are gone now. The authorities must have had them removed as evidence. A few gurneys line the wall, and the metal desk still sits near the back. We follow Alice, padding with soft feet, searching for another door or any sign of where Gerald might be. She moves toward an opening in the back left corner of the room. I don't remember it from before, but there were so many boxes. And, of course, after we read those journals, we left.

We round the corner into the opening. It is a small hallway with an elevator and another door at the end. I am certain that is the same elevator that I was taken on after my so-called reprimanding. As I stare at the elevator, the door at the end rattles, making me jump backward on top of Steve's foot. Alice pivots and pushes us out of the hallway like a mother getting her children to safety. In a flash, the five of us are flattened against the wall on both sides of the opening in the large room. I hold my breath and suck in my stomach as flat as I can get it. I am not sure why I think that is going to help.

Footsteps pound on the floor in the corridor, and Dr. Eckert's voice booms in anger, "I am done, done! No matter what I do, these people are all sunshine and rainbows and praising the Lord." He lets out a deep growl. "I don't need these people anyway!" he shouts.

I almost relax when the light rumble of the elevator door sliding open reaches my ears, but then a phone rings.

"Hello, Mr. President." Dr. Eckert answers in a delightful tone, completely transforming his voice. "I wasn't expecting you to call. Is everything okay? No worries, sir. Everything is going exactly as planned... Oh, yes, I did receive the directions from your advisor, and the process will begin tomorrow on schedule... Tomorrow at 10:35 a.m. eastern standard time is what your advisor documented in the timetable. Is that not correct? Uh-huh. I see. So, to confirm, I am to follow the timetable your advisor sent, and I will receive payment when? But... If you could just divide... Very well, I understand. The job will be completed soon... Yes, sir. You have my word... Good day, Mr. President."

A heavy silence fills the air, pinning me even tighter to the wall.

Get on the elevator. Please just get on the elevator. My heart is beating so hard that my chest is aching. Steve touches my hand. I want to look at him, but I am afraid to move.

The elevator door rumbles, followed by the clack of shoes on the floor and another rumble, which I hope means the door closed with him on it. I relax my muscles and fill my lungs with air. I have been holding in my stomach and taking shallow breaths for so long that my head is swimmy.

Alice motions and takes off into the little hallway again. We hurry behind her. I keep my eyes glued to the elevator door. If Dr. Eckert left, a guard should be coming soon to take Gerald back. Alice doesn't even listen at the door. Instead, she motions for Teresa to put in the code.

"I want to do it again... please let me do it again." Gerald's voice filters through the cracked door.

"No, I am not supposed to administer the program unless Dr. Eckert instructs me to." Claude argues as we push through the door. Claude's head spins toward us. "What's going on?" His eyes open wider. "Mrs. Ellie. Yay. I am so happy to see you."

"Guys, you have to do this." Gerald exclaims, still strapped to the table. "It is amazing." He starts laughing. "He said that I was His child."

Claude moves to unstrap Gerald.

"Alice, you go first." Gerald leans toward Alice when Claude releases the restraint and then turns back to Claude. "Hook those electrodes to Alice. She is going to love this."

"I have done it, Gerald." Alice speaks fast. "It is amazing, but we have to move right now. Come on." She takes his hand as he sits up on the side of the table.

Eileen and Teresa are already waiting by the door.

"One second." Steve says.

I look behind me. Claude is frozen and silent with a cord running from his back to the computer. Steve has the gun tucked under his arm, and his fingers are running rampant across the keyboard. After about ten seconds of speed typing, Steve closes the computer program and yanks the cord from Claude.

"Let's go." Steve utters, grasping the gun with both hands.

"Where are we going?" Claude asks.

The second Alice reaches for the door, it starts to open. We leap against the wall behind it.

"Claude," Dr. Eckert speaks as the door swings into the room, "do you have Gerald unhooked yet? I need him in the testing room." Dr. Eckert stops with the door open shielding us from his view. "Where is Gerald?"

I turn my head toward Steve with wide eyes, but Steve is glaring at Claude, giving him some sort of signal.

"Yes, sir. I am finished." Claude rolls toward the door blocking Dr. Eckert from stepping in further.

In my peripheral vision, I catch sight of Gerald squeezing Alice's hand. Then, Gerald lowers himself and duckwalks behind the table. "I am right here." Gerald rises from behind the table.

"What are you doing back there, Mr. Jameson?" Dr. Eckert questions in a harsh tone.

Gerald lifts his hands. "Whoa. Don't shoot. I was only fixing my slipper. The padding was wrinkled."

"Hopefully, the problem is resolved. Come along. We need to complete one last test."

Gerald steps toward the open door. "I can't wait."

The door closes behind them, and Alice buries her face in her hands. "Why would he do that? Now we have to find him again." Her words come out muffled with her fingers covering her mouth.

"Because if he hadn't, Eckert would have come into the room and found us." I assert. "He was protecting us."

"But Steve has a gun." Alice removes her hands and faces Steve.

"Yes," Steve agrees, "but so did Dr. Eckert. And it would be in our best interest if we did not have to draw attention to ourselves by firing a gun."

"It'll be okay. I know where it is. The testing room is on the second floor of building one." I place my hand on her back.

Alice pulls away, nodding in agreement. But then her body stiffens, and her face turns white. "What if we can't make it in time? Gerald doesn't know how to fight." Alice opens and closes her hands as she paces back and forth.

"We will, but we have to get going." I know I shouldn't be assuring her of something I am not certain of, but it could be dangerous if her mind is consumed with panic.

Steve strides to the exit gripping the gun.

I step up beside him and press my ear to the door. I give a quick nod indicating that I don't hear anything.

He motions me behind him. "Claude," Steve says in an undertone, "you go first."

"No worries. I will lead the way." Claude moves forward, lifts his hand, and pauses. Turning his head toward Steve, he asks, "Where are we going?"

"Building one, floor two." Steve answers in a flat tone.

Claude turns back and places his metal thumb on the pad.

I stare in wonder as Claude touches his thumb to the identification screen. *Hmm. Weird. He must have some sort of identification chip in his thumb.*

Claude proceeds into the hallway and over to the elevator. We wait inside the room until the elevator door glides open, and then in a dash, we pile in. My heart has been beating so fast and hard for so long, the sudden drop to the first floor makes me light-headed. I lose my balance and sway to the side. Eileen grasps my arm, stopping me from crashing into the wall.

The door cracks open, but Claude's hand shoots forward, pushing the close button. "Movement detected. We have to wait." Keeping his finger on the button, he stands frozen like a statue. A minute passes, and he removes his finger from the button. The door slides open again, and Claude rolls forward. Alice goes out first, then Eileen and Teresa follow, Steve and I take the back. Alice crosses from side to side in stealth mode, dodging the locations of the cameras that are etched in her photographic memory. We keep to her pattern, even though Claude is cruising right down the center of the hallway.

I let out a shallow breath when the building two exit appears.

Claude stops in front of the door. "Trouble incoming. Stand back."

Stuck in the middle of no man's land, we have nowhere to go. Alice bolts up beside the door. We squeeze in next to her and hug the wall as tightly as we can.

The door bursts open. "Claude," the guard interrogates in a suspicious tone, "what are you doing all the way out here?" The man's focus is so fixed on Claude that he doesn't even notice us hovering right beside the exit.

"No time for chit chat." Claude rattles off, sticking out his hand to keep the door from closing. "I have to get to building one. I am on a special assignment."

The guard shakes his head and keeps walking.

Claude motions for us to exit. Alice sidesteps into the

doorway and her slipper snags on the threshold, pulling her off balance. In an effort to regain her footing, she thrusts out her hand, slapping the door casing as she grabs hold. The guard whips around with his gun, but Steve already has his lifted with his finger on the trigger. Before Steve can pull the trigger, Claude shifts toward the guard holding his hand out to the side. The guard's weapon flies out of his hand and smacks into Claude's hand with a loud clank.

How? I think, but then I remember. *His hand is magnetic.*

Paying no attention to the gun in Steve's hand, the guard reaches for his pocket. His chest expands as he inhales, and his mouth opens.

Steve takes a step toward the guard. "Don't even think about it? Hands where I can see them, and don't make a sound."

Claude passes the guard's nine-millimeter handgun to Alice and approaches the guard with his right index finger pointing out in front of him. His index finger flips backward, exposing a needle that flies through the air and jabs into the guard's shoulder. The man's body goes limp. Claude catches him with his left hand as he pulls the needle out with his right.

"Is he dead?" Eileen whispers through chattering teeth.

"Of course not." Claude murmurs. "It's a tranquilizer. He is only sedated." He drags the guard over and props him up against the wall.

Bewildered, the question comes out before I even realize it. "Why do you have tranquilizer darts in your finger?" I kneel beside the guard and glide my hand over his pockets. *Bingo.* I slip my hand into his shirt pocket and take out a little handheld device matching the one Teresa took from Four-Fifteen.

"Protection, of course. We are living in dangerous times, you know." Claude answers in a matter-of-fact tone keeping his volume low as he rolls out the door.

With our mouths agape, we turn and file out after him while Steve keeps the gun's barrel pointed at the man. He follows, moving backward until he is outside the building.

I slow down, waiting for Steve to catch up. By the time we

get to building two, Claude already has the door cracked and is peering in. Utilizing the brief moment that we are not in motion, I take my fingers and try to stretch the fabric around my left wrist. I fold it back enough to make a pocket for the small device I took from the guard, tuck the device in the fold, and flip it over one more time to secure it. The fabric makes a ripping sound, but the device seems to be snug, and now my hands are free.

With his arm behind his back, Claude curls his fingers, signaling us to follow. He opens the door wider and slowly inches his way inside. Alice, still clutching the guard's gun in both hands, tucks in close to Claude's back. Eileen goes next, holding onto Teresa's arm.

I hold my breath, and a shudder creeps like spiders crawling down my spine. Steve's hand touches my upper arm. When I glance over my shoulder, he mouths the words, "I love you." I form the words back in silence, and a tear drips from the corner of my eye. The pain woven in the lines on his face breaks my heart. Even more shattering is knowing that he is in pain because of me... because he can't protect me from this nightmare. I smile and give him a quick wink. His mouth curves up as he shakes his head. I turn back and face forward. With soft steps, I close the gap between Teresa and myself, continuously shifting my eyes from side to side in search of any surprises.

Claude rounds the corner into the stairwell. His wheeled feet convert into triangles. The points of the triangles of each foot are opposite each other, so as they turn, he shifts up one step at a time.

Pretty clever engineering. The ingenuity of his design distracts me for a second until the door comes into view. My throat begins to close, and my mouth is so dry that I think my tongue is swelling. *We have no plan, and Gerald could be under attack right now. Or... he could have already been attacked.* The reality of the situation seeps into my brain.

Obviously, Claude doesn't need a plan. He taps his thumb on the screen and pops the door open.

"We are supposed to wait outside the door until it's over." A man's voice reverberates up the stairwell.

Claude moves over, and with furious hand motions, he waves us inside.

A tall, muscular woman has Gerald pinned to the wall. Her knee is pressed into the center of his stomach, and her hands are wrapped around his neck. His face and lips have a blue tint. With frantic motions, Gerald is yanking at her wrists, battling for oxygen.

Alice lifts the gun and aims at the woman's back. "Let go of him, now!" Alice commands with her finger on the trigger. Her hands are trembling, and she is gripping the firearm so tight that her knuckles are white. "I mean it." The end of the weapon shakes.

The woman does not even acknowledge anyone else is in the room, much less flinch at Alice's threat.

I look back for Claude and realize that he must have stayed outside to take care of the problem approaching in the stairwell. *Now what?* My eyes ricochet back and forth around the room. *Eckert has to be watching. We don't have much time. Think, Ellie, think.* I spring forward and yank the woman's long blonde pony-tail, jerking her head back hard. Her grip weakens on Gerald's throat enough for him to pull her hands down and away. She spins, thrusting her foot at my head. I drop and swing my right leg around, sweeping the one foot she has planted on the ground out from under her. She tumbles onto her side. As the woman bounces back to her feet, the door opens, and she collapses in a heap on the floor.

I lift my hand to my mouth as I watch Claude sidle up to the woman's unconscious body and pluck the dart from the back of her neck. I exhale in disbelief and shift my eyes to Gerald. He is doubled over in the corner, gagging and gasping for breath. Alice has her arms around him trying to urge him to stand upright so his lungs can fill with air.

Steve grabs my shoulder. "Ellie, are you okay? Your eyes are bulging from your head."

Gerald must have caught his breath because he steps up beside me. "Can you believe Eckert did that to me? Of all people to put me in here with."

Alice peers over Gerald's shoulder. "Is that Penny?"

"Well," I turn to Alice, "that is Penny's body, but I don't think that was Penny fighting. Something else was in control. When we came into the room, her eyes looked just like Tolliver's earlier today."

"Oh, that was Penny." Gerald confirms. "Don't you remember her busting my nose when I had to fight her in training?" Gerald points to his face. "My nose is still crooked."

"Honey, your nose is fine." Alice's eyes flicker around the ceiling.

"We need to go," I say in reaction to her eye movements. "Eckert will be here any minute." I stride to the door where Claude is waiting. "You know he must be watching this room."

"Um... Claude." I suddenly remember the voice. "What happened with the guards coming up the stairs?"

"Nothing. Before they got to the top, I heard one of them say there was a change of plans." Claude throws up his hands. "I waited outside the door for a minute to make sure they didn't come back."

I nod. "Ok, let's get out of here then."

"Where are we going now?" Claude looks at Steve.

"Out of the complex. Do you know the way?"

"Through the tunnel past the big doors." Claude replies.

My muscles tighten and a pang of guilt stabs through my chest. "Wait. What about the others? We can't leave them here to be bait." I say in desperation.

"We'll have to hope that they will be alright until we can get help. There is no way that we can get the chips from a room full of people and get them out of here without a bloodbath." Steve's face goes white.

I am not sure if he is trying to convince himself of his own words or if he is worried that we aren't going to make it out alive, but he signals Claude to move.

Claude moves through the door into the second-floor hall with the six of us tailing him, and everything goes black.

Steve puts his arm around me, holding the gun in front of us both, but the gun serves no purpose. In a facility built inside of a mountain, no light means abyssal darkness, leaving Steve with no way of knowing where he is aiming.

"Well, well, well," Dr. Eckert's taunting voice echoes from somewhere in the curtain of black surrounding us, "it looks like another failed escape, but congrats to Ellie on another victory. Penny is one of my best."

Steve pivots us around in a circle aiming the gun. I guess he is trying to pinpoint the direction of Eckert's voice, but with six of us and a robot in the midst, I know he wouldn't take the risk of firing.

"I think now would be a good time for you to lower your weapons. On second thought, don't bother. You will only end up killing each other." He chuckles. "It might be a good show. It would be better if Steve and Ellie weren't attached to each other. Let's make the game a little more fun. By the time I count down to one, you two should be properly spaced apart. Three... two..."

Steve drops his arm, and I take one step away.

"One... not as far as the rules call for, but it'll do." Dr. Eckert grunts clearing his throat. "FYI, contrary to your visual restrictions, I can see you, and I do have a gun. So, I wouldn't get too brave."

A whimper filters through the darkness.

"I hear someone crying. Is that my beautiful Joanne?" His tone softens. "Joanne, it isn't like you to display weakness. However, I've been there. I can understand how you must be hurting inside. And to think that you almost had me fooled with your little temper tantrum earlier... acting like you didn't care. But you remembered, didn't you? I knew a love as strong as ours couldn't just die."

"I am not Joanne. I was never Joanne!" Teresa screams.

"What don't you get? The person you think you loved doesn't exist."

"Oh, Joanne," his voice rises with emotion. "There is that spunk I fell in love with. It doesn't matter your name. You are still the same woman. I can still hear your heels click-clacking down the hallway, spouting off 'time is of the essence,' in your drill sergeant voice."

"No, Earl. I am not the same woman." Teresa proclaims. "I have accepted Christ as my Savior. I have been born again. 2 Corinthians 5:17 states, 'if any man be in Christ, he is a new creature; old things are passed away; behold, all things are become new.' Earl, the blood of Jesus has made me new."

"I knew I shouldn't have stopped Don from finishing you." he mutters in a low growl.

The blast of his gun reverberates off the walls.

"Noooo!" Steve shouts. "Teresa!"

Steve's wail of pain for his sister slices through my chest. I reach out for him, but he's not there. A cacophony of cries and screams and shuffling feet bounces through the darkness.

"Steve. Steve. Steve!" *Where is he?* In a frenzy of panic, I turn in circles. A hand covers my mouth. It's a man's hand, but it's not Steve. I duck and jerk from the man's grasp. *Which way do I go?* My stomach twists in a knot. With my arms out, I keep twisting in circles, tiptoeing, and listening for any sound to lead me to the others.

Another hand grasps my wrist and pulls me… a cold metal hand. I don't fight. I move where it guides me. My feet bump into a ledge. *Wait, it's the stairs.* Another hand touches my shoulder and slides down my arm. The hand clutches mine. *Steve. That is my Steve's touch. Thank you, Lord.* He gives my hand a gentle tug, and I follow his lead lifting one leg at a time, searching for the next step. One of my slippers falls off as I wiggle my foot to find the tread. I don't want to be barefoot, but I don't have time to find it. We make it up the first flight to the landing between the second and third floor.

Steve gets me to the bottom of the second flight and then

leans in, pressing his lips to my ear. "Make your way to the top and stay quiet. I have to see if Claude was able to get anyone else."

I know it's selfish, but I grip his hand tighter.

"I'll be back. I promise." he whispers and kisses the side of my head before he pulls back. Squeezing my hand, he slips away.

I turn around and use my hands to help find my way up the steps. My arms and legs quiver as I climb on all fours. *Please keep him safe, Lord. Please let him come back.* My eyes burn from straining in the dark. *I can't do this.* Tears flood my eyes. *Be strong, Ellie. You are not alone. I can do all things through Christ which strengtheneth me. I can do all things through Christ which strengtheneth me. I can do all things through Christ which strengtheneth me. I can do all things through Christ which strengtheneth me. I can do all things through Christ which strengtheneth me. I can do all things through Christ which strengtheneth me. I can do all things through Christ which strengtheneth me.*

I recite the verse in my head seven times, and just as I finish, my hand glides across the top step. Crawling until I reach the wall, I lean back, hug my knees to my chest, and remind myself that I am not alone.

Chapter Sixteen

Digging the heels of my bare feet into the floor, I push myself tight against the wall and close my strained, aching eyes. The deafening blast of the gunshot plays over and over, echoing in my head. *Father, please let Teresa be okay. Please help Steve find her and the others.* My shoulders shudder as I push down the sob that is wriggling its way out. *Lord, please help us.*

I press my face into my knees to muffle the sound in case a whimper escapes with my tears. *Why won't the screams stop?* I clutch the sides of my head with my hands covering my ears. I let out a slow, silent breath. *Finally.* I lower my hands and wipe my eyes. *No, not again.* I cap my hands back over my ears. *Wait.* I stretch my neck and let my hands fall. *Someone is really screaming. I remember now. I heard the same screams when Chey Four-Fifteen was taking me back to building two.* My eyes widen as the whole scene comes flooding back. *I kept looking up the stairs toward the third floor.* I flatten my hands on the floor beside me and push myself to a squat. *This is the third floor.* My heart starts to pound like a sledgehammer busting through the bones in my chest.

The door has to be close. I rise to my feet and inch along

with my back against the wall and my hand extended to the side, feeling for the door as I move. My elbow bumps into something. I shift my hand up. *A thumbprint pad.* Reaching a little farther over, my fingers slide over the door casing and onto the metal door. Pulling my arm back to my side, I breathe in. *Put on your armor, Ellie.* I breathe out. *You can't hear the enemy's whispers if you are drowning him out in your head. 'Yea, though I walk through the valley of the shadow of death, I will fear no evil: for thou art with me; thy rod and thy staff they comfort me.'*

In a quiet, gentle motion, I unroll my left sleeve with my right hand and remove the device. Turning sideways, I find the thumbprint pad again and feel along on the bottom with the tip of my index finger for the small port to plug the device in. It takes a bit of maneuvering in the dark, but I get it plugged in. The screen illuminates like an angler fish in the depths of the ocean. The glow is going to draw attention if I don't think fast. I tap my head. *What was the code? Think. Oh. Zero. One. Zero. Nine. Two. Zero. Four. Seven.*

The lock clicks, and I quickly pull out the device. This time I just slide the device up inside my sleeve. I am not sure why I didn't do that the first time. This unitard is so tight, it fits in there pretty snug.

Cracking the door, I peek into more abyssal darkness. A bloodcurdling cry of pain reaches my ears through the opaque nothingness inside. I slide through the door, leaving it open in hopes it doesn't swing closed behind me. After a few steps, I stop, lost in a sea of black. I don't know which way to go. I force my leg to extend and take another step. Sweat beads pop out all over my forehead and run down my face. A drop falls from my chin and hits the top of my bare foot.

In an instant, I freeze. *My nightmare. I am in my nightmare.* I spin in a circle hugging my arms around my torso. My breathing increases and I open my mouth to suck in more air. *Be strong, Ellie.* I squeeze my eyes tight. *Deuteronomy 31:6. 'Be strong and of good courage, fear not, nor be afraid of them: for the Lord thy God, He it is that doth go with thee; He will not fail thee, nor forsake thee.'* I open my eyes and straighten my back. *You are not alone, Ellie. God is here with you.* I scan the darkness. *There it is.* I twist to my left toward the little stream of light. Clenching my hands into fists, I force another step. *I am not strong enough to do this… but God is.* Chills cover my body underneath the beads of sweat. My feet pad a few more steps across the cold floor. With my hand out in front of me, I grope for the knob. *Wait. There is probably another pad.* I move my hand over a bit and feel for the wall. Just as my fingertips graze the screen, another shriek sends me leaping backward. With trembling hands, I move back to the door and pull out the tiny device. I try to insert it into the port, but I am shaking so badly that I can't hold the device steady enough to connect it.

I swallow hard. *Focus. I can do all things through Christ which strengtheneth me.* The screen lights up, and I tap zero, one, zero, nine, two, zero, four, seven. The door clicks. I snatch the device out and slide it back into my sleeve.

Prickles run down my spine as I stretch my hand toward the door and the sobbing wails that are on the other side. *Now what? I never got this far in my dream.*

I give the door a little push. Bright light floods through the gap and my eyes struggle to adjust as I peek inside. White cabinets line the wall, but my view of the rest of the room is obstructed by the door. *What am I doing? I have no idea who could be waiting for me in there.* A tortured shriek rips through the crack, and without another thought, I fling the door open. *Oh. Oh no.* My pulse drums in my ears, and my stomach is somewhere on the floor.

I run to her side, searching with my eyes for a way to help her. Her head is held in a fixed position by some sort of contraption running across her forehead above her brows, and electrodes are connected to her temples, forehead, and various places on her scalp. A feeding tube runs from her nose to a bag of white fluid hanging on an IV pole. Her body is writhing and twitching in pain beneath the wide straps that hold her to the table, and her wrists and ankles are restrained in metal clamps pinning them down tight. She is yanking so hard against the restraints that blood is seeping from underneath the metal on her wrists and running down her hands. My gaze locks on her pasty, white, contorted face. Her bulging eyes are so dark that I can't distinguish her pupils from her iris, and she resembles a rabid animal with her bared teeth and puffed jaws. A mix of blood and saliva flows in rivers down her chin.

With her fists clenched, a screech that would break glass bursts from her mouth, shaking me from my stupor.

"It's okay, Cynthia. I am going to help you." My voice cracks as I grab the wires and yank them from her head.

A low, droning buzz fades to silence, and her writhing is replaced with tremors that pulse over and over from her head to her feet like the twitch of a snake's decapitated body.

My brain goes numb. *Don't shut down,* I scold myself. *Be strong.* But as I stare at Cynthia's seemingly unconscious body strapped to the table, every card stacked against me crashes down like bricks falling from the sky, pummeling me to the ground. *Teresa has been shot. The others were probably captured by Eckert and his guards. Steve hasn't come back yet. Cynthia is unconscious, and Eckert will probably be in here any minute.* My shoulders hunch over from the weight, and I drop my head. Tears trickle down my face and drip onto the floor. *This is hopeless.* My posture stiffens as those words penetrate through my head. *No.* I lift my head. *For with God, nothing shall be impossible.*

I stride to the cabinets and open each door as fast as I can. *No. Nothing. No.* I move on to the drawers. I slide open the first drawer. *A black tablet.* I hesitate, then shake it off. *I would never get into it.* I reach for the second drawer. *But Alice could.* Yanking the first drawer open again, I grab the tablet, toss it on the counter, and move to the second drawer. *Nothing...* Third drawer... *Bingo.* I pull out an alcohol wipe and one of those tools Dr. Blakely had with the point on one end and the hook on the other.

I race back to the table. *I have to get to the back of her head.* I grasp the feeding tube where it enters right below her nostril and pull in one steady motion until it is completely out. Then, I run my hand around the contraption on her head, but I can't find a release. Bending down, I peer up under the table. *Yes.* I push a stiff metal button, and one side of the clamp unhooks, allowing me to flip it on a hinge off of her head.

I use both hands to roll her head to the side. As I pull in a deep breath to steady my hands, I drop to my knees to put myself at eye level with the back of her head. *Lord, please steady my hand.*

I only have to scrape with my fingernail twice until I snag the wire. Keeping my left nail in the location, I dab her skin with the alcohol pad and insert the needle. Without hesitation, I twirl the tool in my fingers, insert the hooked end in a scooping motion, and slide the wire from her skin.

A few seconds pass, and nothing happens. *It didn't work.* I press my fingers to her neck, and a pulse tickles my finger. "Cynthia. Cynthia," I say right in her ear, "can you hear me? Please, you have to wake up. I have to get you out of here."

Cynthia licks her lips, and her eyes flutter.

"Cynthia, it's me, Ellie. I need you to wake up. Do you hear me? I am going to unhook the straps, and then we have to go." I squat beside the table and pop the releases on the three straps. The ankle and wrist clamps are a little more difficult, but I figured out they work like a child safety cap on a medicine bottle. As I push down on the button, I twist, and the clamps snap apart.

"E-Ell…" Cynthia coughs.

"Yes. It's me, Cynthia. Let me help you sit up." I reach beneath her back and push her up. She swings her legs around to dangle over the side of the table. "Cynthia, listen to me. I am hoping you have the strength to walk. We need to get out of here fast."

Water gushes down her cheeks. "E-E-Ellie." Her voice trembles. "It hurt so bad." Her shoulders shudder with every sob.

I have a hunch, but I ask anyway. "What hurt?"

"The scorching fire… the gnashing teeth ripping and tearing

me apart… you would think it would have ended… that I would have died, and the pain would have stopped… but the torment and agony kept on… My ears are still throbbing from the gut-wrenching screams, screams from people I couldn't see in the thick black blanket smothering me. I couldn't brea-ea-eathe." She breaks down, weeping out of control.

Father, please give me the words. I pull her into my arms. I know we need to get out of here, but on the other hand, we might not get out of here. I might not get another opportunity to tell her. "Cynthia, you know what you just experienced, that is how the Bible describes hell. And that torture will go on for eternity."

"Ellie, I'm not a bad person." she defends.

"No, no. Cynthia, I am not saying you are a bad person. See, Jesus died for all of us. He took the punishment for our sin so that we could have eternal life in Heaven. But we have to accept the sacrifice that He made. We have to believe that He died for our sin. We have to choose to let Him be our Savior and ask Him to come into our hearts. In the book of Matthew in the Bible, Jesus says, 'He that is not with me is against me.'" I swipe the hair from her face as her head lies on my shoulder. "There is no middle ground. We either accept that Jesus died for our sin and live for Him, or we reject His gift of salvation and suffer the eternal punishment ourselves."

Cynthia pulls from my embrace, and her eyes gaze straight into mine. "Ellie, why did you help me?"

"Because you needed help." I say, unsure how to answer that question.

"After what I went through with Dennis, it has been hard for me to believe that someone could love me enough to die for me." Her tired eyes turn downward toward her fidgeting hands. "And Ellie, I know I just said that I am not a bad person, but I can't say that I would have helped me as you did. I can't say that I would have risked everything like you, Steve, Eileen, Alice and Teresa to save other people." She swallows hard, and her voice quivers. "I believe, Ellie. I believe Jesus died for me. I look at you, and this hope and joy radiate from you no matter the situation. And my children, after all their father put them through, they have this unexplainable peace. I want that, Ellie. I need that." She turns her eyes back to me. "And I never want to endure one minute of what I just experienced again."

Smiling, I take her hand. "Then don't put it off. Do you want me to pray with you?"

"Will you hold my hand? I need to do it myself." Cynthia caps her other hand on top of mine. "Believe it or not, I grew up in a Christian home. But one day, I decided that I didn't believe any of it, and then I met Dennis." She drops her head and closes her eyes. "Dear God, I am so sorry. I am so sorry for rejecting you all this time and turning away from you. I am sorry for shutting you out of my life. I am a sinner, Lord, and I ask your forgiveness. I believe now. I believe Jesus died for me. Please take control of my life, Lord. Please come into my heart. I want to live for you. Thank you, Lord. Thank you for sending Jesus. Thank you for giving me another chance. I love you, Father. In Jesus' Name, I pray. Amen."

She lifts her head with the biggest grin spread across her face. We throw our arms around each other at the same time.

"Oh, Cynthia, I am so happy."

"Me too." She squeezes me tighter.

"I am guessing that I missed something pretty big."

His voice startles us, and we both jump back, twisting our heads at the same time.

Steve steps through the doorway, holding the gun down at his side and glaring at us with his eyebrows lifted. Before I can explain, he narrows his eyes and crinkles his forehead. "Mom, I thought Dr. Blakely got you out of here." He moves up beside the table and puts his arm around his mother.

"Mitchell tried, but that nut-case, Eckert, stopped the guard and had me escorted here." Cynthia's mouth curves into a soft smile as she casts her eyes toward me. "But your beautiful wife rescued me, and a second ago, I accepted Jesus as my Savior."

Steve's mouth falls open, and he freezes as if he has forgotten all about our urgent situation. His mouth spread into a toothy smile, and laying the gun on the table, he grabs Cynthia up in a hug lifting her in the air. "Oh, Mom. Oh, Mom! This is wonderful. I am so happy for you."

"There you are." Teresa appears in the doorway. "Mom?" Her pitch rises. Before anyone can speak, she continues with urgency in her tone. "No time for an explanation. We have to move. Eckert won't be out much longer."

"Teresa!" I run to her. "Are you okay?" I put my hand to my mouth and gasp as I take notice of her bandaged shoulder."

"Apparently, Earl doesn't have a very good aim." Teresa lets out a sarcastic giggle. "The bullet grazed the side of my upper arm. That's what took so long. Eileen had to find some first aid supplies."

"Bullet." Cynthia leaps from the table and crosses the room in two strides. "That mad man shot you?" With gentle hands, Cynthia embraces her daughter. "Oh, baby, I am so sorry." She pulls back and looks at Steve. "Where is Eckert now? We have to go before he kills one of you?"

Steve picks up the gun and moves after her.

"It's okay, Mom." Teresa takes her hand. "It seems that the robot, Claude, can see in the dark too, and he has this needle in his finger... he can fire it like a gun. Before Earl pulled the trigger the second time, Claude shot him with a tranquilizer."

"But all the screaming, and then someone grabbed me, and you guys were gone..." I rattle off, still confused.

"A few guards must have heard the gunfire. I don't know. When the security lights came back on, we were on the first floor, three guards were unconscious, and Waves and Claude had all of their weapons." Teresa tugs on Cynthia's hand and takes a step toward the door. "Come on. The others are downstairs keeping an eye on Earl."

"Waves?" I scratch my head as Teresa leads Cynthia out the door.

Steve coughs and mutters under his breath, "I might have made a few adjustments to Waves while I was waiting in Dr.

Blakely's office for him to get you, Teresa, Alice, and Eileen." He leans in and kisses my cheek.

We fall in behind Teresa and Cynthia.

The tablet. "Wait. One second." I sprint across the room and grab it from the counter. In half a second, I am back beside Steve. "Okay. Let's go."

"What's that?" Steve asks and then rolls his eyes up at me when he spots the tablet.

"I don't know." I tuck it under my arm to free up my hands. "I found it in the drawer. I thought Alice might find something on it." I answer as Teresa motions for us to follow.

As they start through the door, Cynthia puts her head a little closer to Teresa, and in a quiet but excited tone, she proclaims, "I accepted Jesus."

Teresa stops, and her eyes dart to her mother. "What?"

"I asked Jesus into my life a few minutes ago." Cynthia's face beams as the words come from her mouth.

Teresa puts her hand to her heart. "Words cannot express how thrilled I am to hear that."

Cynthia pulls on Teresa. "Come on. We can get emotional later."

We tiptoe down the stairs, and I manage to retrieve my shoes along the way, one on each flight. At the bottom, Claude and Waves are positioned over Dr. Eckert, and Alice is wedged between them with her weapon aimed at Dr. Eckert's chest. Gerald and Eileen are standing to the side, both holding guns.

"Finally. What took you guys so long?" Alice looks up. "Cynthia?"

"It's a long story." I say, peering down at Dr. Eckert over her shoulder.

Steve edges up. "Claude, you come with us. Eckert knows I reprogrammed you. Waves, you stay here and keep him sedated for at least another thirty minutes. That should give us time to be completely clear of the mountain. When he wakes up, act like you saved him."

Claude leads as we tread down the stairs to the first level.

"Maybe I should try to get Mitchell?" Cynthia whispers to herself.

My heart drops as I realize she doesn't know.

I glance at Steve. He has his mouth open, but it seems he can't get anything to come out of it.

"M-m-mom," Teresa stutters, "uuu-uuuh."

"Nah." Cynthia answers herself. "He is safe. Dr. Eckert needs him right now. It's best to get you all somewhere safe."

The rest of us exchange a unanimous look of wide eyes and quick headshakes that confirms our agreement. Now is not the time to tell her.

Chapter Seventeen

Nonchalant is no longer an option. Seven people in unitards trudging through the tunnel toward the exit is suspicious enough. Add in a robot at the front of the group and four of the seven people gripping nine-millimeter semi-automatic pistols, and we stick out like a neon sign on a deserted back road.

Claude increases his speed, moving so fast that we are on the brink of jogging to keep up. Gerald brandishes his gun behind Claude, and Steve takes the back with his weapon. Alice and Eileen both have guns in the middle. I have my doubts about Eileen knowing how to use it. I wish she had given it to me, but I wouldn't dare take it from her.

As we dash through the tunnel, I keep an eye on Cynthia in my peripheral vision, hoping her strength holds up. No one else knows the torture she has endured, and now she is practically having to run a marathon.

The first blast door comes into view. It is still open, but a line of guards forming a barrier in front of it storms toward us.

Steve holds his arm out and shifts over in front of me. "Stay behind me. I have a gun."

"Hold your fire. Hold your fire!" Claude's mechanical voice wails like a foghorn and ricochets off the underground walls. He holds out his hand as if he is signaling them to stop, but as he swings his hand around, he shoots a series of darts out of his finger, dropping the whole line in a matter of seconds.

We keep moving without breaking stride. As we start through the first blast door, a giant dark stain on the ground to my right causes my stomach to react, and acid explodes in my mouth. Capping my hand over my lips, I look the other way and try to blot out the image of Dr. Blakely's bloody face in the middle of the stain.

A little bit further up in the corridor, another line of guards barricades the second door.

"Out of the way. Emergency!" Claude shouts orders to the guards. "Out of the way!" Claude lifts his hand.

This time the guards don't hesitate, and they don't rush forward either. They hold their position in a straight-line formation across the opening with their pistols aimed.

The darts fire like a machine gun from Claude's finger. The guards drop one by one in the line, but Claude still isn't fast enough. A few gunshots echo and bounce off the walls. Steve is blocking my view, but he can't block out the howl of pain that pierces my ears or the thud of a body hitting the ground.

"No!" Alice screams.

I step from behind Steve and watch Alice fall to her knees beside Gerald.

Steve charges to the front, firing a shot back, but the last guard has already collapsed from the tranquilizer.

"Help him, Ellie. Please help him." Alice pleads as Gerald shrieks and flails around on the ground.

I kneel next to him, dropping the tablet to the ground. "Gerald, try to hold still."

"I'm hit," he wails. "I'm hit."

"Where, Gerald?" I grab his shoulder in an attempt to stop him from rolling.

"My leg!"

Leg. Okay. At least it's not life-threatening. "Gerald, I need to take a look."

Alice throws her body over his chest to help pin him down, and Teresa grasps his feet.

Oh no. So much blood. Inner thigh. What if it is his femoral artery? Think, Ellie. Tourniquet. "Tourniquet. We need something to use as a tourniquet." I lift his leg and press the heel of my hand as hard as I can to the area right above the wound. *Lord, please help. Mom's a nurse, not me. I didn't go this far in nursing school.*

Gerald's body stills as I put pressure on his thigh.

Eileen runs toward one of the guards slumped on the ground. She unhooks his belt and jerks it from his pants, and then without bothering with the buttons, she rips his shirt open, tearing it from his body. Then, as she turns, she swipes up his gun and tucks it beneath her arm.

Whoa. Maybe it is just an adrenaline rush, but Sis has some muscle strength.

"Teresa," Steve yells without turning around. "Take Gerald's gun and get up here. Alice, I know you're upset, but keep your gun aimed behind us."

Claude flies past, wheeling at warp speed through the tunnel, back in the direction of building one.

As Eileen runs toward me, she yanks the sleeve from the shirt and tosses it through the air.

I grab the sleeve and wind it around his leg to add padding and protect the wound.

Eileen drops next to me and wraps the belt over the sleeve. Sliding the end through the buckle, she pulls it tight. Then using one hand to keep it in place, she twists the other end of the belt around her hand and pulls again. She casts a glance toward me. "I don't really know what I am doing. Do you think I have it tight enough?"

"You tightened it with all your strength, and the bleeding seems to have stopped." I lift my numbing hand, releasing the pressure now that the belt is in place. "I have never done this before either, but I think so."

A noise that sounds like a shopping cart with a bad wheel yanks our heads sideways in alarm.

Claude. I breathe out a sigh of relief at the sight of him speeding back down the tunnel pushing a gurney. Looking Heavenward, I mouth the words, *Thank you.*

"How are we going to lift him?" Eileen speculates out loud.

Claude eases the gurney close beside Gerald's body and squeezes a lever underneath on the side, dropping the mattress flat to the ground.

"Okay, Gerald. We have to get you on the gurney." I speak in a calm voice and squeeze his hand. "We don't want to hurt you by moving your leg, so can you try to lift some of your weight with your arms?"

"Mmm-hmm." Gerald grunts through gritted teeth.

"Okay, count of three. One. Two. Three…"

Gerald bites his bottom lip and scoots with his arms as Eileen and I lift under his back and head. Cynthia guides Gerald's good leg while Claude keeps the injured leg elevated. Once we get Gerald onto the gurney, Claude raises the gurney back up and lifts the footrest to keep Gerald's leg above his heart.

"Steve," I call out just loud enough to get his attention as I scoop the tablet up off the floor and tuck it back under my arm, "we're ready."

Claude lifts a medical bag off the ground, slides it under the gurney, and zooms in front of us, past Steve. Steve follows after Claude with the gun in firing position. Alice and I push the gurney, Cynthia walks beside us, and Eileen and Teresa keep an eye on problems approaching from behind. The tunnel slopes up, and the star-filled night sky comes into view.

Night. It's already dark? The darkness takes me by surprise, but after I reflect on all that has happened since Shelly brought the muffins at breakfast, I am now wondering how long it is until morning.

As we exit, two guards stumble, getting to their feet as we whiz past. Claude has them in a slumber before they even attempt to raise their weapons.

Steve swoops down and grabs one of the guards' automatic rifles as he passes, and Teresa grabs the other.

"Now what?" Eileen calls out from behind as we sprint through the parking lot with a gurney in tow.

"I don't know," Steve voices without slowing. "Maybe those little cars are still by the security building."

My legs burn from pushing the gurney uphill, but considering the situation, stopping for a breather is out of the question. As we jog across the pavement, I scan the lot, which is vacant except for a couple of buses and a line of white utility vans. Moving my eyes around, searching for anything helpful, I pause and do a double-take back toward the vans. *Why is there one silver van... with a black racing stripe down the center of the hood?* My eyes pop out like a bubble-eyed goldfish. The van lurches forward, out of the parking space, and turns toward us. Swallowing hard, I squint, trying to read the side. "Manna From Heaven Pizza Company." Every ounce of air in my lungs rushes out, and my shoulders fall. *I can't believe that I actually thought...* I think to myself, shaking my head in disbelief at my delusion. "Hey, Alice," I say as my mind drifts back in time, "did you name that pizza company?"

"What?" She lifts her gaze from Gerald.

I tilt my head, gesturing toward the van coming across the lot.

Alice glances at the van and back at me with her chin almost hitting her chest.

"Ellie, look!" Eileen's voice bubbles with excitement. "God has sent Mom!"

Steve digs in his heels and comes to a dead halt as the words leave Eileen's mouth. "What on earth?" he mutters. "Uncle Dukakis... Jillian."

I gape at the van in disbelief. *My mother and Dukakis... here. But how?* We met Steve's uncle, Dukakis Denali, after we escaped the facility the first time. It's hard to believe that President Denali was his brother. The two are nothing alike.

The van eases up next to us, and with no regard for her own safety, Mom jumps from the van in a state of hysteria. "What happened? Who's hurt?"

"Mom," the sight of her makes the tears gush like waterfalls down my face, "it's Gerald. Please help him. He was shot in the leg, and there was so much blood. I think it might be his femoral artery."

"Dukakis, put down all the seats. Hurry. We need to get this gurney in the van." she yells over her shoulder as Dukakis steps out of the driver's side door. "Everybody will have to squeeze in around it."

Dukakis looks at the gurney and doesn't ask any questions. He takes off running to the back of the van. A minute later, he appears through the side doors. "Bring the gurney to the back."

Alice and I move at superspeed, and Claude and Steve meet us at the back to help.

Spencer is curled up in a ball on the center console, hiding his eyes and rocking back and forth. As soon as Steve gets to the open doors of the van and he hears Steve's voice, he comes sailing out of the back into Steve's arms.

"Spencer," Herb scolds, "I told you to wait in here."

Herb too. I dart my eyes inside and catch a glimpse of Herb squished up behind the passenger seat.

Claude passes the medical bag to Mom. "Here, I don't know if there's anything that will help, but there is a bunch of first aid supplies in it."

Mom takes the bag, and Claude lowers the gurney. Steve, Dukakis, Alice, and I slide the collapsed gurney into the van.

Mom climbs in after Gerald. "Everybody in. We may need to get to a hospital." Mom orders, wasting no time getting to work on Gerald's leg.

"I don't know if we can. We are all escapees violating the president's executive order." Alice's shoulders jerk. "They won't give him any medical treatment. They'll only bring him back here."

"Cynthia, you can ride up front with me." Dukakis holds the passenger door open.

The rest of us pile in the rear doors tucking close to the side opposite Gerald. Steve helps Claude in first, who manages to wedge in behind the flattened gurney with Herb. Then Steve crawls through, squeezing in the corner behind the driver's seat, and stows the automatic rifle and the nine-millimeter he took from the guards between him and the seat. Spencer curls up on his lap. I go next and reach the other rifle and five handguns for Steve to stow with his weapons. Eileen and Teresa follow, and Alice gets in last, trying to get as close to Gerald as she can without getting in Mom's way.

Herb presses his hand to his chest, knocking his bowtie sideways. "It is so good to have you back. I have been so worried, and Spencer has probably lost five pounds from trembling so much."

"Thanks for taking care of him, Herb." Steve pats Spencer's back.

"Oh, I don't believe we have met." Herb turns to face Claude. "My name is Herb."

"Nice to meet you, Herb. I'm Claude."

Pinching the corner of the tablet between the tips of two fingers, I slip it beneath my legs and then lean over against Steve. He wraps one arm around me, keeping the other around Spencer. I prop my elbows on my knees, holding my arms out in front of me. My eyes water as I sit paralyzed, staring at my hands. Now that the adrenaline rush is wearing off, panic is kicking in. The muscles in my chest tighten, and my shallow breathing causes my head to swim. I don't want to upset Gerald or hurt his feelings by letting him know that his blood on my hands is setting off my OCD, so I try to hide it.

"Ellie, are you okay?" Steve asks in a soft voice.

I notice his eyes are fixed on my stiff hands.

"Yes." I almost don't get the 's' out before my voice starts to crack.

"You are amazing," he whispers in my ear. "Do you know that?"

I gulp, wanting to answer him, but I can't without bursting into tears.

"I can't imagine the battle you had to fight inside your mind to do what you did."

I turn my eyes up to meet Steve's. "Wh-what do you mean?"

"Ellie, I know you. You carry rubber gloves in your car and your purse in case you have to go into a public restroom. Touching other people's hands is a major hurdle for you with your OCD, and right now, your hands are covered in Gerald's blood." Steve reaches down and lifts my chin with his finger.

My whole body begins to shake. "I-I-I w-was afraid he was going to die." I stutter in a barely audible voice.

"I promise you, it's okay. It's Gerald." He smiles down at me. "There is nothing to worry about."

"Thank you. I know that, but it calms me to hear you say it." I lay my head on his shoulder. "Hey, I didn't get a chance to tell you. You know how I found Cynthia in that room?"

"Yeah." he answers slowly.

"That was the door."

"The door?" he asks in confusion. "What door is that?"

I turn my head around and glare at him. "The door in my nightmare."

He glares back at me with eyes as big as doughnuts. "Are you sure?" he probes in a skeptical tone.

"I am positive. The door, the screams, the darkness, my bare feet... it was all there."

Steve seems to be speechless, so I rest my head back on his shoulder.

"Jillian. Sorry to interrupt, but where do I need to go?" Dukakis glances in the rearview mirror.

"Get across the Kansas line. Hopefully, we can find a hotel

that doesn't have cameras." Mom rattles off as she continues to work on Gerald.

"Okay. I am merging on Interstate 70 now." Dukakis yells back.

"Do you think there is anywhere safe we can get some food?" Eileen groans. "I'm getting queasy."

"Well, we haven't eaten all day." Teresa adds.

"You, poor things. Your blood sugar is dropping." Dukakis slides his seat back, pressing Steve over on top of me, and Spencer squeals. "Sorry, Spencer." The van swerves, and the driver's seat jerks as Dukakis tugs at something under the seat.

Cynthia gasps. "Dukakis, do you need help?"

"No, it's good." He moves the seat forward again. "I'll stop as soon as I can find a place that is low-key. But eat these for now. They will get some sugar in your body." Dukakis tosses a whole box of peanut butter cups back to us. "The peanut butter makes 'em a good source of protein too."

Steve picks up the box, takes out two, and passes it to Eileen. "Don't worry. I will feed it to you." He winks at me as he tears open the wrapper.

"Thanks." I wink back. "What would I do without you?"

"What time is it, Uncle Dukakis?" Teresa asks through a mouth full of candy.

"About ten-thirty."

She shrugs her shoulders and mumbles, "No wonder we're starved."

"Are you doing okay, sweetheart?" Mom asks Gerald with that special sympathetic edge in her voice that comes so naturally to her.

I look at her in astonishment. With everything going on, she is one hundred percent focused on the need in front of her.

Gerald twists his head a bit to look at my mom. "Yeah," he chokes out, and then tries to clear his throat. "I am. Thank you. You are amazing. The pain is almost completely gone."

"Don't thank me. God took care of this, not me. Just so happened, everything I needed to treat your injury was in the first aid bag Claude swiped from the facility. There were sealed needles and a vial of hydromorphone for pain, a coagulant powder to stop the bleeding, saline solution to clean the wound, and lots of gauze and bandages." She pauses as her voice starts to crack from emotion. "Gerald, what is even more miraculous is that the bullet barely missed your femoral artery. It went straight through, and all the bleeding was from capillaries."

"Thank you." Alice mouths in a low voice as she bows her head and continues praying under her breath.

"You need to take it easy though, and get plenty of rest, which shouldn't be a problem with the pain meds. And I want us to keep the leg still and elevated for a while." Mom lectures.

"Yes, ma'am." Gerald gives her a salute.

Mom twists toward me on her knees. "Now, let me take care of Ellie." Mom pulls a rag from the bag along with a bottle of alcohol. Scooting a few feet until she is right in front of me, she rocks back and sits with her legs crisscrossed. "Let me see your hands, honey." she says as she pours alcohol onto the rag. She glances at Eileen and back at me. "I am so proud of you girls."

"Mom, I was so scared. There was so much blood. How did you know it wasn't the femoral artery?" I avoid looking at the blood coming off of my hands and keep my eyes fixed on Mom's face.

"If it had been the femoral artery, the blood would have been squirting in pulses like a heartbeat. Gerald's leg was seeping blood." She pours alcohol over my hands and uses some muscle to scrub my palms. "It looked like a lot of blood, but he never lost consciousness, so I don't think he lost a significant amount," she lifts her gaze from my hands to my face, "thanks to you and Eileen. It could have been much worse. There is no telling how much blood he would have lost if you hadn't applied pressure and put that belt on for a tourniquet. That quick thinking probably saved his life." Dropping my hands, she smiles. "All clean."

"Thanks, Mom." She wraps me in a hug and reaches for Eileen next to me, embracing us both. "Get in here, Steve." She pulls him in too.

"Lord, thank you… thank you for taking care of my babies." Mom utters as she squeezes her arms around us.

Mom lets go when Eileen grunts in pain.

"Hey, I see a large truck stop up ahead off the next exit. I'll run in there and grab us some food." The van shifts as Dukakis veers off onto the ramp.

"I'll come and help you." Mom rolls up on her knees. "We are going to need lots of water."

Dukakis parks between two tractor-trailers. "Stay low and keep the doors locked." Dukakis orders. "We'll hurry."

Mom cracks the back door enough for her to slip out.

Exhausted, we all sit in silence. A few minutes pass, and the rear door jerks open. Mom shoves a case of water in and pulls herself in after it.

Dukakis hands her three paper bags and slams the door. He rounds the van and jumps in the driver's seat. "They had one of those grab-and-go hot stations, so I grabbed everything on it plus a few bags of chips.

We all say "thank you" but not in unison, and between the utterances of gratitude and the mixture of rattling paper bags, it sounds more like a bunch of hungry animals.

"Can I eat, too?" Gerald strains to lift his head.

"Of course. If you feel like it, your body definitely could use the nourishment." Mom turns and lowers his leg a bit and then raises the backrest enough for him to swallow. "Eat slowly though, in case the pain medication has your stomach upset."

In about three minutes, all of the bags are empty, and the food has vanished.

My thought processes seem to kick in a little now that I have had some carbs to fuel my brain. "I can't believe you and Dukakis drove all the way out here. Where's Dad?" I ask, hoping there is a good explanation as to why he is not with them.

"I don't know." Mom sighs out loud and stares down at the floor. "When we left your house with Spencer and Herb, your dad didn't speak the whole way home. No matter what I said or asked, he wouldn't respond. I thought he was pulling that whole mute bit again, but a few minutes after we got home, he came out with a duffel bag. He said not to worry and not to be mad at him, but he had to take care of something. I was crying and begging him not to go, but he asked me to trust him and know that he wouldn't leave me in the midst of this chaos if there were any other way. He promised he would be back soon, and then he just walked out the door." her voice trails off on the last words. "About an hour later, Dukakis showed up... said your father had called him and asked him to come to the house and make sure I was safe until he got back."

"Your mom was coming after you guys with or without me." Dukakis joins the conversation from the driver's seat. "So, we all piled in the van and took a twenty-six-hour road trip. And let me tell you, as a preacher, I don't know how many sermons I have done on God being in control and having a plan for us, but right now, I am in awe at the fact that it just so happened we were in the parking lot when you all came running out, Gerald needed urgent medical attention, and your mom is an ER nurse. If that's not God's providence, I don't know what is."

"You know, despite how obvious God's hand is in our escape, a few days ago, I would have argued to my death that it all had to have been a coincidence. The devil had blinders on me." Cynthia holds her hands up. "Thank God He opened my eyes before it was too late."

"Amen!" Dukakis shouts.

Steve lifts his arm around my shoulders and pulls my head into his chest. Safe in his arms, I close my eyes and let my imagination run wild with every possible scenario as to what could have been so important that Dad would have taken off. After a while, the vibration of the van lulls me into a light doze.

Chapter Eighteen

The jerk of the van shifting into park jolts me awake. Out of the side window is a run-down motel with aqua paint peeling off of its stucco siding. Part of the sign has collapsed and is lying in a heap at the base of the metal poles holding it up. The only thing left is 'MOTEL'. Of course, I guess that's all one needs to know. From the looks of the outside, checking reviews probably isn't necessary.

"I'm guessing this is our best shot at a place without cameras." Dukakis opens the driver's door. "I'll see what's available for the night." Dukakis steps out, locking the doors behind him.

Steve bends down and puts his mouth to my ear. "Are you going to be able to handle this?"

"In God's hands, I can. He hasn't let me down yet." I say, winking.

"True. So true."

The driver's door opens, and Dukakis climbs back in. "Good news. They've been having some roof problems, but they have two rooms available that aren't leaking."

"But, Uncle Dukakis," Steve leans around the back of the

seat and peers at Dukakis, "it's not raining. The ground is dry as a bone."

"Yeah, I know. Kind of alarming, isn't it?" Dukakis remarks as he puts the van in reverse. "The rooms are on the other side of the building. I'll back up to the door so wheeling the stretcher in won't be noticeable."

~

WITH THE DOORS on the back open, only about three feet is visible between the van and the door to one of the rooms. Steve and Dukakis rush the gurney inside. Alice helps me conceal the weapons, and Mom takes Spencer.

The two rooms have an adjoining door that is standing open. Double beds take up most of the space, but we manage to squeeze Gerald's gurney against the wall. The bedding is all wrinkled, and the walls and carpet are covered in stains. We all pretend we are standing because we have been sitting in the van for so long, but I am pretty sure that everyone is afraid to touch anything.

"Gerald," I say, scanning the room, "at this moment, I am sort of thinking you are the lucky one with that gurney."

He turns his head to the side rolling his eyes down toward the beds, and his face contorts into a grimace. "I have to say I agree with you. Yuck."

"I'll be right back. Someone put the chain on the door." Dukakis says in a rushed tone with no explanation.

Mom huffs. "First, your dad, and now Dukakis. What is so hard about telling someone where you are going?"

"I wish we had a phone. I need to call Mitchell." Cynthia exhales with a loud moan. "He must be worried sick."

I drop my head. *How could we not have told her by now?* A pang of guilt twists in my gut. *How do we tell her something so painful?*

"I have a burner phone." Mom digs in her purse. "I don't

know why, but Tom insisted that we always have two on hand."
She pulls it from her purse.

"Mom," Steve puts his hand on Cynthia's shoulder, "we need
to talk."

"Why do you have that look on your face, son?" She narrows
her eyes. "You are scaring me."

Steve gulps. "Umm, earlier today, Dr. Blakely brought me
into his office. He was concerned because he hadn't heard from
you yet. He was going to get me out of the complex so that I
could come and find you, but I wouldn't go unless he got us all."
Steve gestures toward the rest of us. "When we were going down
the tunnel, we came across some guards."

Water wells up in Cynthia's eyes like she already knows what
Steve is going to say.

"Mom, I am so sorry. Mitchell was killed."

As soon as that last word escaped Steve's lips, Cynthia
dropped to the floor weeping, the tearing of her heart echoing
through her lips.

"Mom, Mitchell really loved you. He wouldn't have risked it
all if he didn't." Steve kneels beside her with his arms around her
shuddering body.

The door opens and stops with a thud when the security
chain catches. "Uuugh, I forgot about the chain." Dukakis
mumbles. Then he half yells, "Could someone please open the
door?"

Mom slides the chain and pulls the door open.

"Thanks, Jillian." Dukakis plods in with an arm full of large
shopping bags. "I ran to the superstore and picked up some
sleeping bags and clothes for you guys. No offense, but those
unitards sort of stand out." He drops the bags. "I didn't know
what size shoes, so I got a bunch of those self-adjusting slip-on
sneakers and then…" his voice trails off when his eyes fall on
Cynthia sobbing into Steve's shoulder. "What happened?" A
look of concern washes over his face.

"Someone close to her was killed." Mom whispers.

Dukakis mouths, "Who?"

Mom looks at me to answer.

I motion them over to the door. "Cynthia was in a relationship with Dr. Blakely. He was doing some of the testing at the facility, and he had gotten Cynthia released. She was supposed to call him when she was safely home, but she never did. He was helping us escape this morning so Steve could find her. But on our way out, one of the guards shot him. We were escorted back into the facility, which is a long story, but during our second escape attempt, I discovered Cynthia in one of the labs." I take a deep breath. "She wanted to call Mitchell… umm… Dr. Blakely, so Steve had to tell her what happened."

"Oh, brother," Dukakis pinches the bridge of his nose, "poor Cynthia. After everything that Dennis put her through, now this." He squeezes his eyes closed and stands in silence for a minute. Without a word, he pads over and kneels next to her. "Cynthia," he places his hand on her shoulder, "I am so sorry. I can tell you really loved him."

Cynthia lifts her head and pulls away from Steve's arms as she sits up. "Dukakis, I'm never going to see him again. I thought after Dennis that I could never fall in love again. I thought I was incapable of feeling love." Her wailing gets louder. "I didn't even realize how much I cared for him until now. Why didn't I tell him?"

"I'm sure he knew, and it's obvious that he loved you too." He swipes away the tears from beneath Cynthia's eyes with his thumb. "I know it seems so unfair that you didn't get more time with him. I'm not going to sit here and say that I know how you are feeling. God made each of us unique and one of a kind. Only you understand the intensity of your pain. But I can tell you that when I lost Delilah, I was angry. I was supposed to grow old with her." He sniffles and wipes his own eyes. "I was convinced that she was going to get better, and we would have at least two children. And then she was gone, and I was mad. What I am getting at is that God understands whatever emotions you are feeling. He's there to hold you when you cry. He's there to listen if you need to scream."

"But how did you get through it?" Cynthia looks at him with wide water-filled eyes.

"I realized how blessed I was to have been the man Delilah loved. I realized how blessed I was to have had the time I had with her. Some people go through life and never experience true love. And I did."

"He wasn't a Christian, Dukakis. How can I bear the thought of that?"

"Oh, Cynthia," he takes her hand in his, "you hold onto hope. You hope that something happened in the last hours of his life to change that. You don't know what was going on in his heart. He could've talked to God before he died. So, keep your eyes on Jesus and hold on to the hope that Mitchell gave in to the conviction of the Holy Spirit."

"Thank you, Dukakis."

"For what?"

She squeezes his hand. "Caring." Then she shakes her head. "Are you sure Dennis was your brother?"

"Well, we have a lot of family photos together." he says, laughing as he rises to his feet. He holds out his hand and helps Cynthia from the floor. "Okay, I got a sleeping bag for everyone, disinfecting wipes for the bathroom, and a bunch of t-shirts and sweatpants. Just dig through and get what you need."

We scramble for the bags. *I can't wait to get out of this suit that is squeezing the life out of me.* By the time I get a t-shirt and a pair of sweatpants, both bathrooms are taken, so I have to wait my turn. Thankfully, everyone moves fast.

When I come out of the bathroom, Herb's head is spinning... actually spinning in complete circles.

"Did anyone get my charging station from the van?" Herb inquires.

"Yes, Herb," Mom answers, "it's on the table by the door."

"Splendid." Herb rolls toward the door. "Claude, I know you don't have yours, so we can take turns with mine."

"Oh. Thanks, Herb." Claude crosses the room behind Herb.

"Between shooting all of those tranquilizers and racing out of the facility, my battery is getting low."

"You shoot tranquilizers?" Herb twists his head around, looking backward at Claude.

"Yes, from my index finger. Don't you?"

"No," Herb drops his head. "I spray furniture polish from my index finger."

"Really?" The pitch rises in Claude's mechanical voice. "Is it lemon-scented?"

"As a matter of fact, it is." Herb perks up. "Do you want me to spray the table?"

Claude grabs some tissues from a box on the dresser. "Okay. You spray, and I'll wipe."

Do robots get delusional when their battery is low? Maybe it is the same when we go without sleep... but I can't rest. "I know we need sleep," I speak up, "but I can't get Dr. Eckert's phone conversation with the president out of my mind?" I cover my face with my hands and rub my eyes. "Does anybody have any idea what he could have meant by 'the process will begin tomorrow at ten thirty-five'?"

"I was just thinking about that." Alice moves beside me. "That and the comment he made about unleashing monsters. Do you think the two things are related?"

Dukakis spins around. "Hold on. Now I know Jillian said when they took you guys from your house, the officers used excessive and unnecessary force, and her intuition told her something was bad wrong... which, by the way, is why we traveled across the country. Then, we were parked in the lot trying to figure a way in so we could find out what was really going on in there, and you all came running out with Gerald on a gurney. A few minutes ago, you mentioned something about rescuing Cynthia, and her friend was killed helping you escape. Now, you're talking about something happening tomorrow and unleashing monsters. I thought I would let you get some rest before I pressed, but with all the bits and pieces I keep getting, it sounds like we may have a serious situation on our hands."

"Let's stay focused on the facts." Teresa presses her hands together and touches her chin with her fingertips. "Earl was talking to the president when we heard the comment about the process starting. For all we know, the process could have meant a new series of tests."

My mind drifts from the conversation as worry rotates faster and faster in my brain, forming a cyclone of panic. *Bailey, Liz, Cindy, Mable... If Eckert uses them as bait in that room... how could we have left them?* The thought makes me weak. The room grows fuzzy, and static fills my ears. My knees bend under my weight, and a set of hands grip beneath my arms.

"Ellie. What's wrong, Ellie?" Steve yells in my ear as my body touches the floor.

"Oh, no. Let's... her... I need to check... vitals." Mom's voice fades in and out.

Steve's blurry face appears over me, and a cold rag presses on my forehead. As I stare up at him, his deep brown eyes come into focus.

"Her vitals are good." Fingers release from my wrist, and I catch sight of Mom moving in my peripheral vision. "She is probably suffering from exhaustion."

From somewhere close by, Alice lets out a sigh and utters, "Thank you, Lord."

A steady ache lingers in my chest. "We left them." I utter, but my words are wobbly and hoarse.

"What?" Steve narrows his gaze.

"How could we have left them?" I get out a bit louder.

He lifts my head onto his lap. "Oh, Ellie. I know. It's eating at me too. But I don't know how we could have gotten them out. There were too many. We have to focus now and figure out a way to help them."

I rotate on my side and wrap my arms around him. With my face in his stomach, I get control of my tears.

"I'll get her a bottle of water." Mom whispers.

"Oh, man. Are you serious?" Dukakis's voice carries across the room. "So, because you all aren't affected by his virtual demonic experience, he is putting you in a room with someone who has these so-called brain lesions and suddenly transforms into a killer. This sounds like something Dennis would come up with."

They must be filling him in. At the sound of Dukakis' reaction, I flop back over on my elbow and strain to lift my upper body. Steve grasps my arm, and Eileen slides her hand under my back and helps from my other side. I hadn't even realized that she was on the floor next to me. As I get into a sitting position, I notice Alice, Teresa, and Cynthia huddled around Dukakis.

"He did say that he could never be destroyed." Cynthia scoffs.

"Well," Dukakis runs his hand over the top of his head, "if I hadn't been at his execution, I might question it. But since I am a pastor, they let me talk to him beforehand. I didn't want to witness that, but my conscience wouldn't let me leave my brother... so I stayed. He was dead, no doubt."

"Dukakis," I call out, but my voice is too weak to carry. "Duk..."

"Hey, Uncle Dukakis." Steve speaks up and motions him over when Dukakis turns his head. Alice, Teresa, and Cynthia come along behind him.

I manage to manipulate myself up on my knees. "Alice and I were trying to figure out how that virtual reprimanding thing works. It is like demons are clawing at us and whispering in this realistic simulation of hell, but then it all disappears at the sound of God's voice. He tells them that they can't touch us because we have His seal. How can we be battling demons and hearing the voice of God in a computer program created by Dr. Eckert?"

"Hmmm." Dukakis scratches his head as he sits on the edge of one of the beds.

I keep going because I want to tell him everything. "Also, I've been thinking that maybe this has something to do with why we don't have the lesions on our brain." I glance at Cynthia, hoping I don't upset her, but I have to know if anyone else sees the same connection as me. "When I first came in for testing, I had that disc, so Dr. Blakely thought I was asleep even though I wasn't. He indicated that all the people responsible for the violent acts had lesions on the lateral septum of their brain. And before they could release anyone, they had to figure out what had caused the lesions. I believe it has to do with this reprimanding, and we don't have the lesions because Dr. Eckert's program isn't working on us."

"You're right. That's it… but," Alice looks up at Dukakis, "that still doesn't explain how a virtual program has us battling real demons and entering into the presence of God. I can't fathom it is a figment of our imaginations. The peace… the overwhelming peace that overcame me, and the joy that filled me… it had to be real." Alice's voice trembles on the last word.

Steve taps my shoulder. "What disc are you talking about?"

"Oh, I forgot you didn't know about that. When I almost fell going into the train station, Agent Morgan stuck this disc to my arm as he caught me. Come to find out, it canceled out all the effects of the chip in our head. So, when they put us to sleep, I had to pretend."

"That's weird." Dukakis gives his head a quick shake. "Anyway, back to the topic of battling demons. Alice, to answer your question… I don't completely understand it either, but we know the devil will use anything he can to get a foot in the door… television, music, video games. I believe this virtual simulation of Dr. Eckert's could be so dark and satanic that the devil and his demons are using it to enter the person's mind. Maybe I'm reaching, but this theory makes perfect sense if you think about it. Those that are not Christians are being left with scars on their brains. They are having outbursts of anger as if they have relinquished control to some evil force. On the other hand, those that are true Christians have God's seal, the Holy Spirit. So, the demons can't enter because the Holy Spirit already lives inside them."

Steve stares at Dukakis. "When we walked in on Penny attacking Gerald, she didn't even acknowledge we were there. Do you think a demon could have been controlling her?"

Alice turns her head toward me. "Ellie, do you remember when I told you Dr. Eckert mentioned that the chips were working but that he just needed to shock the lesions a little harder?"

I drop my head to stretch my neck muscles and massage my right shoulder with my left hand. "Okay, let's think this through. So, we have a dark, demonic virtual world that could possibly be so evil that demons are preying on that opportunity to tear and eat at a person's mind. And these demons are leaving behind real scars on the lateral septum of that person's brain. Meanwhile, Dr. Eckert has a chip inserted into the back of the person's head with a wire protruding into the lateral septum." I move both of my hands to my forehead and rub my temples with my fingertips. "We know since he uses the chips to put us to sleep, he can control us somewhat through them. So, maybe he can send shocks from those chips down that wire and into the scarred area of the person's brain, stimulating some sort of uncontrollable rage."

Mom stands next to me, holding out a bottle of water. "But why? Why would he want to do that?" Her bottom lip falls. "Oh no. Do you think that's what happened in all these mass murder incidents?"

"I don't know, but aren't these orders coming from the president? We even overheard Dr. Eckert talking to him?" Teresa questions.

"I've been saying it for years." Gerald grumbles. "One way or another, the government will find a way to control us."

Alice paces back and forth, which is one step back and one step forth, considering the small room and how many people are in it. "But on the phone, Dr. Eckert said he received the directions from the president's advisor."

"Oh, now that makes more sense." Cynthia exclaims as she throws up her hands. "I knew Kutchins had never been able to think for himself."

"Ellie, where is that tablet you found?" Steve asks as he jumps to his feet. "Maybe Alice can find something on it."

I point. "I laid it by the television when we came in."

"Find something on what?" Alice snaps her head around at the mention of her name.

Steve grabs it from the dresser. "Ellie found this tablet in the room Cynthia was in. She thought maybe you could hack into it."

"You thought maybe. I'm deeply offended." Alice retorts, taking the tablet from Steve. "Of course, I can hack into it." She grabs a sleeping bag and shuffles over to one of the beds. "Now," Alice dictates, "it is going to take me a bit to search through this. Sometimes, things can be buried pretty deep, especially if things have been deleted." She unzips the sleeping bag and spreads it out on the side of the bed nearest the door. "We need as many fresh minds as we can get to stop whatever is happening, so while I am doing this, you guys try to get some sleep. Gerald has the gurney." She turns to Steve. "Sorry, but you are going to have to bunk with Dukakis. It would seem inappropriate for any of the rest of us. Ellie can bunk with me and stare at you across the small space between the two beds. Cynthia, Eileen, Teresa, and Jillian can take the other room." She leans back against a pillow on the headboard and folds the unzipped sleeping bag over her legs.

Dukakis takes his sleeping bag to the side of the bed next to Gerald's gurney so Steve can have the aisle next to me. Everyone else heads through the connecting door to the other room.

Teresa stops in the doorway and looks back. "Alice, you will wake us if you find something, right?"

"If I find something, you know me well enough to know that the whole motel will probably be awakened by my excitement." Alice reassures her with a smile. "Hey, that reminds me. I haven't had a chance to ask how you guessed the code for the doors."

"Oh yeah, that." Teresa drops her head. "It was our first date."

Alice crinkles her eyebrows, and then her eyes widen. "Your first date with Dr. Eckert. I see."

"I am not sure how we called it dating because we never left the facility." Teresa lifts her head and taps her chin. "We ate at the same table in the dining room, and sometimes we would go for a walk between the buildings. Oh," she giggles, "but our first date was special. Earl ordered pizza."

"I'm sorry, Teresa." Alice tilts her head and presses her lips together.

"For what?"

"I know you were misled and lied to, but that doesn't mean you didn't have real feelings for Dr. Eckert at the time. I know that pain doesn't heal overnight."

Teresa nods. "Thanks, Alice." She turns and carries her sleeping bag into the other room.

I stare at the ceiling, thinking about what Alice said to Teresa and realizing how insensitive I have been. It hasn't entered my mind that seeing Dr. Eckert might have stirred a lot of hurt and pain inside of her. Everyone is settling in, so now that it is quiet, I slide off the side of the bed onto my knees. As I bow my head, I notice Alice is doing the same. With my eyes closed, I block out everything around me and say goodnight to my Heavenly Father.

As I climb back onto the mattress, Steve kisses my cheek. "Goodnight, Ellie. I love you."

"Love you, too." I turn and wrap him in a hug.

"Steve," Dukakis grumbles, "this is only a full-size bed. Does Spencer have to sleep right here?"

"Spencer has PTSD. Sometimes he gets scared, and he needs to be close in case he has a nightmare."

Dukakis lifts his head off the pillow and glares at Steve. "You are telling me that this monkey sleeps in your bed like this at home?"

"Yes… yes, he does." I confirm, cracking a smile.

"Goodnight, Ellie." Steve says in a flat tone, obviously not appreciating my interjection.

"Goodnight." I say back, unable to wipe the grin off my face.

"The monkey snores too?" Dukakis asks in a whining voice.

"No." Alice puts her hand to her mouth. "That's Gerald."

"Oh, brother." Dukakis covers his head with his pillow.

～

"ELLIE, you have been looking over my arm the whole time." Alice stops typing on the keyboard that slides down from the back of the tablet and rolls her eyes over at me. "I appreciate the company, but you need sleep. You almost fainted earlier."

"I can't sleep." I stare at the screen with my head propped on my pillow. "Every time I close my eyes, I think about Bailey and the others. I have to be doing something to help them," I clear my throat, "so I am watching you. And as an FBI agent, I am glad you are not a criminal because, with your skills, you could do some major damage."

"Thanks," Alice says, dragging out her words, "I think."

I narrow my eyes, trying to read the screen without lifting my head. "June thirtieth and July first... the spreadsheet has yesterday and today's date. No," I tap my head, "it's almost morning. Today is the second."

"This is the last file that was open. A list of precise times is listed in one column under the date." Alice details pointing to the times written in military form.

Electrode configuration. I read the top of the next column to myself and move my eyes across. *Voltage.*

"You found this in the room with Cynthia?"

"Yes, it was lying in the top drawer." I utter as I move to the next column. *Subject's reaction level.*

Alice's mouth flies open. "Oh my!"

Subject resuscitated. "He had to resuscitate her." I vocalize the words on the screen as I read. It takes a moment for the reality of it to sink in. When it finally hits me, I press my hand to my chest and gasp for air. "He killed her and then resuscitated her."

"Somebody was killed!" Steve bolts from his bed. "Who? Who was killed?"

Steve's sudden outburst startles Spencer. The monkey yelps

and leaps straight up in the air and comes down on Dukakis's head. Dukakis jumps up, flailing his arms, and falls off the side, wedging his body between the bed and the gurney. Spencer lands on Gerald's chest causing him to thrust his leg up in the air. Gerald screams in agony, and in less than five seconds, shrieks and squeals fill the air as four frightened women followed by two dramatic robots stampede through the doorway from the connecting room.

Dukakis struggles to get out from between the bed and the gurney. "What on earth is going on?"

"Somebody was killed," Steve exclaims, then crinkles his forehead, "I think."

Oops. Me and my big mouth. Of course, right now everyone is looking at Steve, so I turn and look at him too. But he is looking back at me. *He knows I said it.*

"Ellie, didn't you say somebody was killed?" Steve scratches his head,

"Yes," I sit up on the side of the bed, "but you only heard part of it."

"So, no one was killed?" Teresa asks and then stifles a yawn.

Dukakis stumbles around the foot of his bed with his hair sticking out in all directions. "I don't know, but I had a close call."

I cover my face with my hands and shake my head. "No, no one was killed... well, technically, but she was resuscitated, and everything is fine." I look up. "Sorry for the false alarm. Everyone can go back to sleep."

"We're up now." Dukakis sits on Steve's side of the bed, facing me. "Let's hear the story."

"Really, it's noth-"

"Ellie, please tell us." Steve pleads, cutting me off.

"I was watching Alice work on the tablet, and she opened this spreadsheet that Dr. Eckert was using to record results from his testing on Cynthia." I try not to add emotion to my voice. I don't want to upset Cynthia any more than she already is. "One of the columns was labeled 'Subject's Reaction Level'. As Alice scrolled down the column, at one point, he typed in 'subject resuscitated'."

Cynthia half-staggers and drops to a sitting position beside me. "I died?"

"Oh, Cynthia. Maybe not. It said resuscitated, but maybe you just blacked out."

Cynthia twists her head toward me with tight lips. "Ellie, I was blacked out the whole time."

"True." I don't know what else to say.

Silence fills the room as Cynthia stares straight ahead with a blank face.

After a minute, I put my hand on her knee. "Cynthia, are you okay?"

"I am in awe… pure awe." Cynthia's eyes meet mine as she speaks. "Ellie, I got saved after you rescued me. If Dr. Eckert hadn't revived me, that nightmare or whatever he had me in would have become my reality for eternity." Tears trickle down her cheeks. "For years, I was kept frozen in a tube, and now I have died and been brought back to life during a crazy science experiment. But God didn't give up on me. After all the times I have rejected Him and said I didn't believe in Him, He still gave me another chance."

A smile spreads across Dukakis's face. "'The Lord is not slack concerning his promise, as some men count slackness; but is longsuffering to us-ward, not willing that any should perish, but that all should come to repentance' 2 Peter 3:9." Joy fills his tone. "Cynthia, we serve a loving God."

Spencer scampers to Dukakis and rolls his eyes up at him.

"Oh, if you weren't so cute, little guy. Come on." Dukakis lifts him onto his lap. "Hey, since we're up, do you want to share a peanut butter cup?"

Spencer claps his hands, and Dukakis carries him over to one of the bags.

"Ellie," Cynthia addresses me with a soft, hesitant tone, "before we went to sleep, you mentioned something about having a disc in Dr. Blakely's office and that you weren't actually asleep when he was talking about the lesions. Was I in there?"

"Yes, but I wasn't trying to trick you or anything. I was trying to figure out what was going on, and if anyone knew I had that disc, well…"

"No," Cynthia takes my hand, "it's not that. You were doing what you had to do. I just don't understand how… why… if you heard what I said, why you would still rescue me from that room."

"Because, no matter how you feel about me, Cynthia, I love you, and we are family."

"I want you to know that I'm sorry. I didn't mean it. I guess I was just a little jealous. I finally got my son back, and he already had a new woman in his life. And, well, I have changed since then. Even though it hasn't been that long since I said those words, I am not that hate-filled, self-centered woman anymore." Cynthia throws her arms around me. "I love you too, Ellie, and my son is so very blessed to have you as his wife."

A tear drips from the corner of my eye. "Thanks, Cynthia."

I pull back a few inches. "I sort of have a confession myself. When I overheard you and Dr. Blakely talking, I found myself a little suspicious and concerned about what you could be planning. You said something about needing Steve and Teresa out, and that it would be the perfect setup if Dennis hadn't dragged you and the kids into it."

Cynthia lets out a small chuckle, and then a solemn look presses her lips into a frown. "I can imagine that it did sound bad, especially considering what I said about you, but I was only talking about the election. I had these big plans for Steve and Teresa to help me play out the victimized family card, and then we got put back in that complex leading the world to believe that we have something wrong with our brains."

"Oh," it suddenly all makes sense, "and the instability going on in the country is the perfect setup because people will want a change in leadership."

"Exactly," Cynthia pats my knee. "Too bad I'm not running anymore. I could have used a mind like yours."

"Alright," Mom orders, "now that the chaos is over, I want everyone back in bed. We can't fight whatever it is we're fighting without a little rest."

"She's right." Dukakis puts Spencer in the middle of the bed and climbs back into the sleeping bag. "We need all brain cells firing, so everybody better get a few more hours of shut-eye."

Eileen, Teresa, and Cynthia follow Mom back to the other room.

"I am over half-charged. You should take a turn on the charger in case something happens." Claude says as he and Herb follow them.

I lean back on my pillow and turn my attention back to the tablet screen. "Have you found anything else?" I ask, watching Alice scroll down a list of file names.

"Not really. Most of these files are scientific papers written by a Dr. Mordecai Crawley."

"What kind of scientific papers?" I prod.

"The majority of it is a lot of scientific jargon that I don't understand, but they all appear to be experiments involving the brain and mind control." She clicks on a file. "For example, in the introduction of this one, Dr. Crawley states that he can safely put a patient to sleep and wake them up through a wire inserted into the hypothalamus of the brain. He goes on to say that this breakthrough will eliminate the risk of administering anesthesia over and over to patients who require a series of surgeries." Alice exits the document, and the screen display returns to the list of files.

"Well, I guess we know where he learned to torture us. I wonder if this Dr. Crawley knows that his scientific research is being used for malice." I comment as I scan the file names. "Hey, what's that?" I point to a file that reads *SIN_THENATU-RALCHOICE_ALEARNINGAND COGNITIONARTICLE_M-CRAWLEY.docx*.

"Something about how the desire to sin is innate and overpowers morality." Alice opens the file. "His hypothesis for his experiment reads: *The provocation of anger in an individual will result in the innate sinful nature overruling any morality associated with religious or learned behavior.* It appears that he tested his theory through what I believe would be considered unorthodox in the realm of scientific research."

"What did he do?" I move closer to the screen, trying to read the tiny font on the document.

"He took a group of people, five men and five women, and studied them individually, pinpointing their weaknesses. Then he preyed on those weaknesses and aroused anger in each of them." Alice scrolls through the pages of the document on the screen and then stops. "For instance, this one guy was obsessed with his car. Crawley notes that this subject could not stand a speck of dust to settle on the paint, so Crawley took a screwdriver and scratched it."

"Why? What did that prove?" I narrow my eyes in confusion.

Alice turns her head toward me. "Picture it. He gets all these people mad and then locks them in this small room together."

"I'm guessing they vented their anger by taking it out on each other."

Alice nods.

"But what criteria did he use in choosing the subjects? Not all people vent their anger outwardly." *I don't… at least I don't think I do.* My mind stirs as I try to analyze myself. I drop my head.

"Ellie, what is it?"

"I remembered one of my fits of anger. You know when Teresa, who we knew as Dr. Fleming at the time, shot Eileen with that tranquilizer? I thought she had killed or tried to kill Eileen, so I knocked Teresa to the ground."

Alice smiles. "Yes, I remember. You had just gotten your sister back, who had been missing for two years. You didn't know it was a tranquilizer. You thought Teresa had tried to kill her." Alice softens her voice. "Ellie, you believed that she was there to harm your family, and you were protecting them. But... you didn't hurt Teresa because you felt God telling you to turn her loose. And then you asked God and Teresa to forgive you for months after that. A bit different scenario than the ones in this experiment. You stopped yourself before you went too far. And you were taking your anger out on someone you thought was harming your family. These subjects took their anger out on complete strangers. Some people in that room even had some severe injuries. For your initial question, he does not say how he chose the subjects, nor does it document any names. As I said, it seems this experiment is a bit unorthodox. He dug into their thoughts and sought out their weaknesses, and people were left with serious scars... mental and physical."

I sit in silence for a few minutes, still pondering my act of anger. I know Alice is right, but I can't stop thinking about it. Alice somehow always reads my mind because she reaches over and squeezes my hand.

"Ellie, you made a bad choice, and then you asked God to forgive you. It's not like you intentionally sin over and over. You made a mistake. Christians aren't perfect. If there were any perfect people, Jesus wouldn't have had to die on that cross." She leans closer and whispers, "Accept the fact that He has forgiven you and forget about it. It has already been erased."

"Thanks, Alice." I lean my head back on the pillow and listen to Alice tap at the keyboard for a few more minutes. Suddenly her tapping stops.

"Ellie, the puzzle guru is stumped... stumped and a little scared." Alice lays the tablet on the sleeping bag covering her lower body and presses her hands to the sides of her head. "What are we going to do? I honestly believed that I would find something on this tablet. But the reality is we have no proof that the facility is doing anything wrong, and no one is going to take us seriously. All of those people are there because the president ordered them to be. To anyone else, it appears we are the bad guys. We have escaped and are violating an executive order. On top of that, it is believed that we could have something wrong with our brain that makes us go on a killing spree." She turns her head toward me with watery eyes. "Ellie, this isn't like last time. We aren't sneaking into an abandoned warehouse where a few goons with guns aren't expecting us. This is an underground military bunker, built to withstand a nuclear attack, infiltrated with I don't know how many guards carrying automatic rifles and semi-automatic pistols." Alice leans closer. "We don't know what it is we are up against. We don't know what or where something is happening today at ten thirty-five. Maybe our suspicions are all wrong. President Kutchins and his advisor are involved. Homeland Security is involved."

"Alice," I utter in a calm voice, "think about it. We saw Dr. Blakely get shot. Steve and I saw a man get shot on the train. Dr. Eckert is putting us in a room with a person that snaps and tries to kill us. He even admitted it. No, we can't prove it to anyone. But we are not wrong. God is leading us. We just have to be patient. After all, we escaped the facility with Gerald on a gurney, and my mother and Dukakis, who live over half the country away, were in the parking lot in a van big enough to put a gurney in." I glare at her with wide eyes when she looks up at me. "God is with us. He will show us what to do next."

Alice lifts her hand as her mouth stretches into a wide yawn.

"See," I fluff my pillow, "that is a sign we need to sleep."

Alice lays the tablet on the nightstand. "No argument here. I'm exhausted, and I think the sky is already getting lighter."

Chapter Nineteen

It seems like I only touch my head to the pillow before the door clanks, water turns on, and whispers filter through the room. I open my eyes, and Spencer is standing beside the bed with his face only two inches from mine. His mouth spreads into a toothy grin.

"Good morning, my beautiful wife. I made you some coffee."

I lift my eyes. Steve is standing right behind Spencer. "You are amazing. Thank you." I swing my legs off the side of the bed and take the cup from his hands."

"Sorry it's so small. That coffee pot over there only makes a thimble at a time." he laughs. "Believe it or not. I ran the coffee pot three times to get that."

The bed squeaks as Alice gets up from the other side.

"Gerald, where's my coffee?" she chides with a grin on her face.

"Really? Did you already forget that I was shot yesterday?"

She laughs. "I was only joking." She walks over and kisses his forehead. "Good morning, dear."

A moment later, Alice plops down on the bed beside me and

darts her eyes back and forth between Steve and me. "I've been thinking."

"That was fast. You've been out of bed less than a minute. I haven't even had time to take a sip of my coffee yet." I say as I put the cup to my mouth.

Steve sits on his bed across from us.

"Well, time is of the essence, you know." Alice claps her hands together.

"Hey," Teresa comes through the door from the other room, "that's my line."

"Sorry, you're right." Alice retorts, turning up one side of her mouth.

"So," I tap Alice's knee with my hand, "what are you thinking?"

"Well, I actually have three thoughts, but let's take one at a time. First, you work for the FBI."

I narrow my eyes in confusion. "Yes. Yes, I did. But I am fairly certain, considering my current status in the eyes of the U.S. government, that I am now unemployed."

"Probably, but do you have any close contacts there? Someone you could call that knows you well enough to know you are telling the truth."

Steve shakes his head. "No. You know every federal agency has been notified by now of our escape."

"I'll use Mom's burner phone to call Kate. I won't have to say my name. Kate will know my voice, and ever since I met her, she has been enamored by the fact that I was part of the group that stopped President Denali. Hopefully, if she knows I have escaped, she won't verbally acknowledge it is me." I scan the room for a clock. "What time is it?"

"Eight o'clock." Steve answers. "Well, a few minutes past."

"Hey, Mom?" I yell.

Teresa steps to the doorway. "Jillian, Ellie needs to borrow that burner phone."

A minute later, Mom hurries into the room and lays the

phone in my hand. "Sorry, honey, I had to dig it out of my bag." She turns and strides back through the door.

I clutch the phone and pull it to my chest. With my eyes closed, I drop my head, letting the voices around me fade. *Father, please be with those people in the facility. Please keep them safe and help us get them out of there. Lord, please let Kate recognize my voice, and give me the right words to say. Amen.* I open my eyes and tap the screen. "Okay, here goes. Everyone be quiet." I type in the number and hit the call icon.

"Special Agent Kate Matthews speaking."

"Ummm. Yes. Kate, I am hoping you can help me. I have a situation…"

Kate cuts me off. "I'm sorry, ma'am." She coughs into the phone. "You need to speak with local authorities. If they need our help, they will contact us and request assistance."

Did she cut me off because she knows it's me, or is she really directing me to the police? Uuugh. "So—, I take it, you understand?"

"Yes, I am listening." Kate says, emphasizing the word 'listening'.

"Oh, good. I need you to understand that my situation is not as it seems. I am sure in your line of work that people often alter information, or maybe they don't tell the truth at all. And if you look close enough sometimes, I bet you find active volcanoes in the midst of beautiful mountains."

Kate sighs into the phone. "That is an interesting analogy, ma'am. I'll keep that in mind."

"I hope so because the magma would be fatal to those inside, and once it erupts, who knows how many on the outside would be burned by the lava?" I swallow hard. *Please let her have made sense of that.*

"I see. Ma'am, you are a very wise lady, and I appreciate your words of wisdom." she comments in a tremulous voice. She clears her throat and continues. "I will hold on to that and do my best to apply it."

"Thank you." I tap the screen to end the call and blow out the deep breath I've been holding in.

"You, okay?" Steve takes my hand.

"Yeah. She knew it was me, and I am pretty sure she got what I was trying to insinuate. But..." I pause and squeeze his hand.

"But what?" Lowering his head, he leans in and looks up at me with wide eyes.

"But what can she do? She is one agent with the FBI. No one is going to believe her, and if she pushes it, she could lose her job. She can't travel across the country and check it out by herself. What exactly are we expecting?"

"Ellie, I'm sorry." Alice twirls her hair as she stares at the floor. "You're right. I knew it would be a longshot."

"Don't be sorry. You are the only one coming up with ideas, and we have to start somewhere." I pat her back. "Now, if I remember correctly, you had three thoughts, and we only covered one. What is next?"

"The agent that gave you the disc... if he would go out on a limb to give that to you, he might be willing to take the risk to help us."

Gasping, I stretch my back taller. "Agent Morgan... You're a genius, Alice. Ever since I figured out what that disc did, I have wondered why he gave it to me. I kept thinking that Mom must have gotten to him with her speech, but he must have at least had a hunch that something was off about the whole thing. Why else would he have taken that kind of risk?"

"I agree." Steve props his elbow on his knees and rests his chin on his folded hands. "It certainly seems he was having second thoughts about what he was being ordered to do. Or maybe he knows more. But how can we reach him? It's not like he sits in an office all day. He works out in the field, and we can't exactly leave a call back number." Steve looks at Alice and then me.

"That's true." I slump as my hope in that idea deflates.

"Okay. While we ponder on that, what's your third thought, Alice?"

"We have to find your dad."

"What? Why?" I slurp my coffee. "How can he help?"

"Well, last time, he had quite a bit of inside information, and..." Alice hesitates, "and... well..."

"Alice, stop worrying about offending me. You know me better than that." I set my cup on the table and lean back on my pillow. "Say what you are thinking."

She slumps her shoulders. "Ellie, you have to admit it is kind of odd that he would take off without telling your mom where he's going, especially after she just had both daughters ripped from her life again. I can't help but wonder if he knows something else."

I want to tell her she's wrong, but I have been thinking the same thing. How could he run away and leave Mom to deal with this alone? I pull my knees to my chest with my arms and rest my forehead on them, hiding my face. *It's exactly like when he stopped talking when Eileen vanished. I know he thought he was protecting Eileen, but Mom needed him. And now, he's bailed on her again.* I bite my lip and will myself to take control of my thoughts. *Ellie, stop speculating. He loves her. He was shot protecting her. He must have a good reason for leaving.*

"Ellie," Alice's voice cracks, "I'm sorry... I didn't mean to..."

I lift my head. "No, you have nothing to be sorry for. I have been thinking the same thing."

"Well, I hate to keep being Mr. Negative," Steve interjects, "but it's sort of the same scenario. How are we supposed to find him? Jillian doesn't even know how to find him."

"I heard my name." Mom stands in the doorway of the connecting room. "Who's talking about me? I certainly hope it is good things."

"Hey, Mom. We were trying to figure out what to do next."

She glares at me with her hand on her hip. "So, how did that involve me?"

"We were wondering if Dad might know something."

Steve lifts his hand. "Blame me, Jillian, it was me. I said that if you don't know how to find him, how are we supposed to?"

Mom sits on the bed. "Please tell me that your father isn't the only option that you have come up with."

"No, Alice thought of Agent Morgan too, since he tried to help me, but it is the same problem. We have no way of finding him."

"Hmmm." Mom taps her chin. "Maybe I could call the Department of Homeland Security and ask how to reach him. He would have no idea that I am with you guys or that I would even know you've escaped. What could be my reason for calling?" she asks more to herself than to us.

The door rattles with the sound of a keycard. *Hard to believe this place still uses those things. That would be like needing a key to unlock your front door.*

"Room service." Dukakis announces as he pushes the door open with his foot. Plastic bags are looped around his arms, and he is balancing a tray of coffees in each hand.

"Oh, Dukakis, let me help you." Mom bounces up from the bed and grabs one of the trays.

Alice stands and takes the other. "Dukakis, you are the best. Are those biscuits I smell?"

Dukakis holds up one of the bags. "Yep, this one is full of chicken biscuits, and for dessert," he holds up the other bag, "glazed doughnuts. They are still warm too."

Words aren't necessary. The smell has everyone gathered around Dukakis holding hands in less than a minute. Well, everyone except Gerald, and I am pretty sure he was trying to push off the wall and roll the gurney toward the bags on the dresser.

"Let us connect our hearts and minds in prayer." Dukakis lowers his head. "Dear Heavenly Father, we thank you for keeping all of us safe and providing us with food and shelter. Lord, please be with those who are still in that facility and lead us in knowing how to help them. Show us the way. We praise you. We love you. In Jesus' name, we pray. Amen."

Alice puts her coffee on the table by the bed and picks up the tablet. "Now that I am rested, I am going to do a little more searching on this tablet while I eat." She sits with her back against the headboard and crisscrosses her legs. "If I could only find something incriminating enough, maybe the authorities would listen to us." she sputters out through a mouthful of biscuit.

"Hmph!" Cynthia grunts as she carries her biscuit and coffee back to the other room. "If the authorities won't listen, the media will. And when the media creates panic, the authorities will have to act."

The media... that's not a bad idea, I think to myself as I take my spot back on the bed with a biscuit in one hand and coffee in the other. *Of course, we couldn't reveal ourselves to the media, and I doubt they would rock the boat in this situation without a reliable source.*

Mom follows me and sits sideways on the foot of the bed between Alice and me. "What if I call the Department of Homeland Security and leave a message for Agent Morgan? I'll tell them I am calling with an anonymous tip regarding a case he is working on and leave the number for the burner phone."

Steve sits on the side of the other bed listening. "I don't know about that. I am pretty sure your location can still be tracked when you make a call. I think people usually ditch those phones after making a call they don't want to be traced."

"But what about the call to Kate?" Mom asks.

"I was worried about that. But Kate would have to alert somebody that Ellie called her in order for someone to know a call needed to be tracked. I get the feeling Ellie is pretty confident that Kate will keep that call to herself." Steve gives me a questioning look like he is searching for confirmation.

A loud, heavy thud jars the door, making my heart stop for a second as it somersaults into my stomach. I spring up from the pillow, and my spine stiffens. My eyes dart to Steve, then to Alice and Mom. Three more pounding knocks vibrate through the room. Teresa, Eileen, and Cynthia appear in the joining doorway.

Steve jumps to his feet and grabs one of the guns as the rest of us stare, unmoving, at the door.

"Jillian, I know you are in there. Open up."

"You have got to be kidding me." Mom mumbles, pushing up from the bed. She strides to the door and cracks it open. "Tom, what..."

"How could you do this? I know I took off without giving you a good explanation, but when I sent Dukakis to the house, I didn't mean for you to run away with him. Where is that no good, homewrecker anyway?" Dad fumes pushing through the door. "Dukak..." Dad's mouth hangs open as his puffy, red eyes scan the room, stopping on each of us.

Mom clears her throat as she closes the door behind Dad. "What were you saying, Tom?"

Dad's head sinks into his shoulders. "Well, it would seem that I might have jumped to the wrong conclusion." His voice is thick and brittle. "Ellie, Eileen, you're safe." He grabs Eileen, who is standing between the small table and the bed, and squeezes her in a hug. "Oh, thank you, Lord." He releases her and leans over the bed, pulling me up into his chest.

Mom spins around with her hands on her hips. "Tom, what do you mean showing up making accusations? You are the one who called Dukakis, and then you come in here calling him ugly names."

"I know." Dad turns toward her.

"I cannot believe that you actually thought..." Mom takes a step closer. She squints her eyes as she leans in toward Dad's face. "Tom Hatcher," she utters in a barely audible tone, "have you been crying?" Her eyes glisten with moisture.

"Jillian, I have a tendency to think I am protecting you by not burdening you with my worries. Instead of talking to you and asking for your help, I make up my own plan of action, which usually ends up in disaster." His voice trails off.

"Like going two years without speaking and taking off

without giving me an inkling of a clue where you are going?" Mom prods with a touch of sarcasm.

"Yes, exactly like that." He blows a puff of air out of his mouth. "Obviously, if I had consulted you, I would have been here to help our girls." Dad shakes his head in disbelief. "How did you and Dukakis get them out of there?"

"We didn't. God did. We just happened to be in the parking lot when they escaped. And again, that was God's doing. Because they were in dire need of a getaway car, and one needed immediate medical attention." Mom tilts her head and crosses her arms. "I am curious… how did you know I was here."

"Oh, I put this little tracking device on your handbag. Since they took the girls and Steve, I had to make sure I could find you if something happened while I was gone."

"As thoughtful and comforting as it is to know you care that much, if someone forced me from our home, do you think I would have been allowed to take my handbag?" Mom presses.

"I think we have already established that I do not think my decisions through, Jillian." Dad pulls Mom into his arms. "I'm sorry. I'm sorry for taking off on a wild goose chase. I'm sorry for not being there when you needed me. And I'm sorry for showing up here acting like a lunatic. Just know that I only acted like a lunatic because I love you."

"I love you too, Tom." Mom smiles at him and kisses his nose. "Now, will you sit down and tell me what was so important that you took off?"

"Of course, but first, I have a few more apologies to make." Dad gives a little wave as he raises the volume of his voice. "Ummm." He clears his throat. "I owe everyone an apology… especially you, Dukakis." Dad's expression softens, and he walks over to Dukakis with his hand extended. "Sorry, I let my imagination get carried away with me. I appreciate you taking care of Jillian and being there for my family."

Dukakis shakes Dad's hand. "No worries, Tom. The stress is getting to us all."

Dad sits on the edge of the bed by Gerald's gurney. "As you

all already know, I was one of President Denali's legal advisors, and since Kutchins was Denali's vice president, I am quite familiar with him as well. And honestly, this whole executive order thing does not sound like Kutchins." Dad leans over with his elbows on his thighs and presses his hands against the sides of his face. "I felt like my heart was being ripped from my chest when those officers dragged Eileen out of our house. A father is supposed to be able to protect his children, but it was like the day Denali faked your kidnapping. I couldn't stop them. And then we tried to warn Ellie and Steve, but it was too late. When I saw Ellie lying on the kitchen floor, the ground beneath my feet seemed to crumble away. It felt as if I was floating outside my body, and I could hear Denali's voice in my head. It was that speech he was spouting off to me all those years ago, detailing his evil plan to form his personal army and create a new world that didn't know God." Dad starts to rock back and forth as he talks.

Déjà vu... Dad... what's going on? Prickles tingle up and down my spine, and goosebumps pop up on my arms as questions churn in my brain. *The day that Dad came clean about knowing Denali's plan, he sat on the kitchen floor and rocked back and forth. Dad, what do you know? What have you been hiding?*

"When Jillian and I drove home with Herb and Spencer after I watched my other baby get treated like a violent convict, Denali stayed in my head. I don't think I spoke a word the entire trip."

"No, you did not." Mom clarifies.

Dad wraps his arms around his torso as he rocks faster and faster. "His voice got louder and louder. It was so real that I remember swerving when the sound of Denali's fist hit his desk."

I glance over at Mom and notice the blood has drained from her face and her mouth is hanging like a broken hinge.

Dad squeezes his eyes tight, causing the skin on his cheeks to crinkle up. "And then I rememb-"

"Oh. Oh no!" Teresa squeals from the other room. "No!"

Steve grabs the gun again.

"Everyone, get in here quick." Cynthia wails as we are already piling through the small adjoining doorway.

Teresa, Cynthia, and Eileen are sitting on the foot of one of the beds leaning on each other with their eyes fixed on the small television hanging on the wall. Steve had already burst through the door with the gun, so he moves on around to the other side of the room. I follow with my hand clutching the back of his shirt as the news anchor's voice blares from the tiny flat screen.

"So many lives lost, and at this point, authorities appear to be stumped. How could this many acts of violence occur at exactly ten thirty-five this morning at different locations across the city? The question of a terrorist attack has been raised, and even though the Department of Homeland Security refuses to release any details, they have assured the media that this was not the work of a terrorist organization. Just to reiterate for those that have just joined us, multiple attacks in various locations across New York City have left behind a magnitude of deaths and injuries. Right now, the authorities are not releasing any numbers, but we have been told that at least nine attacks have been reported, including one at a retail store, a subway station, a ferry, three restaurants, a convenience store, a public transportation bus, and on a corner in a popular shopping district. As officers are working to respond to so many incidents, the exact locations are not being released at this time. However, one of our reporters was able to speak with a witness to one of the attacks. Jim, could you tell us how the witness described the attack?"

"Yes, Walt." The screen splits, moving the news anchor to one side and showing Jim, the reporter, with a line of shops in the background on the other side. "I spoke with the witness outside the retail store where one of the attacks occurred. The lady stated that the store was fairly crowded. She first saw the attacker when he was staring at the clothing on the opposite side of the rack from her. She remembered that he had this blank look on his face, almost like he was in a trance, but she detailed that there was no behavior that would set off any alarms, so she didn't think anything of it. A few minutes later, she said she had moved on to a table of sweaters, and that is when the sound of metal crashing to the floor startled her. When she turned her head toward the sound, she saw the man in front of the rack that was flipped over on the floor. Her description of his appearance was rather frightful. She stated that his jaws were rigid, and his teeth were bared with blood dripping from the corner of his mouth. His eyes were wide and unblinking. And then, Walt, the scene this woman recounts as she hid behind the table of sweaters reminded me of nothing less than a horror movie. She detailed how this man ripped the metal rods from the rack and began swinging them at shoppers in the store. Due to the graphic nature of her description, all that I can share is that this woman witnessed multiple people being bludgeoned to death before several store employees were able to subdue him. Thankfully the witness was not physically injured."

"Thanks, Jim." The image of the news anchor fills the screen again. "Please stay with us. We will keep you posted as more information surfaces."

Teresa stands up and clicks the television off. Without a word, she sits back down at the foot of the bed.

"I know it's dangerous, but we have to get back in close range to the facility," Alice takes a step towards the door to our room, "and we have to do it fast." She stops with a look of disbelief on her face.

"What? Why?" Gerald shrieks as he leans against the casing of the doorway. His body jerks in alarm.

"Gerald, what are you doing up, and how did you get across the room?" Alice interrogates in a scolding voice.

"I wanted to see what was happening, so I hopped on one leg." Gerald returns the interrogation. "Why are we going back to the facility? Do we have a death wish?"

"I think I can use that tablet to connect to the network.

Eckert said the advisor sent him a timetable. Hopefully, it's in his email, and I can access it." Alice motions to us. "Come on. If we can get that timetable, maybe we can stop what is happening next. And we would have proof."

Gerald balances on one leg and jerks Alice into a hug. "You are brilliant."

"You all do know it's three hours back to the facility, right?" Dukakis asks.

"I know we might not have that much time, but we don't have a choice." Alice runs her fingers through her hair.

"I am going to have to take out a second mortgage when I get back to Virginia." Dukakis mumbles.

"What?" Dad asks, and then his tone drops, and he sighs. "Oh. Dukakis, that van uses gasoline. I can't imagine how much you have spent on fuel driving out here." Dad steps over and puts his hand on Dukakis' shoulder. "Don't worry. I'll pay you back every penny and then some. After all, you have done all of this to take care of my family." Dad taps his chin. "Too bad we couldn't all fit in my little hydrocar."

Mom half-coughs and half-chuckles. "Tom, what do you mean all of us? You barely fit in that car by yourself." She looks at Dukakis. "I'm not kidding. I tried to ride with him in that thing once, and my face was squished against the side glass."

"Make fun of it if you want, but that little thing can go forever on a tank of hydro fuel." Dad says with a smirk. "But since we have no choice but to take the gas-guzzling van, we will use my credit account to fill up."

"It's okay." Dukakis covers his mouth, but I can tell he is smiling from the dimples in his cheeks. "The authorities are more likely to be tracking your location than mine. We better use my credit account for now." Dukakis pats Dad on the back. "It's your daughters that are missing from the facility. I'm sure they are watching for you to use your thumbprint. Speaking of which, when did you use it last?"

"Missouri, right before I crossed the state line." Dad replies with certainty.

Alice helps Gerald into the other room. "Spencer!" she yells.

Steve and I are right behind Alice and Gerald.

"Oh, brother," Steve pinches the bridge of his nose, "this is going to be a trying trip. Ten people in a van with a monkey on a sugar rush."

Spencer is sitting on the floor with three empty doughnut boxes... boxes that held a dozen each.

"Hey, Mom," Steve hollers to Cynthia. "I think Spencer wants to ride up front with you and Dukakis."

Gerald stops halfway across the room. "Alice."

She turns to look at him. "What's wrong?"

"Something has been bothering me." Gerald pauses for a second. "You know how you all think the lesions were caused by the reprimanding, and the reason we don't have the scarring is because the reprimanding didn't work on us?"

"Yeah..." Alice drags out her response.

"Well, the first time I went through it, I wasn't really saved. The reprimanding did work on me. Why don't I have the lesions?"

I already thought about that and came up with my own theory, but now I am curious as to what Alice will say.

Alice takes his hand. "Gerald, I think you don't have the lesions because now you have accepted Christ as your savior. You have accepted His gift of salvation, and as 1 Peter 2:24 says, "... by whose stripes ye were healed." She smiles at him. "You've been made new."

Gerald lifts his head a little higher, and a smile forms on his face. "Yes, I have."

Chapter Twenty

S ince Gerald decided to leave the gurney behind at the motel, Dukakis raised the seats back up, and now the ride is a bit more comfortable. When we came out of the motel, Dad was worried about the cameras in the parking lot of the complex and the possibility that authorities could be looking for Dukakis's van, but Dukakis had already given it a makeover. The 'Manna from Heaven Pizza Company' logos that were on each side had been replaced with magnetic signs that read 'Morning Glory Photography'. A giant monarch butterfly hovers at the corner of each sign, and an array of giant flower decals cover the van concealing the black racing stripe.

I thought Dad was going to hyperventilate when he saw the van's new look. He told Dukakis the goal was not to be noticed, and that people could see that thing coming from a mile away. But Dukakis politely informed him that the authorities would never expect them to be in something that drew so much attention.

Apparently, since Dukakis and Mom had been planning to try and get into the facility, they had stopped at a car decal shop on the way, hoping to find something that would help them get the van up to the parking lot. It seems they had quite a few logos that had been ordered and never picked up, so Dukakis got a good deal on an array of ways to change the look of the van. However, they had purchased the lettering for 'Manna from Heaven Pizza Company' to go with a giant pizza sticker. Mom thought it would be something only we would recognize.

The problem is that a full-size van is not that common, especially with gas prices through the roof and with the government pushing smaller hydro fuel cars. Of course, we are in a van covered in flower stickers, so I am guessing the rarity of a full-size van is the least of our worries.

Dad ended up following us in his HydroMini. He thought if he stayed on our bumper, it would help conceal our license plate, just in case cameras in the parking lot of the facility had gotten a clear picture of it. Besides that, he didn't want to leave his car behind. He asked Dukakis to pull over and let him in the van when we get close.

Cynthia is in the passenger seat again, and Spencer started on her lap, but now he is driving everyone crazy, bouncing back and forth over the seats. Mom and Eileen are sitting on the first row, Steve and I are on the second row, and Alice, Gerald, and Teresa are on the third row with Herb and Claude in the cubby behind them.

"Hey," I pat Steve's knee, "I wish you would say something. I don't think you have muttered a word since we left."

"Sorry," he murmurs, looking straight ahead. "I can't stop thinking that we should have or could have at least tried to do something that might have prevented all those people from dying."

"We had no idea what he was doing or where it was going to happen." I say, wishing I could convince myself and get rid of the guilt. "Remember, all we heard Dr. Eckert say was the process would begin. How could we have possibly known that 'process' meant mass murder, especially when he was speaking to the president of the United States? Well, I suppose that position hasn't exactly been credible considering the last person who was in that office, but this is a new president."

"If someone is to be blamed, it's me." Alice says in a lamenting tone. "It hit my mind last ni... well, I guess it would have been almost sunrise when I was looking at that tablet. I should have pushed to go back to the facility then... but I was afraid." She stares out the side window. Moisture glistens in streams down her cheeks. "Gerald... I could have lost him. And the thought of getting near that place petrified me, so I kept trying to find something in the stored files." She wipes her face. "If only I could turn back time, maybe we could have saved those people."

"Alright now," Dukakis looks in the rear-view mirror and speaks in a firm voice. "No one here is to blame for what happened. This is on Dr. Eckert and whoever else conspired to set this up. No more pity parties. It is a three-hour trip from the motel. By the time you hacked the email, we notified authorities, and someone hopefully listened, it would have been too late. And, Alice," his voice softens, "Ellie is right. We had no idea something of this magnitude was in the making. I mean, this whole thing has so many sides, and honestly, until the whole virtual demon conversation, I was still a little skeptical that we were overreacting and that maybe the president's order was legitimately intended to protect civilians. But now, it's obvious we are fighting against a powerful dark force, and we can't battle this evil if we are looking back. Remember what happened to Lot's wife in the Bible? When she looked back, she turned into a pillar of salt. In the same way, if we stay focused on what we could have done, we become paralyzed, and we can't accomplish what God needs us to. Paul wrote in his letter to the Philippians in chapter four, verses thirteen and fourteen, '...but this one thing I do, forgetting those things which are behind, and reaching forth unto those things which are before, I press toward the mark for the prize of the high calling of God in Christ Jesus.'" Dukakis pauses. "The words you heard from Eckert, 'process' and 'timetable', are clear indicators that more is to come. So, let's focus on stopping what's ahead."

"Wow," Gerald whistles, "that was a good sermon. I am ready to go into battle."

We all roll our eyes toward Gerald.

"Don't look at me like that. I'm serious. That analogy to Lot's wife... that's what it feels like to look back... a statue that can't move in any direction." He bites his lower lip. "Alice, how close do we have to get to the facility for you to access the network?"

"I'm not sure... if I could get close to that security building by the parking lot, maybe." Alice pulls out the tablet.

"Haven't you already checked out all the files on there?" I twist and peer down over the back of the seat at the tablet.

"I'm still hoping to uncover a deleted file or something." Alice slides the back down, revealing the keyboard. "Plus, I downloaded some articles that I wanted to look at using the motel Wi-Fi."

"I am wondering if I should call Kate again."

"Why?" Steve's voice deflates. "Like you said, she is only one agent, and no one is going to take her word for it, especially if it could harm the reputation of President Kutchins."

"Right now, the authorities probably have no clue what avenue to explore in those murders." I lean my head back against the seat. "But you're right. It doesn't matter what I say to her, without hard evidence in her hands, I am setting her up for a pink slip."

"We're getting close." Dukakis interjects. "I would hold off on calling her until we see what Alice comes up with."

"Pardon me, but this monkey is out of control. I could inject him with a bit of tranquilizer." Claude suggests in a calm, monotone voice.

"No." Steve's body jerks, and his head bolts around toward the back of the van. "Spencer, come here."

Spencer bounces over the seat in the same second that Dukakis slams on the brake. His little body flings to the front and slams into the center console between the driver and passenger seats.

"Nice signal." Dukakis puffs, and then he glances down at Spencer. "Sorry, buddy. I guess that's payback for last night." he says with a chuckle.

Mom scoops Spencer up and hands him back to Steve.

"You have to sit still." Steve scolds as he buckles the safety belt around Spencer on the seat between us.

"Wow, he is young there." Teresa utters to Alice behind me.

"What?" Alice's tone reflects surprise at Teresa's comment.

"I'm sorry. I didn't mean to interrupt your reading." Teresa hesitates. "The photo caught my attention. I've never seen a picture of him that young. He looks so different."

"You know Mordecai?"

What? It is probably rude of me to turn around, but my interest is peaked.

"Mordecai. Who's Mordecai?" Teresa pulls her eyebrows together in a look of confusion.

"Mordecai Crawley." Alice enunciates slowly. "Who did you think it was a photo of?"

"I have never heard of Mordecai Crawley, but that is Earl in that photo." Teresa asserts with certainty.

"Say what?" Alice holds the screen closer to her face.

"That is a picture of Earl Eckert." Teresa repeats herself.

Now, Steve is peering over the back of his seat, and Gerald is leaning in close to Alice with his eyes locked on the screen.

Teresa points to the image. "His hair is black in the photo, instead of gray, and he has had some dental work done because his front teeth are straight now. But see the mole on the side of his head and the shape and color of his eyes. And... Earl has a birthmark on his neck. If you look closely, right above his shirt collar in the photo, you can see the edge of it."

"I'll take your word for it, but I don't see the resemblance." Gerald stretches his leg out to the side as he shifts to sit upright again.

Alice turns the screen to face Steve and me.

Those eyes. There is no mistaking those penetrating eyes. I don't have to examine the photo any further. "Teresa's right. Well, obviously, she would know better than any of us," I stumble over my words, "but those are definitely his eyes."

"Is it possible that he could have been brought in like Teresa and had his memory erased?" Steve questions.

A few seconds of silence pass as everyone seems to be pondering Steve's theory.

Alice gives a quick shake of her head. "I don't think so. He has all these files on here that belong to Mordecai Crawley. Why would he have these and not know his real identity?"

"Maybe he found out when President Denali was exposed. That's when Teresa learned who she was." Gerald suggests in a matter-of-fact tone.

"It's possible." Alice puckers her face and twists her mouth to the side. "Nah. Why would he still go by Earl Eckert?"

"Hey, Alice. We are not that far away now." Dukakis calls from the front. "What's the plan?"

Alice straightens and stretches her neck as she looks toward Dukakis. "I've been thinking. Why don't we try the state park? There are a lot of hiking trails, and either Acorn Valley or Cougar's Shadow should put us close to the facility."

"That's a relief. I like your thinking. I don't see going back up the road into the complex parking lot working out all that well, especially in broad daylight… what in the world? What is Tom doing? This is a no-passing zone."

Dad has merged into the lane for oncoming traffic and is moving up beside the van.

Mom glances out the window, and with a loud gasp, she covers her face with her hands.

Dad has his passenger window down and appears to be yelling at Dukakis.

Dukakis rolls down his window. "What?"

Dad is waving his right arm and saying something.

"Okay." Dukakis's window slides back up. "Tom said to turn on the radio."

Mom uncovers her face and watches Dad slow a bit and get back behind us.

Dukakis scans for a station. "I don't even remember the last time I turned this radio on." he remarks as the frequencies skip ahead from one roar of static to another. He stops when a voice cuts through the airwaves.

"... not releasing any details regarding the number of fatalities. Again, for those that just tuned in, some sort of mysterious rioting broke out on multiple crowded beaches along the southeast coast, resulting in numerous deaths and injuries. Authorities are not releasing any information at this time. However, local reporters already on the scene at three of these locations have spoken with witnesses, and strangely, the individual accounts are almost identical and occurred simultaneously around 2:00 p.m. eastern standard time. According to these witnesses, a white van pulled onto the beach, and a group of men, estimated to be in their mid-twenties, exited through the back doors. The white van then drove away, leaving the group of men who started yelling and physically harassing people on the beach... Oh, wait... I think we may have one of those reporters on the air with us now. Hello... John... are you there? John?"

"Yes, I'm here. As you can hear, there is a lot of chaos around me, but I have a gentleman with me that watched the whole scene unfold from inside the snack bar at a hotel pool overlooking the beach. Sir, you said that a group of about six men got out of the back of a van. Can you brief us on what took place after that?"

"I heard a lot of yelling, and when I looked to see what all the commotion was, I saw a white van driving away from a group of men, all wearing the same red long sleeve shirts. I was pretty far away, but I could still see that the men were physically harassing people on the beach, and some started to fight back."

"Physically harassing? Could you elaborate on that?"

"Well, one of the men was shoving a bunch of teenagers that had been playing some kind of game with a ball. Another one jerked up an umbrella and ran down the beach swinging it at people. I even saw one dragging a woman through the sand by her hair. Anyway, I grabbed my phone, but someone by the pool was already talking to the 911 operator. In a matter of minutes, it was pure pandemonium. Fights had erupted everywhere... and not small fights. I'm talking huge mobs swinging at each other. People were getting trampled. Women were screaming and crying and running, trying to pull their children away to safety. Bodies were flying through the air from the midst of the rioting masses. I've never seen anything like it."

"Had you ever seen any of those men before?"

"No, John, I hadn't. But I presume they must belong to some local gang. I thought all this gang stuff had ended, but I can't think of any other explanation."

"Sir, I am so sorry that you had to witness such a tragic scene. I can't even begin to imagine how frightening it must have been. Thank you for taking the time to share your story."

Dukakis clicks off the radio. "I've heard enough. President Kutchins, Dr. Eckert, or whoever is behind this sick plan has got to be stopped." The right signal clicks, and he steers the van into a parking lot. "This little shopping hub looks busy. We'll pick up Tom here."

I look over my shoulder at Alice. Her eyes meet mine, and I can tell she is thinking about that weird anger experiment too.

~

DUKAKIS PULLS the van into a parking space near the trailhead at Acorn Valley. "I cannot believe we broke into a state park. I need something sweet."

"Relax, Dukakis. We didn't break into the park." Dad passes

a candy bar to Dukakis from a box behind the seat. "We entered without paying."

Dukakis's wide eyes appear in the rearview mirror. "That robot did something to the thumbprint pad and opened the gate. Hence, we broke into a state park."

Dad puffs. "Well, if it makes you feel better, we will pay them back later with interest. This is sort of an extenuating circumstance. We can't use our thumbprints this close to the complex, and more people are going to die if Alice can't get that timetable."

Alice sighs. "I still can't connect. I will have to hike a little closer on the trail." She scoots forward in her seat and starts to cross over Gerald.

"Alice, please, no." Gerald clutches her forearm. "I don't have a good feeling about this, and I can't go with you."

Alice smiles at him. "I'll be fine. I am much safer out on that trail than you will be here in the van. Besides, Ellie will go with me."

"At least take a gun." Gerald calls after her.

"I can't. This is a state park." she mutters back.

I climb out of the van behind Alice. We only get a few yards away when Steve, Eileen, and Teresa are right on our heels.

"Do you know which way to go?" Steve asks.

"I think so." Alice steps off the trail into the woods.

"Oh no," Steve's voice drops, and he speaks under his breath. "Please tell me she is not leaving the trail."

"I'm in the network." Alice drops to the ground and starts typing. Then, she jumps up and takes off again. "I lost it."

She is walking fast, and I hustle to keep up with her. Leaves crunch behind me as Steve, Teresa, and Eileen try to stay close.

"Alice," Steve calls to her in a concerned tone, "I don't think it's a good idea to leave the trail. This turns into private property somewhere."

"I don't care," she voices back, trudging on into the woods. "I have to connect to the network, and lives are at stake." Alice digs her heels in and comes to a swift stop in front of a chain-link fence with three strands of barbed wire running parallel to each other along the top.

"Don't touch it," Steve warns. "It is charged with electricity."

Alice drops to the ground and starts typing again. "It's okay. I'm in again."

Steve, Eileen, Teresa, and I stand behind her, darting our eyes around, surveying the area.

"Alright, I have the IP address of the router." Her fingertips fly across the pull-out keyboard. "I'm going as fast as I can." her voice cracks. "Just keep a lookout."

Steve turns in a circle. He stops and freezes with his eyes fixed on a patch of thick brush that is smothering the trunks of a grouping of tall pine trees on the other side of the fence.

Holding my breath, I stare, trying to see what has caught his attention, but I can't decide if the leaves are moving or if it is my imagination creating something to be alarmed about.

Steve pivots his head back to Alice.

I guess it was my imagination.

"Alice, how much longer?" Steve's voice quavers as he opens and closes his hands into fists by his side. "I have an uneasy feeling. Something's not right."

"Almost done with all I can do from here." Alice's cheeks are bright red and sweat beads stand at attention across her forehead. "From the subject lines of these emails, we might have hit the jackpot. The problem is they are all encrypted. I am copying them to the hard drive, and hopefully, we can find a way to unscramble them."

"That shouldn't be a problem. Just hurry and copy them." Steve's eyes dart back to the heavy brush.

Stress lines form wrinkles above Eileen's brows. "Steve, what is it?"

Steve lifts his arm to the side and nudges me back. "Ellie. Teresa. Eileen. Get back to the trail. Now."

I know he is trying to protect me, but I can't leave him and Alice. I take a step backward as the shuffle of Eileen and Teresa's feet fades behind me. My muscles stiffen, not letting me go any farther without them. My eyes follow Steve's gaze through the holes in the chain-link fence. Small piles of leaves rise off the ground amid the cluster of trees.

"Alice, go!" Steve yells as he pulls her up from the ground and pushes us both toward the trail. "Run!" He keeps us in front of him as we weave between the trees.

The spray of bullets cracks and pelts into the trees and dirt all around us. My legs tingle and I force each stride, even though I can feel my knees giving beneath me. *Lord, please help us.* I try to take slow deep breaths, but my chest is so tight that I can't fill my lungs.

Another spray of ammunition flies from the direction of the trail, and footsteps pound the ground toward us. Mom and Cynthia burst through the dense shrubbery, moving past us with guns aimed out in front of them. Mom is in front with one of the automatic rifles, pelting round after round in the distance behind us, and Cynthia is only a step behind her with a pistol. A second later, Dad appears through the brush, firing his own barrage of shots from the other rifle.

The sounds of a raging battle slack off as the storm of bullets fades to a sprinkle and then disappears. We barrel onto the trail. Worry slows my feet and pulls my head around to peer over my shoulder. My slowed pace causes Steve to stumble into me, and frustration fills his face. But I glimpse Mom, Cynthia, and Dad hastening up the trail in the distance behind us, so I turn back around and sprint full speed before Steve has a chance to voice his frustration.

"The van…" Steve points as he gasps for a breath.

Dukakis has already backed out of the parking space and is sitting with the engine running and the side door open. We tear across the pavement and leap through the open door. Gerald grabs Alice's hand and helps her onto the back row between him and Teresa. As Steve and I slide onto the second bench, my heart sinks into my stomach. *Spencer. Where is Spencer?* Then a faint, soft, melodic hum fills the air. My head turns, following the sound to the back of the van where Herb is rocking Spencer.

"See, there they are. Everyone is okey-dokey." Herb soothes.

Spencer lifts his head, and the second his eyes fall on Steve, he wriggles from Herb's grip and soars across the seats into Steve's arms.

Mom and Cynthia climb onto the front bench next to Eileen, and Dukakis hits the button to close the side door. Dad jumps into the passenger seat but doesn't get the gun all the way in before he closes the door. When it hits the barrel, the door bounces back open. Dad reaches for the door with his right hand at the same time that Dukakis slams his foot on the gas. The door swings open wider pulling Dad off balance.

"Tom!" Mom shrieks and thrusts her body off the bench toward the passenger seat.

Just as Dad's body leans out of the van, he catches the grab handle above the door with his left hand and pulls himself back inside. Dukakis is already tearing out of the parking lot when Dad jerks the door closed.

Mom falls back onto the bench with her hand pressed against her chest.

A loud groan flows out of Dad's mouth as he exhales. "You couldn't let me get the door closed first?" he grumbles at Dukakis.

"Sorry. Since the van nor any of us are bulletproof, I thought we were in a bit of a hurry." Dukakis replies with a hint of sarcasm, but then his tone softens. "I really am sorry. I thought you were in."

Alice leans against the seatback hugging the tablet to her chest.

With his eyes filled with tears, Gerald pulls her head over onto his shoulder and presses his lips to her forehead. "Alice, I love y-you." he stammers on the last word.

"I know you do." Alice tilts her face up toward his. "I love you too."

"You don't understand how scared I was when I heard those shots." Gerald turns his face toward the window, and in a nonchalant motion, he swipes the knuckle of his index finger beneath each of his eyes.

Alice snuggles her head beneath his chin. "Oh… oh, yes, I do." She points to his leg.

Dukakis's heavy eyes glance back at us in the rearview mirror. His face is flushed, and he dabs the perspiration running off his forehead with a napkin. "So, now what? Did we get what we needed?"

Alice sits up. "I'm not sure. I copied the email files, but they are encrypted. I have to find a way to unscramble the data."

"I told you that wouldn't be a problem." Steve reassures. "All we have to do is plug the tablet into Herb."

"Dukakis," Alice's tone fills with urgency, "we need a safe place to stop the van so we can study these emails."

"I'm on it." Dukakis says as the van accelerates. "Maybe we can go back to that shopping hub where we left Tom's toy car."

"Ha-ha." Dad retorts with his nose tipped up in the air. "Go ahead and make your jokes, but it cost me almost nothing to drive over halfway across the country."

Sirens wail in the distance. "New plan." Dukakis veers off on a side road. "We have to find a place for a van makeover." After a few more cuts and turns, the van bounces down a narrow gravel path and screeches to a halt. Thrusting the transmission into park, Dukakis flings his door open. "Come on, Tom. Help me."

Dad climbs out, and Steve passes Spencer to my mom and exits out the side door to speed up the process.

My heart is pounding too hard to sit here, so after a minute, I leap from the van too and start peeling off decals. *At least I can't hear the sirens anymore.*

Dukakis hurries behind us, affixing new logos that read 'Open Road Shuttle Service'. Then he unrolls a yellow and black checkered stripe, and Steve helps him stretch and smooth it down the center of the hood.

I notice Dad open the passenger door and slam it back. He jogs to the front and starts ripping off the front license plate.

"What are you doing?" Dukakis asks, peering over Dad's shoulder.

"Putting on new license plates." Dad pulls the clips off and removes the Virginia plate. He picks up a new one off of the ground next to him, places it on the frame, and presses the clips on.

"New Mexico?" Dukakis's volume rises a few notches. "Where on earth did you get New Mexico plates?"

"I borrowed them from a motor home back in the state park."

"And you don't think they will notice their license plates are missing and report it?" Dukakis rattles off so fast that his words almost run together.

"Probably not. It was hooked up in the campground, and by the looks of their supplies, they are going to be camping a while." Dad stands up and heads to the back of the van. The rest of us follow. He kneels and starts replacing the rear plate. "Chill out, Dukakis. We will return the plates before the people ever know they are missing. I'm sure when we explain why we took them, the folks will understand."

As we climb back in the van, Steve drops onto the seat beside me and then pops back up. "Hey, Teresa. Trade seats with me. We can check out those emails while we are moving."

Chapter Twenty-One

"It is so nice to be needed for something besides house cleaning and monkey sitting." Herb boasts. "I mean, it's not that I don't enjoy cooking, cleaning, and singing lullabies, but I feel that I could be using all this information stored in my hard drive for greater purposes."

Steve reaches over the back seat and plugs the tablet into Herb's control panel. "Well, if you can unscramble these encrypted emails, maybe you can get a job with the Department of Homeland Security. If any of those officers know the truth about what is happening in that facility and are keeping quiet, there may be a few job openings."

The van moves forward, then backward... forward then backward... forward then backward... Dukakis struggles to get the huge full-size van turned around on the little gravel road. With every shift in direction, the van jerks.

Alice tries to type on the tablet's pull-out keyboard. "It's a little hard to type like this, Dukakis."

He finally gets the van turned around, but then he pulls to the side as much as he can since it is only a one-lane drive. "I'm going to park right here until you do your thing with that computer. Nobody is around, and if someone does show up, I'll say we are lost." Dukakis pulls out a candy bar and twirls his hand in the air. "Now have at it."

"While you guys are checking that, I'm going to see if we are on the news." Dad clicks on the radio and turns the volume low. But within five seconds, he is cranking up the sound, and as the words of horror flow through the speakers, a solemn hush falls over us.

"… a morbid scene for authorities responding to what appears to be the result of road rage incidents across the country that have all occurred on crowded rush-hour freeways. In Los Angeles, a tractor-trailer entered the Santa Ana Freeway going the wrong direction. We don't have many details at this point, but we've been told that several cars veered out of the way on the exit 133 ramp as the truck built up speed. It then entered the rush hour traffic that was nearly at a standstill and wiped out multiple vehicles before coming to a stop. The driver jumped from the truck, ranting and yelling at other drivers. Another driver pulled a gun, and from the description given to us by a witness, this was an illegal automatic weapon. From there, all we know is that this spurred other drivers to pull weapons, fights escalated, and hundreds of people were killed, some from the spray of stray bullets. What makes this story even more unbelievable and tragic is that similar incidents occurred at relatively the same time during rush hour traffic on Interstate 27 in New York, Interstate 95 in Miami, Interstate 4 in Orlando, Interstate 40 in Nashville, Interstate 95 in Southern Connecticut, and other reports are still coming in. Speculations and theories are filling the web as to what could be spawning the horrific madness that has consumed so many locations across America today. We have seen speculations about terrorists and cults, but at this point, remember these are rumors. Nothing has been released or confirmed as to the cause of this sudden chaos."

Dad jabs the radio button, and the reporter's voice is gone. "Alice, hurry. We need something… anything that we will get the authorities to believe us."

Alice types away and glides her middle finger across the touchpad.

Gerald whistles. "Whoa, that's a lot of folders. Are all of those emails?"

"I didn't have time to pilfer through the folders, so I copied everything associated with Eckert. I found two different email accounts that he had accessed using the network. I am guessing one is personal and one is professional… maybe." she adds, staring at the screen.

"How about that one… *Presidential Correspondence?*" Gerald points.

I lean my head over the back of my seat and strain to get a glimpse as Alice taps the keyboard. A list of emails appears. Alice clicks on the first one, which appears to be from the White House with *Follow Up on Meeting* in the subject line.

Alice's eyes flick back and forth as she scans the screen. Her mouth moves as if she is reading to herself, and then, after clearing her throat, she reads aloud. "Dr. Eckert. Thank you for accepting our proposal and agreeing to head up the research in determining the cause for what appears to be brain malfunctions in my predecessor's Soldiers Against Crime trainees. Since you were a primary overseer in his program, it seems only natural that you would be the best candidate in pinpointing the cause. Please respond as soon as you have any findings to report. Sincerely, Office of the President of the United States."

Alice glides her finger across the screen. "Okay, here is where he replied several days later. 'President Kutchins or To Whom It May Concern. I have conducted a CT scan on the perpetrators that you had escorted to my lab. Lesions in the area of the lateral septum were present and consistent in each of the subjects. In our meeting, you theorized that this could be an aftereffect of cryogenic preservation. However, I have noted that at least one of the perpetrators was never cryogenically frozen. Of course, no conclusive studies have been performed, but just upon my initial observations surrounding these specific subjects, I believe the lesions are a result of a virtual reprimanding procedure used for behavior modification in the trainees. Please advise as to how you wish to continue. Sincerely, Dr. E. Eckert Ph.D."

"So, he knew what was causing the lesions before that Executive Order was ever released." Eileen notes with a hint of hostility.

"It appears so." Alice sighs and taps the touchpad. "Okay, on to the next one." She takes a deep breath and starts reading. "Dr. Eckert, I wanted to inform you that I will be issuing an Executive Order within the next few weeks requiring all parties that were held in President Denali's Soldiers Against Crime training facility to return to Cheyenne Mountain Complex. A member of the Presidents' Council of Advisors on Science and Technology, Dr. Damien Seaver, will be reaching out to you with detailed instructions. From this point forward, Dr. Seaver will be your contact in regard to this project. He and I have discussed the uncertainty of this volatile situation, and he has some excellent ideas on how to control these sporadic aftershocks left behind by President Denali's program in a way that will create a better quality of life for the citizens of our country. He and I both agree that, considering your familiarity with the subjects and the complexity, you are the one to head up this operation. You should hear from Dr. Seaver today as preparations must begin immediately. However, in the interest of national security, I will follow up with you personally as needed. Sincerely, Craig T. Kutchins, President of the United States of America."

"Steve, you're a science and tech person." Gerald stretches his neck and peers over the top of Alice's head. "Have you ever heard of this guy?"

"No," Steve shrugs. "But that doesn't mean anything. I'm sure there are lots of great scientists that I haven't heard of."

"Well, here is an email from him. Let's see what he has to say." Alice lifts her leg and rests her foot on the edge of the seat, using her knee to prop up the tablet. "Dr. Earl Eckert. First, I want you to know how pleased I am to have the opportunity to work with you on this project. I am impressed by your research and the developments that you have made in the areas of mind control and behavior modification. I have thoroughly studied the progress that you have made through the years, and I know that you are familiar with my work as well. I believe this current situation has presented itself for a reason. While the side effects left behind by President Denali's little scheme are tragic, I am certain that a treasure can be found in the midst of this misfortune. By combining the advances that you have made in your research with my extensive studies on primitive war and its effects on a sustainable population, I am confident we can utilize what now appears to be a problem to create better living conditions for the citizens of our country. As for our plan of action, I am currently collaborating with the President on his Executive Order and the protocol for the Department of Homeland Security to follow in apprehending the subjects and transporting them to Cheyenne Mountain Complex. I have been informed that the complex has remained intact and untouched since the investigation was completed, so much of the equipment you need should still be on hand. I have a crew en route now that will assist you in adding extra security measures. These subjects may be hostile about being ordered back to the facility after only having attained their freedom for a short time. Therefore, new security measures must be awakened and instructed to react to even the slightest hint of opposition. My crew will provide you with what is needed for awakening and instructing security. In addition, Dr. Mitchell Blakely has agreed to return and help you test, evaluate, and monitor the subjects. I will be in touch with more details and a timetable of events. The Executive Order is planned to be issued in two weeks. However, that timing may be moved up if panic sets in early. As for now, get set up in the complex and prepare the brain modules for behavior modification in concordance with your study on mimicking sham rage in humans. I have found your capacity to evoke aggression without any external stimulus fascinating, to say the least. Please inform me of any issues that arise. Sincerely, Dr. Damien Seaver." Alice leans back and blows out a heavy breath. "This email was sent almost two weeks before the police station explosion."

"Save that email, and p-please hurry up." Cynthia's voice trembles as she stares down at the floor. She doesn't turn around, but her panic is obvious. Her body is quivering so badly that the hair on top of her head is shaking. "Find the timetable so we can call the authorities."

Dukakis twists his head and glares at Cynthia with one cheek full of chocolate and peanut butter. "You made sense of all that gibberish."

"The details in that email are limited, and I assume the allusions were vague on purpose. However, based on what we already know, some of the wording indicates…" Cynthia swallows hard, making a loud gulping noise. She doesn't finish her statement. Instead, she lets out a low moan.

"Mom," Steve moves forward and squeezes in next to me and Teresa, "I get that returning us to the facility was never about finding the problem and helping us. Dr. Eckert already knew the problem. And mind control, behavior modification, primitive war… all sound frightening, but what are you thinking? How does any of that relate to creating better living conditions for Americans?"

Cynthia sniffles. "Did you pick up on the phrase sustainable population? Many theories are in circulation as to why people engaged in primitive war, such as the argument that the desire to kill is an innate trait. Most probable is the desire to dominate or gain status. But one theory is that even though those engaged in this primitive war had no cognitive awareness of its natural purpose, the casualties decreased the population, keeping the number of people in a certain ecological area in line with what it could sustain or support." She twists her neck and looks back at Steve. "When a population exceeds what its ecosystem can provide for, you end up with famine or disease, or in a modern society, an excess of people that the government has to provide funding to care for."

Steve drops his head. "Combine that with those long wires protruding into our brains and Eckert's mention of unleashing monsters, and it sounds like a government-approved internal genocide. The government reduces the population and the amount needed in their budget for welfare while keeping their hands clean." He lifts his eyes and gazes at me with worry lines etched in his downturned mouth. "Eckert is using mind control to create murderers. When he unleashes his monsters, survival of the fittest kicks in, and the fight for dominance is on. In essence, the population takes care of its own downsizing."

Alice gasps so loud it sounds like she sucked in all the air in the van. Our eyes all shift toward her at once. She sits frozen with her mouth agape staring at the tablet.

This can't be good. "Alice," I choke out, "what is it?"

"We got trouble." Dukakis starts the engine.

Flashing blue lights are easing down the gravel road in our direction. Steve grabs Spencer and shouts out directions for switching positions. It seems like pandemonium with ten people, two robots, and a monkey rotating and flipping at warp speed over the seatbacks all at the same time, but somehow it works. Everyone is sitting nice and proper and quiet before the police car even comes to a stop in front of us.

I watch through the windshield as two officers who appear to be local police attempt to creep from their car with stealth. With their guns drawn, they lurch toward the driver's side door of the van, one behind the other. As they get closer, I notice the one in front has some sort of purple stain down the front of his shirt.

I wonder how they chose who was going in front.

They approach the open window.

"Good afternoon, officers." Herb addresses them in a calm, professional-sounding voice. "What can I do for you?"

The front officer's mouth falls open and his eyes bulge out from his face. "Uhhh. We received a call from one of the farmers out here. Said a van had been parked out here for a bit. He was concerned since this is his private drive."

"Oh, my. I do apologize." Herb puts his metal hand to his forehead and shakes his head. "I had one last pick-up, but I seem to have taken a wrong turn. I was just trying to locate the correct address before I started into motion again."

"I see." he says, still pointing the gun at the window. "D-do you have a license to drive this thing?"

"Of course," Herb replies, then stretches his neck lifting his head higher. "I am licensed to drive a commercial vehicle in all forty-eight contiguous states, plus the District of Columbia." He raises his right hand, waving his fingers. "Do you need my thumbprint?"

"N-no. U-uuh. That's okay. Where are you headed with all these people?"

"Oh." Herb gives a little happy bounce. "We are off to the state park. That is, as soon as I pick up my last customer."

The officer lowers his gun. "Well, we didn't mean to frighten you, but you are trespassing on private property. And with the reports coming across the scanner about a dangerous group in a full-size van, you probably alarmed the owner."

"Certainly. We will be moving on along. Oh, dear," Herb moves his face closer to the window, "is that a grape jelly stain?"

The officer looks down and rubs the front of his shirt. "Oh no. My wife is going to have a fit."

The other officer moves around from behind. "Well, I told you to get the cream-filled instead."

"No worries." Herb pulls at his pinky finger. "You just need to pretreat with an oxygen-based bleach, which I just happen to always have on hand." Herb holds out his hand and squirts the stain. "No pun intended."

"Pretreat. Huh." The officer tugs at the shirt fabric. "Thank you."

"Well now, we wouldn't want your wife to be upset, would we?"

The officers start back to their car.

Herb waves as he presses the button to raise the window. "Have a good day, gentlemen."

Steve's head appears from the cubby behind the last row of seats with Spencer's arms clutched around his neck. "You pretreated the stain on his shirt?" The irritation is clear in his voice.

"If I hadn't, his shirt could have been ruined. Hmmm." Herb puffs, then mumbles, "It's your fault anyway. You are the one that gave me furniture polish and oxygen-based bleach instead of tranquilizer darts."

Steve and Spencer climb over the seat. Spencer bounces to the front and sits on the center console between Herb and Dad, and Steve slides in on the second bench with me and Eileen, who had to shift back beside me so Dukakis could occupy the front row. Teresa had to leap to the back to give Eileen her seat.

"Let's focus." Dukakis orders in a stern voice. "Those officers need to see this van moving out behind them, and Alice still needs to tell us what her drama was about before Herb turned our shuttle transport into a laundry service. Herb, do you actually know anything about driving? You need to stay in the driver's seat until we know they are way out of sight."

Herb narrows his eyes at Dukakis, and his pupils glow red. "Do I know anything about driving? I'll have you know that I have a solid-state drive with a zettabyte of storage. That means I have at least ten million times the storage of the human brain." He spins his head back to face forward and starts the van. "Okey-dokey. Safety first." He talks in a low monotone to himself as he buckles his seatbelt. "Adjust mirrors. Apply brake. Shift into drive. Hands at nine and three."

"Oh, brother," Steve groans, "what have I created?"

"Here we go." Herb announces, and the van crawls forward.

As if our thoughts are intertwined, all of our eyes fix on Alice.

"I-I f-f-found the t-time t-table." Alice stammers. She takes a deep breath and closes her eyes. "We have to find a way to reach Agent Morgan."

I prod. "I know that, but what did you find?"

"There are four phases." Alice's words come out at such an

enormous speed that it's hard to keep up. "Phase one has today's date, July 2, and is titled, 'The Exposition: Setting the Scene'. Phase two, dated July 3, is titled, 'Rising Action'. And phase three, dated July 4, is 'The Grand Finale'." Alice looks up from the screen.

Panic and anticipation flood through my body, and my hands tighten into fists.

"And phase four?" Steve raises his eyebrows.

"The date reads July fifth with a plus sign after it, and it's titled, 'Aftershocks'." Alice answers and then moves her eyes back to the tablet. "Only four things are on the timetable for today, which leads me to believe this is more of a testing-the-water phase. Of course, three of them have already happened."

Gerald peers over her shoulder. "That timetable isn't that detailed. How are we supposed to stop it if we don't know which ball game?"

"What do you mean?" My voice cracks, and I open and close my hands seven times.

"I think you are misreading it." Alice mutters to Gerald. "There is an -s at the end." She raises the volume of her voice. "The last entry on today's timetable says, 'MAJOR LEAGUE GAMES START TIME 7:05 P.M.' I think he means all of the 7:05 games, and since this is Friday, not only will there be a lot of night games, but a lot of people will be in attendance at each one."

Chills pierce like needles down my spine. "I can't help but think about the anger experiment of Crawley's that we read about in the motel. He was provoking people to anger and setting them up to take out their aggression on innocent bystanders." I face Steve. "You're right. He is unleashing monsters, but he is not intending for the monsters to do the killing. He just needs them to start the killing... get people stirred up... arouse anger. And when people get stirred up and angry, sometimes they let their emotions overrule doing the right thing, and survival of the fittest or the fight for dominance kicks in." I turn and cast my eyes on Alice. "And just like in Crawley's experiment, I think the plan is to get people mad, and then they will take it out on whoever is within reach."

"And what better place is there to get people fighting mad than a ballgame?" Mom rubs her temples. "I've never understood it. Some people act like they would be more than willing to kill over their favorite sports team."

The van lurches to a stop. Dukakis blocks Mom from sliding into the floor, but Spencer flies off of the console and smacks into the radio controls.

"Oh, my. These brakes are touchy. Sorry about that." Herb says. "Anyway, we are back to the main road. Should I just turn in the opposite direction of the police car?"

Dukakis moves toward the driver's seat. "I'll take it from here, Herb."

As Steve helps Herb get stowed away behind the back row of seats, he stays in the loop of the conversation. "I'm afraid to ask, but what is 'Rising Action'?"

Alice clears her throat. "Here's a quick overview." She glances up over the top of the tablet. "And keep in mind that 'Rising Action' is on a Saturday and on July third, which means not only the weekend but one of the most popular vacation weeks of the year." She looks back down and begins to read. "We've got the New York City subway, twenty major amusement parks, Las Vegas strip, the Statue of Liberty, Grand Central Station in New York, Union Station in Washington D.C., Willis Tower in Chicago, Pike Place Market in Seattle, Atlantic City Boardwalk in New Jersey, Mount Rushmore…" Alice lifts her eyes. "Do you get the idea?"

Steve has settled back in the seat next to me. "Pretty much every major tourist attraction in the U.S. when the most tourists are traveling."

"You got it." Alice confirms. "Then, for the 'Grand Finale', all the major fireworks' displays… the one from the Brooklyn Bridge and the East River in New York City, the National Mall in Washington D.C., Philadelphia, Downtown Nashville,

Miami..." She stops and takes a deep breath. "We really don't have time for this whole list."

"Can you send that timetable and those last two emails, the one from the president detailing Dr. Seaver as the contact and the one written by Dr. Seaver, to this phone? I'm going to call Kate and send her copies of these files." I tighten my muscles and try to push down the tears that are forcing their way into my eyes. "Maybe if she sees the proof, she will help us find Agent Morgan, and they can get agents en route to the stadiums."

"What's the number?" Alice says as she taps the screen.

I read the number off of the phone, and then I lower my head and close my eyes. I feel Eileen grasp my hand, and Steve's arm wraps around my shoulder.

"Dear Heavenly Father," Eileen prays aloud, "thank you for protecting us in that park and helping Alice intercept this information. Please be with Ellie as she calls her friend, Kate. We know you have given Ellie this friendship for a reason. Please help Kate to believe Ellie and to take this information seriously. Lord, please give Kate the knowledge of how to proceed with this information. We pray for all those who have been affected by this, those who have lost loved ones, and those trapped in that facility. Please guide us. Show us what you want us to do and help us to do it. In Jesus' Name. Amen."

Chapter Twenty-Two

With my heart in my throat, I barely choke out a "goodbye." I tap the screen to end the call and look up to find myself encircled by penetrating eyes bearing into me, waiting for a report on the part of the conversation they couldn't hear.

I lean my head back against the seat. I don't want to see all the disappointed expressions as I share the mediocre news.

"Ellie, please tell us what she said." Fear and impatience fill Gerald's voice behind me. "Did she believe you? She knows those emails are real, right?"

"She knows me. She knows I would not make this up or send her fake documents." I squeeze my eyes tight. "The problem is getting someone to believe her when the evidence incriminates the President of the United States and one of his advisors."

Mom lightly smacks the back of her seat. "You've got to be kidding. After the last president, you wouldn't think the president's involvement in a heinous crime would seem so far-fetched."

"Yes, I know, Mom. But Kate is afraid they are going to turn it around and make us look like the masterminds behind the plan. We are the ones who found the evidence, and we are the ones that have a timetable documenting attacks that have already taken so many lives, so many that they still do not have a definite count."

The van bounces as Dukakis turns into the shopping hub parking lot. "So, let me get this straight. Kate thinks they are going to convince the American public that a group of ten people, a monkey, and two robots are behind this. I hope they make sure to include that this is the same group that risked their lives to save the world before."

"Kate's probably right. The government has already locked us back in that facility." Gerald makes a noise between a grumble and a growl. "Lately, it seems the government has the power to fabricate anything it wants."

"Alright," Alice stretches up tall, "we have to do something. A lot more people are going to die, including our friends in that facility."

There is the Alice I know. The puzzle guru that takes the lead. "You have that look in your eye." I stiffen my shoulders and gaze at the determination on her face.

"What look?" Alice meets my gaze. The question pours from her mouth, but her hardened facial expression says that she knows what I mean.

I lift my eyebrows. "The look that says you have a plan, and it is going to entail taking a lot of risks which goes against every grain of my cellular composition."

"If you mean the look that says I am not going to be afraid anymore. God gave me Gerald, and He didn't let me lose him. God even sent your mother to take care of him. And as I sat here listening to us just now, I realized that God has brought us together in this place at this specific time, and I don't believe He wants us to sit back and wait. God is telling me it is time for us to take a leap of faith. I feel it in my heart." Alice's voice gets louder as her resolve gets stronger with every word.

"Wh—" Steve starts to ask a question.

"Wait. Don't stop me now. I'm on a roll." Alice declares. "I know you all are not going to like my idea, but…" she pauses, balls her hands into fists in her lap, and closes her eyes, "we have to get back into the facility." She rattles off so fast that it is almost as if she is hoping we don't hear her. "Now, I am sure you are thinking that I must have a death wish, but Eckert is the key. He is the expert behind this whole mind control thing and the one most likely to be calling the shots, so if we can stop him, we at least postpone the events on the timetable." She opens her eyes and stares straight at me.

"You're right," I assert with an edge of certainty in my tone. "Our only choice is to go after Eck——." I jump at the vibration of the burner phone in my hand. I glance down and my heart flutters at the text message on the screen.

> *I'm scared. I know you, and I know you are telling the truth. I can't sit back and do nothing. God led me into my career field to protect innocent people. I tried to talk to the Special Agent in Charge. He told me that I would be asking for a prison sentence if I even suggested the documents were real. So, with a lot of searching, I found Agent Morgan. He wouldn't talk to me about anything. I hope that I haven't hurt you with my actions, but I followed my gut and gave him this phone number. I thought he might talk to you. I'm sorry. I didn't know what else to do.*

"It's Kate. She found Agent Morgan and gave him this number." The phone rings as the last word comes from my mouth. I swallow hard, tap the screen, and put the phone to my ear. "Y-yes." I stammer as my mind whirls with indecision about how much I should say or not say to him.

"It's me. Look, the thing at the station… I only wanted to help you stay safe." his words are a bit muffled, like he is covering his mouth.

"Why?" I question with boldness in my tone.

"Because you are one of the reasons that I'm still alive."

I don't know how to respond, so I hold the phone and wait for him to continue.

"You all are in over your head. Do you understand? This is not like last time."

"It seems to me that it is a lot like last time. A bad person in a high position has decided that he should have the power to decide when a person's life will end. It's called murder, regardless of the social or political status of the person committing it. And, in case you have forgotten, as an officer for the Department of Homeland Security, it is your responsibility to protect the American people." As tears from my rising temperature flood into my eyes, my voice gets strained.

"I know. I know. Everything you said is true, but by the time we prove the evidence that you have is authentic to the people that matter, it will be too late."

"I understand. Thanks for the help before, and thanks for not turning in our location."

"You're welcome, and I am sorry that I can't help you." He at least sounds sincere.

"Oh, I don't know if it matters, or if you already know... but are you familiar with Dr. Earl Eckert?" I ask, not knowing why it suddenly seems important.

"Yes, he is the scientist in charge at the facility. I read the emails you sent detailing his supposed assignment."

"Did you know his real name is Dr. Mordecai Crawley?" I probe, wondering how much Agent Morgan is aware of.

"No, I didn't, but then again, I don't know that much about Dr. Eckert." he responds in a dry tone.

"Well, maybe if nothing else, you could figure out why he changed his name."

With a soft sincerity in his words, he replies, "Will do. Stay safe, you hear."

"I am, and I always will be safe in the arms of Jesus. I hope you are too."

The line goes dead. I lean over with my elbows on my knees and drop my gaze to the floor. I can almost feel all the eyes in the van burning holes straight through me like lasers. Steve's hand brushes my hair behind my ear, and a soft hand falls on my back.

"Ellie, it's okay." Alice whispers. "Our plan doesn't involve Agent Morgan anymore. He is too far away to help, and we could never trust anyone that he might be able to reach out to in this area to help us anyway."

I lift my head and nod. "So, what's the plan? How are we going to get back in there?"

"Very carefully." Alice proclaims.

"Please tell me there is more to your plan than that?" Steve's forehead wrinkles in concern.

"When we escaped the facility a couple of years ago, security outside was not so tight. Only one of the checkpoints had security, and well, if you remember, they were sleeping. The twenty-ton doors were sealed, so I suppose they saw no need to be alarmed enough to have any extra surveillance outside. But now, both checkpoints are manned, and Dukakis, I am wondering how you and Jillian got through the gates."

"Simple," Dukakis pulls out another candy bar, "we were in a pizza delivery van. I had a stack of pizzas. I stopped at the first point, told the guard that pizza was being provided to all the staff for a job well done, and handed a couple of pizzas out the window. The guard waved me through, and I did the same thing at the second one." Dukakis takes a bite of the candy and holds up the bar. "People love food, right Gerald?"

"Are you serious?" Dad sighs. "You broke into a government facility with pizza?"

"I am going on the hope that they are still transporting people in, and the twenty-ton doors are still open. But if they are, that means security will be extra tight outside, especially after our escape." Alice glances at my dad and then at Gerald. "I don't care how much food we throw at them, they are not going to let a full-size van by those guard offices. Mr. Hatcher, this is where you and Gerald come in. Mr. Hatcher, that little car of yours is similar to the little security cars. And Gerald, before you argue, you are not able to go into the facility with us anyway. There is an entrance to a parking lot before you pass the first guard office. One camera is aimed at the entrance to the lot, but I think if you drive quickly, even if anyone happens to be looking at that camera feed, they will think it is a security car." She lets out a shallow breath. "That's what I am hoping anyway. Mrs. Hatcher, where is the medical bag that Claude gave you?"

"Under the back seat where you are sitting." Mom starts to get up from her seat.

Alice bends down. "I got it." She pops back up with the bag. "Yes, thank you." she mumbles to herself as she pulls out a small bag of individually wrapped syringes. "Steve, can we load some of Claude's tranquilizer in these."

"If he has enough left." Steve takes the bag of syringes.

"No worries," Claude interjects. "I tossed a few vials in the side pocket of that bag in case I needed a refill."

Alice opens the side pocket and pulls out a small white box.

Steve takes the box from Alice and passes it along with the syringes to Mom on the front bench. "I think loading these things with the right amount is your field of expertise."

"Okay, we have to hurry up, so on with the plan." Alice begins talking faster. "Mr. Hatcher, after you park in the lot, go up to the guard office and act as if you are lost and in need of directions to the state park entrance. I suspect there will be two guards, but…"

"Alice, I got this." Dad interrupts. "You want me to find a way to inject them with the tranquilizer. I'll find a way. I am guessing that Gerald and I are then to take the car and move to the second guard office?"

Alice glances at me, and I know she is thinking about when my dad got shot and how we were sure that we had lost him. "You know, never mind." Alice shakes her head. "That's too big of a risk. There must be another way."

"What about Claude?" Cynthia suggests. "He can shoot those tranquilizers."

"No," Dad argues. "Claude needs to go into the facility with you, and we can't risk something happening to him before you get in. Not only that, but Claude can't fit in the car with Gerald and me. Gerald can't go into the facility, nor can he take Claude by himself limping around with a gunshot wound."

"I guess that part is set then?" Alice moves her eyes around to each of us as we nod in agreement. "Alright, the rest we will have to wing. No way we can plan when we don't know what we are going to encounter."

"Would we blend in better if we put those horrible suits back on?" Eileen questions.

Alice shakes her head. "Dukakis, Tom, and Jillian don't have one, and we will be carrying guns, so the suit isn't going to matter." She makes a gurgling noise and lowers her voice. "Besides, I cut mine into small bits at the motel anyway."

I can't help but crack a smile at her comment.

"Don't laugh. Those things were awful and you know it." Alice complains. "Not only were they fifty sizes too small, but whoever designed them certainly did not take going to the bathroom into consideration." She claps her hands together. "Gerald and Mr. Hatcher can go now. We will wait five minutes and proceed in that direction. That will give Steve a chance to load more of the tranquilizer into Claude. There is a side road just before the first guard check. Dukakis can pull the van off there and wait until you call us with an all-clear. Any objections?"

"More than you can count." Dad chokes out in a mumble. Tears are pooled in his eyes, and his bottom lip quivers.

With her own eyes full of tears, Mom slides from the front seat onto her knees and stretches her arms around Dad's neck in the passenger seat. "Oh, Tom. I'm scared too. But you know the girls we raised. They are going to do this with or without us, and I have to be thankful that God is letting us stand in this battle beside them."

Dad rests his chin on the top of Mom's head as he pulls her close. "And to think we thought God was finished with our little army, and here we are again."

Spencer had been so quiet that I had almost forgotten about

him. It's a strange phenomenon for him to sit still for that long. In a swift leap, he projects himself from the center console to the front bench in the tiny space between Mom and Cynthia and grabs both of their hands.

"I guess he has watched you guys enough to know that in times of distress, you need to call out to our Father." Cynthia lowers her head and closes her eyes. "Dear Heavenly Father, please be patient with me. I'm new at praying, so I'm just going to talk to you like this is a conversation. I understand Tom and Jillian's tears because I haven't had Steve and Teresa back in my life for that long. I'm terrified of losing them, but Jillian's words a minute ago made sense. Thank you, Lord, for letting us be here in this battle with our kids. And as I say these words, I think I am having an epiphany because as much as we love our children, You still love us more. And You are not only going into this battle with us, You are leading us. I wasn't in this army the first go around, but I am glad You recruited me. My life is Yours, Lord. You created me for Your purpose as You did everyone else here. Lord, I ask that you would protect us, guide us, and help us to stop this evil from harming any more of your children. In Jesus' Name, Amen."

"Amen." we all say together.

"Are you ready, Gerald?" Dad stretches his neck to see Gerald all the way in the back.

Gerald hugs and kisses Alice, then wobbles to the side door. "Yes, sir. Let's go."

"Girls," Dad blows a kiss to each of us, "hold on to that and don't let go until I can give you another one. I love you!"

With tears trickling down our cheeks, Eileen and I reach out and grab the floating kiss and pull it to our hearts. "Love you too." we say back.

Dad opens the door and smiles at Mom. "I love you, Jillian."

Mom repeats the words back to him right before he closes the door. Spencer wastes no time taking over Dad's spot in the passenger seat. Dad helps Gerald hobble to the tiny car that sort of looks like a spaceship with its domed bubble-glass top. Dad opens the door, the only door, which is located on the driver's side, and through the glass, I watch as Gerald gives Dad this 'you have got to be kidding me' look before he eases in and slides over to the passenger side. Dad climbs in after him, and when he closes the door, the side of Gerald's head is smooshed against the curved glass dome.

Mom turns and looks back at the rest of us. "I told you that car was made only for one person."

Chapter Twenty-Three

Clutching Steve's hand, I sit stiffened on the middle bench between him and Eileen. The only sound inside the van is my heart pounding in my ears. Dukakis veers onto a small side road not far from the first security gate and circles around so the van is facing the main road.

Now we wait.

I drop my head, trying to push out all the negative thoughts of what could possibly be going wrong right now that are passing back and forth through my brain.

"Never forget," the warmth from the whisper in my ear calms the thrumming beat of my heart.

I turn my head and whisper back, "be not afraid... for the Lord thy God is with thee whithersoever thou goest."

"He is with your dad and Gerald right now too." He lifts his eyebrows like he is waiting for me to acknowledge that I'm okay.

I open my mouth to tell him I know that, but before I can muster a sound, the phone vibrates in my lap. In less than a second, I whip it up to my ear. "Dad."

"Sorry, but it's me. I tracked the ping of our last call. I don't want to know what you are up to, but my stomach has been twisted in a knot since we talked. Then when I did a quick search on Mordecai Crawley, my heart joined my stomach. For the last five minutes, I have been trying to convince myself that you are misinformed and that Dr. Earl Eckert has nothing to do with Dr. Mordecai Crawley."

"I told you that Eckert must have changed his name."

"Mordecai Crawley committed suicide ten years ago." Agent Morgan spouts through the phone. "I don't know what is going on... I don't know anyone well enough in that area to get you trusted help... and I don't have enough time to cough up proof to make them believe me." So much emotion pours through his tone that he pauses for a deep breath. "I have contacted authorities in all the areas of the seven o'clock games tonight. I told them we had a tip that there could be trouble at those games similar to the instances that have occurred previously today. They are supposed to send whatever authorities they have available to those locations."

"Thank you. I have a hunch that the troublemakers would have been transported out of Raven Rock Mountain Complex. Maybe you could track any large vehicles or flights out of that area."

"I will work on that." He swallows so hard that I can hear it through the phone. "I am praying for you all. Be careful."

I lower the phone back to my lap. "Mordecai Crawley is dead." I announce, not sure what it means, or at this point, what it matters.

"So, the whole thing is over, right?" Mom's lips curve slightly up. "If Crawley is Eckert..."

"No... I'm sorry. Crawley committed suicide ten years ago. He can't be Eckert." I blurt out before she gets too excited.

"Well, then somehow Earl's photo was placed in that article by mistake." Teresa assures us. "I don't know Mordecai Crawley, but the photo I saw was Earl Eckert. I am certain of it."

The phone vibrates again. *Please be Daddy.* "Hello."

"It's showtime, sweetheart. Gerald and I are at the second gate."

~

THE VAN SLOWS for the speed bump and then picks up speed past the first security gate. We wind around the curve to the second guard building. I know I just heard his voice, but the image of him lying on the ground beside that truck with blood covering his chest creeps into my thoughts, stealing the breath from my lungs. I hold my breath until I take in Dad's form, strong and intact, standing in the doorway of the security office... *wearing a guard uniform.* I blink and do a double-take. *Gerald too?*

Dukakis rolls the window part way down as Dad steps out. "Please tell me you didn't strip the guy down and steal his clothes."

"No," Dad snaps back. "The laundry service must have dropped off clean uniforms. A bag with two uniforms was hanging on the hook by the back door."

I can't help but smile when I notice the shirt is a bit tight in the stomach. His pale skin is glowing where the fabric is pulled apart between the buttons.

He walks around the van with Gerald limping behind him. Both of them have rifles hanging from straps on their shoulders. They climb in the side door.

"Gerald and I have decided that you all are not going in without us!" Dad barks out.

Before Alice gets a sound out of her open mouth, Gerald flings his hand up. "Before you say a word, it is not up for debate."

Dukakis eases on up the road into the parking lot.

A single whimper squeaks from Spencer's mouth as he jumps from the passenger seat and climbs under the front bench. Steve leans over and pulls him out from under the seat in front of us.

"Spencer, I know you remember what those bad people did to you in there, but we have friends that are still inside and need our help. I need you to think back to that warehouse where we stopped the plane and you guys rescued me, and I need you to be the Spencer that led the way."

Spencer sticks out his bottom lip as he listens to Steve's motivational speech.

"Okay?" Steve looks at him like he expects Spencer to suddenly snap out of his fear, but Spencer doesn't respond or even move, for that matter.

Several of those transport buses are in the lot, and Dukakis squeezes the van between two of them. "Alright, let's move." Dukakis pushes the button, and the side door slides.

As soon as a crack appears in the door, so does the tip of an automatic rifle aimed at Steve. Spencer squeals and leaps on the barrel, thrusting the tip toward the floor, and then somehow flips his body around. With his hands pushing the barrel against the floor, he pushes off, shoots through the air, and plunges both feet into the guard's face. The guard grabs the edge of the door as his head jolts backward. A few strands of hair move and tickle my ear as something whizzes with a light whistle past my head. The guard grabs his neck and falls to the ground. Spencer grunts, and with an angry jerk, he pulls the gun the rest of the way from the man's hands. I glance behind me in time to see Claude closing up his finger.

Dukakis peers out the side door from the driver's seat, and his shoulders slump. "This is going well. We're not even out of the van yet." he mumbles.

"Beep… beep… beepity-beep… beep."

Every head in the van turns toward the back. Claude's eyes are flashing in sync with the beeps, and then his body starts to vibrate.

"Oh," Dukakis blows out a puff of air, "what a relief. I thought a bomb was about to explode."

With wide eyes, I cast a glance at Steve. *Is he smiling?*

"Do robots have seizures?" Gerald asks with an edge of concern.

Claude stops, and the lights in his eyes go dark. "No, I am not having a seizure. I am trying to send Waves a message."

"Well, that could have been helpful long ago." Alice raises her voice. "Why didn't you say something?"

"You can do that? Like telepathy?" Gerald asks in wonder.

"No. No. No... I mean yes... Ooooh. You, people, are confusing." Claude's head trembles.

"What Claude is trying to communicate is that he is a computer. He is not telepathic." Steve explains in a calm monotone. "Eckert must have had the robots connected on the same frequency so they could communicate. That means he can send Waves a message if Waves is close enough for him to send a clear signal. Sort of like walkie-talkies, but in a code that cannot be heard... unless it's Claude adding dramatic sound effects." He gives his head a quick shake. "But even from here, being in this close of proximity, it is questionable because Waves is inside of a mountain, and we are outside."

"Oh... sorry, Claude. Please continue." Gerald makes a continuing motion with his hand.

"I am finished." Claude replies with a similar wave of his hand. "He will message back when he has put the cameras in a loop. In other words, he is setting up the cameras to play the last five minutes over and over so we will not appear to be there if anyone is watching. Then he will leave a gurney at the end of the tunnel."

"Brilliant!" Alice exclaims. "But won't the guards question why Waves is pushing a gurney through the tunnel?"

"Waves has a reputation for being a bit different, so no one really pays attention to what he does." Claude's mechanical mouth curves up. "His programmer had a bit of fun in creating his personality. I guess humans would say that he marches to the beat of his own drum."

"Well, while we are waiting, we need to do something with this unconscious man lying by the side of the van." Mom points. "If anyone does come by, he is definitely an attention-grabber."

Dad jumps out and rolls the man under the van. He climbs back in wiping the sweat from his forehead. "Claude, couldn't you just have asked Waves to take out Eckert, and then we wouldn't have to risk our lives going in?"

"Uuuum." Steve twists his mouth to the side. "When I adjusted Waves programming, I only instructed him to help and protect us. I did not input code that would make him harm Eckert unless he was posing a direct threat to us. And let me add that I did that before we had any knowledge of what Eckert and… uh" he pauses, "Seaver were up to."

"Grab your weapons. We are clear for takeoff." Claude reports.

Between the rifles that Dad and Gerald came out with, and the rifles and guns we left the facility with, we each have something to carry… well everyone except for Spencer and Herb.

Mom tosses the strap of one of the rifles over her head so that the strap crosses her body. "Blessed be the Lord my strength which teacheth my hands to war, and my fingers to fight." she proclaims in a bold voice.

Outside, Steve moves in front of us to peer around the nose of the van. It's only about six-thirty, so there is no darkness to shroud us. Dukakis is on the other side since he exited the driver's door.

"Do you see anything?" Steve whispers to him over the hood.

"Nothing, but I didn't see that one coming up to the side door a while ago either." Dukakis responds, looking in both directions.

"Alright," Steve glances over his shoulder at the group, "I'll take the front behind Claude. Dukakis and Tom, you two cover the back. Everybody else, tread softly in between. Herb, make sure the ladies stay safe in the middle." He makes eye contact with Gerald. "The gurney is at the entrance. Can you make it that far?"

"Don't worry about me. I'll make it fine."

Steve grasps the rifle and moves out behind Claude.

I follow, gripping the nine-millimeter in one hand and holding Spencer's hand with my other. Taking wide strides and soft steps, I hunker low as we file behind the row of buses in the lot.

An eerie silence surrounds us... no traffic, no voices, not even the quiet hum of electricity or the rustle of a leaf in the wind. At the end of the row of buses, no other options are before us. We have to trudge into the wide open. As we round the last bus and head for the path to the tunnel, a guard steps into the path with his rifle aimed. With ten weapons aimed back, the guard hesitates a bit too long, and Claude drops him with a dart.

I keep my face forward but scroll my eyes from side to side. I count my steps to seven and start again. Behind me, a light brushing noise and then a clank unnerves me and interrupts my counting. I realize it must have been someone picking up the guard's rifle, so I resume counting backward instead.

The entrance to the tunnel comes into view along with four guards sitting on the ground with their backs leaned against the outside wall. *It's too far. Claude's dart won't make it.* Bile rises in my throat as one of the guards spots us and aims his rifle. I jerk Spencer behind me even though I know a spray of bullets from an automatic rifle would take us all down. But at the same time the tip of the rifle points in our direction, a red mohawk appears in the opening of the tunnel, and one... two... three... four guards drop. A shiny metal hand waves and disappears back through the opening. I exhale and roll my eyes toward Heaven. *Thank you, Father.*

Waves is out of sight, but the gurney is there, right where he said it would be. Steve motions and Gerald sticks the gun in his belt and lies down. Steve shakes out the sheet Waves left on the gurney and covers Gerald from the neck down to cover his uniform. Dad moves forward to push the gurney since he is dressed as a guard and the rest of us try as much as possible to stay directly behind him. Claude continues to lead the way. The twenty-ton doors are still open. I'm not sure with their current timetable of events why they are still transporting people in for testing, but I guess they have to play the charade out to the end. At the first door, the guards don't even flinch at the sight of

Claude or the sound of the gurney behind him. Of course, robots and gurneys are probably pretty common occurrences around here. Claude hits them with darts before they have time to realize that we are behind him.

The guards at the second door are a little more alert, maybe because they are closer to the action inside, but Claude still moves before they get a chance.

Claude stops at building one and sticks his metal thumb to the pad.

It worked. Either Eckert doesn't know Claude isn't here, or he's been too busy being a supervillain to care.

We step through the door into building one behind Dad, who is still pushing Gerald on the gurney. The hall is vacant, for now.

Spencer doesn't make as much as a whimper. Protecting Steve from that guard at the van seemed to give him a new determination. Maybe panic and fear were consuming him because he had too much time and nothing to focus real energy on. Maybe he just needed to have a real purpose, not one made up in a video game.

Claude wheels on along toward the goal, Dr. Eckert's office.

With the realization that my entire family's lives are in imminent danger, my OCD kicks in, and the thoughts of every scenario on the other side of that door crash against my skull, making the vein in my forehead throb. At this point, I regret that we did not at least make a tentative plan of action. *Be not afraid... for the Lord thy God is with thee whithersoever thou goest.*

Dad steers the gurney up against the wall, and Gerald flips the sheet back and slides to the floor. I watch Claude move to the thumbprint pad as I will myself to steady my knocking knees. *There is an eye scanner like on Dr. Blakely's door. Claude won't be able to open that door.*

Claude presses his thumb to the pad and puts his eye in front of the little screen. The red laser shoots out, at the same time, Claude shoots the red laser from his eye. The streams of light collide, the screen shuts down, and the lock clicks. He glances over his shoulder with a slight grin. In an undertone, he utters, "Waves taught me that." With his finger ready to fire the dart, Claude puts his other hand on the door applying only enough pressure to make a crack. He wraps the hand with the tranquilizer around the edge of the door and pushes in a slow swift motion. "Let's go." he orders.

Inside, Eckert is slumped over in his desk chair with the tiny dart protruding from the side of his neck.

Dad pulls handcuffs from the pocket of the uniform. "Here." He tosses them to Steve. "I found these in that security office."

"Perfect. See if we can find tape or rope or something for his ankles." Steve says as he pulls Eckert's arms behind the chair and latches the cuffs.

We spread out in the large office, searching drawers and cabinets for anything that will work. I move to a credenza with a hutch attached to the top along the back wall. The top cabinets are full of binders, so I bend over and tug open the drawers. I look inside a small black case in the top drawer. *A bag of those little tools and alcohol pads.* I sit the case on the countertop and move to the bottom drawer. *Bingo.* I grasp a handful of wire ties.

Boom. The blast pierces through my ear drums. I thrust my hand out in front of me to stop my fall, but the force from the explosion is too powerful. My elbow gives, and I slam into the credenza. Pain shoots through my forearm, and it takes my brain a second to catch up and send the message to my body to get up. I scramble to my feet.

Eckert's chair is on its side by the door. Steve is on his knees, pushing himself up beside Eckert. Everybody else must have been on the outskirts of the room because they appear to be fine. Spencer is with Herb in the corner with one hand over his eyes... *oh-oh no.* Claude is bent over where only fragments of the desk remain. *The explosion... it was Eckert's computer.*

"Claude!" Steve dashes toward him.

Claude stands upright, twists his torso back and forth, and then his neck. "All good." He taps his chest. "Military steel." He winks at me. "Spaceship material right here."

With my hand pressing against my heart, I jog back over, grab the wire ties, and toss them to Steve. "Hurry. I can't believe the guards aren't here already." I grab the case from the counter with the package of tools and alcohol pads.

When I turn around, Claude is already by the door.

"Wait, we can't go yet." Alice stares unblinking at the smoke where the desk and computer used to be. "We may have Eckert, but that doesn't guarantee that some sort of program isn't already running. He could have something set to activate those wires at a certain time tonight... I was going to check his computer... but..." She turns to Claude. "Can you contact Waves? I could use that computer in his room."

Claude makes his beeping noises, and his head starts to vibrate again.

Steve rolls his eyes as he aims his gun at the door.

The beeping and shaking stop. "He's on his way." Claude announces.

In less than a minute, the door swings open. "Row, row, row your boat gently down the stream. Merrily, merrily, merrily... whoa." Waves gawks at the smoke and debris. "So much for keeping a low profile."

"I will go with Waves." Alice orders. "You all go on ahead and get Bailey and the others."

"No." I blurt as soon as the words come out of her mouth.

"Ellie, we are going to jail if the authorities show up." Dark circles rim Alice's eyes. "Until Morgan, Kate, or somebody can prove those emails are real and investigate this place, we are the bad guys. Our goal was to stop Eckert and help our friends. We have no choice but to make the most of our time."

"I'll go with Alice and Waves." Gerald grabs Alice's hand.

I know she's right. "Alright, if Gerald is going with you."

"I'll go out first." Waves bops his head side to side, and with every hard bop, his spiked mohawk vibrates. "Merrily, merrily, merrily..."

Alice and Gerald turn down the hallway behind Waves. I'm not sure, but I think I heard Gerald humming along. The rest of us hoof it out the door toward building two. When Claude is right in front of the entrance to building two, the door swings open. The guard nods at Claude in recognition and starts to hold the door open, but then he spots us. In a snap, Claude has the guard in dreamland before his hand ever touches his gun.

I point to a door on the left. "This is the room where Bailey and the girls are." I place the gun under my arm and open the little black case. "Here, take part of these, and you guys go get the men that were in your room. Herb and Spencer can stay with us, and Claude can go with you."

Steve kisses my cheek. "Okay. We'll come back here when we're done."

Claude uses his thumb to open the door. He waits until we are inside and then pulls it closed behind us.

I swallow. I blink. I bite my bottom lip. Nothing works. Tears flood my face despite my effort to push them back. The room is silent. I shift my eyes from cot to cot. Every cot is filled, but no one lifts their head. No one wiggles a finger. No one trembles or even flinches. No one cries or whimpers. No one moves or makes a sound. I wonder how long they have been like this. *Since we left? Could they have spent the last twenty-four hours without food or water?*

Eileen's hand touches my shoulder. "Let's get busy. We'll start in the back and work forward. Hopefully, as we wake them up, they won't be too weak to help." She takes the bag from my hand and passes out tools and alcohol pads.

I wipe my face with the back of my hand. "Mom, come on. You can watch me do the first one, so you'll know how to find the wire." I plod with heavy feet to the back. When I look down at Bailey's still body, the guilt of leaving her consumes me all over again. *Lord, please help my new friend to understand why we couldn't take them all. Please help her to forgive me.* Kneeling beside the cot, I scrape a couple of times with my fingernail until I snag the wire. Pressing my left nail down hard, I wipe her skin with the alcohol pad and insert the needle. Without hesitation, I flip the tool over and insert the hooked end in a scooping motion. The wire slides from her skin.

With her mouth frozen in a circle and her eyes fixed on Bailey's still unmoving body, Mom shakes her head.

"It takes a minute, or at least, with Cynthia, it did."

Mom gives a quick nod and goes to the next cot.

Bailey's arm twitches and her eyes flutter.

"Bailey. Come on, Bailey." I say into her ear. "It's me, Ellie. I need you to wake up."

Her eyes pop open, and she rolls onto her back and stares at me, or maybe it's more of a glare. I'm not sure yet.

"E-E-Ellie?"

"Yes, it's me, Ellie. We've come to get you out of here, and there isn't much time. Can you try to get moving while I help wake the others?"

She moves her head up and down in slow motion.

I hop up to my feet and move down the line, and soon between Mom, Teresa, Eileen, Cynthia, and me, we are nearing the end of the first row. All the women are weak, but I think everyone will be okay. I squat and start to work on Cindy, remembering that first day... her broken spirit curled on that cot... and then the prayer that lifted her from that cot and into our group. Just as I pull the wire from her head, the door bursts open.

The barrel of the gun stops only a few inches from my head. "When their locations started to disappear, he told me it had to be you. You just don't know when to stop, do you?"

One of the guards must have found him. I don't move, and I don't answer either. My mind is going in circles, whirring like one of those old hard drives with the spinning disc, starting and stopping in search of an answer. I don't have one. But then, there is a beep, a faint beep right behind Eckert, beside the door.

For a split second, Eckert twists his head to find the source. As he does, the gun slightly moves with him. In my peripheral vision, Herb is lifting his fourth finger. I slap the tip of the gun down as Herb squirts Eckert right in his eyes and Spencer pounces on his head, pulling Eckert's hair with both hands.

Eckert falls to the floor, screaming in pain with his hands pressed to his eyes.

"Not only do I have oxygen-based bleach, but I am loaded with the hard stuff too… chlorine bleach. You will want to flush that out immediately and seek medical treatment." Herb leans over and lifts Spencer from Eckert's head. "Nobody messes with my family."

Claude walks through the door, and Eckert collapses to the floor. "Why was he screaming? That was hurting my ears."

Steve, Dad, and Dukakis slide in behind Claude. The skin on their faces is pale and stretched tight from their widened eyes and dropped chins.

"Water… we need water." Mom says in urgency.

"Right here. I have a bottle." Bailey yells. "Let me fill it." In a second, she comes running from the bathroom.

Mom pulls Dr. Eckert's eyes open one at a time and slowly pours the water into them.

"Seriously?" Dad looks at Mom in disbelief.

"Tom, I have taken an oath. I know he could lose his eyes if I do not flush them with water." Mom explains. "Now, I have done the right thing as a medical professional with the resources available to me. So, are you all going to tie him up again or what?"

Teresa and Eileen jerk sheets off the cots. In less than a minute, we have him tied up in so many sheets that he looks like a mummy. Then, we use more sheets to tie him to the legs of one of the cots, which are bolted to the floor.

"Where are the men from your room?" I ask Steve, noticing no one else is with them. "Didn't you get them?"

"We got their wires out and woke them up, but we left them in the room." He rests his hand on my shoulder. "Ellie, I know you have a heart of gold, and you want to get all these people out of here tonight."

I look at him, not liking where this is going... but I know he's right.

"Ellie, do you know how many rooms in here are full of people? Some are even restrained. If we march these people out of here, how are we going to transport them?"

I nod.

The door swings open again, and Steve whips around, lifting his rifle.

"Hold your fire." Waves throws up his hand as he rolls in the door with Alice and Gerald behind him. "Who's that?"

"Dr. Eckert." Claude answers.

"But," Waves twists his head and points back to the door, "he was... I thought..." he scratches his head and mumbles to himself, "maybe I've been singing 'Row, Row, Row Your Boat' a little too much."

I move my attention to Alice. "Did you find anything?"

"Yes, but it's not good. I don't know how these wires work, so I don't understand the code or what is happening. But a program is open now, and someone is manipulating it."

Who else could be controlling it? I think as I have my doubts that Dr. Eckert would entrust the success of his plan to anyone but himself. "Maybe he has it set up on a prescheduled program like you were talking about earlier." I suggest.

"No, a person actually has the program open somewhere in here and is manipulating the code as we speak." Alice argues with a tone of confidence.

I rub my temples. *Eckert doesn't seem the type to relinquish control, but it doesn't make sense either that he could manage this whole facility full of people alone.* "Waves. Waves!" I have to yell to snap him from his apparent fascination with mummy Eckert.

"Oh, sorry." he moves closer to me.

"Waves," I continue, "besides Dr. Blakely, has there been anyone else here in charge or helping Dr. Eckert?"

"Let's see." he taps his metal chin and starts mumbling the entire scenario in a low tone as if he is searching for the answer to my question. "Homeland Security officers bring people on buses. Guards escort them in. Those that are waiting for testing go to the five dorms and buildings six through ten. Building one is testing, building two through four are negative tests, and building five is positive tests waiting to be transported out." He opens his eyes wider and lowers his hand. "No. There are lots and lots of guards, some robots, and Dr. Eckert."

"You say lots and lots of guards, but we really haven't encountered that many." I cast a glance at Steve, wondering if he has noticed the same.

"That's because most of them are patrolling the areas with people waiting for testing and the positive test buildings. Oh," Waves points his index finger, "and the transport buses going out to Raven Rock."

"What's in buildings eleven through fifteen?" Alice inquires.

"Beat's me." Wave's shoulders make a grinding metal sound as he shrugs.

Alice and I turn and look at Teresa.

"How would I know?" Teresa retorts, but then as we move our eyes away, she continues, "But, building fifteen was remodeled into President Denali's personal shelter. I never saw it, but it might be worth taking a look. The problem is that the only way to get there is past the buildings that Waves says have the most guards."

"Okay, there are too many of us to get there in time, and besides that, we left the gurney in building one." Alice talks so fast that I can barely keep up. "Ellie, Steve, Teresa, and I will go. Claude has the tranquilizers so he can lead us. Waves can stay with the others just in case any guards show up."

Gerald opens his mouth, I assume to argue, but Alice stops him.

"Gerald, please," her voice cracks. "People are going to die. This is the only way." Alice takes his hand. "I promise I will be fine, and I can't take a chance on you trying to make it that far. I can tell you are in excruciating pain now. Your face is pasty white, and sweat is running off your forehead."

He nods. "You're right," he says to her, "just be careful. I need you."

Mom's arms squeeze around me as I step toward the door. "Ellie, I am so proud of you. I love you, baby." Her lips brush my cheek, and before Mom pulls back, she moves her mouth closer to my ear. "Ye are of God, little children, and have overcome them: because greater is He that is in you than he that is in the world."

Tears form in the corners of my eyes, and my lips curve into a smile. When Eileen and I were little, Mom would recite that verse every night as she tucked us in. "Thanks, Mom. I love you, too."

"Alright, we have to go. Time is running out." Alice steps up behind Claude.

Steve looks at Mom, Dad, Cynthia, Eileen, Gerald, and Dukakis. "Keep your guns on this door at all times. And Waves, no singing. You need to be on guard. Herb…"

"No worries. You can count on me to keep everyone safe." Herb salutes.

Spencer jumps on Steve's shoulders and wraps his arms around his neck.

Steve drops his head.

"It's okay." Alice pats Steve's arm. "Spencer can come. He did get us out of quite a few fixes last time. Come to think of it, he very well may have saved me from being shot."

Claude opens the door. Alice, Teresa, and I grip our nine-millimeter pistols, and with Spencer on his shoulders, Steve pulls the rifle up in both hands.

Please, Lord, guide us. Please help us to find the person controlling the wires in those people's heads before it's too late.

"Anyone up for a game of charades?" Waves voice filters through the door as it closes.

Chapter Twenty-Four

Not again. I stop in my tracks and listen. *Nothing.* I let out a shallow breath. *I am just hearing things,* I try to assure myself.

We turn the corner. Another yelp of pain… a man's voice.

I am not hearing things. A man is screaming.

Steve, Teresa, and Alice freeze in their tracks.

"It's coming from my room." Claude moves to the stairwell and peers up toward the second floor.

Be strong. Someone is in trouble. With the gun out in front of me, I grit my teeth and speed past Claude taking two steps at a time. *I can do all things through Christ which strengtheneth me. I can do all things through Christ which strengtheneth me. I can do all things through Christ which strengtheneth me. I can do all things through Christ which strengtheneth me. I can do all things through Christ which strengtheneth me. I can do all things through Christ which strengtheneth me. I can do all things through Christ which strengtheneth me.* I stop at the door, and my lungs deflate. I realize that my mad dash in front of everyone was all for nothing because I need a thumbprint or a code to get through the door.

His hair-raising shriek pulls my arm upward. I aim the gun at the door.

"Stop!" Steve grabs my arm.

Claude wheels in front of me and puts his thumb on the pad. He gives the door a gentle nudge and then pushes on through. "Oh, dear."

"Chey Four-Fifteen." I gasp.

"How do you know?" Steve gives me a puzzled look. "All the guards look almost identical."

"Think about it. Four-Fifteen was supposed to be guarding the door, and we escaped. Then, I helped Cynthia escape." I point to Four-Fifteen. "This is exactly what he was doing to Cynthia. As punishment, Dr. Eckert is making Four-Fifteen take Cynthia's place as his lab rat."

Claude taps on the computer, manipulating through different screens.

"Wait," Alice says to Claude as she strides up next to him. "Can you go back? Was that his brain?"

Claude taps a button, and an image of the brain appears. In the center, bright blasts of color shoot out from the center in pulses. Four-Fifteen's body jerks with each pulse, and he lets out a scream when the blasts pulse out through the whole image.

"Shut it down." I beg.

In a second, the humming buzz of electricity fades, and Four-Fifteen's body goes still.

"Is there any of those tools in here for the wires?" I scratch with my nail, feeling for the tip of it.

"Do the guards have wires too?" Steve gapes over my shoulder.

"Well, something has him knocked out." I scrape with my nail a bit slower. "Yep, I feel it."

Claude hands me a tool from the drawer.

It takes a bit longer than with the other ones, but I finally wiggle the wire from his head. One look at it, and my stomach contracts. This is a thicker wire with a hard bead on the end and tiny filaments extend from it like hairs.

"Four-fifteen," I nudge his arm. "Four-fifteen, can you hear me?"

He doesn't move.

I put my finger to his wrist. He has a pulse, and his chest is rising and falling.

"Something's not right about his brain." Alice points to the only area with color on the screen. "See. He only has activity in his brain stem. He is in a vegetative state."

"Come on, Four-fifteen. Wake up." I speak right into his ear.

Spencer climbs onto the side of the table and pries Four-Fifteen's eyes open with his little fingers. When nothing happens, he makes a little monkey noise and shrugs.

"Ellie, the only brain activity he has is in his brain stem, and that is minimal. In other words, his brain is only firing enough to tell him to breathe and make his heart pump blood through his body. He is not going to wake up." Alice's eyes glitter with moisture. "Ellie, we have to hurry. Time-"

The door flings open. "Time is of the essence. I couldn't agree more." As soon as the statement leaves her mouth, the gun flies from her hand and sticks to Claude's open magnetic hand, and the woman falls to the floor with a tranquilizer dart protruding from her shoulder.

Teresa drops to her knees beside the woman. With a trembling finger, she points to the woman and looks at Steve. "Did you know? Did you know about this?"

Steve doesn't answer. All of the blood appears to have drained from his face, and he doesn't seem to be able to move his lips.

"Steve," she snaps, "did you know I had a twin?"

He shakes his head. "No. No, I-I definitely was not aware of that."

Teresa stands and backs away. Without a word, she lifts her gun and opens the door.

Claude rushes to get in front of her, and the rest of us race to catch up.

As we leave the room, I cast a glance over my shoulder. The

sight of Four-fifteen makes my heart feel like a boulder in my chest. "I'm sorry. I'm so sorry, Four-Fifteen."

Chapter Twenty-Five

"I can't believe she didn't tell me." Teresa mumbles through gritted teeth. "How could she keep something like that a secret?"

Steve touches his hand to the small of her back and tilts his head closer to hers as we speed walk down the long corridor of building two. "Sis," he says in an undertone, "I'm sure Mom must have had a good reason for not telling you. Before you get upset, give her a chance to explain. After all, she's been through a lot too."

Teresa's hardened jaw softens, and the corners of her lips droop down. "Listen to me. Like I am one to pass judgment on anyone." Her hands begin to tremble. She puts her left hand over her right hand to help her steady the gun. "I'm sorry. I shouldn't have acted—"

Steve cuts her off. "Don't worry about it. As much as it caught me off guard, I can't imagine what a surprise it must have been for you."

Claude is making record time. He barely pauses at the exit door to glance both ways in the tunnel. The buildings are set up in a grid pattern. Claude turns right, leading us down the tunnel past building four, then he turns left again into another tunnel that leads us between building three and building six.

I was expecting him to slow down and use a bit more caution as we approached six, but Claude is still sailing. Steve, Teresa, Alice, and I keep our guns aimed in front. Spencer walks beside Steve, clutching his leg.

No guards. Weird. I was certain we would encounter trouble going past building six. *Why is Claude going so fast?* I toss my eyes sideways at Steve and notice that he is in a half jog, practically dragging Spencer along.

Up ahead, I see an intersection of the tunnels. Pressure builds in my chest. *Why doesn't he slow down?* Blood pumps hard through my arteries, and every nerve ending in my body is on high alert. With my finger on the trigger, I grip the nine-millimeter pistol in both hands, readying for what could be around the corner.

Claude speeds right on past the intersection. For a second, there is a scurry of footsteps. Without stopping, Claude's body pivots, turning in a complete circle at his waist. I get to the intersection just as three guards collide with the floor.

Teresa screams. I glance back, and one of the guards has her by the ankle. She aims her gun, but she doesn't fire. Instead, she rears back with her other foot and kicks him in the head. "I am not in the mood!" Teresa barks in a gruff tone without moving her lips.

The guard isn't moving, but Claude fires another dart anyway.

"Did you see that?" Teresa blows out a breath as she glances back over her shoulder. "That guard's eyes were closed. His hand shot out and grabbed me like a reflex in a dead snake."

Before I can respond, more footsteps pound from somewhere down the hall. Between the clomp of our feet and the hammering of my heart, I can't determine if it's one or a hundred storming, and the echo inside the mountain makes it hard to tell how far away they are.

The tunnel veers to the left, and as we round the curve, the guards are right there, traveling at the same max speed as us. All I can figure is that the guards must have been anticipating descendants of the Anakim because they have their rifles aimed way over our heads and they almost trample right over us. I expect Claude to fire his darts, and I am guessing Steve, Alice, and Teresa must be banking on the same because we pass up the split second we have to shoot. But Claude has no time to react. The guard in front crashes into him, and then we are all in a tangle. A giant hand grasps my wrist, pushing and twisting my hand down that is holding the gun. I try to tighten my grip, but the nine-millimeter falls out of my hand and hits the floor. My arm is pinned at my side, and my face is pressed against the guard's chest. I don't stand a chance against his weight, and my feet slide across the concrete floor as he pushes against me. *Be strong, Ellie. Push,* I keep telling myself because I know if I am too close, he can't maneuver that long rifle to aim it at me. *Push. Push.* Grunts and groans and shuffling feet mixed with thud after thud of body after body clashing with the floor resonates all around me. *Push. Push. Just a little bit longer. Where is Claude?*

"Something bit me." The guard's voice thunders above me and then trails off. He stops pushing, and his rifle clanks to the floor. Holding his ankle, he hobbles backward.

I reach for my pistol and grasp onto it just as a gunshot reverberates through the tunnel. I whirl around, this time ready to fire with no hesitation, but Claude finally has the situation under control. Guards scatter the floor in a peaceful sleep. All of the guards except for one who is lying in a puddle of blood in front of Teresa. Steve's rifle is shaking in his hands, and he still has it aimed at the guard with the hole through his chest. Teresa is holding her neck, gasping for breath.

Oh no. She can't breathe. "Teresa." I dart up beside her.

Alice races up on the other side and gently tries to tug Teresa's hand from her neck. "Try to relax and take small breaths."

Holding up one finger, Teresa nods and coughs at the same time. From the looks of the red finger marks, a hand must have been gripping her neck pretty tight. I rub my hand across her back until she sucks in a deep breath.

Teresa inhales a few more solid breaths. "I'm good."

I turn back to Steve, who is still staring at the lifeless guard on the floor. Spencer is patting Steve's leg as if he is consoling him.

"Steve," I walk over and put my hand on his shoulder, "are you okay?"

"I didn't want to. I know these guards have wires and probably have no clue what they are doing, but I didn't have a choice. He was going to kill her." he says in a dry tone. "It all happened so fast. By the time I got my gun loose from the guard in front of me, I thought I was already too late. Her head was flopping like a ball on a string."

"I know. It's okay. You saved Teresa's life." I reassure him. "We all would have been killed if we hadn't rounded that curve at the same time as them. They were as taken by surprise as we were."

"Funny how the echo in this tunnel messes with the sound. I don't want to think about what could have happened." He turns his gaze toward me. His eyes glisten with a hint of moisture. "We better get moving."

When I look up, I realize that building fifteen is within sight, which must have been the reason for the rush of guards. As we start forward again, Claude nods to Spencer. "Well done, little guy. I appreciate the assistance back there. I didn't know monkeys could bite that hard."

Spencer's mouth spreads into a toothy grin.

Claude stops in front of the door to building fifteen. No guards remain, out here anyway. I am trying not to think about what could be waiting on the other side of the door. As Claude approaches the security pad, I set my jaw and tighten the grip on my gun. He presses his thumb to the pad and lowers his eye to the screen. Again, he deflects the laser from the screen back with the laser from his eye. The screen flashes: "SECURITY CODE REQUIRED".

We all turn to Teresa.

She shrugs and steps up to the keypad. "I'll give it a try." She taps zero, one, zero, nine, two, zero, four, seven. The lock clicks.

Claude eases the door ajar an inch at a time.

Bending my elbow, I point the tip of the gun up, preparing to aim as soon as I get through the door. Every organ in my body is trembling. I keep telling myself that I am or was an agent for the FBI. This should be routine for me, but this is different. This is personal in a way that I can't explain. I hold my breath and step behind Claude. Steve touches my arm and motions for me to stay behind him, but I need to go in first. I will not cower in fear to whoever is in here. I think of Psalm 56:11 and let the words engrave themselves in my mind. *In God have I put my trust: I will not be afraid what man can do unto me."*

I scan the room, in awe of its hominess. I expect a hallway with doors on each side, like the other buildings, but instead, we walk into a large room with a sectional sofa, bookshelves, and beautifully painted landscapes hanging on the wall, framed to look like windows. A crystal chandelier hangs in the center of the ceiling. The room is trimmed with tall intricate dark-stained crown and base molding, and a wooden door stained to match exits the back. It is stunning, that is until I look behind me.

By the blank stare on Steve's face, his shock is obvious. The entire back wall beside the door we entered through is a mural of Steve's father, the infamous President Dennis Denali.

"Come on, let's check out what's through that door." I point to the back of the room.

No thumbprint or keypad is required. Claude twists an old-timey brass doorknob and gives a push. A bullet buries itself in the door casing.

Claude jerks the door closed. "That room doesn't seem to have the same cozy, welcoming feel that this one has."

I scramble past Claude, and with a swift shove, I thrust the door open, swooping the barrel of the nine-millimeter around the room, aiming at nothing but side-by-side computer screens lining the perimeter. The only way out is through a steel door to the left. I motion toward the door and take off across the room.

Claude wheels past me. I keep forgetting that Steve programmed him to protect us. He stops next to the door, but again, no thumbprint is required. I guess President Denali didn't want to have to deal with all of that once he was inside this building.

I reach for the doorknob, but just as my hand brushes it, the knob is pulled away from me.

"You really don't give up, do you?" He steps toward me. His grating voice sends chills down my back. "This time, I would say you would have wished you had, but you won't be around to wish anything. You got lucky with that explosion in my office. You were supposed to be standing by the desk. But that's the thing about you." he smirks. "You are never acting, or reacting, or doing anything that you are supposed to." He moves his eyes around the room. "None of you people are. You even went and ruined my sweet Joanne." Dr. Eckert points to his chest. "Well, this is enough explosives to destroy all of building fifteen." He extends his hand with his finger resting on the detonator.

"Earl," Teresa's face softens, "I've been thinking a lot about you."

"Save it. I am not falling for your little acting debut." He lifts the detonator a bit higher.

"No, you don't understand, Earl. I know our relationship could never work. I've changed, and well, the person you were involved with wasn't real anyway. But I need to ask you a question. I don't want to die without knowing if you truly loved me back then, or if it was lies and deception like everything else surrounding this place."

"Joanne, you know I loved you. I never stopped loving you," his finger trembles on the button, "but as they say, there is a thin line between love and hate."

"Earl, do you remember our first date? We never got to leave the facility to go on a real one. We usually had dinner in the dining room, but our first date was special. You spread out that blanket on the floor of the arena and pretended we were on a picnic in the park. You even had a basket with sandwiches."

"How could I forget?" he shifts his head to the side and curves one side of his mouth up.

"Earl, did you know you loved me then?" Teresa asks lifting one brow.

"I loved you long before that."

Teresa nods. "That's all I wanted to know."

As she finishes her sentence, something snaps behind Eckert's back.

Eckert jerks his head around to find Claude standing right behind him.

Claude reaches out with his index finger and pokes the button on the detonator. "It doesn't work anymore."

Eckert's face goes blank, and he stands there motionless. Then, in a swift move of his hand, he reaches for a handle sticking out of his waistband, but Claude is still so close that Eckert doesn't stand a chance of even touching the weapon before he collapses to the floor.

Alice strides to the computers on the wall and starts typing on one of the keyboards.

"Teresa," Steve says in a calm, matter-of-fact tone, "I don't think you have a twin sister."

"Me either." Her lips form a straight line as she glares down at the man on the floor. "And we need to move fast because that is not Earl."

"Are you sure? Because this is the computer that was being used to run the program." Alice questions as she continues to pound the keys on the computer.

"I am positive." Teresa affirms. "Remember when I told you all about our first date?"

I widen my eyes. "You were testing him. You told us that you ordered pizza on your first date." The photo of young Mordecai Crawley flashes in my head. I recognized him as Dr. Eckert by his distinctive eyes, eyes that are so deep and dark, but at the same time, have a strange glow. I didn't get a look at the man in Dr. Eckert's office, but neither the one in the girls' room nor this Dr. Eckert had those weird eyes.

"Well, either the real one was here, or the fake one was running the program. Either way, I have to figure out how to shut this down." Panic floods through Alice's voice.

I look over her shoulder. A timer showing minutes, seconds, and hundredths of seconds is flashing as it counts down on the screen. *Activate electrical discharge in 1:25:13.*

A heavy silence falls over us as we watch every hundredth of a second vanish before our eyes.

"Think, Alice, think." Alice says to herself. "Only a minute and fifteen seconds left. Why is nothing working?" Her fingers fly across the keyboard.

"Thumbprint required to disable." A computerized female voice instructs as the words appear at the top of the monitor. "Thumbprint required to disable."

Alice jumps to her feet and pulls at Eckert's limp body. Steve gets on the other side to help. She presses his thumb to the pad.

"Print not authorized." the voice announces.

"I told you that's not him." Teresa's voice cracks.

Alice goes back to typing with violent strokes. "Fifty-eight seconds."

I nudge Steve's arm with my elbow. "That means the real one was just in here." I mumble in an undertone as I pass the gun to my left hand and wipe the sweat from my right palm on my pant leg. I nod toward that metal door. "We have to go find him."

A discordant mixture of squeaking and clomping shoes against the concrete floor seems to come out of nowhere.

I switch the gun back to my right and pivot. "Alice, keep working. We got you covered."

We stand with our guns lifted toward the wooden door where the sound of the approaching stampede is growing closer.

Is that...

"Please, please, Lord, don't let us be too late." Mom's voice echoes through the open door.

At the sound of Mom's frantic prayer, we lower our guns.

Agent Morgan barges through the door with his gun drawn, and Kate bursts in right behind him.

"Is everyone okay?" He aims the gun around the room before his eyes fall on Dr. Eckert's form on the floor.

Before I can express my shock at their presence or answer Agent Morgan's question, Mom, Dad, Dukakis, Cynthia, Eileen, and Waves pile into the room.

"That may not be Dr. Eckert." Agent Morgan says with a tight grip on his Colt 45.

"It's not." I mutter, looking back at Alice. "And we need his thumbprint to stop the program from activating those wires."

"Seven seconds." Alice's voice quavers.

Waves zooms around the huddle in the middle of the room and presses his metal thumb to the pad.

"Authorization complete. Activation canceled."

All eyes in the room move from the "00:02:32" frozen on the screen to Waves.

"I am guessing from your puzzled expressions that you are questioning my ability to replicate Dr. Eckert's thumbprint." Waves taps his fingers on the desk. "It's quite an amusing story, really."

"Waves." Steve's frustration rings in his tone.

"To summarize, I scanned his thumbprint one day because I wanted to copy this arcade game he had downloaded on his computer." Waves lowers his head.

"Timer initiated. Activate Electrical Discharge in 05:00:00."

"Oh no. No. No." He has restarted it from somewhere else.

"He's not going to stop. We have to find him." I don't wait for Agent Morgan to stop me. I stride across the room and pull open the metal door. The room is pitch black, with only the light filtering from the open door. I shift the aim of my gun from side to side as I glide my hand along the wall.

Agent Morgan steps through and feels along the other side of the door. He must have found the switch because a faint light illuminates a short corridor with a door off each side and one at the end.

I open the door on the right and step in. "All clear." I say, backing out. "Bedroom."

Agent Morgan looks into the door on the left. "Bathroom. It's empty."

We walk side by side toward the door at the end. Kate has her gun right behind us. I don't know if the others are following.

"Do you hear that?" Kate whispers.

"Yes, but what is it?" I crack the door, and the rumbling sound gets a bit louder.

Agent Morgan pulls a small flashlight from his pocket and storms through the opening into a rugged tunnel with jagged granite walls. Kate and I follow as he shines the beam of light in front. The pitter-patter resonating from behind us cues me that the others are coming too.

The tunnel becomes brighter, and as we round a bend, a large circle of sunlight and trees appear. Agent Morgan says something, but the roar is so loud now that I cannot hear. We exit the tunnel and find ourselves in a thick forest of trees on the side of the mountain. Kate points up.

A short distance from us, a helicopter is hovering above the trees. Morgan takes off running in the direction of the helicopter. Kate and I jog after him but dig in our heels when we take sight of the ladder swinging above the treetops. Dr. Eckert is halfway up the ladder hanging from the helicopter.

Kate lifts her gun.

"Don't shoot!" Agent Morgan yells above the roar. "We need him alive."

"Why?" she retorts.

"There is no Dr. Damien Seaver. We need to know who is responsible for this."

I feel a nudge in my back as the others come to a stop behind us.

"If we don't shoot him, he is going to get away." Kate shouts back. "That is unless you know how to fly."

At the word 'fly', Waves comes bouncing by, moving in the direction of the ladder.

"Oh, brother!" Steve exclaims as Spencer scampers past us, gaining ground on Waves.

Waves gets right beneath the ladder. His spiked mohawk raises and flips to the side. Then, he tucks his arms tightly to his body, and the red spikes of hair start to spin. Within seconds, he lifts off the ground. Spencer claps his hands, and with a giant leap, grabs onto one of Waves' rotating feet. As they lift into the air, Waves gives a quick glance down at the little monkey hanging from his leg, and in an amplified voice, he breaks out singing the chorus of "Wind Beneath My Wings."

"You have got to be kidding me." Agent Morgan mutters to himself.

Waves gets even with Dr. Eckert's head, and Spencer jumps toward the swaying ladder. Steve lets out a gasp that drowns out the sound of the helicopter, but then his gasp transforms into a hoot when Spencer makes a hard landing on the center of Dr. Eckert's back, latching onto his shoulders with both hands. Between the swing of the ladder and Spencer's impact, Dr. Eckert loses his grip.

Spencer and Dr. Eckert fall through the air, changing Steve's hoot back into a gasp. Waves' mohawk stops spinning for a second and he drops straight down. With his arms extended and one finger pointed, Waves shoots a dart and wraps his arms around Eckert just as his body goes limp. As they descend, Spencer's hand slips from Eckert's back, and a high-pitched monkey squeal whistles like a bottle rocket as the flailing animal plunges into the top of a tree.

Steve and Agent Morgan take off. I race after Steve toward the tree, and Kate goes after Agent Morgan in search of Waves and Dr. Eckert.

Standing beside the trunk of the tree, I wrap my arm around Steve as he gazes up through the thick leaves.

"I'm going up."

He didn't say that. Yes. Yes, he did. "What? What are you doing?" I exclaim.

Steve jumps and pulls himself onto the lowest branch. And, seemingly out of nowhere, Spencer swings right into Steve's arms.

A half-sigh of relief escapes. Only a half because I realize that our five minutes have to be over. I turn and run back up the mountain. "Alice! Where's Alice?"

"Honey," Mom wipes the sweat from my head, "you don't look so good. You are going to collapse if you don't calm down."

"Where's Alice? The five minutes…" I grab onto Mom's shoulder.

"Alice and Eileen stayed up to work on that program." Mom answers. "Ellie?"

The trees spin, and bright light fills my vision. Mom's voice fades, but I feel her hands grab my waist.

Chapter Twenty-Six

Muffled voices fill my ears. I fight against the weight of my eyelids, but I manage only to crack them. Through the narrow slits, Steve and Mom come into focus. Both of them are staring straight down at me with worry lines between their brows. I blink a few more times and get my eyes open.

"What happened?" I mumble.

"You fainted and scared us to death. That's what happened." Mom rants. "Steve told me you haven't been eating right. Your little body must have given out."

Between their towering faces, I spot that crystal chandelier above me. *I am on that fancy couch.* I swing my legs to the side and pull myself up. *Yep. And there is giant President Denali covering the wall. Alice. The five minutes.* "Alice. Where's Alice?"

"I'm right here." She sits beside me and drapes her arm around my shoulders.

"The five minutes... how many people are dead?" The room starts to spin.

"No one is dead, and no one got hurt." She smiles and winks. "I found a glitch."

I drop my head over on her shoulder. *Thank you, Lord.*

Agent Morgan's voice pulls my head back up. He is standing in the doorway with Kate.

I curve one side of my mouth up. "You know I have a lot of questions."

Kate giggles. "I figured you did." She walks toward the sofa with Agent Morgan following. Kate sits on one side, and Alice slides over so Agent Morgan can sit on the other. "And just so you know," she says, "authorities are at the main gate as we speak, working to get everyone here cleared for release. Now, let's see if we can give you a quick rundown to answer your other questions." She nods to Agent Morgan.

"Oh… where to begin." He sighs. "Well, for starters, when I spoke to you the second time and told you Mordecai Crawley was dead, Kate and I were already on a plane en route here to the complex. I had no doubts that you all were going to try to stop Dr. Eckert, and the bits of information I kept uncovering had me terrified. However, with a lot of puzzle pieces that didn't fit together, Kate and I had no choice but to go out on our own. On the flight here, I discovered that Dr. Mordecai Crawley was most likely going to prison. Not only was he doing experimentation with cloning humans, which the law prohibits, but he was also using extracted DNA from subjects and attempting to create clones of them without their permission. When Dr. Crawley's body was discovered, he had left a note indicating that he would rather end his life than spend it in prison."

"But the body they found was not Crawley, was it? It was a clone." I twist my mouth to the side as I run the scenario through my head. "Considering he was going to prison for cloning humans, did the authorities not question the identity of the body?"

"No, because according to the records, none of Crawley's attempts had been successful. That, and the blood sample matched."

"Because they had the same DNA?"

"You got it. They didn't see a need to perform an in-depth DNA analysis. If they had, it probably would have revealed an irregularity where a base had been copied incorrectly. Anyway, let me move on to the next puzzle piece, Dr. Damien Seaver. As of right now, I am still waiting to hear from the Office of the President as to how he is affiliated with this person and what credentials were verified in Dr. Seaver's appointment as an advisor, because the closest match I found was a Dominick Seaver who happens to be a ninety-year-old retired farmer. I personally think that Dr. Eckert and Dr. Seaver are one and the same. However, the ultimate question asks what part President Kutchins plays in all of this. Is he the mastermind behind this plan or a pawn in someone else's game? I mean, I never thought of President Kutchins as one that would take action without the leadership of Congress, but everything that has happened has come from Executive decisions."

"Excuse me for interrupting," Alice speaks up, "but I've been thinking and running all these things through my mind as you were talking. We are all aware that President Denali had this evil and twisted plan to drop poison from a plane that would wipe out humanity except for a select few he had kept safe here in this mountain. He was erasing the memories of these select few in hopes that they would no longer have any knowledge of God because his sole purpose and intent was to repopulate the earth with people who would follow him instead of God. And today, we have personally witnessed Dr. Eckert's success in cloning humans since we have run into a multitude of Dr. Eckerts and another Teresa. That being said, I am questioning the originality of those guards because quite a few of them look alike."

"If I may interject for a moment, Alice." Agent Morgan lifts his hand. "I believe you are right about that. We ran fingerprints on a few of them, and there were no matches. I am no scientist, but I have been told that just as identical twins do not have matching fingerprints, neither do clones. Therefore, blood samples have been extracted from those same few guards and sent for testing. Sorry for interrupting, but I wanted to clue you in while you were on the topic. Please continue."

"I'm glad you did. Now I feel like we are on the same page."

Alice clasps her hands together. "I think it is safe to say that deception has been a dominating factor in America since President Denali. He had the American people eating from the palm of his hand. They thought after he put an end to the identity theft crisis that he was going to save them from all their troubles. And look what he planned to do to them. Look what he told us when we were brought to the facility for training. We thought we were chosen to protect Americans." Alice swallows hard, and her voice cracks as emotion pours through her words. "And then we were brought back here again, but this time we were led to believe that something was wrong with us." Alice darts her eyes back and forth between Agent Morgan, Kate, and me as if she is sizing up our reaction. "The Bible speaks about deceivers and deception. Matthew 7:15 warns us to 'beware of false prophets, which come to you in sheep's clothing, but inwardly they are ravening wolves.' It seems to me that we have had a few sheep turn out to be wolves. Then, 2 John 1:7 says, 'For many deceivers are entered into this world, who confess not that Jesus is come in the flesh. This is a deceiver and an antichrist.'" Alice pauses. "I'm sorry, but I do not believe that this is a population control thing, even as morbid and disturbing as it would be if that were true." Tears fill her eyes. "We are still being deceived. Dr. Damien Seaver is a pseudonym. I hadn't realized it until Agent Morgan was talking about the name and I pictured the letters in my head. The first initial is 'D'. The last name is Seaver."

"Deceiver." The word passes through my lips as only a whisper.

Cynthia, who has been standing by the door beside Dukakis, takes a step and falls to her knees. Her arms quiver as she covers her pale face with her hands. "He said that he could never be destroyed." she says in a zombie-like voice. "It was his clone that was put to death."

"Hold on," Agent Morgan reasons. "I think we are getting a bit carried away. I highly doubt if Dennis Denali were still alive that he would have remained hidden all this time. And I am inclined to believe with the facts before us now, that Dr. Earl Eckert has been the mastermind behind this plan from the get-go. Even with President Denali's demented plan to destroy the world, it was Eckert's mind control procedures that were being used to accomplish the mission. And here Dr. Eckert is again, with his mind control tricks in another attempt to destroy humanity. But instead of dropping poison, he is invading people's minds and turning them into murderers. We know from history it is not that farfetched or hard to believe that with the least bit of provocation, some people will choose to destroy each other. He's been setting humanity up to destroy itself."

"No. It's Dennis. He is still trying to create a world where he is the only power." Cynthia mutters from her position on the floor.

"Agent Morgan, I am not saying you are wrong," Alice says, glaring at the mural on the wall. "I am only asking that you at least consider my theory, because if I'm right, this isn't over."

"I will." he nods. "I want this to be over."

Alice stands and extends her hand to me. "I am ready to go home." she says as she helps me to my feet.

"I- finally- made- it." Gerald's words come out between heavy breaths as he stands bent over in the doorway. "What- did- I- miss?"

Alice shakes her head. "You hobbled all the way here."

Claude zooms to the door. "I'll grab a gurney."

"What happened? Where are we going?" Gerald looks around the room.

"To the airport. Jillian and I are going to fly us home." Alice wraps her arm around Mom's shoulders.

Mom laughs. "I'll let you have the pleasure. If you remember correctly, my last flight didn't leave the ground."

~

I PLOD my way into the kitchen. "What time is it?"

"Five o'clock in the evening." He stands up and gives me a kiss. "I just woke up a few minutes ago myself."

I shrug. "Well, it was already morning before we went to bed." I sit down at the table. "Alice didn't land the plane until four a.m."

"So good to be home." Herb wheels over to the table and places a cup of coffee in front of me.

"Oh… coffee." I clutch the cup in my hands. "Thank you, Herb."

"We have toast too." Steve passes me a plate.

I look over at Spencer sitting on the other side of the table with three banana peels lying in front of him. "So… it seems that his PTSD is healed."

"Well, maybe," Steve says without making eye contact, "it wasn't PTSD after all. I'm not saying he wasn't afraid after everything that happened, but," he coughs and then mumbles under his breath, "maybe I felt bad after that first nightmare, and then maybe I spoiled him a little too much." He tilts his head and cracks a grin. "I'm just saying, maybe."

I roll my eyes toward him and curve up one side of my mouth.

Tapping his fingers on the table, he continues, "And I was thinking that maybe we could go next week and pick out some nice jungle wallpaper for the extra bedroom, and I could move Herb's charging station in there so Herb would activate if Spencer were to get up in the middle of the night. What do you think?"

A full smile spreads across my face. "I think that I like your thinking."

As I pick up the knife to spread peanut butter on my toast, the doorbell chimes.

Steve pushes back from the table. "I'll get it."

A moment later, Steve comes back into the kitchen with Agent Morgan. "Want some coffee?"

"No, thanks." Agent Morgan replies. "I know you don't need

company right now, but I wanted to stop by and let you know that everyone has been released and transported home."

"What about the people whose test showed lesions?" I ask.

"No worries. They are allowed to go on with their lives as normal." He must notice my look of confusion because he coughs and continues to explain. "One of the initial perpetrators, the one from the grocery store shooting, had detailed in his statement to the authorities that Eckert had called him into his lab a week prior to the incident with the claim there could be something wrong with his brain. Yesterday, authorities decided his story might have had some truth to it, so they checked, and sure enough, a long wire was protruding into his brain. It turned out to be the same with the other imprisoned perpetrators as well. Honestly, I am not sure what will be done concerning them. Obviously, they committed horrific crimes, but on the other hand, they were not in control of their actions. For the ones with the lesions... yes, they have scar tissue in their brain, but every ounce of research says that they are still in control of their own choices. Therefore, unless they choose to break the law, they are free to live their lives... and hopefully, find Jesus along the way if they haven't already."

"And President Kutchins?" Steve questions.

"He has resigned, but he is admitting no involvement or knowledge of wrongdoing. He apparently didn't bother to check out Dr. Seaver's credentials. He said Dr. Seaver's name was already listed as a member of the President's Council of Advisors on Science and Technology, therefore he saw no reason to question it."

"What about all those people that were killed?" I exclaim. "He may have thought it was to control the population, but murder is murder."

"The emails prove that, and he was arrested as soon as he resigned." He leans against the door casing. "And the guards were clones. Their DNA was a match to a platoon of Navy Seals that went missing on their return home. There were sixteen men. We don't know what happened to the men, but the guards were all clones of them. Hence, why so many of them looked the same."

"Sixteen men cloned over and over." Steve shakes his head.

"I am curious about something." I twist my chair around. "If Eckert had this capability to clone, then why didn't President Denali make an army of clones instead of abducting and deceiving a bunch of young people?"

"I spent all night at that facility searching for hard evidence." Agent Morgan points to his ruffled hair. "I guess you can tell that I haven't been home yet. But it appears Eckert's clones have some issues. Some of his documentation noted that he had not overcome the reproduction issue. Denali wanted his army to repopulate, which would be impossible with Eckert's clones. On top of that, in order to make adult clones, the rate of cell division is so rapid that his clones age at lightning speed. And it seems that with the progress made in the area of cryonics at Denali's facility, Eckert has been experimenting with cryopreservation in his clones to see if it would slow the process. According to his notes, the guards had been frozen, which, in essence, stopped the aging process until he needed them. Once they were thawed, I found no documentation on the results of aging. I would think the rapid aging would just pick back up where it was before the cryogenic preservation." He puts his hand to his mouth to stifle his yawn. "Anyway, I am heading home to get some sleep. I will talk with both of you soon." Agent Morgan turns to leave the room and stops. "Oh, by the way, I wanted to give some closure to Alice's concern, so I made a few phone calls. Dennis Denali was fingerprinted when he was taken to prison. The fingerprints matched. The man is dead. Through a thorough investigation, I intend to prove that Earl Eckert was continuing with President Denali's plan to destroy mankind. And I have not discarded my theory that Eckert was behind this from the beginning. I believe President Denali was a cover and a means for Eckert to put his plan in motion." Agent Morgan waves, and a few seconds later, the front door clicks.

Steve sits back down at the table and grabs my hand. "We have a lot to give thanks for."

We lower our heads and give praise to God.

Steve lifts his head, but he doesn't let go of my hand. "Do you remember when Alice was talking about deception?"

I turn and look at him with a curious expression. "Yes. What about it?"

"I was just thinking about all of the deception and all of the lies that we have been told." He moves his eyes to meet mine. "But everything in God's Word has proven true... over and over again."

Squeezing his hand, I smile. "'And ye shall know the truth,'"

Steve joins in, and we finish together. "'... and the truth shall make you free.' John 8:32."

Epilogue

The roar of crashing waves fills my ears as the skin on my heels melts away, leaving raw flesh.

"I told you there is no place to run." his deep voice fumes as he drags my body across the scorching sand.

I gaze up at the blue sky and the wispy clouds that feather across it like random brush strokes in a painting. Then it disappears. The burning sand, the blue sky, and the bright sun all fade. Now my feet bounce over roots and rocks, and I am encompassed in a canopy of green.

He shows no mercy as his hard hands squeeze around my wrists. A door creaks open. He lifts my body and drops me into the chair. "Eat." he orders. "And show a little more respect. Without me, you die."

I lift my head and stare straight into the face of pure evil, but I am not afraid. "You… you don't give me life. 'He that hath the Son hath life; and he that hath not the Son of God hath not life.' That's from God's Word… 1 John 5:12."

His feet pound against the dirt as he trudges back to the door. "Eat." he hisses.

"I will eat for his sake, not yours." I take an orange from the bowl.

He stops with his hand on the door and glares at me over his shoulder. "At least we agree on something." He turns back, and the door slams behind him.

∾

I GASP as my body shoots straight up in the bed.

Steve clicks on the lamp. "Ellie, what is it? Are you having nightmares again?" he asks through a yawn with his eyes only half-open.

"He's alive." I mutter. "Steve, your father is alive, and he wants the baby."

A second of silence passes, and then Steve leaps to his feet.

"Baby? What baby?" he asks me with wide eyes. "Ellie?"

Acknowledgments

Thank you to my amazing husband, Steve, for encouraging me to step outside my comfort zone and chase my dream. Thank you for supporting me in all of those hours, typing on my computer, and thank you for listening when I needed to talk about it.

Thank you to my wonderful children, Landon and Layna, for believing in your mom. You never doubted that my book would get published. And thank you for being my social media consultants and telling all your friends about my book.

Thank you to my mother, Carolyn Bryant, for her countless hours of proofreading and all her work in promoting my book.

Thank you to all those who read my first book and requested a second. Words cannot express how much your outpouring of support and positive feedback touched my heart.

Thank you to my publisher for giving me the opportunity to share my faith through my writing.

And most of all, I thank God for surrounding me with so much love and support, for nudging me on when I couldn't think of what to write, and... for everything... because without Him, I could do nothing.

A look at: The Final Remnant

By Terry James and Heather Renae

After the disappearance of nearly half the world's population, Caden Johnson is convinced God totally sucks. In fact, He can take His holiness and shove off. The world is crawling with mutant animals and invisible monsters—who all enjoy human being with a side of fries. And what is God doing? Watching it burn.

But when Caden hears his little sister might be alive—and stuck on the other side of the world—he decides things are *going* to change. Dragging his brother along, and armed with nothing but a baseball bat, he sets off to keep what's left of his family alive.

In a gang he hardly trusts, and enemies at every turn, Caden must face the Cosmic Bully he's learned to hate all his life… Or die trying.

A unique blend of genres, The Final Remnant is teen fantasy and apocalyptic Christian fiction at its best.

AVAILABLE NOVEMBER 2022

About the Author

F. D. Adkins is a Christian fiction author and freelance writer. Her hope is to pass along the comfort that comes from having a personal relationship with Jesus while offering her readers a brief escape from life's struggles through an action-packed story full of suspense, twists, turns, love, and a few laughs. In other words, her passion is sharing her faith through fiction.

She has been married to the man of her dreams and her best friend for 23 years. She loves spending time with her family, reading, writing, and always enjoys a good cup of coffee. She also has a soft spot in her heart for all animals especially dogs.

She lives in South Carolina with her husband, Steve, their two teenage children, Landon and Layna, and their dog, Lucy. She posts stories of faith and devotions weekly on her blog.

9 781639 771202